Wild Man

ALEXANDER CHARLES

Little Bear Publishing
PO Box 1106
Libby, MT 59923

Paperback ISBN: 978-1-7366898-0-6
eBook ISBN: 978-1-7366898-1-3
Library of Congress Control Number: 2021906252

Editor: Arlene Prunkl
Cover Art: Kelsey Dzintars
Developmental Editing: Anika Hanisch
Light Copy Editing: Savannah Cottrell
Book Designer: Jamie Tipton

CONTENTS

Wild Man is a fiction tale based on The Bauman Story
as told by Theodore Roosevelt in his book titled,
The Wilderness Hunter, published in 1890.

☙

ACKNOWLEDGMENTS

I want to thank my wife, Laurie, for her unwavering support and my Editor, Arlene Prunkl, for her advice, encouragement, and many insights into the nuances of the literary world.

PROLOGUE

We are naturally intrigued by stories, but most of the time, even if the story is a great one, the fascination lasts but a moment. Like ornate snowflakes that melt in our hands, they quickly fade, and we wipe away the lackluster residue, even as the words vanish from our thoughts.

But to me, and to my people, the stories I grew up hearing are something else entirely: treasured, transformative, they withstand the test of time, and they carry a wisdom to be passed along so that others may also learn from them.

Most of these stories were spoken, not written. They were passed along from grandparents and parents to children and grandchildren while sitting around a campfire inside a tipi or lodge, often well into the night. They were treasures, kept safe within the minds of human beings, and though these treasures were shared freely among my people, the vaults in which they were stored had always remained full.

But as the years slowly rolled past, I watched the stories fade, one by one, like the buffalo that once thundered across the prairies like a great roiling sea.

I am an old man now, and nobody wants to hear my stories. But I have stubborn blood in my veins, a pen in my hand, and a story on my tongue—and the paper that lies before me has no choice but to hear it.

When my father, Gabe, was young, he was smitten by romantic tales of the Wild West and stories of mountain-man adventures. Later, after the hands of time had turned, and the wisdom earned from countless knocks on the head had cleared his senses, he would entertain another theory as to his wild westward wanderings.

He had answered the siren call that beckons deeply from the cavernous soul of many a young man. It happens when they come of age and feel the urge to break away from their roots. Blindly, they venture, as if moved by some indomitable force, like the spawning salmon's perilous journey to its place of origins—back to the beginning of things.

Though Father had convinced himself that his wanderings stemmed from a yen for freedom and adventure, he would come to understand it was a yearning for something else entirely: a search for something good, something better—the irrepressible search for Eden.

Eventually, he would come to realize that Eden had come and gone—it was nowhere to be found. The farther he traveled along this lonesome, never-ending trail of heartache and pain, the more he discovered he was only moving farther from his Eden, the twisting trail taking him to places where creatures ripped flesh with fang and claw, and dreadful demons lurked in the dark shadows of the forest.

But at the age of nineteen, oblivious to what lay ahead, my father departed from his Kentucky home with a friend in the spring of 1832 and headed for St. Louis, where they would catch a keelboat ride north into the heart of beaver country. Their goal was to become free trappers, live by their own rules, and enjoy the freedom of mountain men.

But no sooner had they arrived at Fort Union on the upper Missouri than his friend changed his mind and caught a ride back home, claiming he'd endured enough ridicule from the half dozen brash keelboatmen who boasted of being half alligator and half horse and had done their level best to live up to the bodacious claim. My father had both thicker skin and a thicker physical constitution, which made him a more difficult target for taunting.

He traveled as far as he could by boat, and then, along with a mob of greenhorns led by a captain, he set out on foot to trap the various rivulets and arteries of the Rockies. After a week of hard trapping and few pelts, he got separated from his fellow trappers and, by chance, happened upon a pair of free trappers who persuaded him to join up with them.

The following pages tell the rest of the story.

Walter "Running Fox" Bauman
February 2, 1901

Chapter One

Time to Move

Gabe Bauman leaned over the small creek, scouring dirty pans and utensils from the evening meal, while not far away, his two associates, Bill Branch and André Choteau, took their ease by the light of the campfire.

His task complete, he rose and glanced at the stars glistening brightly above the crags. Choteau lazily stirred the campfire with a stick while Branch slurred twisted verses between gulps of whiskey.

Sweet Laura McDoon, a fair lass was she,

Shone bright as the moon, but not so at me.

I smiled, I winked, but she called me a sap,

Then her face turned to stone when my trousers fell down,

and I landed forthright in her lap.

Gabe gathered the items to the sounds of the two mountain men snorting and guffawing. Sighing deeply, he swallowed his chagrin and returned to the campfire just as Branch belched loudly. "When you get to be a real man, greenhorn, I might give you a sip," said the drunken trapper.

"*Oui,* monsieur. You wouldn't want him to burn his tender lips."

They laughed loudly at the Frenchman's derisive joke, which Gabe ignored. He had grown somewhat immune to their persistent jabs. Several weeks previously, he had accepted the fact that it was his own fault, his own naivety, and his trusting nature that had got him into this mess—a weakness his father had warned him about.

Gabe had been enthusiastic and eager to learn when Branch first hired him as camp-tender, hunter, and apprentice trapper. But after thirty days of hard riding, deep in the heart of the Rockies in search of beaver, the "majesty of the mountain" had lost its luster.

Then, they had found the honey-hole, and the real work began. After a solid week of relentless, sweaty labor, he had grown numb from skinning, fleshing, and stretching beaver after beaver. The hard work was somewhat tolerable since he had been raised in the backwoods of Kentucky and was accustomed to the strenuous life. His nineteen-year-old chiseled body bore witness to that fact. But, though physically capable of meeting the rigors of the trapper's life, he'd grown mentally weary of his two new companions.

"What the hell do you keep looking at, Frenchy?" slurred Branch as he took another swill of whiskey.

Gabe glanced up at Choteau, who stared bug-eyed into the alder brush that grew on the other side of the gurgling creek that trickled ten long paces from their campfire. The Frenchman blinked nervously as if bracing himself for either rebuke or insult, then sat down tight-lipped near the fire, the muscles of his jaw pulsing as he clenched his teeth.

"I told ya a dozen times we got nothin' to worry about. Them damned Kootenai ain't comin' back in here," said Branch cynically as he peered into the willows.

Branch's words appeared to be of no consolation to the Frenchman. A few days earlier, when he and Gabe had been alone skinning beaver, he said he'd seen and heard something unusual: a vague flash of brown, a soft shuffling of underbrush—*and it was no damned bear!* Or so the Frenchman claimed. Apparently, Choteau's apparition had him spooked again.

According to Choteau, he had been sitting by the fire to keep warm, while Branch and Gabe slept contentedly. A movement in the trees across the creek caught his attention, and he listened carefully to pinpoint its location. Then came soft footfalls in the dark forest, and suddenly, he noticed two eyes peering back at him from just inside the foliage reflecting an eerie red from the light of the campfire. Choteau said he tried waking Branch, but he was half-dead drunk.

He had thought the eyes might be those of an owl at first, but when a rock whizzed by his head, landing with a loud thud behind him, he realized it had to be something else. Couldn't have been a bear. But he claimed when he raised his musket to shoot, whoever or whatever it was quickly ran off and disappeared into the forest, leaving the nervous Frenchman bewildered. The morning after the incident, Gabe was cooking breakfast when he overheard Choteau arguing with Branch about what he'd seen, but Branch had just scoffed.

Now, as the night settled in, Gabe couldn't help but notice Choteau's frenzied demeanor. Either his tormentor had returned, or the Frenchman was turning into a lunatic right before his very eyes. Perhaps the steady diet of beaver meat, along with the constant badgering from the vitriolic Bill Branch, had finally pushed the Frenchman to the point of hallucination.

Choteau's fretting glances were contagious, and Gabe soon found himself looking into the darkened forest for anything unusual. If it were Kootenai, they would know soon enough, and he sat and inched lower against a log whenever Branch tipped back his brown jug, peering toward the alder-lined creek and the shadowy forest beyond.

"I bundled up the last load of fur, sir," he said to Branch, mostly to break the tension. "Not sure if we can pack much more on the mules." Gabe found that using the formal *sir* was usually an effective means of currying favor with Branch, or at least minimizing his sardonic jabs. But this time, it had little effect.

"You bell-head!" Branch taunted. "Am I gonna have to show you again how to properly pack a mule? Hell, I figure we can get at least one more days' worth of trappin' loaded on 'em."

The hobbled mules and horses grazing in the meadowed flat behind the camp snorted in the distance, then snorted again. Gabe and Choteau cocked their heads in unison toward the animals. They were clearly protesting the presence of something. But what? Branch corked his whiskey and placed it beside him. Silence. Dead silence.

Rubbing his chin, the way he always did when in deep cogitation, Branch stared toward the darkness. "We better get some—"

A twig suddenly snapped behind the thick willows across the creek some thirty yards away, breaking the calm like a gunshot. In one fluid motion, Choteau grabbed his rifle, cocked it, and wheeled in the direction of the noise.

"Hold on," said Branch under his breath, suddenly sober. Quietly, he took up his own rifle, rolled to his feet, and stumbled backed behind the protection of a root ball.

"Damn it! I told you I saw something," whispered Choteau in his thick French accent.

Clink! Out of nowhere, a pebble bounced off the skillet near the fire, then another landed on Branch's bedroll. "What the hell?!" he yelped.

Choteau reacted as if the pebble were a cannonball, ducking down tightly against the base of the closest pine tree.

Gabe stared intently into the dark shadows of the forest, determined to confirm the presence of Choteau's tormentor, but when another pebble landed nearby, he quickly realized he was completely exposed, sitting in the open by the light of the fire. Jolted into action, he grabbed his trade musket and ducked behind a pine tree.

Branch's lusty stories of frontier battles had made him eager for his first skirmish, and with a white-fingered grip, he nervously pulled back the hammer on his rifle. The hammer's click broke the jittery silence like a clap of thunder. Gabe glanced at his boss, expecting a rebuke, but Branch only squinted into the forest with his dark, piercing eyes.

Choteau knelt poised, his rifle shouldered. All three carefully surveyed the surrounding timber for any sign of movement, but nothing stirred. They watched and waited until the pale face of the moon rose over the high mountain basin. Finally, Branch relaxed and ran his beaver grease-stained fingers through his grimy, graying beard as he always did when he was about to come up with a new plan.

"I'm telling you, there's something out there!" Choteau's voice quivered as he spoke.

Over the past month, Gabe had observed how Branch approached problems more pragmatically than the edgy Frenchman—always thinking, always coming up with new angles to bring resolution or get what he wanted. But one thing remained constant: the primary goal of Branch's mission never changed, only the expediency with which it was to be achieved. Their mission was simple—trap the hell out of the basin as quickly as possible and get out, and Branch never let them forget it.

Dismissively, Branch remarked, "If it was Blackfeet, they woulda fired by now. Maybe it's other trappers tryin' to spook us outta here. Annoying as hell, though. Just move, ya sons of bitches, and I'll give ya somethin' to think about—right between yer eyes."

But Gabe could tell even Branch was more nervous than usual when he suddenly barked, "Go fetch the horses, kid."

Gabe uncocked his rifle, slung it over his shoulder, and grabbed a handful of lead ropes before huffing into the darkness toward the grazing horses. He hated being called "kid" but knew Branch meant business. The horses were their means of escape, and it would be disastrous if the troublemaker scattered or stole them, which would leave them on foot with no means of getting gear and fur out of the mountains.

He paused for a moment and scanned the terrain for danger. Stunted spruce trees ringed the grassy meadow, reflecting silvery moonlight, which made night walking relatively easy without the aid of a torch. But this night was different. Gabe felt an odd presence, and a tingle went up his spine as if something was watching him. Steeling himself, he set out, taking pains to avoid tripping on one of the many protruding tussocks of grass or stepping into one of the scattered bogs that lay hidden near the edges of the adjacent beaver lakes.

As he cautiously made his way across the grassy flat, he continued to scan for any sign of Indians. He recalled looking down on the small Kootenai village from a ridgetop, where he had been ordered to stay with the horses while Branch and Choteau hiked down to speak with tribal leaders just before the three trappers had entered the remote wilderness drainage.

Unlike their territorial cousins the Blackfeet, the Kootenai seemed peaceful enough: gentle whispers of smoke emanating from quaint, conical tipis, laughing children running about, and chattering old women preparing fish. Their village near the mouth of the drainage was a difficult one-day ride from where the trappers' camp was situated near the first of a series of high mountain lakes.

Ahead, dark, four-legged shapes appeared on the edge of the timber on the other side of the meadow. "Easy, boys. Easy," he said reassuringly. Their unmistakable clomping, hobbled gait confirmed them as the horses and mules, and not the herd of elk that occasionally drifted like ghosts into the meadow at night to feed.

As he drew closer, the moonlight made it easier to see the animals. They turned and faced Gabe in unison with protesting ears perked, sensing feeding time might soon be over. His horse was the easiest to catch, so Gabe always caught it first, making it easier for the others to relinquish their freedom.

The stout chestnut gelding he had named Juniper had become his friendly confidant—always listening attentively whenever he needed to vent after one of Branch's frequent tongue lashings. Though Juniper was just another one of Branch's horses, it was Gabe's to ride, and the two had bonded—perhaps because they shared the same abusive blighter.

But it wasn't just Bill Branch who harangued him. Choteau, who was amicable enough when alone with the young trapper, would often transform into a draconian taskmaster when in the presence of Bill Branch, barking orders like a field general. To make matters worse, the sycophant seemed to better tolerate Branch's truculent disposition and bouts of inebriation whenever Gabe was on hand to receive his boss's frequent verbal abuse.

Approaching the horses carefully, he whispered, "Hello, good fellow. Hello, Juniper, my friend."

Juniper sniffed his hand and gave a half-hearted snort before nodding his head, finally yielding to the braided leather lead rope, which he deftly tied into a halter for guiding the horse back to camp. Next, he unhobbled the other horses, who were familiar with the routine. Since Juniper was the lead horse, the others soon followed in line as they started toward camp.

Before striking out for camp, he looked up at the multitude of stars and bright round orb, its moonlight reflecting upon the lake, a stark mirror image of the knife-edged peaks that ringed the basin. It was a breathtaking image, and he paused for a moment to take it in before returning to the oppressive reality of the camp.

Staring at the brilliant display of stars, he remembered how his father would often take him out on clear nights to gaze at the heavens. "God is up there," he would say. "He's up there, watching." Gabe wondered if his father was, at that very moment, in the field in front of their Kentucky homestead, looking up at the same stars. Suddenly, he felt a lonely pang of regret and a sudden urge to get moving.

Turning toward the camp, he gave Juniper a little tug to urge him ahead. They had taken a couple of steps when, without warning, his horse snorted and wheeled. He groaned as searing pain shot through his hand when the lead rope stripped across his bare palm.

"Whoa, boy! Easy, now," he said firmly, clenching his fist as he beat down the pain. The other horses and mules stood stiff-legged, facing Gabe several paces away. "What's the matter, boy? You've never done that before. What's the matter, eh?" But as he approached Juniper, it became clear that the horses and mules weren't looking at him, but at something beyond him.

Cautiously, he scanned the moonlit basin. Nothing appeared out of the ordinary at first, but then he saw something—the indistinct outline of an odd, rounded figure on the edge of the meadow, rising above the stunted spruce. The horses snorted in succession as he squinted and shielded his brow from the moonlight to better see it.

"Choteau? Is that you?" he hollered. But there was no reply, and the shadowy figure suddenly disappeared like a mirage.

Gabe had spent enough time wrangling horses at night to pay little heed to the shifting shadows that often play tricks on the eyes—but Choteau's story and his constant fretting made him feel uneasy and wary.

Once again, he secured Juniper and talked to him softly, stroking his neck until he calmed down. Watching for any signs of movement among the spruce along the far end of the grassy flat, he led the procession back toward the camp.

As they crossed the flat, the animals suddenly seemed cooperative, eager to follow toward the security of the camp, and didn't take long to cover the distance. Approaching quietly, he tied off the horses and mules to their respective trees that served as temporary hitching posts, a short stone's throw from the campsite. As he cautiously stepped near, he could see Choteau and Branch through the trees, talking and staring intently into the moonlit alder brush, oblivious to Gabe's presence.

"There! I saw it again!" cried Choteau as Gabe stopped just inside the timber adjacent to the campsite.

Something dark flashed within the foliage on the other side of the creek. Branch wheeled and fired. A white plume of smoke and sparks from the gunpowder shot out from his rifle barrel like a fire-breathing dragon. The tethered animals jumped at the gunshot, which echoed across the basin and back again. Something large erupted and crashed through the brush, then darted through an opening in the timber.

"I saw it!" shouted Choteau. "I saw it!"

Gabe ducked behind the nearest tree and watched.

Branch quickly reloaded and blurted, "Don't just gawk, Frenchy! If ya see him, shoot him!"

But the creature seemed to have vanished like a specter, and once again, the forest withdrew into a deathly stillness.

"Did I get him?" Branch shouted. "I was on him, that's for damned sure! Was he a Koot?"

Choteau turned to Branch, mouth agape, stupefied. "No! It was no Koot!"

"Well, what, then? Trappers?"

"No. It—it looked like a man, but much bigger, with hair—lots of hair like a bear, but—but—not a bear."

"Damn, Frenchy, make up your mind! Was it man or beast? Can't be both!"

But Choteau just stared into the alders, wide-eyed and trembling as if he'd seen a ghost. Gabe moved closer and inadvertently stepped on a small branch, which snapped under his foot. The two trappers spun around with rifles pointing directly at him. Gabe covered his face and yelled, "Don't shoot! It's me!"

"Damn it! Bauman, ya nearly got yourself killed!" shouted Branch. "Get down, ya damn fool greenhorn!"

"What did you shoot at?" asked Gabe just as a foul odor hit him square in the nose. "What's that awful smell?"

"Somethin' was in them trees watching us all right. I couldn't tell what it was. Damned Injun or bear, I wager. I got a glimpse of the sneaky son of a bitch. Think I hit him. Let's go look for blood." Branch cautiously emerged from behind the root ball and stepped toward one of the nearby panniers. Retrieving a bear grease-soaked strip of linen, he wrapped it around a stick to make a torch and lit it using the campfire. Gabe followed close behind Choteau as they cautiously crept ahead, crossed the creek, and entered the alder patch. Gabe twisted his way through the thick foliage until they stopped in front of him, looking closely at the ground. "I knew I hit him," announced Branch.

"Did you find blood?"

"No, we found a pair of bear spectacles and the four moccasins he left behind," Branch said, sneering. "Of course we found blood! Damn! That smell! Did you break wind again, Frenchy?"

Choteau glared at him. "If anyone has a bad case of the winds in this camp, it would be you, monsieur."

Gabe stifled a chuckle at Choteau's verbal jab. But Branch couldn't deny it, so he didn't bother to reply.

They continued slowly, wrestling through the dense mishmash of alder. Ahead, a weak blood trail appeared: a couple of thick congealed drops spattered on the foliage that sparkled in the torchlight like menacing black eyes. The blood trail soon entered the old-growth forest opposite the brush and alders. Branch raised the torch to get a better view.

"The trail goes up the mountain," Choteau said. "Not a lot of blood. Flesh wound, eh?"

"Maybe," Branch said. "I don't think he'll be bothering us any-more tonight. We'll leave at first light."

⁂

In the morning, they quickly packed and were headed down the trail by daybreak. Choteau appeared relieved to be leaving the haunted valley, and it seemed to Gabe that tensions faded with each step closer to the Kootenai River. As usual, Branch led the pack train while Choteau brought up the rear. It didn't bother Gabe; he felt more comfortable when Branch's jeering eyes were on the trail and not on him.

Gabe glanced back at Choteau, who kept looking this way and that, clearly still on guard from the previous night's disturbance. Branch, however, was his usual self, oblivious to everything except the trail in front of him and their enormous load of beaver, frequently checking the large bundles to make sure the precious cargo was riding well.

Weary from skinning beaver the day before and a fitful night's rest, Gabe's eyelids grew heavy, his shoulders slumped, and he slowly surrendered to his fatigue as they plodded along. But the calm didn't last long.

"What's a damned lowland skunk doing up here in the high country?" Branch barked.

The disgusting smell from the night before had returned, but Gabe only glanced at Branch and Choteau, then yawned. He shrugged apathetically at Branch's observations, closed his eyes, and once more drooped his head, disregarding the horses irksome snorting at the foreign smell wafting across the trail.

It was always wise to heed the olfactory powers of the horses to give warning. Odors that lingered in the thin air of the mountains could be a sign of danger ahead and a harbinger of possible annihilation. Gabe was well-aware of this from Branch's constant harping at him to pay closer attention to his surroundings, but Gabe had yet to see much urgency. His time on the trail had been without incident up to this point. *Just one more moment of rest,* he thought. *What harm could a skunk bring?*

But when Choteau, riding at the end of the procession, finally caught wind of the pungent smell, he hollered, "That is no skunk, monsieur!"

Gabe sat up and recognized the distinct smell from the night before, when they had followed the blood trail: a mixture of fresh bear dung, skunk juice, and dead fish that turned his stomach and singed his nose hairs.

Gabe turned in his saddle to see Choteau scanning the upper reaches of the massive trees lining the bottom of the canyon. Suddenly, the Frenchman pointed and shouted, "There it is!"

Choteau wheeled his horse, which caused the already tense pack string to startle and jump in an undulating twine of stomping, snorting chaos. The Frenchman leaped off and yanked his gun from its scabbard. Gabe followed where he aimed with his eyes, but there was nothing out of the ordinary—only gnarly limbs that jutted from the enormous cedars like giant outstretched arms.

"Did you see it?" Choteau shouted.

"See what? All I see are big trees and branches," grumbled Branch. "Stop slowing us down."

Choteau pointed up in the trees. "I tell you I saw it!"

Branch shook his head, mumbling profanities under his breath as he heeled his horse in the ribs and continued down the trail.

Choteau stood there, staring into the canopy of the forest until Gabe broke his spell and urged him on. "Come on, André! You're going to get left behind." Pulling back on the reins, he slowed Juniper until the Frenchman mounted his horse and hurried to catch up, glancing nervously into the canopy above as they plodded on through the forest of giant cedars.

Chapter Two

Creatures of the Mountain

M*orning pushed gently against the dark spell of* night, the pre-dawn glow illuminating the entire mountain basin. Far below, the men appeared as small as ants, scurrying and shuffling, their garbled voices and hurried clanking echoing faintly off the canyon walls. High on the ridge above the camp, watchers watched through the ferny canopy of a giant fir tree.

When the procession set out and finally disappeared from the valley floor, the watchers silently and skillfully descended. The Younger swung playfully on the last limb some twenty feet off the ground, then flipped himself to the ground, landing on massive feet with a dull thump. The older one, the big dark Gray, was less playful. Favoring his left shoulder, he lumbered down and lay next to a small spring that gurgled from a fissure in the mountain, while the Younger plucked seeds from pinecones.

Moments later, a clenched fist appeared in front of the Gray. Giant fingers slowly opened, revealing the gift, a handful of pine nuts. The Gray rolled over and looked up at the Younger with melancholy but appreciative eyes. He accepted the pine nuts, popped them in his mouth, then gave a soft, high-pitched coo as the Younger disappeared, once more ascending to the upper boughs.

The Gray sat up, cast his eyes around, and winced when he put his hand down on the ground to push himself up to a sitting position.

Clutching his shoulder, he gave a deep, guttural *humph*. Most of the blood had dried after the bleeding stopped sometime during the night, leaving a thick, crusty mat of coagulated blood on his silvery-gray fur. The Gray stood, his colossal nine-foot frame towering above the nearby alder brush. He stepped toward the spring, knelt, and washed the dried blood caked on his hand and wrist. The Younger soon came down the tree with another handful of pine nuts, which the Gray accepted with a gentle coo.

A clattering of rocks on the mountainside above them sent the smaller one scurrying back up a tree while the Gray stood silently, intently listening and sniffing the air. Then, yawning, he sat and rested his massive arms on bent knees. There he remained, calmly watching a bobbing dipper fluttering in and out of the spring as it searched for larvae.

The brush suddenly parted, but the Gray ignored the swishing and rustling—his nose had already told him what approached from the forest, and he continued watching the dipper, mesmerized as it dove in the water and popped out with a bug, mysteriously managing to stay dry.

A soft call came from behind the Gray, and soon, a large Alpha female stepped near with long, powerful strides, her large, hairy breasts and ponderous belly clearly indicating that she was pregnant. Kneeling, she emptied an armful of pinecones next to the Gray, who answered with a pleased *a-mmmmm* and deftly began removing the nuts and eating them one by one. Without hesitation, she hunkered down next to him and gently picked dried, crusty flakes from his blood-matted shoulder until she had worked her way to the wound.

A rustling behind them and tentative footfalls elicited only a soft *arooo* from the Alpha. The Younger stepped near and looked curiously over her shoulder as she gently pulled long hairs from the deep wound until a trickle of blood began to ooze. The Gray didn't flinch as she rubbed a mossy paste into the round hole, then performed the same procedure on the hole located on the other side of his muscular shoulder. He continued eating pine nuts while watching the dipper, smiling each time it popped out from the spring and performed its bobbing dance before diving in again.

When the Alpha had completed her treatment, the Younger jumped up, grabbed a protruding branch of a nearby pine tree fifteen feet off the ground, and nimbly swung himself up. He looked down at his mother and they made cooing sounds to each other.

She was an impressive specimen in her own right—nearly seven feet tall with massive shoulders and forearms—but the big Gray dwarfed her when he finally stood. She stared at him sadly as he lumbered to a nearby fallen log and sat down with a handful of cones.

She looked up at the Younger, who was standing on a big branch with his arms folded, and vocalized: *Whuh-whuh, whaa. Whuuuh ohhh.* In response, the Younger clambered even higher up the tree, disappearing into the canopy. A few seconds later, pinecones began dropping from the upper reaches, landing with a clatter in a small opening, well-away from the resting Gray. She began picking them up and piling them near the Gray, who leaned against the log and stretched out his long, powerful legs. He looked at the cones, and soon, his fingers went to work, their supple agility incongruous for hands of such size. After chewing a few mouthfuls, he closed his eyes for another nap.

A jay fluttered above the Gray's head and landed on his knee. He squinted, opened an eye, and picked up another cone, then carefully removed some seeds that he fed to the bird one at a time. The gray bird chirped as if to say thank you, and the Gray repeated the identical call. Soon, another jay flew down, then another, also demanding the tasty seeds.

Before long, the cones stopped dropping, and the Younger climbed down to remove and eat the pine nuts. The Gray rolled to his knees, stood, and stretched to his full size, rubbing his wounded shoulder. Shaking out the stiffness, he reached down and picked something shiny from the ground near the fallen log.

He had found it near the creek, close to where the man-beasts slept. At first, he thought it was a rock, but it was much too smooth. On one side was the figure of a man-beast holding a rabbit and on the other side there appeared to be what looked like the leaf of a fern. It appeared ridiculously small in his giant hand as he studied every nuance of the strange shiny object, rubbing his fingers over the ornate designs pressed into it. Curious, the Younger approached, but when he reached for the it, he was met with a glare and a low grunt: *Garoof.* The Younger quickly stepped back submissively, looked down sheepishly, and stepped away.

The Gray promptly launched himself off the bench and headed down the mountain, leaving the others behind. With long strides, he soon covered the half mile to his destination—an opening at the base of a steep cliff. He sniffed the air before squeezing himself through the narrow entrance to a cave and then emerged into a large chamber.

A sliver of sunlight illuminated an array of items he had collected, carefully arranged on a rock ledge inside the cave. The Gray approached the cache, glanced over his shoulder, then carefully added the smooth shiny object to his collection. He paused to examine each in turn, marveling for a moment at each unique shape and intricacy.

His focus was broken when the Alpha female called faintly just outside the cave, *Cooaah, cooaah,* which startled the Gray. He picked up the shiny object he had just laid down and held it to his chest with both hands, glancing protectively toward the entrance. *Garooo!* he yelled, the sound echoing deep into the cavern. He opened his hand and held it in the narrow beam of light to study it one final time, then gently placed it on the rocky shelf with the other items and exited the cave. The worried Alpha and the Younger were waiting patiently when he emerged, greeting the Gray in their own way, with unspoken gestures, subtle facial expressions, and head movements.

Before clambering back up the mountain, they looked as if on cue toward the hazy, smoke-clouded camp to ensure the intruders were gone for good. The threesome had come to fear only one thing—the loud, brazen man-beasts. Wherever they camped, it seemed danger or death was near. The creatures had learned to avoid them, preferring the darkness of the forest or the steep upper reaches of the mountain, where they could go about their business in peaceful obscurity.

Feeling a sense of relief, the Gray looked forward to returning to their normal routine and visiting their favorite feeding areas lower on the mountain. The Younger, especially, seemed pleased—for the man-beasts had killed many beavers, which had saddened him. The three had spied upon the man-beasts from a safe distance high on the mountain for many days until the Gray finally had lost patience.

Moved by frustration and hunger, he had come down the mountain for several nights to toss pebbles at them, hoping to get them to leave.

He wasted no time leading the group to the lake below, where they would find ripe huckleberries and wild raspberries growing abundantly in scattered patches. Disappearing into the foliage, they silently traveled down the mountain into a familiar drainage. They foraged here often, where they could find enough berries to fatten themselves for the long, cold months ahead. After filling his belly on berries, the Younger would often hide in the bushes along the lake. Here, he would watch the beavers go about their business gathering green alders and willow branches, which they would ferry across the water and store in a tangled mass next to their domed lodges. This underwater cache would provide food for the furry rodents during the coldest months of winter, when a thick layer of ice prevented them from foraging on the alder and willow brush growing along the lake shore. The Gray didn't mind the Younger observing them, hoping he would learn the wisdom of storing a cache of food for later use.

But sometimes, the Younger grew bored watching them go back and forth from the brush to their lodge with their loads of branches, and he would crawl atop their lodge and hide. His dark fur blended well with the brownish gray of the beaver lodge, and he would wait until an unwary beaver swam close and then pop up from the lodge, which would frighten the beaver into slapping its tail on the water.

This kept the Younger amused until the Gray grew impatient. After giving the Alpha a knowing nudge, she would then call to him. Obediently, the Younger would leave his curious friends with the huge, orange teeth and return to the task of filling his belly.

It was a good year for berries, but as the first wisps of snow brushed the mountaintops, the Gray sensed winter's icy fingers would soon grip the mountains. Amid the lush greenery near the lake, they peacefully fed until the lingering smell of smoke from the man-beast camp sent a chill up and down the Gray's spine, colder than the icy winter winds that screech across the high peaks. The smell of the man-beast camp reminded him of his wound. The gray whisps of smoke had become a dark, foreboding remembrance that lingered stubbornly in the crisp autumn air of the basin.

$\mathcal{A}$foot

Gabe sensed that trouble seemed to be following them like a wolf nipping at their heels. Since hastily retreating from the remote mountain basin, they had been delayed by bad weather, broken tack, and sore horses.

One evening, several days after the strange encounter with their mysterious tormentor, they camped along the trail near a meadow, where the horses could rest and graze. Sometime during the night, however, two of their stock broke free of their hobbles while the trio slept soundly in their tattered bedrolls next to the campfire. But fortunately, the tracks of the two deserters eventually merged with the main trail and headed east—along the same path that would lead the trappers to their final destination, where the mountains met the northern plains.

One of the missing animals was Branch's riding horse, and, unfortunately for Gabe, the despotic mountain man requisitioned Juniper, forcing Gabe afoot. As the distance grew between him and the pack train, so did Gabe's hatred of Bill Branch.

His eyes watered, momentarily obscuring his vision, as he struggled against the frigid east wind that blew through the broad, timbered valley. He blinked and rubbed his eyes, stumbling along the trail as he tried to keep up with the pack string that inched farther and farther ahead of him. An icy numbness permeated his moccasin-clad feet from the last stream crossing, causing each step to sting. Taking a deep breath, Gabe glowered at Branch and Choteau as they disappeared into the timber ahead of him, riding comfortably dry.

Frustrated and cold, he paused and sighed in frustration when he heard the familiar sound of the horses splashing through yet another stream crossing. He had hoped they would stop to let the horses drink, giving him ample opportunity to catch up—but not this time. The tracks of the two escapees now appeared fresher. Through a gap in the timber, Gabe caught a glimpse as Branch angrily kicked his heels into Juniper's ribs, prompting the horses to surge ahead through the frigid water.

A man on foot could circumvent the stream crossings by taking an alternate route around the serpentine streambed, but the horse trail cut through Blackfeet and Salish country, and the natives had grown increasingly intolerant of trappers. The stories Branch told about cold native justice were still fresh in his mind, and a man alone on foot would be an easy target, so it was critical that he keep pace with the pack train. As they cut through another oxbow bend along the stream, he ran to catch up.

Wonderful, he thought facetiously as he approached the deep stream crossing, watching in frustration as the last pack horse, heavily loaded with beaver plews, disappeared into the timber on the opposite side.

Gabe took a moment to assess the water's depth and flow. He looked down into the deep pool of crystal water, then up and down the stream for a shallower section. Logjams and thick brush quashed any hope of a drier, more suitable crossing. Gabe was tough for a young man his age, but even so, he didn't relish the idea of soaking his leathers up to his waist in the frigid water. Perhaps, if he jumped, he might make it across to the bank on the other side.

The sound of the pack train drifting farther down the trail was like an unrelenting goad—it was time to move. Quickly, he backed away from the bank a dozen paces, then sprinted forward and leaped. For a moment, in mid-flight, he thought he might make it—until he lost momentum and landed with a splash just short of the bank. He cried out as icy mountain water sank its teeth into his flesh, taking his breath away. Holding his rifle high above his head to keep the powder dry, he lunged ahead and crawled out of the water onto the bank. Scrambling to his feet, he stood on the shore for a moment in shock. Exasperated with Branch and the entire misadventure, he clenched his fists in anger and tightened every muscle in his body against the biting cold until he felt the veins on his neck bulging.

"Aaargh!" he blurted angrily before marching on, water seeping from the seams of his soaked moccasins as he hurried to catch up with the pack train that seemed to have vanished as if swallowed by the thickly timbered forest.

After another mile or so without sighting the trappers, Gabe finally noticed the horses and mules tied to nearby trees just off the trail. He gave a deep sigh of relief, slowed his pace, and soon detected the smell of an upwind campfire. Silently, he slipped forward along the trail until he caught a glimpse of Branch and Choteau easing ahead of him toward the wispy smoke that rose above the trees.

Gabe was not surprised by the sight of campfire smoke. It was the only trail for miles that cut directly through the mountains to the northern plains and was frequented used by trappers and native tribes.

Gabe's frigid legs and sore feet made it easier for him to dismiss the idea that the camp might hold a potential enemy. It was the fire he coveted, and the chance to thaw out and dry his soaked leathers. He quickened his steps until he finally caught up with his callous cohorts, who cared little about leaving him behind.

As he moved closer, he noticed that their demeanor and body posture seemed unusual—as if they were on a hunt. Gabe slowed and circled to the left, keeping concealed by the forest, until he finally drew parallel to their position. It was only then that he could see their quarry.

There, in a small meadow, not far from the Flathead River, camped a young Blackfeet boy roasting a freshly killed rabbit above a small fire. Tethered next to him was his horse—along with their missing animals. It was obvious to Gabe that the two strays had simply followed the main trail, stopping, as herd animals often do, at the comforting sight of others of their kind.

The young man must have been pleased when the animals suddenly showed up unannounced at his campsite. Perhaps he was looking forward to the praise he would receive from his Elders after delivering them to his village. But Gabe figured it would be an easy task to reclaim them without any trouble, for the boy appeared to be just a whippersnapper, no older than twelve or thirteen.

Gabe glanced to his right. Hidden just inside the timber, the two trappers watched as the brave saddled his horse. Then Branch tapped Choteau and motioned him forward toward the camp. They wasted no time. While the brave bent over the fire, tending his rabbit, they moved in.

Soon, the unmistakable angry voice of Bill Branch broke the calm of the forest. Instinctively, Gabe stepped forward, emerging into the small campsite clearing. He watched as Branch grabbed the terrified young brave by the collar, nearly lifting him off the ground, while Choteau calmed the animals to keep them from bolting. The boy stared up at Branch with wide-eyed fear as the mountain man growled at him menacingly with his wolfish teeth bared.

Gabe had seen that look of violence in Branch's eyes before and knew it meant trouble. "Let him go, Branch. Let him go!"

Ignoring him, Branch reached for the handle of the long-bladed Green River knife that hung on his hip. Gabe sprinted to intervene as Branch pulled it from its sheath and placed the pointed blade against the boy's midsection, holding him close. Gabe dove, grabbing for Branch's arm just as he began the thrust. But Gabe fell short, his fingers slipping from Branch's elbow, and he landed on the ground next to them with a thud.

"No!" Gabe bellowed as he rolled over and looked up.

The thrust was quick and deep. The boy looked at Gabe, stunned, terrified, and then again at the menacing Branch. His knees buckled, and he collapsed to the ground next to Gabe.

"Damned horse thief!" spat Branch contemptuously as Gabe rolled over and knelt beside the young brave.

Horrified and in shock, the boy grabbed Gabe by the arm, his desperate, pleading eyes begging for help as he coughed and gasped for air, spraying droplets of blood. Gabe blinked as blood spattered his face and ineptly held his hand over the boy's wound, trying to stanch the bleeding. His efforts didn't help, but it was all he knew to do. As blood oozed around his fingers, he looked around in panicked desperation. Perhaps Choteau could help. But the Frenchman gave little heed to the fracas as he casually examined their missing horse and mule for signs of injury.

Gabe looked down again, wondering why the boy had camped here, all alone. He had heard stories of native customs—vision quests or tests of manhood. *He shouldn't be here. This isn't right!* he thought as he felt the world spin upside down in a wild state of confusion.

As the boy's life slipped away, and the light in his eyes faded, Gabe removed his trembling hand from the stab wound and hung his head, nauseated by the senseless waste of life. He couldn't help but notice the young man's handsome features and well-groomed appearance. A wave of indignation swept over him, and his breath quickened as he turned, glaring up at Branch. The filthy, uncouth mountain man stood in stark contrast to the young, handsome brave, the dichotomy vivid and perverse. As Branch strolled nonchalantly toward Choteau and the animals, Gabe's indignation welled into a rage.

"What the hell did you do that for?!" he cried as he rose from his kneeling position beside the boy.

Choteau stepped away from the horses. "He was a voleur, a dirty Indian horse thief."

Nearby stood the boy's horse tied to a tree, and a few yards farther was the rabbit he'd killed for breakfast, still cooking over the small fire. Branch walked back to Gabe, knelt, and wiped his bloodied knife on the brave's pant leg as the boy spontaneously convulsed and belched out blood—one last gasp before slipping completely into the blackness of death.

"Don't just stand there, kid!" barked Branch. "Go through his things there and get anything we might be able to use."

"This horse of his will trade well," Choteau said as he looked it over.

"Yeah, but we need to wash off all those damn Blackfeet paint marks before we leave here."

Gabe could not hide his chagrin and defiance from the wary Branch, who grabbed him by his coat collar and snarled, "You work for me! Do as yer told!"

Branch clenched his jaws and bared his pointed yellow teeth. They were the first thing Gabe had noticed when he'd first met the man—those wicked, wolfish teeth. He often wondered if they'd been chipped into points during a skirmish, or if Branch had sharpened them that way on purpose.

Branch shoved him toward the Indian's horse. Gabe clenched his fists, primal rage whirling, moving him toward a precarious edge where he could feel the animal within baring his teeth, his mind slipping into a wild feral state. Just as he was about to completely lose control and tear into Branch, Choteau came forward, and both men stared him down. Outnumbered, he stomped away and reluctantly began looking through the boy's belongings, still trembling in a state of shock.

"Always, kid. Always do what you're told. Nothing more and nothing less. Let's eat!" His words were hollow and far off. Gabe looked up as Branch smiled for the first time that day, marching to the campfire with his usual cocky self-assurance.

Gabe looked at the nicely roasted rabbit and could almost taste its sweet, savory flavor. But thoughts of eating food after the violent murder he had just witnessed made him sick inside. He looked again at the rabbit and walked away.

"What? Not hungry?" Branch said.

Gabe remained silent in protest.

"Fine by me," Branch said, sneering.

Once out of eyesight, Gabe ran to the nearby stream and vigorously washed the blood from his hands, his stomach still churning. Thick ribbons of red dispersed into opaque vermillion clouds, then dissipated altogether in the flowing water—gone like the life of the young brave.

Looking down near the water's edge, the reflection staring back at him startled him until he realized it was his own, his brown hair and eyebrows appearing black against the stark paleness of his face.

Cold beads of sweat formed on his forehead and broke free, dripping down his brow, running down the sides of his face, until a sudden tingling sensation swept over him. Nauseated, he stumbled over to Juniper, the only object of sanity in his view, and stroked his neck. Immediately, he thought of his father, remembering how he had stroked the neck of Lilly, their Shorthorn milk cow, and how he had felt almost jealous of the ample affection and kind words his father lavished upon her before the daily milking. But as he stroked Juniper's neck, it seemed to make sense why his father loved that old cow so much, and why she always seemed to give more when Gabe's father did the milking. It was so simple that he was surprised he hadn't thought of it earlier—they were friends.

The sudden epiphany brought a sharp pain—one he hadn't felt in a while, as if his heart had doubled up and then abruptly fallen to the pit of his stomach. He breathed deeply, trying to stave off the sickening feeling in the hollow of his gut and continued stroking Juniper's neck, the warmth driving away the icy chill in his hands, but not the trembling.

Choteau and Branch made short work of the rabbit. Gabe had to look away when Branch peeled back the young brave's scalp—a trophy to gloat over or trade for a few handfuls of lead shot or gunpowder. After he'd finished, Branch ordered Gabe and Choteau to toss the body into the stream. Gabe watched, benumbed, as the corpse rolled with the current until it disappeared into a deep trough in the belly of the river.

Chapter Four

Trail to Rendezvous

*G*abe rode with an empty gaze at the rear of the pack train, his head swirling as if he'd been concussed with the butt-end of a rifle, still struggling to reconcile what had just happened. For some strange reason, the last memory of his mother kept tormenting him, perhaps induced from the trauma he'd just witnessed. He tried humming a song, but the memory wouldn't go away. It kept coming back, again and again, jolting him like a schoolmaster's switch and blistering his conscience like a branding.

The expression on her face seemed frozen at the pinnacle of despair: the anguish distorting her natural beauty, the open-mouthed wail so discordant with her gentle voice. But more than anything else, it was the look in her eyes—the profound look of incredulity and dismay. It was a look that haunted him. Then, from her loving lips, came the words that pierced his soul. As he trudged along the trail, Gabe wondered if his mother and father would ever welcome back their weary prodigal. Even more, he wondered if he could ever find the courage to face them.

A wide stream crossing distracted him from his dispiriting thoughts. He was thankful to again be seated firmly on Juniper's back—perhaps now, his leathers would finally start to dry. By all appearances, the two men in front of him had no misgivings or regrets over what had just happened, as if completely impervious to any needling of their deadened consciences.

Gabe was well-aware of their intentions. Their focus now was only on what lay ahead, and they rode with stoic purpose toward a makeshift trading outpost set up on short notice by agents of the Rocky Mountain Fur Company to horn in on their competitor, the Hudson's Bay Company, and capitalize on the few remaining regions still holding beaver. Choteau and Branch called it a Rendezvous—a marketplace where beaver pelts were exchanged for hard cash or trade goods to replenish much-needed supplies.

Branch had educated Gabe regarding the entire plan. They would trap beaver and sell the pelts to fur traders at the Rendezvous, who would then ship them to hatters in England, who would then extract the beaver felt to make expensive hats coveted by both rich and poor alike.

The more Gabe thought about it, the more he believed Branch's "plan" seemed more like a scheme. The circular brown pelts that had seemed so innocuous at first now appeared stained by the blood of the young brave, soiled beyond remedy by the avarice of Bill Branch and André Choteau.

Gabe remembered his long journey from the woods of Kentucky. The cottonwoods lining the Missouri River had prevented him from seeing the changes in the landscape as they crept against the muddy current of the river. One morning, he climbed the steep banks overlooking the river, and the first thing he noticed was the relentless, unbridled wind that roared across the plains. It seemed the farther they traveled, the more unforgiving it became, pressing the prairie grass flat, stinging any exposed flesh and burning it red as if from a scorching sun. Whenever it diminished to a growl, it blew the tall grass like undulating waves of a great golden sea.

The mountains appeared as blue-gray monoliths on the distant horizon, growing larger each day until they rose from the plains like the toothy jaw of a dragon, with snowcapped granite peaks so high it seemed they nearly brushed the stars. Gabe never forgot the feeling of amazement when he'd first entered those mountains. The roaring wind receded to a purr, the air was pristine and fresh, and the chalky river waters became crystal clear with riverbeds of rounded stones in various shades of purple, red, and blue.

But now, the glory of his memories had been tainted, and the shining mountains that had seemed so full of promise at the beginning of this trek now took on a darker hue. The cascading waterfall that gushed down the side of a mountain along the trail, the jagged peaks where he'd watched mountain goat kids frolic and play, and the many other sights that had previously stirred his soul now seemed dull and blunted.

The face of the dying boy kept flashing across his mind. Branch's big Green River knife had done a thorough job, but its sharp edge had cut something in Gabe as well, and he could almost feel its cold steel pricking against his heart. He looked at the fragments of the boy's blood stubbornly clinging in crevasses along his fingernails, just as the youth had struggled to cling to life. Quickly, he scratched and rubbed to remove the dried blood and along with it, the memory.

Gabe gazed up at the monochromatic mountain landscape that now seemed ominous, even dead. For the first time in his life, he doubted the presence of God. He could still see God's footprints in the majestic snowcapped mountains and His fingerprints in the gilded wings of the graceful golden eagle circling overhead, but he felt as though God had vanished from this place—flown away to a heavenly Xanadu far beyond the stars to a garrison where He could avert His unsullied eyes from the madness of men.

His dream of being a mountain man had been dashed, thoroughly crushed, and it lay gasping on the ground in the throes of death. His only hope was to complete the transaction that had begun several months before—get paid after they sold the beaver and either find another mentor or make his way back to Kentucky. He had friends and kinfolk there who might put him up until he could find work somewhere.

He looked at his calloused, grimy hands as Juniper gently rocked him back and forth in the saddle. He thought of his mother again and how she was so meticulous, making sure he kept himself well groomed and presentable. *If Mom could see me now,* he thought, chuckling despite himself, *she'd hand me a bar of soap and a brush and pour me a bucket of hot water.* In her honor, he made himself a silent promise to scrub himself clean the first chance he got.

His father's words echoed in his mind: "Nature's a hard schoolmaster with no mercy for fools." Gabe hadn't understood those words until now, and though he'd hated schooling, he suddenly realized that the lessons he learned in the small classroom back home were much easier than the education he'd received over the past couple of months. The mountains, so alluring and majestic when viewed from afar, had taught him hard lessons. Foremost was that freedom from rules and accountability brought a host of problems. The structure and conventions of his life in Kentucky, including his parents' oversight, which he had despised, were now beginning to make sense.

As he pondered this, he realized that even among the trappers, there existed a harsh set of rules—a social order akin to a wolf pack with Branch as the undisputed alpha wolf. Initially, Gabe had struggled with the urge to argue with his harsh employer, but each time, he was quickly nipped. Eventually, he had to surrender to the rules of the pack, finding it easier to just shut up and do as he was told, imagining himself a captive Israelite and Branch his whip-happy Egyptian overlord.

The mountains had a separate set of laws—uncodified and perhaps harsher than those found in either the civilized world or on the trapline. The unfortunate souls who failed to heed these rules usually didn't fare well, and no trapper survived long by traveling haphazardly through the treacherous mountain landscape alone.

He learned there were specific travel corridors, established and used by indigenous people for generations. These routes entered the vast wilderness at specific points on the Rocky Mountain front, dictated by geographic soft spots in the otherwise craggy teeth of the mountains. Just as blood flows through the body, these routes started as arteries, then split into veins and then capillaries as they penetrated deeper into the rugged terrain. It took many years for a man to learn the obscure pathways scattered throughout the vast sea of mountains, as well as the many dangers to avoid. As they snaked their way along the turquoise waters of the Middle Fork, Gabe reluctantly acknowledged to himself that likely few people knew these travel routes better than Bill Branch.

But this trail seemed pleasant by comparison to some of the others they had suffered through. It meandered through lush meadowlands and dense stands of lodgepole forests dotted with the occasional patch of larch trees whose needles had turned a brilliant yellow as autumn settled upon the mountains.

After nearly a week of hard riding, Gabe could see from the many fresh horse tracks on the trail that they would soon arrive at their destination. More importantly, he was encouraged by the prospect of meeting other trappers. He wanted out. His overbearing, murderous boss had purged him of every idyllic notion about the mountain-man lifestyle.

Even though Gabe was considered a greenhorn by his two counterparts, he felt a sense of pride about one thing—they couldn't argue he hadn't proven himself highly capable and well-suited to the challenges of the trapper's life. He was confident in his raw physical strength, and he wasn't afraid of anything, including Bill Branch, even though Choteau had told him that it wasn't unusual for an inept apprentice to mysteriously disappear from Branch's employ.

It didn't take long for Gabe to realize that Branch had little use for people; they were just another tool, like a knife or hatchet to be used until broken, then quickly cast aside. He managed to remain in Branch's good graces by doing the work of two men, but the occasional semblance of repose was met with swift rebuke. He did his best to avoid testing the boundaries of his boss's limited patience, but it was futile, and he found himself becoming calloused to the verbal jabs and stringent demands of apprenticeship.

Soon, they topped Marias Pass. Far in the distance, beyond the long gauntlet of rugged mountains, lay the broad expanse of the northern plains. A sense of relief and hope made him sit up in his saddle, for the end of their journey was near. As the pace quickened, Gabe could sense his compatriots' eager anticipation of cashing in on their huge catch of fur.

The trail descended gradually toward the Two Medicine River, where other trappers had already started gathering in a nearby meadow. A few brave men risked traveling by canoe, which offered quicker access to prime beaver country when safe water levels permitted. But river travel brought danger from logjams, rapids, and bandits eager to relieve trappers of both furs and worldly possessions. For these reasons, Branch preferred to lead his expeditions by horseback, which provided a quick means of escape if ambushed.

Just when the prospect of a new and different course had lifted Gabe's spirits, Branch turned abruptly in his saddle and scowled, "From this point on, I do all the talking."

Gabe immediately felt a tightening of his jaw and a swelling of anger. *Count to ten,* he thought. *Count to ten before speaking and then bite your tongue if you open your mouth.* It was the advice his father always gave him. Gabe knew it was a weakness—his tendency to blurt whatever was on his mind instead of keeping his mouth shut. The words always found a way to well up and escape his lips, despite the wise advice, especially whenever he got angry. This time, however, he fought the urge and held his tongue, for he had a plan.

Branch's posture indicated he was poised to act quickly upon any sign of trouble. He threw a hawkish glance at the men near the river's edge and appeared to recognize one of them, perhaps a former trapping associate. The man's presence seemed to put Branch at ease, and he nodded to acknowledge him as the three rode by. Several other trappers near the river unloaded meager pelts from beached canoes. They lifted their heads and stared at their pack string, heavily laden with fur, but seemed to divert their eyes when they recognized the unmistakable face of Bill Branch.

The sight of smoke rising from tipis and campfires quickened Gabe's pulse. This would be his first Rendezvous. The sweet smell of roasting buffalo made his mouth water and stomach growl. The steady diet of dried, greasy beaver flesh had thoroughly flogged his palate, and he longed for anything besides rodent meat. *Perhaps the tight-fisted Branch would relent and barter for steaks,* he mused to himself.

The trail offered scant game aside from the occasional rabbit or grouse. Most of the backcountry deer and elk had either been shot or had grown wary of trappers, leaving their hiding places to feed only during the dead of night.

Lately, he had been tortured by a recurring dream about his mother's cooking, starting with a freshly baked pie. His nose wouldn't let him forget the sweet aroma of cinnamon and apples. In his dream, the pie always sat cooling unattended on the windowsill outside the kitchen of their small log cabin, just out of reach. He tried purging the thought of the pie, but that only ushered memories of other scrumptious vittles: roast beef, smoked ham, sweet potatoes, corn—and the butter, *mmmm*, the butter, spread thick on freshly baked bread—it made his mouth water and his stomach growl like a hungry grizzly bear.

His favorite breakfast included his mother's scrambled eggs, whipped in cream and fried in bacon fat. But lately, his conscience nagged louder and louder and the cornucopian fantasies of her scrambled eggs had become tainted by the memory of chicken eggs neatly aligned along the split-rail fence behind the barn. When his parents were not around, he would sneak eggs from the henhouse and use them for target practice. All went well until his parents discovered his transgression. He would never forget the beating he received for that offense, or how his courageous mother dove between him and his father after the tenth hard belting on his backside with the razor strap.

Now, after having been denied a decent square meal since St. Louis, he wondered what hobgoblin of hell would ever possess him to destroy a perfectly good egg. As they rode, he suddenly had another epiphany—how could he have been so heedless of his parents' efforts to scratch out a living and keep two meals on the table each day? But the memory that truly pierced his soul was of how callous and indifferent he had been to the tears of his mother after she found the fragments of eggshells lying on the ground beneath the fence.

Compared with his Spartan existence since leaving home, Kentucky was a land "flowing with milk and honey." But these were just halcyon memories now, buried under piles of skinned carcasses, diminished by dangerous trails, and pierced clean through by Branch's sharp tongue.

At least at the Rendezvous, Gabe might find respite from the daily fight and perhaps recuperation for his weary soul. It was an unspoken rule that the Rendezvous, for the most part, was a safe zone, where warring parties set aside differences to openly trade without the threat of hostility. The fact that everyone was well-armed to quash any misbehavior undoubtedly helped facilitate a measure of acceptable decorum.

As they entered the encampment, Gabe was pleased to see a group of Indians and mountain men preparing for a footrace while raggedly clad ruffians placed wagers and lined the perimeter to cheer them on. The congenial hubbub of activity helped ease his troubled mind. He had been looking forward to this moment, eager to test his skill in the contests Choteau had spoken of.

As the men lined up to race, Choteau whispered to Branch, "Better hide that." He pointed to the scalp of the Indian boy hanging from his saddle horn. "We've got Blackfeet in camp." Gabe scowled and grit his teeth as Branch hastily moved the scalp to a saddle bag.

"Never let an opportunity for profit slip by" was one of Branch's mottos, regardless how heinously obtained. Gabe scanned the slatternly trappers, who appeared to be of the same ilk as Branch, and he resigned himself to the fact that the ne'er-do-well would no doubt find a willing reprobate to trade something of value for the scalp.

The sight of a couple young Blackfeet men gave Gabe a disquieting sense of foreboding as he remembered the boy Branch had killed on the trail. The last thing he wanted was for the ire of the Blackfeet to be kindled when they were in such proximity to the band's main village, especially since he might have to cut through their territory to reach the Missouri River and catch a boat ride back to St. Louis.

The horses startled when an official fired his flintlock pistol to start the footrace. As the runners bolted toward the finish line, the crowd held up jugs of whiskey and cheered raucously, a clear indication that many were well on their way to inebriation.

At first glance, the hodgepodge mixture of Indians, English, and French presented an eclectic cross-section of humanity that seemed to congeal in relative harmony. But after listening each night to Branch and Choteau, it came clear that underneath the thin veneer of civility was an edge sharper than a beavertail dag, brought on by cultural animosity and the economic upheaval from the dying fur trade.

In short, most of the beaver had been trapped out, which made both the natives and the mountain men even more hungry for fur.

The older trappers could sense the tension in the air. Take away a man's food, or his means of obtaining it, and atrocities are sure to follow; civility is cast aside and replaced with barbaric lawlessness. Make a man hungry enough and he transforms into a lower life form— a feral beast more dangerous than a grizzly.

But for Gabe, the dark clouds rising on the economic landscape played second-fiddle to what was unfolding before his eyes. He looked on with growing enthusiasm as the winner of the footrace was quickly awarded a braid of tobacco and a jug of whiskey. "I want to run a race," he said impulsively as they rode by.

"Forget it," Branch said. "You'll never outrun them Blackfeet. They run like bloody damned deer. Besides, you've got work to do."

Gabe sighed deeply and eyed the menagerie of trappers and Indians gathered around small campfires. Perhaps he could find an amicable, honest soul who might take him in. But all he saw were scruffy, wind-weathered trappers as wild as the rugged mountains they had just crawled from. The encampment was abuzz with the discordant sound of various tongues and dialects, some bartering zealously for trade goods, while others haggled using widely known sign language. Many of the natives and trappers were clearly multi-lingual, and Gabe suddenly felt witless and out of place. The power of trade, and the benefits it brought, had perhaps forced them all to take greater pains to understand one another—at least when it came to negotiating.

As the three plodded toward the rough-hewn log cabin at the far end of the meadow, folks stopped what they were doing momentar-ily and stared in disbelief at Branch's pack mules carrying massive bundles of beaver plew. They passed a small group of buckskin-clad mountain men practicing for the ax-throwing contest. Next to them, a few Salish women haggled with a crusty trapper as they tried to trade a blond wolf pelt for a bright red wool blanket.

On the surface, the Rendezvous appeared to improve native life, but Gabe noticed something sinister flowing beneath the thin veneer of gleeful trading—the amber liquid that swept the natives away. He saw what it did to Branch, and he was puzzled why others seemed blind to its deleterious effects. Some of the natives called it firewater.

The few who saw its evil, mostly wizened old warriors, stayed clear of it. Those who didn't were smitten by it and became easy prey for the unscrupulous.

For Gabe, the whiskey was a double-edged sword. It made Branch surly up to a point, but if he consumed enough, it eventually made him groggy. One benefit was that Gabe learned a lot about Bill Branch from Choteau's campfire stories, spoken in hushed tones while the drunk trapper slept soundly under the effects of whiskey. Some of the tales seemed dubious but judging by the reactions of the trappers at the Rendezvous, Gabe wondered if they perchance had a measure of truth.

Several men quickly stepped aside, giving Branch a wide berth, while others spat tobacco rancorously, just out of eyesight, and mumbled under their breath as they rode past. The mixture of fearful and disdainful stares spoke volumes—Branch's reputation preceded him like a murder of crows. His hawkish face, furrowed brow, and steely gaze that seemed to look straight through a man elicited an instinctive reaction suggesting a malevolent notoriety.

Despite all this, even Crooked Bill Branch, the name men called him behind his back, had a sliver of kindness in him. Gabe had noticed it early on during his apprenticeship, an occasional lapse into a kind of fatherly patience—but only well after his whiskey had run dry. Even Choteau admitted Branch hadn't always been a stone-hearted killer. The frontier had hardened him over the years like a flint spearhead. According to the Frenchman, when Branch was doused with whiskey on a rare blood moon, he would sit by the campfire, quote tearful verses, and speak forlornly of the woman he'd left behind in Old England.

Choteau said her name was Julia Trimmer, a nobleman's daughter he had met at a poetry gathering. At one time, Branch had fancied himself a bit of a bard, and he wooed her with heartfelt verses until his romantic words finally melted her heart. Soon, the two were stealing away to quiet places to do the things lovers do. But when her father discovered the covert affair, he was incensed and hurried her away to an undisclosed location, refusing to allow his daughter to marry a common landholder.

Branch had then sunk into a deep depression and even contemplated suicide. It was a friend who rescued him and set him on a different course—a hatter who claimed to know of a sure path to riches. His seductive stories of American rivers teeming with beaver ripe for the taking captured Branch's imagination, and a plan unfolded—he made an oath to become wealthy trapping beaver, return to England to stake his claim as an equal to any nobleman, and win back his love.

He saw her one last time six months after their plans had been thwarted. It was just a glimpse as her overprotective father whisked her into a carriage, but it was a glimpse that pierced his heart, for she was obviously well-on with child.

Seeing her again, in such a condition, made Branch even more determined to succeed. But as the years slowly passed, the wilderness had a transformative effect on him, as it did on so many others. Bite by bite, the jagged fangs of the mountains had chewed away the chains of social construct that had tightly constrained him until Branch was completely freed from them. The lover's oath he had so desperately clung to was forgotten, swallowed up by the mountains, drowned in the blood of beavers, and lost among countless skirmishes.

It was difficult to imagine the former William Branch, gentleman poet. The only Branch Gabe knew was the rugged, cynical mountain man who seemed invincible. Forever etched in his mind was the sight of battle scars mapped across Branch's body. Gabe noticed them the few times the hardened trapper had removed his shirt to scrub off the grime after a long sweaty day of fleshing beaver. The leathery skin of his sinewy body was marred by old knife, arrow, and bullet wounds. On his left side, just under the skin, rested a .53-caliber ball, where it had lodged after nearly passing entirely through his body during a skirmish with the Shoshone. Privately, Choteau claimed Branch surely survived the life-threatening wound on sheer meanness alone. Removing the lead ball resting under his skin would have been an easy task, but Branch preferred to leave it where it was lodged—as a souvenir, or perhaps a talisman bargaining chip with superstitious natives should the need arise.

Choteau said the tribes farther south claimed he had been touched by the Great Spirit, naming him White Medicine because of his stubborn refusal to die. Branch never objected to the moniker, fostering their perception of his invincibility with embellished storytelling. Though he doubted some of the claims, Gabe was under no illusion and was fully aware that Branch's warped mind had a manic bend, capable of turning dark on a moment's notice at any perceived show of disrespect, and he had learned the hard way to always be on guard.

Chapter Five

The Trade

C*ampsites were scattered along the perimeter of* the meadow, and as they approached the small makeshift trader's cabin tucked against the trees, the staring vagabond trappers passed around brown jugs of whiskey and laughed obnoxiously as they pickled themselves.

Gabe was struck by the sight of a short, portly man who stood looking over the encampment from the doorway of the cabin with an odd sense of glee written on his face, as if pleased with the sight of the developing crapulence. Something about the man, the self-assured way he held the collar of his coat and the wide grin on his face as he squinted over his spectacles, made Gabe suspicious. As they dismounted and stepped toward the cabin, the trader's rapacious disposition quickly changed when he recognized Branch. Without hesitation, he waddled into his cabin, sat down behind a roughly hewn desk, and feigned looking busy.

Inside the dingy cabin were stores of trade goods neatly stacked and awaiting customers, transported via keelboat from Fort Union, then by primitive wagon to the Rendezvous. Included were rifles, axes, tomahawks, knives, as well as gunpowder, shot, and a wide assortment of trapping supplies—all marked up to reap a hefty profit.

The ladies weren't forgotten, either. The wares included a variety of household items from wool blankets and clothing items to cooking utensils and colorful adornments of little value, but they were greatly treasured among the native women and perfect for a good fleecing.

Gabe soon noticed the stockpiles of rank spirits—set back away from the flapping buffalo-hide front door to better protect the hoard from pilfering hands. When the trader offered Branch a jug of whiskey before trading, Gabe caught on to his game—use the whiskey to grease the wheels for unscrupulous negotiations. But Branch was much too shrewd for that game.

"You can't pull the wool over my eyes, Smith," Branch said. "You can keep yer whiskey—until after the trade, of course."

It was widely known that it had become illegal to use whiskey for trading with the natives, but Smith obviously didn't care, shrewdly aware that nobody would enforce such a law in this remote corner of the frontier.

The chubby trader laughed and refilled his lamp with the toxic liquid, then reached out his hand to Choteau and Gabe. "Douglas Smith, fur trader." Gabe introduced himself and shook the man's round hand, which felt cold and soft, like a greasy ball of lard.

Smith plopped down on an upright section of log, his ponderous belly hanging over his belt like a heavy whiskey keg. He tilted his dome-topped, beaver-felt derby over his eyes, opened his ledger book, and squinted through spectacles that hung precariously on the end of his stubby nose. With a quill in his pudgy fingers, he jotted down Branch's name, his jowls quivering.

"I thought you were buying at Fort Piegan," groused Branch.

Smith grinned obnoxiously and looked up at him over his spectacles, a bead of sweat forming on his brow. "I left them boys and joined up with Rocky Mountain Fur. The Blackfeet went on the warpath and burned down the damned fort."

"The hell you say!" Branch shook his head. "Ain't this Hudson's Bay territory?"

"Bull! Who told ya that? I don't give a rat's ass what Hudson's Bay says anyway. They think they own this country. Besides, I'm offering nearly two dollars more for a prime pelt than those cheapskates."

"I won't say a word," replied Branch, smiling.

Smith rose and retrieved a wooden measuring rod. "Let's take a look at these furs of yours," he said before waddling out the door, eager to inspect the large catch of beaver. Gabe, Choteau, and Branch had little choice but to follow.

Choteau muttered, "What in the name of Heaven does a man have to eat to get that fat?"

Branch chuckled and murmured, "I hear he can eat half a mule in a single setting."

"What's that?" Smith asked. But before they could reply, he approached the horses and remarked, "Say, that's quite a load of beaver!" His squinting eyes opened wide and lustfully darted up and down at the fur, then he eagerly untied a bundle, touching his upper lip jubilantly with his thick, fat tongue.

Branch swaggered closer, arms folded across his chest, grinning confidently. "Ever see beaver fur like these?"

Smith rummaged through the pile, measuring and remeasuring, stroking the plush fur again and again. He cocked his head back and looked up at Branch. "I haven't seen a catch like this since..."

He stuck out his bottom lip, then pursed them, trying to hide his excitement. The plews were plush, heavy, and enormous. Smith continued to caress them, one after another, lovingly, as if petting a purring cat. For a moment, he appeared transfixed, mesmerized by the heavy pile of pelts stacked at his feet. Retrieving from his pocket a small bone tool etched to gauge the thickness of a pelt, he measured feverishly, then announced, "These all appear to be select quality dark heavyweights—jumbos." He shook his head in disbelief.

Branch puffed out his chest, smiling. "Yup. Told ya so, Smithy. Best beaver in a thousand miles," he boasted, "and only *we* know where to get 'em."

Soon, a curious crowd had gathered near Smith's cabin, eagerly watching and listening as he performed his inspection for any hint or clue regarding the locality where they had obtained the beaver plews. Gabe overheard one of the men in the crowd say, "Listen, Jones, before the day is over, I'm gonna find out where they got 'em." He glanced at the man and recognized him as the one Branch had nodded to when they first arrived.

Gabe stepped back and watched as the excitement grew, like a prairie fire, throughout the encampment, as the camp denizens chattered eagerly and discussed how they would return to the mountains to find more beaver. After seeing Branch's catch, they knew they had to be out there somewhere—swimming in the untouched arteries and veins of the mountains. They must be found and trapped quickly—before others found and extirpated them completely. Seasoned with intoxication, new plans were hatched, with bulging eyes and waving arms, to go deeper into the mountains, and this time, the trappers would redouble their efforts.

"Now, where'd you boys say you got these?" said Smith, rubbing his chin.

"I didn't say," Branch replied.

"That, my friend, is a trapper's secret," added Choteau, grinning.

Smith finished counting out the pelts and unlocked a heavy steel box full of gold, silver, and copper coins. He sorted and counted the coins, placing them atop one of the beaver pelts. "I can pay you the balance in supplies," he said with a grin. He looked up at the two mountain men, eagerly awaiting their response. Smith was clearly excited by the encampment's reaction to the enormous catch of fur, no doubt aware the men would drink whiskey and sit in circles around campfires, chattering with renewed vigor to extract the creatures from every pond and rivulet in the mountains.

Branch and Choteau stared at all the coins Smith had placed on the bundle of pelts and then stared at each other. They seemed bewildered, as if the payment was more than expected. In the next instant, Branch broke into a happy laugh, and he and Choteau grabbed each other by the forearms, danced a jig, and let out a loud whoop that could be heard throughout the camp.

"It's beer and skittles for us, Choteau! Beer and skittles!" Branch said boisterously.

Smith chuckled at their reaction until his jowls jiggled. He could barely contain himself, almost forgetting to lock the box of coins before hastily beginning the task of hauling the heavy bundles of fur into his cabin.

Chapter Six

Eagle Claw

G*abe's first impulse was to help the portly trader* haul the furs into his cabin, but Smith's rabid demeanor stopped him short—as if he might possibly catch his disease if he got too close. Beads of sweat dripped down Smith's forehead and off the end of his nose as he hauled load after load, disappearing into the small cabin, then tucking them out of sight in the dark, dingy depths.

Gabe pondered the scene as he waddled to and fro, noticing how the trader strangely resembled the beaver in his never-ending task of building dams when moved by the sound of trickling water—only it wasn't the trickle of water that drove Smith, but rather the tinkle of coins and what they could bring him.

Out of the corner of his eye, Gabe watched as Branch gleefully sorted the coins and placed them in leather bags until only a few copper and silver ones remained. He picked them up, held them in the palm of his hand, and stared at them—the precious coins. After a moment of contemplation, he grinned, picked up a large silver one and put it in the biggest sack. The remaining pittance he put in a small leather pouch. Gabe quickly turned away when Branch faced him and shouted, "Greenhorn! Catch!" tossing him the small pouch.

Gabe turned, caught it, and tucked it in his coat pocket, not bothering to count his hard-earned pay. The feathery weight of the bag confirmed Branch had doled him but a paltry lick-up. Gabe chuckled mirthlessly at the absurdity of the payment, considering all the work he had done for the mountain man. His herculean effort to hack a path into Branch's beaver paradise was worth at least a quarter share, by any honest man's standards. But Gabe had moved beyond indignation and no longer cared about the coins, for the trail to the Rendezvous had brought things to light.

Gabe watched as Branch, without hesitating, grabbed his rifle and walked to the center of the camp. He raised his gun and fired it into the air, which immediately got everyone's attention, then hollered, "I'm here to tell ya that there's still fur to catch. You just need to go farther and deeper into the backcountry, boys. They're still out there! Looky here!" Branch then held up the bag of gold and silver coins and brazenly boasted, *"Yeeeehaw! I'm a rich man!"*

Bemused, Gabe tried to decipher Branch's new game. The mountain man had just rattled the chains of the beast, and soon, the entire encampment would be buzzing with fresh plans. But why would he invite attention by teasing everyone? Were his antics part of some carefully orchestrated scheme, or was he just rubbing their noses in his triumphant success?

Branch's celebratory mood spread throughout the encampment like a fever. The trappers stood around chattering and gesturing wildly, completely unaware of their ailment: greed. *More* was what they wanted—always more, never less.

Two trappers soon approached Branch and Choteau as Gabe busied himself tending camp while eavesdropping on their conversation.

"George Johnson. How's the trapline?" said Branch by way of a greeting.

"Bill Branch. Good to see ya. This is my partner, Thomas Jones." Johnson smiled as Jones reached out his hand, but the wary Branch ignored the gesture and murmured half-heartedly, "Pleased to meet ya." Branch nodded toward Choteau and said, "This is André Choteau, my partner. He trapped many years with the Hudson's Bay outfit. Damn good beaver man. Choteau, this is George Johnson and—what was your name again?"

"Thomas Jones," the man replied.

Branch nodded indifferently, while Choteau extended his hand and greeted them with his heavy French accent: "Pleasure to meet you both."

At first glance, Johnson appeared to be the manifest embodiment of a mountain man. He wore a silvery brimmed wolfskin hat that rested atop a head of brown hair that just touched the top of his shoulders. A row of four-inch decorative fringe ran along the sleeves of his jacket, with another row that wrapped around his shoulders. Even more astounding—his meticulous attire appeared brand new, not weathered or stained from sweat and blood like all the other trappers.

He was adorned with the classic mountain-man accoutrements: a coveted Green River knife tucked in an ornately beaded sheath, a fine leather belt lined with silver medallions, and a polished powder horn fashioned from a mature bull buffalo. But most impressive of all was the grizzly-claw necklace draped across his chest, its six-inch claws symmetrically spaced with colorful beads.

While Johnson appeared burly enough to take on a griz single-handedly, his brown beard was unusually well groomed and coiffed. Unlike Gabe, whose thick, calloused hands bore the hallmarks of hard work, Johnson's hands were small for his body size and relatively callous-free. Appearing almost soft, they were devoid of the typical patina induced by bloodstains and beaver grease—even his fingernails were clipped, trimmed, and clean.

Johnson had a gaudy disposition to match his remarkable outward appearance. His stride was excessively confident, with a wide swagger, as if he had learned to walk from the grizzly bear whose claws adorned his puffed-out chest. He had a way of posturing himself a bit past upright, with his chin and nose tilted back slightly, as if at any moment, he might sprout a wide-flaring fan of tom-turkey feathers. Moreover, the manner in which he turned his head to the left or right was reminiscent of a proud mountain buck displaying impressive antlers.

Likewise, Jones was also an interesting sight to behold, appearing better suited as a judge or cleric rather than a rugged mountain man. His wide-rimmed black hat and matching black wool coat reminded Gabe of the country preacher who made his rounds every other week near his Kentucky home to preach to the settlers. Jones was more slightly built than most men, but appeared wiry, with short hair, a clean-shaven face, and a square jaw to match his sober countenance.

"That's one helluva catch you got there," Johnson said with a chuckle.

Branch was quick to reply: "There's more where that came from, boys, and I know right where to get 'em."

Gabe glanced at his boss when he heard the timbre in his voice shift and saw the subtle smile on his face. "Let the games begin," muttered Gabe as he unloaded panniers from the pack mules, for he knew from Branch's wry smile that he wanted something from the two trappers. But what?

After months of being victimized by Branch's psychological gamesmanship, Gabe took pains to avoid falling prey to his manipulations. However, he found it amusing whenever Branch directed his cunning wiles at the gullible Choteau. It was like a game—to decipher Branch's next scheme before it inevitably revealed itself. There wasn't much else to occupy one's mind in a trappers' camp when bored by the daily routine.

Why would he say that to Johnson? Gabe wondered. *Was it bait? No. A seed. Yes, a seed.* Crooked Bill Branch was wise to the darker motives that fester within a man, and he observed that Branch often started his game by planting thoughts or ideas—ones that would take root in the fertile soil of a greedy mind. Already, he was tilling, cultivating, and sowing, plotting for what lay ahead, confident his seeds would sprout and bear fruit. *But what weed will emerge this time? And what noxious fruit will it bear?* If Gabe had his way, he wouldn't be around to find out. Nevertheless, he continued to listen for clues as he worked to set up their campsite a stone's throw from the trader's cabin. He wanted to get his chores out of the way so he could tend to more personal matters—the contests.

Branch and Choteau abruptly ceased their celebratory chatter and began staring intently at something across the meadow. Gabe naturally turned to see what had caught their attention and spotted an unusual-looking Indian man emerging from the timber riding a striking brown-and-white paint horse and leading another laden with a decent catch of beaver plew.

He stood out from the others, the brownish tint of his hair contrasting with the jet-black color of the other natives'. As he moved closer, it became apparent his skin and hazel eyes were also lighter than the others.

"Damn 'breed," Branch spat. "That there's the worst kinda animal—half human and half Injun."

"That's Eagle Claw. The Blackfeet call him the White Warrior," replied Jones. "I wouldn't tangle with him. He's crafty as a coyote and bites like a rattler."

Unfazed by the cold stares, Eagle Claw stopped his horse at the fur buyer's cabin and nimbly hopped off. He left the reins hanging loosely on the ground, apparently confident his well-mannered horses wouldn't run off while he unfastened his bundle of beaver pelts. The warrior possessed a quiet dignity, which stood in stark contrast to the uncouth mannerisms of Branch and his ilk.

The weapons he carried gave fair warning that he wasn't to be trifled with. His belt was adorned with colorful beadwork, and snugly tucked under it was a long-handled hatchet. Its four-inch blade tapered to the eye, with an equally deadly man-killing pike jutting opposite the blade. A Hawken rifle with decorative brass tacks lining the edges of its maple stock hung outside the scabbard from a rawhide strap tied around his saddle horn. Hanging from his hip was an eight-inch beavertail dagger with a blood-brown patina obtained from frequent use, and a smaller one was tucked in a sheath fastened to one of his knee-high moccasins.

Gabe caught the Indian's eye and said, "Nice catch." The man acknowledged him with a wary nod as he removed the bundle.

"Don't be friendly to Injuns, boy!" Branch exclaimed loud enough for Eagle Claw to hear. "Specially a damn 'breed like that one. Nothin' worse than a 'breed. He'll smile at yer face and take your scalp first chance he gets."

Gabe expected a reaction, but the man once again ignored the insult and the demeaning attitude of the trappers. He plopped down the bundle of beaver fur and retied the straps to his elk-antler pack saddle, still unfazed by their stares.

Then, to everyone's surprise, the brave looked at Choteau and amiably said, "Bonjour, Monsieur Choteau. Mon père me disait toujours, 'Couche avec un serpent, et attend-toi à être mordu.' Méfiez-vous, mon ami."

"What the hell? Do you know him? What did he say?" barked Branch, as if insulted that the man had spoken out loud.

Choteau's eyes shifted nervously under the searing heat of Branch's probe and replied, "Hell, no, I don't know him! We might have crossed paths—once."

"You didn't answer my question, Choteau. What did he say, damn it?"

Choteau nervously paused as if his tongue had turned to stone. Finally, he blurted, "How should I know? The damn 'breed speaks poor French."

"He said something about laying with a snake," remarked Jones.

As the brave picked up his bundle of fur, a slight grin spread across his face, then he turned and entered the cabin.

"Would you look at that?" Choteau pointed, as if desperate to change the subject.

Gabe looked up from the ring of rocks he was busy constructing for a firepit. Across the meadow, a white man with a black beard and an attractive native woman walked arm in arm toward the cabin. She walked with a pronounced limp, and when they came closer, it became clear that something had horribly disfigured her; the left side of her head was badly scarred, her left eye sagged lazily, and thick strands of white hair grew from a slight depression just above her left temple.

Then, the tall, raven-haired woman walking behind them caught his eye. He stopped what he was doing and found himself staring at her as the trio approached. She was stunning. Her dark eyes sparkled with an energy that matched her confident stride, and she was obviously in fine fettle judging from her stature and how her buckskin breeches fit snugly around the graceful curves of her hips.

"Damn! I'd take a squaw like that any day," Choteau remarked.

"Not that one," said Johnson with a laugh. "That one's a hell-cat. She'd gut you clean while you sleep, and you wouldn't know it till you woke and tried to take a swig of whiskey!"

The woman saw them staring at her and frowned in disapproval. Gabe averted his eyes and continued his duties. His father had always told him it was rude to stare, especially at a woman. But he soon found himself peeking again, impulsively, as if his eyes had a will of their own.

"Who is she?" Choteau asked, appearing pleased with the distraction from Branch's inquiry about the half-breed.

Johnson spoke up: "She belongs to that Kootenai tribe up on the Tobacco Plains, and she ain't to be trifled with. She killed a man who gave her unwanted advances near the mouth of the North Fork. Saw what was left of him—saw it with my own two eyes. Cut off his manhood and slit him open, clean as a whistle. Cut him into pieces like he was a fresh-killed mountain buck, then scattered him around for the ravens and coyotes and wolves."

Gabe hesitated before placing the last rock around the firepit and studied her while she waited impatiently near the doorway, again finding it nearly impossible to take his eyes off her. Johnson's claims seemed absurd, given her innate beauty. He had heard plenty of embellished mountain-man stories and had learned to put little stock in them.

"Stop hornswoggling me, Monsieur Johnson," replied Choteau. "Nothing so lovely could do such a thing. I'd love to play a tune on her fine set of Cupid's kettle drums."

Suddenly, Branch shouted, "Damn it, Gabe! Stop gawkin' and get to cookin'. I'm hungry!"

Gabe took a deep breath as he absorbed the rebuke, then gave full attention to his duties. Still, he managed to observe the woman and the other newcomers from the corner of his eye as he worked. After a few moments, the half-breed stepped out of the cabin with a bundle of supplies and visited with the dark-bearded man and the two women waiting near the doorway in their native tongue.

Branch muttered to his cohorts, "Teach the kid everything I know about trappin', and I still have to play nursemaid. I could swear sometimes the kid's been brained."

"We French call the greenhorns *mangeur de lard*—the pork eaters. They rank lowest among all trappers," Choteau said. "At Hudson's Bay, I would beat such a lout with a beaver's tail."

"Well, if he doesn't get our camp set up soon, I'll beat him with more than just a beaver's tail."

An angry clatter erupted near the entrance of the small cabin. It was Eagle Claw speaking loudly to the bearded man in the Kootenai tongue, gesturing forcefully with a pointed finger at Branch. One thing seemed obvious—the four knew each another, and the bearded man used assuaging tones and words to soften the growing anger of the brave. The bearded one was obviously a white man, but his attire appeared more native than many Indians in the encampment. In addition to the ample breechclout around his waist, colorful beads were woven into the braid of hair that draped over his shoulder and two eagle feathers protruded from behind his head. Choteau had said it happened sometimes—a white man who turned Indian. His demeanor appeared to calm the brave and, apart from his paradoxical appearance, he seemed to subtly possess a characteristic Gabe hadn't seen in a while—integrity.

The brave finally stopped gesturing, gathered his horses, and stomped off toward a small camp situated on the other side of the meadow, a long stone's throw away, where he tethered them to trees alongside several other horses. He unrolled a deerskin tarpaulin and sat down next to a small fire to inspect his trade goods, occasionally looking up to glare at Branch.

Curiosity tempted Gabe to walk over and strike up a conversation. But when Johnson and Jones departed for their campsite, he hurried to finish cooking, for Branch would now be focused only on food. More importantly, the gathering of men near the hatchet targets indicated that another contest was at hand, and Gabe didn't want to miss out.

Chapter Seven

The Contests

Branch and Choteau sat across from each other, wolfing down the goulash Gabe had prepared. The thick, gray soup consisted of the usual fare: cornmeal, chunks of dried beaver meat, wild onions, and wapatoo, which Gabe had collected during their trek to the Rendezvous.

Having lived on jerky and berries for the past few days while making their hasty departure, the men ate ravenously. It was on these occasions, when eating was more necessary than talking, that Gabe found consolation—preferring the chomping, belching, and flatulence of his disheveled comrades over Branch's harsh culinary critique.

The ax-throwing contest was announced as Gabe finished his last bites. Branch and Choteau threw down their plates and departed for the contest. Gabe quickly scoured the pots and pans, grabbed his ax, and ran to join them. He arrived as contestants finished making their practice throws at an upright log. Glancing at the first-place prize, a coveted English muzzle-loading pistol, Gabe gladly paid the entrance fee, which nearly emptied his small bag of coins, then marched to the end of the line.

Gabe blended well with the others awaiting their turn, yet he somehow felt out of place. He had become a diametrical contrast to the young man who left home six months before. He normally kept his straight, brown hair short, but it now draped well over his ears, and he had to part it in the middle to keep it from hanging over his eyes. His chin had sprouted a sparse growth of whiskers, and despite the meager diet, he had somehow managed to grow nearly two inches and now looked over the heads of the trappers waiting in line ahead of him.

The only clothes he'd brought on his long journey west were the ones on his back. The cotton shirt his mother made had worn threadbare from the hard work, sweat, and grime. He had replaced it with a poorly sewn shirt he'd fashioned from buckskin that hung loosely off his broad shoulders. Gabe was careful, however, to keep his brown wool coat from wearing out, keeping it safely bundled in a buckskin bag. It was essential and often the only thing that kept him warm during foul weather. He had also made for himself a set of rough leggings to protect his breeches from wearing out when breaking trail through thick buckbrush and devil's club. He would attach them to the leather belt near his hips with rawhide straps and kept snug with bands of the same around his knees and ankles. He used a simple strip of rawhide tied in a knot around his waist to hold his sheathed knife and keep his buckskin shirt tight against his torso.

Gabe had become well acclimated to the strenuous nature of living in the wilderness. He rolled up his shirtsleeves, revealing well-muscled forearms. His physical stature alone was enough to keep away most of the swaggering bullies who, like boar grizzly bears, were eager to display their dominance.

Two men designated as officials measured the proximity of each throw to the bull's-eye. The target was a small, dark circle carved on a cedar slab secured to a pair of upright logs, roughly seven paces from the toe line. As the roguish trappers took their turns and their marks were tallied, Gabe's confidence grew.

The official barked out, "Bill Branch, you're next!"

Branch turned to Choteau, grinned, and boasted loudly, "The pistol will be mine!" Carefully taking aim, he hurled the ax, which flew spinning toward the target, hitting the outer edge of the black circle in the middle of the slab. Choteau slapped him on the back as the officials measured the mark and conferred with each other before announcing, "We have a new leader—Bill Branch!"

Gabe smirked when Choteau handed a fresh jug of whiskey to Branch, who took a swill and danced obnoxiously in premature celebration, knowing full well his antics only agitated the other contestants.

"Next up—Gabe Bauman!" yelled the official.

Gabe was so busy amusing himself with Branch's buffoonery that he almost missed the call. Jolting to attention, he turned to face the target and stepped up to the line. He focused first on the target, then on the small mark in the center of the bull's-eye. Just as he threw the ax, Branch cavorted dangerously close to the throwing lane, and the ax whistled inches from his head. Branch instinctively ducked and landed clumsily on the ground amid the laughter of well-seasoned trappers.

"You damned fool kid!" Branch scrambled to his feet, fuming with anger.

"Sorry about that, Mr. Branch, sir."

The officials measured the throw and announced Gabe as the winner, to the cheers of the other mountain men. But Gabe had known he'd won as soon as the ax left his hand. "Just a lucky throw, I guess," he said modestly, but inside, he was bursting with pride as he went to collect his prize.

Branch shot him a disdainful look. "Don't worry, Bauman. I'll get square with you in the shoot-off."

Gabe was too excited to care about Branch when the official handed him the new pistol. He paused to admire it, cocking the hammer back and dry-firing it at a nearby stump. The weapon was well balanced, the trigger was crisp, and the iron sights sharp. Gabe was well pleased with his prize.

There was little time to celebrate, for the main event was about to begin—the shoot-off. The contest was a test of a marksmanship, a necessary skill that mountain men took great pride in. The rifle was the frontiersman's most essential tool and shooting with accuracy often meant the difference between life and death. With rifle in hand, a man could both feed himself and defend against a charging grizzly or bandits bent on pillaging or murder.

Just when Gabe turned to make his way to the adjacent marshaling area, he was startled by the outstretched, sinewy arm of the breed. "You did well," said the stoic brave.

Gabe reflexively stepped back. The brave smiled faintly and again thrust his hand out.

"Oh! Much obliged." Somewhat befuddled, Gabe noted the man's vicelike grip when he reached out and shook his hand.

"I am Eagle Claw, of the Kootenai people," he replied in well-spoken English.

"Will—will you be entering the shoot-off?" Gabe asked after introducing himself.

But before the brave could answer, a slovenly trapper hollered, "Ain't no 'breed gonna walk away with that Hawken, that's for damned sure!"

Eagle Claw ignored the insult and walked away, fading into the crowd that made its way toward the shoot-off. Gabe wasn't sure what baffled him more, the brave's unexpected congratulatory gesture or the fact that he spoke fluent English. After enduring a month of Branch's twisted machinations, he found it difficult to trust anyone and had grown wary of the hidden motives that drive men to do the things they do. Still, the man was remarkably civil for a "breed" that would supposedly take a man's scalp the moment his back was turned. For a moment, Gabe was distracted from the hubbub, pondering Eagle Claw as he approached the target area for the shoot-off.

The officials silenced the raucous men and explained the rules, which were relatively simple—get two shots off within thirty seconds at a target set at fifty paces. The man whose two shots measured closest to the bull's-eye would win. This required the shooter to make both shots count. The prize—a coveted .53-caliber Hawken, the premier muzzle-loading rifle of the frontier.

One by one, the trappers came forth to pay their fee until Gabe, the last person, stepped up to the official and dumped out the few remaining coins in his pouch.

"Sorry, son. That not enough—"

Before he could finish his words, Gabe pulled the new pistol from his belt. The official instantly stepped back at the sight of the pistol in his hand, but relaxed when Gabe handed it to him as payment for his entrance fee. The official gave a sigh of relief, then accepted his fee with a look of incredulity, and handed him a paper target and five silver coins in change.

The first contestant stood stoically waiting at the toe line, marked fifty paces from the target. He held his rifle by the end of the barrel with the butt resting on the ground, which was the proper starting position. A hush came over the crowd as the official held up the hourglass. "Go!" he shouted, flipping the hourglass over on a log slab.

The shooter burst into fluid motion, as if he had performed the routine a thousand times: he uncorked the powder horn, poured some into the upright end of the barrel, and recorked the horn. He then retrieved a patched round ball from a leather pouch, tapped it into the end of the barrel, and forced it down several inches. Wasting no time, he pulled out the ramrod mounted under the barrel and shoved the ball down its throat until it reached the back end of the barrel. Pulling the hammer back, he popped open the round, brass box embedded in the rifle stock, grabbed a small percussion cap between his thumb and forefinger, closed the lid, and inserted the cap on the nipple resting beneath the hammer.

The shooter threw the rifle to his shoulder, found the target, and fired. A cloud of smoke spewed out the end of the barrel and hung in the air for a moment, obscuring the target. He appeared uninterested in whether he had hit his mark and was already reloading his rifle for the next shot. But he wasted time glancing at the sand slipping through the hourglass, fumbled for the cap, and dropped it into the tall grass. Visibly nervous now, he parted the grass this way and that until he finally found it. Hurriedly, he placed it on the nipple and fired, just as the official shouted, "Time!" The crowd cheered, but the celebration was in vain—the hurried shot had missed the mark by several inches.

A cloud of blue-gray smoke formed and spread until it hung above the encampment like a ghost. Some shooters were quicker than others, but their shots were off target, while others' shots were true, but they were too slow in reloading. Gabe grew increasingly optimistic about his chances as the contest continued.

However, Crooked Bill's first shot squarely hit the bull's-eye. The second was a bit rushed. Impaired by his growing state of intoxication, he fumbled and dropped the lead ball in the tall grass while reloading. But instead of searching for it, he shrewdly grabbed another from his pouch. Just before the time ran out, he fired and grazed the bull's-eye. Only Choteau and a few others cheered when the official announced he was the new leader.

"Let's see you top that, Bauman!" Branch jeered as he stepped aside to rejoin Choteau.

Gabe didn't flinch or react to the challenge. He just stood by, patiently waiting at the end of the line with his well-used trade musket cradled in his arm. It wasn't a rifle sought after or coveted by the mountain men, so he never worried anyone might steal it. Rife with dings, chips, and rust, it was gnarly in appearance. The stock had been cracked and repaired with rawhide by its previous owner—a deceased Blood Indian. Gabe never worried the unfortunate man would come looking for it. Branch had made sure of that after prying it from the gravely wounded brave just before he killed him. He'd handed the beat-up rifle to Gabe, trading the dead man's scalp for enough lead and shot to keep him hunting for camp meat whenever the need arose. Most trappers would have considered the gift useless—a "Yorkshire compliment," as Branch called it—but Gabe was happy to have the weapon nonetheless. Unlike his father's Kentucky rifle that he had used many times to take down game at well over a hundred yards, the bare-bored musket was only accurate out to fifty yards, perhaps sixty at best or seventy on a prayer; it would be a waste of good powder and shot to risk shooting at game much farther than that. Gabe was a naturally good shot, and a few tips from Branch had helped him become even better. Gabe had used the trade musket enough to learn its many idiosyncrasies and foibles until the old relic seldom missed its mark. Despite its tattered appearance, it was all the rifle he needed for this contest, and he waited in line with eager confidence.

Finally, it was Gabe's turn, and the opportunity he'd been longing for—to prove to Branch and Choteau that he was an equal among men and no longer a greenhorn. The many hours of practice and marksmanship he had learned since he was a boy would crystalize into this moment—when he would hold up the Hawken in victory.

The official called Gabe's name, but his voice seemed hollow and far away, having already gone to that place inside himself where time seemed to stand still; his focus was singular—the target in front of him. He felt no excitement or tension when he stepped to the toe line, and he purposely slowed his heart and breathing in anticipation of the shot. When the official signaled for him to go, he didn't react in the hurried manner of the others. Instead, he smoothly and methodically loaded his musket without taking his eye off the target. He had learned that good shooting hinged on rhythm and timing: when to hold your breath for the shot, timing your heartbeat, and when to apply just enough pressure on the trigger to break the sear at the perfect moment, releasing the hammer.

He took aim, and the rifle seemed to fire on its own, almost too quickly. But only Gabe knew the shot was true. The onlookers assumed he had missed, but when they saw the lead ball had smacked the bull's-eye dead center, they erupted with cheers.

The raucous applauding caused him to lose focus and his heart began to race with adrenaline. He closed his eyes, stood still, and breathed deeply. Once again, he willed his heartbeat to slow, his pause confounding those who wanted him to hurry. Precious sand ran through the pinch in the hourglass. Some of the men sighed in disappointment, and he overheard Branch muttering to Choteau, "That delay just gave me the Hawken." But his discouraging words only made him focus more.

Those who had placed wagers cried, "Load up, kid! Load up!" When Gabe finally reached the state of calm he needed, some of the frustrated trappers had already begun walking away. He went into motion, every movement fluid and smooth. A hush fell over the crowd, heads turned, and men froze breathless. The gun sprang to his shoulder, and just before the last grains of sand dropped through the hourglass, the old trade musket bucked.

Onlookers squinted and strained to see through the smoky haze. Running toward the target, they hovered over the officials, craning their necks as they stared, dumbfounded, at the two holes merged into one.

A disheveled mountain man forced his way in and peered between the two officials, then turned with wide eyes to the crowd and shouted, "It's another bull's-eye!"

The crowd erupted with cheers and descended upon Gabe, who wasn't overly surprised at the final results. He looked at the rowdy, weather-browned wave of humanity enveloping him with a sudden sense of trepidation, which quickly turned to joy when they lifted him on their shoulders and hoisted him in the air. Gabe smiled and laughed, then held up his fist in victory. For the first time, he felt like a mountain man and not a greenhorn, for he had bested the best.

The official presented him with the new Hawken rifle amid the cheers and jostling of the mountain men. He held it in his hands, studying every detail, and as he did, the noise of the crowd faded, and their celebratory shouts seemed far away.

When he was much younger, Gabe would use a chair to retrieve his father's rifle that hung from the fireplace. The weapon was strictly off-limits, and he had received several whippings with the switch for taking it down and handling it, after which he was careful not to get caught.

As Gabe admired the Hawken, he remembered how he would run his fingers along the long, heavy barrel of his father's rifle, feeling the smoothness of the brass inlays and admiring the tiger-stripe maple stock. Most of all, he'd loved to practice aiming at things, but at just five years old, he had difficulty lifting the ten-pound rifle to his shoulder, and on occasion, he would rest it on the windowsill and take aim.

The Hawken was his—all his. For a moment, he thought he might be dreaming and that taking his eyes off it would somehow make it disappear. At length, he looked up and beyond the circle of men, and there stood Crooked Bill Branch—eyes red with hate and his face contorted in a jealous scowl. He had never looked at Gabe that way before, with a palpable loathing—the same look he gave the Indian boy just before Branch thrust his knife through his heart. "You lucky bastard!" shouted Branch. "This ain't over!" And he turned and stomped off toward their camp.

Chapter Eight

Revelation

Eagle Claw bided his time while the crowd dis- persed, then made his way to where the men had lined up to shoot, careful not to draw any attention. Looking down into the thick grass, he studied the ground near the toe line. The shooting skills of the young trapper were impressive, but he was more pleased he had out-shot the foul-mouthed overlord whose sharp words bit like a wolf.

He glanced around to see if anyone was watching, then moved the matted grass aside with his moccasin-clad foot until he found what he was looking for. Checking again for any possible onlookers, he reached down and recovered the round lead ball Branch had dropped during the shoot-off. Holding it tightly in his hand, he made haste back to the encampment, where his family sat in a circle around a small campfire waiting for his return.

As he approached, a familiar voice came from the campfire adjacent to his tethered horses. "Who won this time?" asked Dawn, his half-sister. The sound of her voice seemed disturbingly loud, and Eagle Claw quickened his pace to get closer, hoping she wouldn't speak again.

"Not so loud," he admonished her in the Kootenai tongue. "Speak Kootenai, not English. There are too many ears."

Dawn rolled her eyes, smirked, and whispered, "Yes, brother. Can I whisper in English?"

Eagle Claw ignored her catty remark and sat next to her in the vacant spot in the small circle, and said, "The trapper who won the pistol—the younger one. He also won the rifle."

"Must be a good shot, eh?" said Eagle Claw's stepfather, James Harrison.

"Yes. He defeated the mean-looking gray beard. I spoke with Two Spears from the Salish, and he said they call the gray beard Crooked Branch."

"I've been watching him, brother," replied Dawn. "I think you are right. He is the one who came into our village looking for beaver. He and the other one—the one they call Frenchy."

"I am certain they are the ones. But I don't remember the younger one who won the contest. Were there not only two of them?"

Eagle Claw's mother, Singing Bird, who preferred to remain silent, finally spoke as she gazed at the glowing embers of campfire: "Yes. There were two. But they walked into camp on foot." She paused for a moment, then added, "Maybe the younger was waiting somewhere in the trees, watching their horses." Her words were deliberate and her demeanor like calm water as she carefully pushed an alder branch into the fire with her left thumb.

Eagle Claw acknowledged his mother respectfully, for he always listened closely whenever she chose to speak. He glanced down at the gnarled fingers of her left hand, twisted like juniper roots, then at her scarred face and head. He never saw the disfigurement as offensive or ugly, for it was the face of his mother. The beauty of her unmarred side more than compensated for the other—the sparkle of love and light in her good eye outshining the darkness surrounding her gruesome blemish. At first, the mutilation had been as troubling to her as it was to others, and whenever she went for water, she was careful to avoid seeing her reflection. But in time, she came to accept the deformity of her once-perfect face, particularly when she realized it kept the men at bay.

Aside from her handicap and the strange patch of white hair, her injury had caused another mysterious change—she began having visions and dreams, ones that would come to pass. The visions came randomly at first, but as she grew to embrace her new "gift," as James called it, she learned to harness and control it. The natives said she was "touched." Aside from those close to her, she mostly kept her visions to herself, as they were often strange, beyond interpretation, and only brought fear and confusion among those who heard them.

Eagle Claw sat in silent contemplation at his mother's words. Finally, James squinted and replied, "I was hunting the day those men came to our camp, so I'm no help. Are you sure it was them? We must be certain. We don't want to start trouble. Not here. Not now."

Eagle Claw nodded and looked across the meadow, where Branch and Choteau were talking and drinking. "I was at the river fishing and only saw them from a distance, but it must have been them. I recognized Choteau, the Frenchman, and who could forget the face of the gray beard? Did you see the big beaver, eh? Only one place I know where beaver grow that big."

James sighed, as if resigning himself to Eagle Claw's keen observation. "White Cloud would know. He is the one who spoke with him."

Eagle Claw felt the kindling of righteous indignation, fanned by the brazenness of Branch and his men. His feelings conflicted with the values James had taught him: to be at peace with oneself and others, to show kindness, to not seek revenge but leave room for God's wrath, to turn the other cheek, and on and on. He understood the words, and at times believed and followed them. But in this moment, they seemed foreign—outlandish words, like a language he could not bring himself to understand.

The sacred canyon behind their camp was important for their survival. When winter lingered, and meat supplies ran low, brave warriors were granted permission to trek deep into the area for the beaver whose meat would help them survive until spring. If the beaver were trapped out, the Kootenai would have to journey to the plains, braving the deep snow and dangerous mountain passes. There, they would hunt for buffalo, while the Blackfeet lounged inside their warm tipi lodges, growing fat on buffalo tallow. Using snowshoes to chase them on foot into deep snowdrifts, they would run them through with spears or arrows, butcher them, then pack the meat over the mountains to their winter camp on the Tobacco Plains.

But it wasn't just the beaver pelts and the absconded food source that chafed at Eagle Claw. It was the spirit of the trespass and the slow, unwelcome crush, like a giant foot stepping down upon them, followed by the gleeful twist of the foot, as one would step on a bug.

Eagle Claw clenched his jaw. "I am certain it was them. Those devils lied to us! They snuck into the sacred land, even after White Cloud forbade them."

In a calming tone, James replied, "We must not judge rashly, my son. We will pray and take this concern to the Elders, and then we will smoke and decide our course of action."

Eagle Claw abandoned the argument and scooted toward his mother. "Let me have your hand, Mother," he said softly. "Please."

She hesitated a moment, then reached out her gnarled hand. Eagle Claw gently pried open the contorted fingers and placed in her palm the lead ball Branch had dropped. "Tell me what you see, Mother."

She looked down at the ball. Suddenly, her fingers snapped shut around it and she gazed out above the encampment, trance-like, the pupils of her eyes growing wide before rolling back in her head.

As the minutes passed and she remained in that position, jerking occasionally as if being poked by something sharp, Eagle Claw grew concerned and wondered if he had gone too far. Just as he was about to grab her wrist and take away the musket ball, she fell back, then opened her hand and dropped the ball on the ground, trembling and gasping. Eagle Claw quickly helped her to sit up.

"What is it, Mother? What did you see?" asked Dawn, who sidled to her, and held her hand, calming her terrified panting.

"I saw the raven, the gray beard, the Big Man. I saw a great beast—the bear. It came fast from the fog and opened wide its jaws, then—death. That's what I saw—death."

Eagle Claw placed his hand on her shoulder and gave her a drink of water. "What do you mean, Mother? What do you mean by death?"

"It was cloudy at first, like a mist that shifted and moved, until the visions came silently, but rapidly. I saw the one they call Crooked Branch laughing like a cackling raven, drops of thick, dark blood dripping into a pool at the base of a tree, and ravens fluttering away—one with something in its beak—an eye, I think. There were thousands of wriggling maggots, the looming figure of the Big Man in a dark forest. Then, the fog returned and there appeared, emerging from the fog, a great bear. Though it churned up the rocks as it charged, it made no sound. Its eyes were locked as it ran, as if about to pounce on prey. Long, thin strings of saliva stretched from its mouth as it sprinted closer and closer, its massive jaws opening as it stretched out its neck for the bite. And when the beast opened wide its jaws and clamped down—everything went black."

Her words dampened Eagle Claw's indignation. He sat bewildered and tried to make sense of her vision, the word *death* still echoing in his mind. In his travels, he had seen it happening to other tribes: conflict, bloodshed, starvation, disease. Death had come to the land; perhaps not in the form of a bear, but death nonetheless. He could feel its ominous encroachment like the great shadow of a mountain, growing larger and speeding faster at the setting of the sun.

The little band sat quietly now, the growing revelry on the other side of the camp a petulant reminder of unwelcome changes and the uncertainty of things to come. The trail that stretched from the Two Medicine River to the Valley of the Salish to the Kootenai River and beyond, the trail they had used for eons to move to and from hunting grounds and to trade with other tribes, the trail that had helped bring them life, was now bringing death.

Eagle Claw looked on disdainfully at the obnoxious debauchery of the encampment and suspected more of them would come now: trappers, adventurers, fortune seekers, and settlers. He heard the traders calling it "progress," but his mother's words confirmed his thoughts—that "progress" was really regression and death cloaked in crafty disguise. The beavers were the catalyst, and the trail the trappers would use to find them led straight to the Kootenai fish camp.

His father spoke of large villages to the east filled with roads and people. They were sure to come now, with their insatiable appetites for more and their persistent pushing—always pushing. Eagle Claw had carefully studied men like Crooked Bill Branch, and one handful was never enough—not even two. They were never satisfied until they had it all, and even then, they would still crave more. Eagle Claw remembered James referring to them as broken cisterns that could never be filled, no matter how much was poured into them.

"Will you be coming with us?" asked James.

"No. My horses need rest," Eagle Claw said. "I will stay tonight and leave in the morning. Perhaps I can discover more about them."

Eagle Claw was confident he would gain more information from his covert investigations. He understood the nature of a secret—like a small but powerful creature that even the strongest of men could not contain for long. The little creature would twist and turn and slip from grasp like a wriggling fish, or flitter away like a mountain jay from person to person until known by all, its familiar flight aided by the sotting of rotgut whiskey.

James looked him directly in the eye and said, "Be careful. I sense trouble brewing. These free trappers will get drunk tonight and then there's no telling what will happen."

"Whiskey!" Eagle Claw said. "Devil's drink. I won't be tricked by it. It reaches up from your belly—only to steal your heart."

Dawn assisted Singing Bird to her feet, and they began packing for departure. When finished, Eagle Claw helped them load the horses for their long trip to the fish camp. If they left within the hour, they would get over the pass to the first campsite near the Middle Fork—a safe distance from the coming dissipation of the Rendezvous. Eagle Claw approached his mother and hugged her, then helped her into the saddle. As she waited for the others, she reached out to him and gently touched his shoulder.

"Be safe, my son," she implored. "There is an evil in this place."

Eagle Claw smiled and squeezed her hand, interpreting her concern only as love. But he was uncertain what trouble the night would bring and did not take her words lightly. The presence of evil seemed obvious, but he had no idea how to contain it. Nevertheless, he was more concerned with her safety and the safety of his sister and James than his own and felt relieved they were setting out for home.

☙

Every now and then, Dawn would glance sideways and peek from the corner of her eye at Gabe. She had noticed him earlier but kept her thoughts to herself.

Aside from his makeshift attire, she noted his brown-eyed, youthful face with a few flecks of whiskers sprouting from his chin, and his impressive, broad-shouldered physique, a half-head taller than the others. She felt an instant attraction but was under no illusions. Ascertaining a man's intentions was a necessary skill for any woman on the frontier if she valued her own dignity.

Simply stated, most of the men she encountered outside the village were as randy as billy goats. Laws common to the civilized world to punish wrongdoers did not exist on the untamed frontier, and the godless had no compunction in sowing their seed in unwelcome soil. There were plenty of men roaming the mountains with no moral barricades to stop them from having their way with an unaccompanied or unwary woman.

Dawn was keenly aware of this fact. Nevertheless, she found herself uncomfortably intrigued by Gabe, who stood out among the others. She tried to ignore his appealing strength, confidence, and the respectable way he carried himself—distinctly out of place among his rough companions. But she found herself unable to disregard him, and it angered her.

She tightened the cinch on her horse and found herself glancing again at Gabe. This time, he seemed to be staring back at her from his campsite across the meadow. Contradictory feelings of loathing and longing swept over her like a rude gust of wind. Her heart quickened, and she looked away, again annoyed at herself for her feelings and for letting her guard down.

A voice came from behind her. "Be alert, my sister," said Eagle Claw, "and keep your rifle ready and your knife sharp."

She smiled and nodded as the small group gathered to go over final details of their long and hazardous journey back to the fish camp before James's customary prayer for safety.

Chapter Nine

Parting of the Ways

G*abe had built a fire suitable for cooking a quick* meal, another steaming kettle of trapper's stew, but this time with fresh biscuits that sent a rich aroma drifting across the encampment. Crooked Bill had invited George Johnson and Thomas Jones to join them around the campfire for the meal, which unfortunately meant there would be no second helpings to help sate Gabe's perpetual hunger.

The feast was by design, and Gabe knew it, which made Branch's inevitable critiquing even more agitating. It was times like this, when lips were loose and minds soft, that Branch relished: an opportunity to boast of embellished exploits and bask in the dingy glow of his own self-adulation. Gabe ate quickly, sitting a few paces away from the others and the warmth of the fire, lost in speculative contemplation of his uncertain future.

"Not bad grub, Bauman," said Johnson between bites.

Just as Gabe was about to thank him, Branch cut him off. "Not bad? What have you been eatin', Johnson? Weasel marinated in wolverine piss? Polecat seasoned with buffalo chips? I gotta hand it to Bauman, he can sure fix a fine plate of bow-wow mutton."

Choteau laughed mid-bite and choked, spitting a mouthful back onto his plate as he tried to collect himself. Johnson raised an eyebrow and shoveled another spoonful into his maw as Choteau finished his uncontrolled laughter, cleared his throat, and heartily lapped up the regurgitation. Gabe shrugged it off, semi-amused at Branch's uncanny ability to string together a tapestry of insults in varying shades of excrement.

Without waiting for a reply, Branch carelessly tossed his plate aside and started in: "We was comin' off the Salish River when we caught a damn Injun who stole our horses!" he crowed.

"What'd ya do, Bill? Shoot 'im?" slurred Johnson.

"Hell no! No need wastin' good lead on a thievin' Injun. I stuck him. Stuck him good!" Branch grinned, wild-eyed, as he thrust his arm forward in a grotesque mime of the kill strike.

"Stuck 'im clean up to Green River," added Choteau.

"*Shhht!* I'm tellin' this story," Branch growled. He pulled his long-bladed Green River knife from the scabbard on his hip and looked at the maker's mark halfway up the blade, which read GREEN RIVER KNIFE WORKS. His rapt audience exchanged sober glances as he again made a sharp upward stabbing motion. "He put up a helluva fight, but I stuck 'im way past Green River, by God, and then I asked if'n it was hard to breathe with that blade stickin' in his throat!"

As Branch told the story, it brought to Gabe's attention how much he had grown to despise the man. He leaned forward and glanced at the trapper, infuriated with his lies, remembering how he murdered the helpless boy. For a moment, Gabe was back on the trail, lying on the ground next to the fallen boy—the horrific memory flashed as the young brave coughed blood while gasping for air.

Jones and Johnson paused, then laughed forcefully, more out of fearful self-preservation than genuine humor, Gabe surmised, as the gloating Branch slid the knife back in its sheath. The disgust and rage he felt toward the mountain man had been building up for days. Like ice dams that back up the rivers in early spring, then burst forth without warning when the water pressure reaches its apex, Gabe rose and blurted, "That ain't how it happened, and you know it!"

The blustering storytelling abruptly stopped, and they all stared wide-eyed at Gabe. Branch stood, awkwardly off balance, and glared menacingly, then his eyes danced here and there as if he were searching for the nearest rifle.

Gabe was dumbfounded by his own words, but it was too late to take them back, having impulsively spewed them from his mouth like a good retching.

"What the hell do you know, kid? You were back on the trail afoot, trying to catch up to us!"

Branch's words were suddenly sharp and clear, as if his own wrath had cured him from his semi-guttered state. But this was nothing new. Gabe was always amazed how his boss could magically summon sobriety, even during his most intoxicated state, as if he'd been drinking water rather than rotgut.

"Branch is right!" shouted Choteau like a good sycophant.

Distracted by another passing of the jug, the men laughed hesitatingly at first, as if asking permission, then obnoxiously when Branch took the jug from Choteau and tipped it back. He kept one bloodshot eye on Gabe as he took another swig. Gabe stepped back a couple of inept paces, as if pushed by an ominous force. When Branch made no effort to approach, he turned and looked at the other trappers scattered across the meadow, wondering what inevitable consequences would result from his infraction, hoping for a miracle way out.

He felt like a trapped beaver, struggling vainly to escape his captor. Then, he saw them—the three he'd seen earlier talking with Eagle Claw by the trader's cabin. They were mounted and riding toward the trail leaving the encampment. *The trail, yes, the trail,* he thought—the one he had just ridden in on that morning, the one that led to the Salish and then to the Kootenai camp. The one that led away—away from Branch and the likes of him.

In an instant, he knew exactly where they were going. The three paused and turned to wave goodbye to Eagle Claw. Gabe instinctively took two steps toward them, as if he might suddenly break into a sprint, catch up to them before they disappeared, and beg to join them. They were only two impulsive steps, but they were the most cathartic steps he'd ever taken—two yearning steps toward freedom.

Gabe's heart sank when they dipped out of sight. He looked over at Eagle Claw, warming himself by a fire on the other side of the small clearing. The man stared back at him from across the meadow for a moment, then looked back at the fire as if ill at ease with Gabe's stare.

Johnson and Jones finally got up, and as they staggered to their camp, Gabe could feel a stiffening tension from Branch's full scrutiny.

Branch turned to Choteau and ordered, "Go hobble and turn out the stock." It was Gabe's job to tend to the animals, and he was surprised when Choteau complied. Without a word, the Frenchman retrieved the hobbles, untied the stock, and led them through the timber to pasture. Perhaps he sensed what was to come and didn't want to be around for the inevitable confrontation. A sudden release of adrenaline caused Gabe's heart to quicken.

"Sit down, Bauman," said Branch firmly.

Taking a deep breath to collect himself, Gabe stepped toward the fire and sat down across from his boss, mentally bracing for the tongue lashing. *Here it comes,* he thought. *Just like a hundred times before.* Gabe would listen, nod, and take the rebuke, but not hear a single word. He would retreat—inside the walled fortress he had built inside his mind, where he would chant invalidating brickbats until Branch had finished his tirade.

"Congratulations on the Hawken, greenhorn. You really took the egg. Looks like all that training I gave ya paid off."

Gabe was befuddled by the compliment, even though it was laced with self-congratulation. For a moment, he felt appreciative. Gabe raised his brows and blinked twice. Then, just as he was about to reply cordially, he came to his senses. *What's he up to now?* He chose his words carefully, shrewdly. "Thanks ... Sir. I just did how you taught me." Even through the rising heat of the campfire, Gabe could smell Crooked Bill's acrid whiskey breath.

Branch's response began calm and low, then gradually built into a crescendo of anger. "You know, kid, shootin' at a paper target is one thing. To survive out here, you gotta be able to draw down on a man and make that shot count. No hesitation. Take that Injun back on the trail. Now if we'd'a let 'im go, like you wanted, and taken back our horses, the first thing he'd'a done was scurry straight back and claim we stole *his* horses, which were really *our* horses! Get it? We'd have the entire Blackfeet Nation on our ass!"

"Um-huh," replied Gabe in a slightly patronizing tone.

"Don't give me that 'um-huh' humbug!" barked Branch, pointing his gnarled finger. "You don't survive in this country bein' weak, kid. You'll lose your scalp and end up dead. Maybe put your partners at risk, too. That little stunt you pulled on the trail coulda brought it all down on us. You don't let a thievin' Injun go free. Ever! That's my rule number one."

Gabe felt a welling of indignation as Branch's rebuke pushed him past the limits of his tolerance. He stood and looked directly into Branch's piercing eyes. Like a flood, the words rushed from his mouth: "Rule number one this, rule number one that. Everything is always rule number one with you! Well, let me tell you what *my* rule number one is: Do unto others as you would have them do unto you. Ever heard of that rule?"

In a flash, Branch sprang across the campfire, sending the cooking tripod flying, kicking up glowing embers, as he tackled Gabe to the ground. The lunge took Gabe by complete surprise, and before he could roll over, Branch had grabbed one of the rocks from the fire ring and swung to kill. At the last second, Gabe saw it coming and jerked away, the rock glancing off his temple. He felt a sharp pain that shot clean through his head, and everything suddenly went black.

ево

Branch lifted the rock above his head for a second blow—but hesitated when he realized others had overheard them arguing and were watching from their campsites. He looked down at the impudent kid, unconscious, blood trickling from the side of his head. Reluctantly, he tossed the rock aside and breathed hard.

Rapid shuffling footsteps approached from the meadow. "I almost killed him, Choteau. I almost killed him," said Branch angrily. "Damned mouthy bastard!" But, when he looked up, it wasn't Choteau, but the half-breed. The man stood poised within striking distance, the only movement coming from the hatchet in his hand, which he rhythmically spun as if it had a life of its own. Branch paused and wisely stepped back, scanning for Choteau, but he was nowhere to be seen. Somehow, the brave had gotten the jump on him and had him dead-to-rights.

The half-breed knelt and examined Bauman, keeping an eye on Branch. Feeling Bauman's chest, he muttered, "He is still alive."

"You want the son of a bitch? You can have him," Branch said, sneering. As the Indian dragged Bauman away, he felt relieved to be getting rid of the kid and thankful the brave hadn't used that wicked-looking hatchet on him.

Chapter Ten

ℜemembrance

The clickety-clomp of horse hooves always had a hypnotic effect on James Harrison. As they journeyed from the Rendezvous to the Kootenai village, his thoughts drifted aimlessly. He had recognized a couple of the Blackfeet men at the Rendezvous and wondered if they remembered him. They were one of several tribes he had ministered to, spending two winters with them before an unpleasant parting of the ways.

James was a convincing preacher, but although they had accepted many of his teachings, he was unable to completely win them over. He remembered feeling as if he'd failed in his mission. He departed the Blackfeet village under the bombardment of rocks and horse dung, unsure of himself and his future. Despair and thoughts of suicide had overwhelmed him as he rode along the wildering way until he stumbled upon Singing Bird. Though he kept it to himself, it was she who had saved him.

He reflected on that day, the dreary clouds that hung in the sky, and the deep gloom that had swelled within him like an incubus, whispering biting words in his ears: *failure, worthless, inept, fool.* Even the horse he rode seemed to feel the weight of his sorrow and had slowed to a dull, plodding pace. He thought about how they'd mocked him, even the children had lined up to jeer him as he rode away. Two years of his life—gone. And although he had known where the westward trail of his departure would take him, James was hopelessly lost on it.

After five dreary days on the trail, he had recalled a series of high cliffs overlooking the river valley. He had prayed there on a previous excursion and decided it would be a good place to do so again—like the "high places" spoken of in the Bible, where the priest would go to pray. He had thought perhaps the elevated bench would bring him nearer to God; perhaps there, the Lord would better hear his pleading and take away the painful, derisive voices that echoed in his mind.

But when James rounded a bend in the trail, his dark thoughts were interrupted by the sight of several dozen carrion birds circling above the cliffy bench where he wanted to pray. After clambering up the steep abutment to the bench, he saw that they were ravens, perched in the trees, poised like angry, beaked gremlins, cawing their displeasure at his intrusive presence. As he moved closer, James saw what appeared to be a heap of garments and fur near the edge of the precipice. He approached cautiously, rifle in hand, until he realized that the mélange of garments was a person, a Kootenai woman to be precise, by the way she had dressed and adorned herself.

Her blood-stained forearms seemed to tell the story in a single glance. She appeared to be grieving, having slashed her arms in the custom of the Blackfeet women, mourning the loss of a husband or child—a practice unusual for the Kootenai. But when James purposely snapped a twig, she remained motionless, as if already dead.

Venturing closer, he noticed the gashes weren't superficial, but deep, the pools of drying blood wide and thick. Her angry wounds were much too serious for the purpose of grieving. The self-inflicted cuts seemed intentional—to permanently end her pain as well as her life. But upon closer inspection, and despite the blood loss—the woman was somehow still alive. James's despair suddenly vanished, like the ravens that had flapped away when he approached too close.

He scooped her in his arms and descended to the river, then cajoled her with tiny sips. After wrapping her in a buffalo skin blanket, he picked the flies and maggots from her deep wounds and applied bandages, employing what medical skills he had learned to inch her back from the edge of eternal darkness. He then built a shelter and a fire, and he stayed by her side for many weeks, nursing her back to health.

As a missionary, James quickly learned to speak the native languages wherever he preached. But the Kootenai language was foreign to him, and when Singing Bird was well enough to speak, he could scarcely understand a single word she spoke. Fortunately, he soon discovered she knew the Blackfeet tongue, which he also knew well.

Singing Bird had been fearful at first, but like all human beings, she understood the universal language of compassion. When he had gained her trust, she recounted the story of her young son's horrific death and how her husband had blamed her for it, divorced her, abandoned her and her son, Eagle Claw, then headed north to join a different Kootenai tribe. She spoke mournfully about Eagle Claw, whom she had left with her sister, and how much she regretted leaving him.

And then she told James of the vision she had had while atop the cliff.

She awoke in a vast field of golden grass with long whiskered heads. When she sat up, there stood the Big Man, the great beast of legend. It towered above her. She fell back, horrified. Her knees became weak, and she struggled to stand. Finally, she managed to find her strength, but when she turned to run, she collided with an enormous tree that stretched high into the air. Stunned by both the tree and the Big Man, she turned around, but he was gone.

She reached out and touched the great tree. It had a strange surface, smooth and white, and had a door similar to that of a lodge, and high above, at the top of the tree, its limbs swung around and around in a great circle. She was staring at the limbs when suddenly, one of them struck a bird, and it fell to the ground, landing near her with a dull thump. She walked to the bird and looked down at its mangled body.

Then, Singing Bird noticed on the field, stretching to the horizon, many hundreds of these strange white trees with limbs that spun in a circle, and she saw that each one had killed many birds. She looked around and saw that the vast forest of "killing trees" covered the once-verdant plains and had taken the place of the buffalo.

Suddenly, the field was gone, and the ground where she stood was flat and hard, like the surface of a smooth rock, decorated with white and yellow stripes. She turned slightly, and once more, there stood the Big Man, but he was farther away than before. This time, she didn't try to run. She just gazed at the Big Man—and he at her.

She heard a strange noise coming from behind her. It sounded like the roar of the waters near her village. She turned just as strange wheeled carts, like the white man's wagons, charged past her, yet there were no horses pulling them. They were of many colors, their surface shiny like flint, and all around her, they spewed foul odors and screamed past so fast that she could not move. Finally, she could stand the noise no longer, and she bolted to get off their trail, but one struck her, then another and another, until they had completely broken her body and rendered her unconscious.

When Singing Bird awoke, she found herself on a flat path, hard as stone. Alongside her stood a tall barrier of woven wires, and on the other side of the path the evil wagons roared mere feet from her. She backed against the barrier, but they continued passing her like a stampede of buffalo, as if she wasn't there.

Somehow, she managed to climb the barrier, the wires cutting her badly as she clambered over the top. Barely visible in the distance stood the Big Man. Again, they stared at each other. Perhaps he knows the way back to my village, *she thought.* Perhaps the Big Man can help me away from this dangerous place. *She began to move toward him—surely he would know how to escape this madness and show her the way home.*

She came to the place where the Big Man had been standing, but he was gone again. Now, as far as the eye could see, the land was covered with strange, leaf-like things of various shapes, sizes, and colors that blew in the wind. They were everywhere, and the land lay like an open wound that smelled worse than rotting fish. Large, metal wagons pushed the mass of leaves into heaps, and white, cawing birds swooped in and picked at them. Ugly squirrels with hairless tails ran here and there, everywhere, and maggots wriggled amid the stench of death.

In despair, she looked at her feet and there saw a jagged metal fragment. Reaching down, she picked it up with trembling hands and studied its sharp edges with tearful eyes. Yes, the edges, the sharp edges would save her. And she cut her arms again and again, until the world went black a second time.

When she finally opened her eyes, she saw the face of a white man, a black-bearded white man, and he was carrying her in his arms.

ᐸᔓ

As he swayed in his saddle, James's mind wandered, drifting back and forth in time, thinking about Singing Bird's vision and how he had come to love her. Though he could never understand her vision, he could see beyond the ugly scar that marred her face to the beauty of her soul, and he was pleased to make her his wife. A smile, barely perceptible to him, lifted the corner of his mouth when he remembered those days. His failures had taught him much since that time: forgiveness, forbearance, faith. But most of all, he had learned that the pathway to the light meandered through the labyrinth halls of service to his fellow man. As they made their way to the village, James wondered what new lessons God had in store, for he had long accepted that the lessons would never cease as long as he walked the earth.

They had several campsites to choose from along the trail, but there was one in particular that James avoided and always circumvented. But, lost in memories of days gone by, he'd forgotten to veer off the main trail to avoid that place of darkness, and when he finally looked up, he realized he was right in the middle of where he didn't want to be.

On the edge of the small clearing was a tree, a white-barked poplar, and near its base a bleached white bone protruded from the ground. James was startled when he looked up from his musings and saw it, as if the small piece of bone were a giant horned monolith, a charging white buffalo emerging from the forest floor.

Dawn recognized the place in the same moment James did. "Father! We're not camping here!"

"I know. Damn it, I know!" He kicked his horse and led them quickly down the trail. It wasn't like James to use profanity. In fact, he never used curse words, and neither did the Kootenai. Almost immediately, he regretted the indiscretion. "I'm sorry, dear," he mumbled, feeling awkward.

Singing Bird said nothing, but he knew by the way she stiffened in her saddle and stared straight ahead that she felt the darkness of that place. He sensed the tension building inside her, just like her other forebodings, and her palpable urgency to move farther down the trail. He heeled his horse into a trot when she began humming the prayer song she often used to drive away the demons and perhaps the horrific images that were flashing across the horizon of her mind.

James found the clickety-clomp of the mules' and horses' hooves suddenly discordant and perverse. He chastised himself for his lack of attentiveness and tried to think of other things to distract himself from his crimson memories. But it was to no avail.

∾

It was early spring, and the deep snows had melted just enough to permit travel. James and Dawn had been hunting and had decided to camp just off the main trail, next to a big white poplar tree. James had marched off to find a rabbit or grouse for dinner while Dawn gathered wood for a fire. : Like a pretty songbird, her lilting tune flittered in the thin mountain air as she collected kindling and firewood. Dawn told James what happened after he left.

The two men must have heard her singing and humming. While she placed rocks in a circle for the fire pit and arranged the kindling before building the fire, they quietly worked their way close and hid behind the nearby trees—watching.

Sneaking up behind her was an easy task, her singing probably dampened the sound of their footfalls, and they quickly had her gagged with a leather thong. She told James she tried to scream through the gag, as she stared in horror at their crazed eyes and salivating mouths, as if they were starving and she were a piece of rare venison. James had taught her how to defend herself and she put up a good struggle, but she was no match for two grown men. Soon, they had her subdued, using the large poplar tree and several others to stretch out her arms and legs, immobilizing her so she wouldn't break free during the ravishment.

The larger of the two wouldn't stand for the smaller, weaker one to watch, so he sent him off down the trail. He then turned his attentions to Dawn to comfortably enjoy his pleasure without the distraction of gawking eyes.

Dawn fought against the ropes until her wrists bled. He got down on his knees and straddled her, looking down at her with lustful anticipation. Huffing a demented, guttural laugh, he pulled out a rust-pitted, long-bladed knife from the sheath that hung from his hip. She stared in horror at the knife as the man leaned back and, one by one, snipped the elk-sinew cords on the front of her breeches. She glanced at her horse tied nearby and her rifle hanging hopelessly out of reach on the saddle horn. She bit hard on the leather gag at the sight of his slovenly face, his crazed eyes, and the thick thread of drool streaming out of the corner of his mouth. She kicked vainly against the cords holding her legs as it came to full light what he was preparing to do.

He had worked her breeches down to her knees when a dull thud jerked him forward onto his hands and knees. He looked down at her with his mouth slightly agape. A second later, off in the distance, came the *kapoosh* of a muzzle-loader. His heavy beard seamed to pull his bottom lip away from his yellowing teeth. Thick, dark blood pooled and arced over his lip like a dark shiny worm before breaking free, dripping onto her cheek. She jerked her head away as if he were about to strike her with a rock or club.

Coughing, he sprayed blood that spattered her face and shirt, grunted painfully, then rolled off to the side. He tried to get up and go for his gun, but the next round hit him on the back of the leg. He squirmed across the snowy ground, still coughing as he reached for his rifle leaning against the big poplar tree.

"Shoot him, Sven, shoot him!" The man called to his buddy. Sven didn't reply. He was choking on his own blood after James had cleanly slit his throat.

Then, a blur flashed over Dawn and the rifle was snatched from the man's hand before he could cock back the hammer. He tried crawling away but was too injured to get far.

She seemed shocked at first, when James suddenly appeared, looming above her, looking upside down at her from behind. "Are you all right?"

The words, and the nonchalant way he said them under the circumstances, made her angry. She frowned and mumbled, flaring her nostrils as she bit down on the leather gag.

"Oh, sorry." James reached down and cut the gag and the ropes holding her hands.

Dawn yanked up her breeches, stumbled to her feet, and faced him. "Do I look all right?" she replied incredulously. She stared at her attacker, but it was clear he wouldn't be causing any more trouble. The first bullet had taken him squarely through the shoulder blade, perhaps nicking a lung. It wasn't enough to kill him outright but enough to incapacitate him.

"Let me look at those wrists."

"Forget my wrists! I'm fine. I want to shoot him. Let me shoot him! *Let me!*" The words spilled off her tongue like the snow slides that came crashing down the mountain in deep winter in an unstoppable rush that shook the ground. James felt the rumbling deep in her soul—the violent mix of rage and fear, driving her to reach desperately for James's rifle. "Give me that gun, damn it!"

"Enough!" James shouted.

She stopped talking, but her fury remained, her wrath fixed in her eyes. It was only the horrified look on James' face that seemed to make her take pause.

James looked her in the eye and continued. "I want you to go get on your horse and lead mine to the next camp. It's not that far—the one by the stream up ahead. You know the place, right?"

She glared at him. "Yes, I know the place. What about the other man?"

"Don't worry about him. He won't be bothering us."

Without hesitation, she stomped over to the horses and led them down the trail.

With his rifle cradled in the crook of his arm, James stepped over to the groaning trapper and looked down at him with a fleeting shade of pity—as if looking down at a wounded rabbit or squirrel.

As the stench of the slatternly man permeated his nostrils, the thought of what the thugs tried to do to his daughter crashed into his imagination with full force. An uncontrollable rage coursed through his veins, causing his jaws to clench and his fists to tighten. James felt the muscles of his body swell, as if transformed by something dark and primal. Something inhuman, a beast inside him, had taken control.

The trapper struggled with what little strength he had, but it didn't take long for James to stretch him out using the same cords he had used on Dawn. He cried out desperately for help when James pulled out his flint-bladed knife and cut loose the leather threads on the crotch of his breeches, just as he had done to Dawn.

"You bastard!" bellowed the man, showing his blood-smeared teeth. "You son of the devil!"

James paused for a moment at those words, "son of the devil," and a little voice in his head grew urgent and loud. It was a voice that echoed from the past, preaching words he had preached many times to others: "Do not take vengeance, but leave room for God's wrath..."

But James gritted his teeth harder and pushed the words down, slamming a lid on them so he couldn't hear their imploring echoes. Although he had thwarted the attempted rape of his daughter, the damage had been done—he had seen it in her eyes and heard it in her voice. The reprobate had overshadowed her light with his darkness, fracturing the tender edge of her soul. There would be no room for negotiation, no hope for mercy—for judgment had come to the trail.

James grabbed hold of the trapper's crotch and pulled out his limp, slimy tool. The man wriggled and emitted a horrific whimper, but James kept pulling and stretching it until he'd nearly lifted the man's hips off the ground.

"*No! No! Please!*" came the plea, the man's voice trembling violently.

James looked at him and said pensively, "Maybe … maybe right now I *am* a child of the devil … or perhaps an angel of God."

He was surprised by his own words, as if it weren't him talking, but someone else. But he was even more surprised at how easily it came off—his root of pride and the essence of his manhood. One swipe of the knife—*schlllp*—and it was gone. He tossed it aside, as if it were a snake about to bite his hand, then grabbed a handful of snow and scrubbed his hands vigorously. He shook the melting snow from his hands and stood for a moment, watching blood squirt from the man's crotch with each heartbeat pump, gloating over his convulsive sobs and moans.

But he wasn't done yet. The good leg came off next, just below the knee. Fortunately for the luckless trapper, he lost consciousness shortly thereafter and bled out well before James had finished.

Later, it would be the blood that James remembered most—the giant scarlet sweeps and blotches across the stark white snow, and the salty, metallic smell of it. Ever since that day, whenever he had to field dress a deer or elk, he would take a deep breath and work quickly to avoid the stabbing reminder of the trapper's acrid guts.

When finished, James dispersed the body's various parts across the area, making it easier for the ravens and coyotes and bears to discover the fleshy repast and not miss a single morsel. After washing his blood-stained hands in the snow, he took a shortcut through the timber. When he broke into the clearing, he found himself staring down the barrel of Dawn's rifle. She looked blinded by rage, and her shaking trigger finger turned white as she began to squeeze.

"It's me! Don't shoot!"

Startled, she stared at the blood-stained sleeves of his jacket as he waved his hands. "Sorry," she said, lowering her rifle. "Two men rode through a few minutes ago, and I wasn't taking any chances."

His eyes shifted to her blood-spattered face and shirt, and he inhaled sharply. He noticed how her normally soft, tender eyes were suddenly piercing and sharp, her breathing quick and short—like someone fresh in the middle of a skirmish. It was only then that James recognized the full measure of changes the day had wrought. There had indeed been a branding—a permanent searing of the mind. Somewhere between the scarred edges of terror and lamentation, a deep, smoldering canyon had been burned in them both.

James wondered whether he would ever see his sweet, innocent, happy daughter again. Would she be able to put behind her the image of the drooling, grunting swine, his wild eyes and venous cauliflower nose, and the smell of his fecal breath in her face? He didn't feel a single pang of guilt. That would come later, long after the fires of rage had gone out. In the course of time, he came to regret dispersing the trapper's sundry parts for the scavengers to feast upon. After all, even Judas Iscariot had received a decent burial.

James built a gigantic stone wall around those cardinal-colored memories until his only nagging reminder was how the traumatic event had come to transform his daughter. He watched her grow hard and jagged, and witnessed her trust of men wither and die.

To compound the problem, shortly after the incident, Dawn began grilling him with questions about Eagle Claw—why were his features so different from those of other braves?—as if she innately already knew the truth. Finally, he relented and told her everything, how before Eagle Claw was born, Singing Bird had been brutally raped and that Eagle Claw was her half-brother—fathered by a vagabond trapper who had nearly killed Singing Bird with a vicious head blow to keep her from fighting while he had his way with her, and how she had spent nearly a month in and out of consciousness before eventually recovering.

From that moment forward, Singing Bird's disfigurement caused by her rapist became an ever-present reminder to Dawn that no man could be trusted, and she had come to treat them as if they were diseased—and touching one, or being touched by one, would cause certain death. Thus, she came to despise all men. The only exceptions were James and Eagle Claw, the only two men she ever trusted.

❧

Stewing over the gruesome memories, James rode well in front of Singing Bird and Dawn. He kept an ear open, just enough to hear the horses' hooves as they plodded along and the occasional soft tones of womanly conversations, to reassure himself they were close behind. It was a tough ride and seeing the white bone of the trapper by the poplar tree had triggered a violent trembling in his soul. Heavy stones in the wall James had built around that memory had been loosened and must now be repaired; blood-stained snow had been exposed that must again be painstakingly covered.

They rode until the setting sun had nearly put the day to bed. They dismounted, set up camp, and, after a quick meal, nestled under their buffalo robes. And as James held Singing Bird close, he prayed that a good night's rest would quell his disquieting stabs of remembrance.

Chapter Eleven

Story Time

E*agle Claw did his best to ensure that Gabe was* comfortably bundled near the fire. The young trapper wasn't about to wake up from his forced slumber anytime soon, but Eagle Claw figured he'd be safer in his camp than left for dead or propped against a tree near Branch's camp. Gabe's associates had piled his gear in the meadow between their two camps—an apparent sign he was no longer welcome. Eagle Claw checked on him again before slipping into the hodgepodge circle of humanity at the center of the encampment, where all the trappers were gathered to hear news and tell stories from the trapline.

But Eagle Claw wasn't there to tell stories. He hoped to get information about the source of Branch's beaver catch and felt confident he would succeed once the whiskey took hold, loosening the tongues of the mountain men, which were normally as tight as a snapped trap when it came to disclosing information as to the whereabouts of fur. And as he'd predicted, as the night closed in and the brown jugs were passed around the circle from one mouth to another, stories were shared, and secrets revealed.

After several passes of the jug, Eagle Claw sensed the unspoken derision of the others when they noticed him abstaining. It was customary to always drink at these events; to decline was tantamount to sacrilege—akin to passing on Sunday communion. Abstinence was taken as a subtle disapproval of the orgy, exposing for a moment the ugly beast of dissipation feeding voraciously among them—and on them.

However, it was clear to Eagle Claw that most of them, including Crooked Bill Branch, were already too drunk to hold him accountable for his perceived self-righteous refusal to partake. The obnoxious Branch grabbed the jug before the tipsy trapper next to him finished his swig, spilling the amber liquid down the sides of his dirty beard and onto his greasy buckskin shirt to the laughter of the crowd. Branch gulped hard, then inhaled deeply, visibly reacting from the concussion of the potent liquor. Staggering to his feet, he struck an orator's pose and commenced with a sauce-tarnished elocution, which surprised Eagle Claw. He hadn't expected any sort of showmanship from the rough mountain man.

"We were trappin' one time, Choteau 'n' me," began Branch. "I can't say when, but it were somewhere up in the godforsaken Yaak country or thereabouts." He paused and took another drink while the next person impatiently waited for the jug with eager outreached hands. Branch's tongue seemed to sag under the dull, heavy weight of the whiskey as he told the story. "We rode up a hidden canyon— secret canyon—when an eerie feelin' come over us. We rode until our horses refused to go on. Somethin' was a-spookin' 'em." He tipped the jug back again, slightly missing his mouth, the whiskey spilled down his beard and onto his leather shirt. Branch laughed at his faux pas, which caused the others to laugh—except for Choteau, who sat staring blankly at the campfire.

"Now, one night, we hear a strange animal cry. It weren't no cougar ... it weren't no bear." The audience gradually stopped laughing. It seemed odd to Eagle Claw how the white men showed little tolerance for such tales when sober—tales of strange forest creatures and beasts that could kill a man without a qualm, then feast on his flesh. But now, when inebriated, they listened with rapt attention.

"Then, we done saw it—in the campfire light, starin' at us just inside the timber, its eyes glowin' red in the firelight. Then it stood up ... and ... and it towered above the trees. For the first time, we was afraid."

He paused, wide-eyed, before errantly passing the jug back to Choteau, to the ire of the person next in line. The Frenchman took a sober sip, still staring trance-like into the fire. The circle of men was deathly quiet.

Branch continued: "Then, an ember from the fire flicked up in the air and landed near the thing. It turned the other way like it were a-scared of the spark. That's when I saw 'im good. His shoulders was wide as a buffalo, and he was taller'n a tamarack." He paused again, which caused his listeners to grow restless and look at each other with disquieting stares.

"What the hell was it?!" yelled one of them impatiently.

Branch snapped out of his trance. "Whaddaya mean, what was it? It was that damned ol' Skookum—the Wild Man of the woods."

A disappointed sigh came from some of the trappers, while others rolled their eyes disparagingly. But Eagle Claw's heart thumped in his chest at the word *Skookum*, and he felt his temples throb as a slow, burning anger welled up inside. He fought to maintain his composure as he noticed a couple of the crusty old-timers nodding to each other and exchanging stone-faced glances. He glanced at Branch's cohort, the Frenchman, who sat uncomfortably expressionless, as if holding a secret he couldn't tell yet wanted the whole world to know.

Then came a distracted murmuring. Branch was losing his audience, so he continued loudly, which once again got everyone's attention: "An' you know what I done? Hell, I shot 'im in the ass an' hollered, 'Get the hell outta here, you hairy son of a bitch!'" Branch held up the whiskey and hollered, "*Yahooooo!*"

A few of the tipsy trappers, hungry for anything to howl at, erupted with laughter, except Choteau, who got up shaking his head, farted loudly, then walked to the edge of darkness to relieve himself. The rest of the rowdies found this funnier than Branch's story and roared with laughter.

The clueless Branch joined them, laughing obnoxiously thinking the crowd was laughing at his story rather than Choteau's perfectly timed flatulence. "That damn Skookum took off a-runnin' like the devil was after 'im, an' I ain't seen 'im since."

Eagle Claw felt no compunction to laugh or even crack a smile. A handful of the men gazed blankly downward and remained silent, while most of the Indians listening behind the circle of trappers were grim-faced as they listened to the story. One by one, they rose and walked away into the night, quietly disappearing into their tents, tipis, and makeshift shelters.

Eagle Claw understood their reaction. To those who had lived their lives in the wilderness, the Skookum, Big Man, or Wild Man, as some called him, was no laughing matter. Only the foolhardy or unwise made jokes about the creature, and to do so was sure to invite trouble or certain ruin. To his people, the Kootenai, the Big Man was as real as any other creature; Eagle Claw knew this fact better than many in his own tribe. And the creature was Big Medicine to the Elders, who saw him as an omen and a protector of all things wild and untamed. Though Eagle Claw didn't share this view, he understood from experience that the Skookum was not to be trifled with.

More importantly, Branch's story convinced Eagle Claw that Crooked Branch and his men surely must have trespassed on their sacred grounds—a place where the Skookum roamed. The Elders must be told as soon as possible.

Chapter Twelve

Unlikely Friend

D*aybreak was but a dim prospect when Eagle Claw* rekindled his campfire and knelt close, blowing the embers back to life to drive away the morning chill. He carefully nursed the burgeoning red glow, adding grass and twigs until they caught, then fed more sticks and dried pieces of wood until the fire was fully kindled.

Nearby, the young mountain man he rescued the night before began moving like a slow-moving worm under the blanket Eagle Claw had wrapped him in. He had decided he should help the young man, just as he had seen his father do many times for those in need. The Bible stories his father had read to him, like the one about the Good Samaritan, taught him that helping others was what civilized human beings did. "Be merciful, for God is merciful—abundantly merciful," James would say. The words goaded Eagle Claw until he finally surrendered to them and came to the aid of the young trapper.

But more significantly, Eagle Claw felt sympathy for the young man when he saw how the men had mistreated him and how he'd endured and stood resiliently against the nipping wolf pack. Eagle Claw could relate to that kind of abuse. Witnessing the maltreatment of the young trapper had stirred bitter emotions that percolated from the depths of his soul where he had kept them entombed.

Gabe moaned, gently touching his head. "What happened? Where am I?"

"You don't remember?" Eagle Claw sat by the fire and crossed his legs.

Gabe rolled over, facing the fire. He squinted and sat up, pulling his knees toward his chest, then rolled his head in a circle as if the movement would somehow get his brain to start working again.

At length, he looked up at Eagle Claw and pointed at him. "I remember you. You were at the contest ... the ax-throwing contest. And you shook my hand."

"Yes. My name is Eagle Claw, remember?"

"Oh, yeah. Right. I'm Gabe Bauman—I think," the young man said. Gingerly, he placed his hand over the visible lump on his head and moaned. "Wait! Branch!" he blurted in sudden recollection. He spoke so loudly that Eagle Claw saw Branch stir in his bedroll near the campfire across the meadow.

"Yes, Branch. He hit you with a rock. You are lucky he didn't kill you. Seems like you must have a pretty hard head, eh?"

Gabe peered at him with a furrowed brow. "Wait. Did you just make a joke?"

Eagle Claw fought back a smile. "Here. Drink some water."

Gabe accepted the flask. "You know, you speak pretty darn good English for a Kootenai."

"Thank you. My father is English. He is a man of God and speaks many tongues. He also taught me French and Blackfeet."

"That must come in handy for you." Gabe sipped some water.

"At times, yes. Sometimes, I'd rather not know what men say when they think I don't know what they're saying."

"I heard you speaking in French to Choteau. Do you know him?"

"He stumbled into my camp one night, nearly frozen to death. I fed him some food and let him warm himself by the fire. Perhaps he didn't remember," Eagle Claw said wryly. He changed the subject. "Are you hungry? I have food."

"That's very nice of you, but I—hey?" Gabe paused, still looking dazed from the blow to his head. He glanced here and there. "What am I gonna do? I have no horse. Maybe Branch has cooled off by now."

Again, Eagle Claw looked toward Branch's camp, where the men were stirring. From what he had witnessed the day before, he thought it unlikely Branch would take the young trapper back, but it wasn't his fight. "They piled your gear over there." He pointed toward the small heap some thirty yards away. "They'll be rising soon. Maybe you can go talk to them."

Gabe struggled to his knees to get up, but Eagle Claw stopped him short. "No. Wait. They haven't woken yet. Before you go over there, I must ask you something."

Gabe sat back down with a painful sigh, holding the side of his head. "Sure, why not? Go ahead. Ask away."

Eagle Claw pointed at Branch and his men slowly stirring. "Those two you were with, Branch and the Frenchman, they came to our village not long ago. They wanted to make a deal—a trade. They asked permission from our elders to trap fur in the high mountain valley above our village; in exchange, they would give us some of the fur."

Gabe lowered his eyes sheepishly. "I wasn't with them when they talked to your elders. They made me stay back with the horses."

"Ah," said Eagle Claw, nodding. "So that's where you were. My mother is so clever." He recalled what Singing Bird had said before they left for home, when they sat together around the fire discussing the trappers. Her intuitions had always amazed him—how she could somehow put things together and trace the multitude strands of a spider's web back to its beginning. "What did Branch tell you after they spoke to our Elders?"

"He said the chief didn't care how many beavers we trapped. Just to leave a few to repopulate the lakes."

Eagle Claw nodded with pursed lips as feelings of anger and satisfaction quickened his pulse; satisfied that he had confirmed his suspicions, but angry that Branch and broken his word and deceived the Elders.

Pointing at Branch and his men with righteous indignation, he replied, "Do you know what Branch is called by the other trappers? He is known as Crooked Branch. He earned this name because his words and his spirit are crooked. And I can tell you this truthfully— Branch lied to you, and he lied to our Elders. He did not receive permission to trap there—in the lakes above our camp. That country is sacred to my people. We are sworn by covenant with the Creator Spirit to be guardians of this land. What you and your friends did was a terrible trespass." He glared at the group of offensive mountain men milling around and gathering near the fire as vindictive thoughts raced through his mind.

Gabe was silent, and his face grew sullen. After several moments, he looked directly at Eagle Claw and spoke: "It wasn't my decision to trap there, and they never said anything about it being sacred land. I'm ... I'm very sorry."

Eagle Claw glimpsed a simmering anger etched in Gabe's eyes as he rose, arms folded, and faced Branch's camp while Branch and Choteau shuffled about. The young trapper's jaw muscles pulsed as he clenched his teeth and pressed his hand against his head. Shaking the light dusting of autumn hoarfrost from his blanket, he draped it tightly around his shoulders to ward off the morning chill and glared at them.

Sensing what Gabe was about to do, Eagle Claw replied, "When you talk to them, tell them I speak for my Elders, and they are not welcome to trap on our sacred lands."

"What if they don't take me back? I have no horse."

There was a hint of meekness in Gabe's voice, reminding Eagle Claw of a young male wolf driven from the pack, skulking at a safe distance with his tail between his legs, silently hoping the alpha would take pity and accept him back.

The two watched as George Johnson and Thomas Jones rode up to Branch's camp and dismounted. Branch stood straight and firm, his chafing voice announcing to all that the alpha wolf of the encampment was officially awake.

"Now is your chance," Eagle Claw said in a firm, prodding voice.

The young trapper hesitated before walking pensively toward their camp. Eagle Claw quietly followed at a distance, rifle in hand, working his way in—close enough so he could monitor and intervene if things got out of hand.

When Gabe came into their view, the four mountain men looked up, startled, and reached for their rifles, but relaxed when they saw he was unarmed. Eagle Claw quietly slipped behind the log hut then into the stand of poplar and pine that ringed the encampment to better conceal his presence. Cautiously he crept closer.

"What the hell. If'n it ain't the greenhorn!" shouted Branch. "How's your head, kid?"

The others jeered and laughed, to the pleasure of the caustic Branch.

"Is there a reason why you moved my stuff?" asked Gabe.

"Is there a reason? Hell, yeah, there's a reason! I ain't puttin' up with a smart-ass twirp like yourself who doesn't know when to keep his damned saucebox shut. You're done here, kid! Besides, Johnson and Jones here are fallin' in with us, and I flat don't need yuz anymore."

"So what am I supposed to do, Branch? I don't have a horse."

"That's your problem, Bauman. You shoulda thought of that before you went an' popped off. Whaddaya gonna do now, cry? You think I'm gonna give you sweet ol' Juniper as a gift? His name ain't Juniper anyways. I call him Fleabag, a name that suits us both just fine. Look around." Branch gestured at the mix of trappers scattered around the meadow. "There's still a few Blackfeet and Salish here. Maybe you could see if any of them need a good squaw to cook and bend over, since ya love them damned Injuns so much."

Gabe's posture changed. He stood straighter, and his fists tightened as the four laughed at Branch's sardonic remarks. The tone of the conversation, and the expression on Gabe's face told Eagle Claw things were about to get out of hand.

"You lied, Branch!" Gabe proclaimed loudly. "Eagle Claw told me all about it. You said we were free to trap back in that basin, but that wasn't true, was it? Why did you lie?"

Trappers emerging from their makeshift lodges stared in Branch's direction. The crusty mountain man seemed happy that he had a growing audience. "Now, ya see, boys, this here is exactly what I've been sayin'. He just shoots off at the mouth. Who gives a pile of wet bear shite what them Injuns said? My rules say a free trapper is free to trap wherever he damn well pleases. And we're headed just a straight as an arrow right back there, boy!" His words caused Eagle Claw's hackles to go up, and his grip tightened on his rifle as he inched closer.

"Well, let me tell you this, Branch. You and your 'boys' here are not granted permission there. Those words come straight from Eagle Claw. So put that in your pipe and smoke it!"

But Branch only laughed. "You're a funny one, Bauman. In fact, you're so damn funny, you could make a stuffed bird laugh. I ain't never seen a greenhorn quite as lippy as you, that's for damn sure!"

"Maybe we should cut out that cussed tongue of his, Branch," remarked Johnson, fiddling with the handle of his sheathed knife.

Through the stand of poplar trees, Eagle Claw noticed Gabe's attention drawn to something. Following his eyes, he spied the Hawken rifle leaning against a pannier next to Branch's bedroll.

"That's my rifle!" blurted Gabe as he charged toward it, pushing Choteau out of the way. He grabbed it and held it tight, looking it over carefully for damage.

Just then Branch hollered, "Grab him, boys!"

Before Gabe could react, the three had him subdued. Branch jerked the Hawken from his hands, tossing it carelessly into the tall grass behind the panniers. Jones and Johnson had him by the arms, but he kicked and stomped until Choteau grabbed his legs and held them tight. Eagle Claw darted through the timber until only a single bush separated him from the men holding Gabe. Outnumbered four to one, he waited for the right moment to intervene.

"You know, Bauman, I've killed men for much less," said Branch, sliding his Green River knife from its sheath.

"Hurry up. He's squirmin' like a brained rattler," shouted Johnson.

"Hold 'im tight, boys. This won't take long."

Eagle Claw's heart pounded with anticipation as he neared the point where stealth must give way to action. He peered around the bush that stood between him and the trappers just as Branch placed the Green River knife just under Gabe's sternum. The others grinned and continued to hold tight as Gabe struggled. But they all froze when there came an unmistakable click from Eagle Claw's rifle. The devilish grin on Branch's face abruptly vanished, and as he turned to the source of the sound, his eyes grew wide when he found himself looking down the barrel of a rifle.

"Let him go," said Eagle Claw calmly.

"You goddamned filthy 'breed. You—" Branch stopped short when he saw Eagle Claw's trigger finger tighten, and he quickly changed his tune. "You heard him, boys—let him go." His eyes shifted here and there as he looked for a way out of the predicament.

The three mountain men let go and stepped away, each warily moving farther apart, then shifting to form a circle, like a wolf pack. As they circled wider, Eagle Claw sensed his advantage slipping away, and he began retreating as each man backed toward their rifles.

Branch seemed to find his lost bravado and glared at Eagle Claw. "You filthy 'breed! Your mother was a whore and your father a buffalo. First, I'll skin you alive, then I'll tie you to a post and burn you alive like them Iroquois do back east, then after that, I'll stake you out on an ant pile and let 'em eat you alive. And when I'm done doin' that, I'll fry your ass in bacon grease and eat you alive!"

"Come, let's go!" Eagle Claw shouted at Gabe.

"What about my Hawken?" Gabe was frantically moving panniers and scanning the camp for his hard-won prize.

"Forget the Hawken!"

"Your friend is smarter than he looks, Bauman. Better listen to him," Branch threatened.

Fortunately, by the time Branch's men had retrieved their weapons, a number of camp denizens had risen and drifted closer. Branch's men noticed them and appeared hesitant to engage in a full-on battle. But Eagle Claw took no consolation, for it was clear he had worn out his welcome. When it came down to it, he knew the trappers would never side with a half-breed.

He was relieved when Gabe gave up his search, and the two of them backed away until they reached the small pile of gear in the middle of the meadow. Fortunately, Branch had no use for Gabe's old trade musket, which lay on the ground next to the gear. They rummaged through the pile and found Gabe's powder horn and possibles bag, which he opened to confirm its contents: lead balls, shot, wads, flint, and various tools needed for his rifle. Gabe grabbed them, his rifle, and another armful of his belongings, and the two carried the items to Eagle Claw's small campsite.

Eagle Claw spoke first. "It won't be difficult to bundle your gear. There's not much of it. We'll tie it up and drape it over your lap and tie the rest behind your saddle."

"Wait a minute. What's happening here? What's the plan?"

"What's the plan?" Eagle Claw asked incredulously, surprised that Gabe seemed oblivious of the precarious nature of their situation. "The plan is to get out of here—now! The numbers are not in our favor. I have two horses. You can come with me, or you can stay here—by yourself—*all alone*." He emphasized the last words like a slap to wake up the naïve young trapper to the stark reality that faced him.

Eagle Claw had been in these situations before—outnumbered, outgunned, facing imminent death. He could sense the moment as keenly as a grizzly could smell a gut pile from a mile away. He kept an eye on the four men watching from across the meadow, their rifles in hand, while he loaded his horse and secured his gear to the leather straps hanging from the pommel and saddle horn.

"Go with you? Where are you going?"

"To my village, of course. To my people. To the Kootenai." He stopped and looked Gabe in the eye. The young trapper seemed clueless, and Eagle Claw could feel himself growing impatient. "I'm not waiting for you to come to your senses." He grabbed the reins of his horse, quickly mounted, and looked down at Gabe anxiously.

After glancing one more time at Branch and his men, the young trapper finally bundled up his few items in his bedroll and secured them to his horse, then quickly grabbed his musket and, as soon as his butt hit the saddle, Eagle Claw set out, and the two cautiously crossed the meadow toward the trailhead. Eagle Claw placed his rifle in his lap, urging Gabe to do the same, pointing it in the direction of Branch and his men as they rode past. By now, the entire Rendezvous encampment had groggily crawled from under their blankets and were staring, like surly grizzly bears waking from deep hibernation.

Eagle Claw looked over his shoulder every few paces until they were out of rifle range. As they rode past the half-dead denizens of the camp, he recognized their look: a look of uncertainty and bewilderment, teetering on the edge of hostility. It was unsettling to be in the presence of that look, and he kept his mind alert and his body taut until they were well beyond the encampment.

The two rode for hours—silently. Eagle Claw was no longer concerned with what lay behind. His focus was now on what lay before them on the perilous trail and the events that might unfold at its terminus. They certainly had enough able-bodied warriors in the tribe to resist Branch and his men, but would the Elders listen this time, or would they instead, like so many times before, decide to "smoke on it" and do nothing?

As they gradually put the miles behind them, he silently practiced the speech he would give. It would be a good speech, a strong speech—one that would stir his village into action. Then, he thought of Gabe and wondered if he had done the right thing by helping him. Eagle Claw had a wife and child of his own eagerly waiting for him at the village. He didn't relish the idea of bringing home a stray trapper. Perhaps the tribe would give Gabe a horse to help him on his way—he could only hope. The Elders, and James, would know what to do. The young trapper was certainly safer on the trail with him than with the murderous gang he had just left behind.

‹••›

Gabe, on the other hand, thought only about the trail behind him and the harping voice in his head telling him he was going the wrong direction. His home in Kentucky was east, not west. The events of the past day were mostly a blur. His head was splitting with pain, and during the night, he had been haunted by a nightmare that shook him to his core—the same one he'd frequently had as a young child.

He wondered why the nightmare had returned. Was it the blow to his head or something else? Searching for an answer, he thought about the young Blackfeet boy Branch had murdered. He remembered Branch's face when the hardened trapper had grabbed him and pulled him close after killing the boy. He'd noticed things he hadn't seen before—black pimples that cratered in the crevice where his nose and face came together, thick bloodshot veins that funneled into the corners of his eyes, the twisted satisfaction in his quivering grin, and his snake-like eyes that seemed to turn from brown to morbid black. It was a face that reeked with the very essence of evil.

He had recognized the same malevolence when Branch's men held him tight and he'd felt the sharp tip of Branch's Green River knife just under his sternum.

As he rode behind Eagle Claw, memories he had tried desperately to bury flashed through his mind—the blood of the Blackfeet boy oozing through his fingers, the horrific memory of his own father lying on the ground with blood streaming from his nose. They were moments in his life when he had felt the sickle of death about to swing clean through him. The nightmare was like that—like the sickle of death. Whatever the cause, it troubled him that it had returned.

The dream always started the same. He was falling—or perhaps more accurately, descending—slowly and precariously. There was just enough light to see the conical shape of gray sand moving down toward a black hole, just big enough for him to slip through. Initially, he assumed the sand was white and only appeared gray from the lack of light. However, after many recurrences, he came to realize that it wasn't white at all, but the dingy gray of death itself. In the same instant that he became aware of the sand, he realized he was moving with it, toward that infinite black hole that drained into the Stygian caverns of oblivion.

He grabbed vainly for a handhold, but the sand slipped through his fingers like air. Swimming with hysterical fear against the current, the last thing he always remembered was the feeling of utter hopelessness, sliding inevitably downward, downward to the pinch-point that led to eternal darkness—the nexus of all evil, the crystallization of all his fears. As he drew near the hole, he could see them, far below, the thrashing, undulating horde with hairless warty heads and pointed ears, their mouths lined with rows of sharp teeth, their clawed, craven hands reaching upward to catch the next flesh that might perchance slide through the maw.

His faithful mother had come to his rescue whenever he had the dream. Finding him in a cold sweat screaming unintelligible words from an ancient primal tongue, she would wake and comfort him. Though his parents were God-fearing, taking great pains to point

Gabe toward the narrow path, it was that dream, and the pure terror of slipping into that dreadful place of darkness, that drove him toward the outstretched arms of God.

But the nightmare he had the night before was slightly different this time. He was swimming hard against the current of sand and amazingly making progress when a clawed hand reached through the hole and grabbed him by the ankle. As he slipped into that black pit filled with writhing creatures, his father appeared above him. Reaching down, he grabbed Gabe's hand and pulled him up, up toward the blissful light. He felt himself stretching against the force above and the force below, and as his father pulled him higher and higher, the scarred, gnarly arm of the evil below came into view, then the demon's snarling head. Its snapping jaws were lined with fanged teeth, its forked tongue flicked hungrily, and a maniacal smile was carved into its ashen face. Its long, pointed ears, wart-covered head, and evil countenance were all what one would expect on the face of a demon, but its eyes—its cruel, piercing eyes—were those of Crooked Bill Branch.

The dream had jolted Gabe as if he'd been struck by a bolt of lightning, and as they rode, he thanked God that he was finally free of the diabolical trapper. He thought about Branch's ruthlessness—how he had killed the boy and brazenly stolen the Hawken—but he still found it difficult to fully comprehend Branch's demented nature. Shortly after being hired, Gabe came to realize that Branch was, in fact, a notorious schemer, and his newest skilamalink seemed obvious: bait a couple of greedy trappers with hollow promises and lure them into helping him trap out the Kootenai's sacred lands. Gabe's father had always told him: "A man's wicked deeds trail behind him like a goblin. Eventually, the goblin catches up, and woe to that man when it does." As Gabe thought about his former boss, he wondered to himself if that giant, fanged goblin would ever catch up to Bill Branch. It didn't seem fair that the villain always seemed to get the upper hand, no matter how heinous his crimes, and it made Gabe question things—it made him question God.

Dreary cogitations kept Gabe preoccupied along the serpentine trail until he remembered the beautiful raven-haired woman and realized they were traveling precisely to the camp where she lived. The winsome epiphany swept his worries to the far corner of his mind, and the formerly bland, monochromatic mountains became vibrant and alive. Even the birds, whose bright songs had fallen on deaf ears since leaving the Rendezvous, suddenly came to life and filled the air with exuberant melodies.

Feelings of contentment and freedom grew, and the dark shadow of Crooked Bill Branch faded with each step they took away from the encampment. Then, he realized that something else was missing—the chafing sound of Branch's voice. Like a lifting fog, he became aware of things that previously escaped his attention: the forest grouse perched on a limb of a larch, pecking for its yellow needles; the inquisitive weasel that hopped up on a log to survey them as they passed, and the eagle that swooped from the sky to grab a trout with its talons from just beneath the surface of the adjacent stream.

The warm autumn sun gradually drove away the morning chill, and Gabe felt more alive with each breath of crisp mountain air. As they rounded a bend in the trail, a black bear sow with two cubs padded leisurely through a patch of huckleberries, lapping up the sweet treats with nimble tongues in preparation for winter's long sleep. They were so engrossed in their feeding, they hardly acknowledged the horses, which snorted one by one as they stepped into the scent cone of the thickly furred bruins.

Eagle Claw paused after passing through a stand of birch trees along the river bottom and motioned for him to come forward. Gabe urged his horse ahead until he was even with Eagle Claw. There, on the broad edge of the meadow, stood an enormous bull elk with his harem. His bugle was answered by a younger challenger, nearly equal in size, partially concealed just inside the adjacent timber. Before long, it mustered enough courage to emerge and enter the arena, ears laid back and ready to battle for the harem.

Gabe had seen elk before and had killed a couple of small ones for camp meat, but he'd never witnessed a battle between two mature bulls. He asked if they could shoot one, but Eagle Claw whispered that killing one here, so far from the fish camp, would only slow them down. Besides that, it would be too much meat for them to carry and most likely would spoil before they could get it safely to camp. Nevertheless, Gabe was pleased when Eagle Claw insisted they watch the fight to see which one would triumph.

The challenger approached and lowered his antlers, then the two, in unison, squared off as the cows and calves watched between mouthfuls of meadow grass. *Do they care who wins?* Gabe wondered. *Do they even have a choice as to which one will be their suitor?* The bulls' antlers clattered as they locked horns, the sound echoing throughout the valley as they churned up the ground. After a half hour of strenuous combat, they were both spent, and their tongues were hanging out—both unwilling to give up. They stood locked together, pushing each other back and forth a foot or so, but neither with the strength to dominate the other.

The herd bull finally gave one desperate surge, got a foothold, and hooked the challenger with one of its saber-pointed tines. The loser quickly retreated into the timber with the herd bull hot on his heels. He let out a victorious bugle to announce he was still king before returning to his harem. Undeterred, the loser let out a defiant piercing trumpet call inside the nearby timber to let the herd bull know he hadn't left the area and would return to challenge him again when he had recovered from the fight.

Gabe wanted to discuss the elk battle with Eagle Claw but sensed he wasn't in a talkative mood. Besides, Branch had preached silence on the trail, especially when in the heart of Blackfeet country, and it appeared Eagle Claw was somewhat familiar with that sermon. It made sense to ride quietly on this trail. Men talking loudly could signal danger to anything or anyone within earshot. It was a distinctive, discordant sound that traveled far in the broad valleys, echoing along rivers, and bouncing off rocky cliffs and crags, possibly reaching the ears of a potential enemy.

But according to what Choteau had told Gabe, the trail hadn't always been rife with danger. The peaceful surroundings belied the ever-present existence of peril, where each twist of the trail could bring an unwelcome encounter with either man or beast. The fur industry was groaning, like a ravenous behemoth, from the scarcity of beaver. The crisis, born of unchecked greed, had left both mountain men and Indians hungry and desperate. Some had even resorted to ambushing, robbing, and waylaying unwary travelers. These men had sinister motives, played by a different set of rules, and had no compunction about enriching themselves at the expense of others.

As Gabe and Eagle Claw rode through the large meadow, the herd of elk trotted toward the security of the timber with their odd nose-in-the-air gait. They had gone only a few paces into the forest on the far side of the meadow when Eagle Claw abruptly stopped his horse, dismounted, and pulled the bow from the elk-hide scabbard that hung from his saddle horn.

Gabe scanned the terrain to see what had prompted his companion's actions. He tried to ask, but before he could get the words out of his mouth, Eagle Claw put his finger to his mouth, calling for silence. Then, he put two fingers over each ear and made the universal Indian sign for *rabbit*. After silently stringing his bow, he pulled a raven-feathered arrow from the moose-hide quiver slung over his shoulder and nocked it. He crept ahead, leaving his horse unattended, which afforded the steed a moment to get a few mouthfuls of grass. Gabe watched as Eagle Claw moved silently through the underbrush. In one fluid movement, he drew and shot.

Gabe's eyes followed the arrow's path until it hit its intended target. Only then could he see the rabbit where it had been hiding in the grass near the trail. The arrow had hit with lethal results, pinning the animal to the ground. After it stopped thrashing, Eagle Claw retrieved the arrow and checked the flint arrowhead for damage before wiping away the blood on a tuft of grass. He picked up the rabbit, already beginning its fall transformation from forest brown to snowy white, and looked it over, sizing it up for a meal, then carried his prize back to the horses.

"Dinner," he said with a smile.

Gabe acknowledged him with a nod. Eagle Claw tied the rabbit by its hind legs to his saddle, and they continued their journey.

As the sun began to drift toward the western horizon, Eagle Claw scanned the area to make sure no one was watching from the shadows, then turned off the main trail. The detour led upward toward a finger ridge higher on the mountain, a safe distance from the vulnerabilities of the main trail. Gabe surveyed the small, secluded hideaway some distance off the beaten path and was pleased to see a grassy meadow, where they could graze their horses and camp for the night after the day's long ride, thinking it would be a perfectly quaint place to build a small cabin.

"We camp here tonight," said Eagle Claw softly.

Chapter Thirteen

Skookum

W*ithout a word, the two unlikely traveling com-*
panions unloaded their gear and put rawhide hobbles on the horses'
front feet before turning them out to graze on the nearby grassy
bench. The hobbles restricted movement and would prevent them from
traveling far, making it much easier to catch them in the morning.

Gabe was finding it a challenge relating to Eagle Claw's conspicuous silence and found himself biting his tongue whenever he was about
to start a conversation. But when he noticed Eagle Claw unwrapping
an ornately beaded parfleche, his curiosity got the best of him.

"What's that?" he asked loudly.

Eagle Claw was painfully slow to reply, as if the question itself
was a violation of decorum. "I traded a half dozen beaver pelts to a
Blackfeet three moons ago. Pretty colors, eh?"

"No, I meant the things in the bag."

"My tools to build us a fire?"

Gabe had always used a strike-a-light to start a fire, but this was
new to him and he was interested in seeing how the contraption
worked. Quickly, he gathered some firewood while Eagle Claw
gathered a few large rocks to form a fire ring.

Gabe peered over Eagle Claw's shoulder as he meticulously
arranged the items. He began by placing a handful of tinder and

kindling on a dry patch of ground in the center of the fire ring. Next, he strung a small bow and looped a spindle stick around the string. Placing a fireboard over the wad of tinder, he used a fist-sized rock with a divot in the center as a spindle and pressed down as he vigorously worked the bow back and forth, causing the spindle stick to spin rapidly. Within a minute or two, thin wisps of smoke started to rise from the hole he was boring into the fireboard. After a few more rapid strokes, he had created a small ember, which he carefully tapped from the fireboard onto the kindling. Gently, he blew on the ember until the tinder caught fire, then carefully fed the fledgling flame dried grass, followed by kindling, then larger sticks until the fire was well established.

"That's amazing!" Gabe exclaimed with a chuckle. "How did you learn to do that?"

Eagle Claw smiled wryly and replied, "Old Indian secret."

His faint levity put Gabe's heart at ease for a moment. Eagle Claw placed a couple larger logs on each side of the fire, then skinned the rabbit, secured it on a spit, and used the two logs to situate the rabbit above the fire. Gabe's mouth watered at the sweet tangy smell of roasting rabbit while they unpacked their bedrolls and then they sat down to warm themselves while it cooked.

"My stomach's growling," Gabe said impatiently as a crispy brown patina slowly formed on the rabbit, and he eyed it like a mountain lion ready to pounce. But Eagle Claw didn't reply. He only sat and gazed into the fire as if lost in contemplation.

The lack of conversation made Gabe uneasy until Eagle Claw finally broke the silence. "When everyone was gathered around the big fire at the Rendezvous last night, Branch told a story about the Skookum. He said he shot and wounded it."

His words were startling—not because of his sudden interest in conversation, but because of Branch's bodacious claim. The brave locked eyes with him, as if waiting for a reply. Gabe averted his eyes and stared into the fire soberly, a loss for words, wondering why Branch would make such a boast.

"Was it true or was it just more lies of the Crooked Branch?" asked Eagle Claw insistently.

Gabe replied incredulously, "Branch said it was either the Kootenai trying to scare us or a bear. He said nothing about a Skookum."

But the persistent brave continued to probe: "What about you? Did you see anything strange when in our sacred lands?" Thinking Eagle Claw was making another joke, an impulsive grin formed on the corner of Gabe's mouth, until he met the brave's steely gaze.

Gabe stared into the fire and replied, "I saw something when I was gathering the horses on the night before we left, but it turned out to be nothing—probably just a pine tree or a speck in my eye. Choteau said he saw something, though, and Branch shot at it. Frenchy seemed more spooked than Branch—said it was covered in hair and walked on two legs, like a man, only bigger. On the trail out, he claimed to have spotted something high up in the trees, too. Crazy talk." Eagle Claw said nothing and stared stone-faced into the fire.

"That Frenchy … he's different. Branch says he's too superstitious, believing too much in tall tales told by Ind—" He stopped short and felt his face blush. Gabe glanced sheepishly at Eagle Claw, whose stern expression remained unchanged. Embarrassed by his near slip of the tongue, Gabe continued blithely, "Choteau talked to me later about what he saw, but I think he was trying to pull another prank on me— with me being a greenhorn and all. You know, trying to scare me."

Eagle Claw grabbed a small log and placed it in the fire. Gabe was relieved after a few minutes when he removed the roasted rabbit and portioned him half—perhaps now, he would change the subject. Gabe quickly began gnawing off bites of roasted rabbit flesh, blowing out air rapidly as the sizzling meat burned his tongue.

"We seldom go into the canyon where you trapped the beaver," said Eagle Claw after several bites. "We intentionally built our camp there at the mouth of the drainage because other tribes are afraid to go there. It is a sacred place to my people, but there are also many dangers there. The old ones tell many stories about this place."

"Why do you consider it sacred?"

His question caused Eagle Claw to pause. His cold demeanor relaxed as he stared into the fire as if it had hypnotized him for a moment. Then he began to speak. "It has been sacred ground for as long as I can remember. There are powerful spirits there. A long time ago, two braves went into the canyon and were never seen again. It is a very dangerous place for men. We only go there when necessary—to catch beaver when our winter food runs low. Only the bravest among us are permitted to enter the sacred lands, and only if they receive the blessing of the Elders. To do otherwise is to test the patience of the Great Spirit and invite trouble."

Eagle Claw's story sounded sketchy, like those of Branch when he jinked him with tall tales around the campfire at night to try and scare him. Gabe felt an impulsive grin forming at the corner of his mouth, and he couldn't help but raise his brows in disbelief.

Eagle Claw glanced up at him and visibly reacted to Gabe's body language, and his next words came chopped and quick. "We try not to speak of the sacred places to outsiders who don't understand these things. The white men call us superstitious savages. They hear of our legends and call them 'fiction tales' for the weak of mind. It is offensive to us," he added bitterly, "when foreigners speak this way about things they know nothing of."

Gabe's grin faded, and he felt bad that he had offended Eagle Claw. Swallowing nervously, he nodded and replied, "Well, I guess we all have our legends. All I know is that I didn't see anything back in that drainage."

Eagle Claw pursed his lips and stretched out his legs next to the comforting fire as if to assuage his anger. "Do you believe in God, Gabe Bauman?" he said abruptly.

The question took Gabe by surprise. "Sure. Of course I believe in God," he blurted.

"But you cannot see His face or touch His hand. Yet you believe anyway. Perhaps because you see other signs of His presence, eh? So it is with the Skookum. Though you did not see it with your eyes, if you would have looked more closely, you would have found its sign—a track, a string of hair, its strong odor, or its wild cry in the night. 'The secret things belong to God, but the things revealed are for us and for our children.' This is spoken of in the Bible. Do you know this?"

Gabe sat back, a piece of half-chewed rabbit hanging from his open mouth. He was at a rare loss for words—Eagle Claw's statement made sense.

"Perhaps someday, God will reveal things to you, Gabe Bauman, and then you will think differently, eh?"

Gabe nodded humbly and finished his meal in silence. Without saying goodnight, he crawled under his bedroll, still perplexed by Eagle Claw's wisdom and his unexpected quotation of scripture. After what seemed like an hour pondering the words, he finally faded to sleep.

∽

Eagle Claw was restless, disturbed by their conversation, and stayed awake by the fire. The talk of the Skookum and the hypnotizing tongues of flame from the campfire ushered ominous memories from his childhood.

He remembered it was late summer. Singing Bird needed meat for the evening meal, so she summoned young Eagle Claw to stalk through the woods with his bow to shoot a grouse or rabbit.

At only six years of age, he had already proven himself capable of bringing home small game with his bow and arrow, and he took great pride in using his skills to be a provider. Mostly, though, he found peace in the woods, far away from the bullying boys who plagued him incessantly.

Eagle Claw knew just the place where he could find a rabbit for his mother—a nearby spring, a mile or so away, where cool clear water trickled from a source deep within the mountain. It was a watering hole where the wild forest creatures came to slake their thirst on hot summer days. Bears often soaked in the cool water that collected in pools below the spring, so he always took precautions not to invite trouble by blundering in carelessly.

He grabbed his bow and arrow and set out for the spring. After hiking in the hot sun, he looked forward to quenching his own thirst and hoped there were no bears at the watering hole. As he approached, he could hear the faint gurgling of the spring and crept cautiously ahead. Peering through the brush, he was relieved to see a fat rabbit. After getting a drink, it hopped to some nearby grass and began nibbling. Slowly and silently, Eagle Claw crept forward, pausing only when the rabbit sat on its haunches to look around for danger. Taking care not to disturb the loose rocks under his feet or step on a twig, he stalked closer until he had worked his way into killing range. He waited until the rabbit lowered its head to grab another mouthful of grass, then drew back his bow and released the arrow, hitting its midsection with a dull *thwack*.

The arrow pierced completely through and buried itself in the moist soil on the other side of the rabbit. It began thrashing wildly, trying to break free, but the arrow was buried deep enough into the ground that it held firm. To Eagle Claw's shock, after failing to free itself, the rabbit began squealing loudly. He ducked behind a bush and waited patiently for it to stop, knowing the cries might summon a bear or cougar. Besides, he had been bitten before when handling a wounded rabbit and didn't want to repeat that mistake. Not only that, but pulling the arrow free before the rabbit had succumbed could also give it a chance to bolt, making recovery more difficult.

However, unlike the other rabbits he'd killed, this one stubbornly refused to die, and wouldn't cease its piercing cries. He searched for a big rock or stick to finish it off, but the high grass around the perimeter of the spring concealed almost everything. Eagle Claw remembered some larger rocks farther back on the trail where he had begun his stalk, so he grabbed his bow and sprinted to find one. Soon, he came to a small rocky chute on the side of the mountain where he found a few hefty rocks.

He didn't hesitate. Grabbing one, he ran back to the rabbit, raised the rock over his head with both hands, and brought it down hard on its head. The rock performed better than expected, popping out both the animal's eyes with the heavy blow and silencing it in mid-squeal. Relieved, Eagle Claw sat down next to his prize to catch his breath. He cupped his hand and drank from the spring to quench his thirst. He loved the earthy taste of the mineral-rich water and couldn't seem to get enough of it.

After his belly could hold no more, he was ready to head home. But just as he was about to reach for the rabbit, a foul odor burned in his nostrils. It was a thick, pungent scent, like that of a skunk. Then, he heard a heavy footfall and something large pushing through the alder brush behind him. He grabbed his bow, leaving the rabbit behind, and darted behind a thick bush a dozen yards away, hoping it wasn't a bear.

The odor became stronger and the footfalls quieter until the small ravine fell into a deathly silence. The boy slowly raised his head, peering through the tangle of brushy stems, his eyes darting back and forth to see what could have made the noise. He blinked and looked away, but only for a moment, and when he turned again to check on the rabbit, something caught his eye.

Suddenly, he saw it, as if it had appeared from nowhere—an enormous creature. It was kneeling, facing away from him, and it seemed to be studying the rabbit. Its back and shoulders were visible through the brush, but Eagle Claw dared not stretch higher to get a better view for fear of being seen. At first, he thought it was a bear, but when it stood up on two legs, still facing the opposite direction, it became obvious that it was much too tall to be a bear—and its shape and form were that of a man.

Eagle Claw's heart raced, and his breathing quickened as terror pulsed through his veins. Immediately, he remembered the stories told by the old women of the village about the demon of the forest: the Skookum. He had been warned to never wander far from the village, for it would hunt for children to catch and eat them.

The thought of its teeth sinking into his body filled him with panic. He wanted to run but feared it might see him and snatch him, so he tried to stay as still as possible. Just as he was about to bolt, the creature took a step toward him. Eagle Claw ducked lower, trembling as his eyes tracked up its body from its giant feet all the way to the top of its head.

The beast held up the dead rabbit and sniffed it curiously. It turned its head slightly so that Eagle Claw could see part of its face. Dark, grayish hair covered its head like a thick hat that extended down to its brow. Its eyes were like two coals set deep under a pronounced brow. Its nose was bigger and wider than a man's, and its slightly downturned lips made for a serious, somber countenance. The face, though fearfully intimidating, appeared more human than animal.

It pulled the arrow out and dropped the rabbit. It studied the arrow, sniffing it curiously, more interested in the tiny feathered shaft than the dead rabbit. It then touched its pointed tip and winced when it pressed too hard against its finger. It let out a grunt and rubbed a massive thumb against a fingertip, dripping blood. Then, it knelt, shoved the arrow back through the rabbit, and stood upright, holding the arrow and the skewered rabbit, which looked like a small gopher held by its massive hand. Suddenly, the wind shifted, and the creature alertly sniffed into the breeze, as if alarmed by something it had smelled. When it turned the other way, trying to locate the source of the smell, Eagle Claw sensed the worst and ran—as fast as his legs could carry him.

He crashed through brush and over deadfall, then sprinted through the creek and the mountain meadow blanketed with tall grass and lumpy tussocks. He glanced back before re-entering the forest at the far end of the field. To his horror, the creature stood watching from the opposite side of the meadow. Its enormous size and ominous glare made his heart race. Moved by fear and adrenaline, Eagle Claw ran farther and faster than he had ever run before. He ran and ran until he could run no more. Finally, he collapsed close to the creek drainage where tall grass grew.

He tucked himself beneath a drooping tussock and curled into a fetal position to make himself small, then closed his eyes. Primal dread coursed through his veins, and his heart pounded inside his chest. He wanted to get up and run farther, but his legs would not obey—he was completely spent, and his ribcage heaved in and out as he fought to catch his breath. After a few minutes had passed, his breathing was less labored, and with his little hand, he groped at the ground until he found his bow—a worthless piece of wood and sinew against such a creature, yet somehow, it gave him courage.

Suddenly, his eyes flashed open. He strained to hush his labored breathing as the sound of something large approached from behind. Instinctively, he froze, and closed his eyes, trying to make himself as still as possible. He remembered the fawn he and his sister had found lying perfectly still in a grassy meadow. *Yes, the fawn,* he thought. *I will pretend I'm the fawn.* But the steps came closer and closer until he could hear the alder brush rattle softly as the thing crept up behind him. When he smelled the familiar skunky odor, his heart began to race again. Every fiber in his body wanted to run, but he knew he could go no farther. The most courageous thing he could do was remain motionless. The brush across his face tickled and itched, but he maintained his resolve and didn't move, thinking only of the fawn and of his own family. He thought about how he would hold his baby brother by his hands and help him to balance on two legs. He wanted him to walk, so he could teach him how to hunt. "Come on. You can do it," he would say, but his brother would just collapse in a lump and lay there, smiling at him, kicking his legs excitedly.

The minutes turned into an hour, and Eagle Claw's thoughts drifted back and forth nervously, calmed only by the gentle summer breeze. He was startled when a gust of wind caused the drooping grass to again tickle his face. He had lost track of time and couldn't remember how long he had been lying there. Somehow, he seemed farther from home than ever before, even though he knew the village was but minutes at a hard run. Remembering his mother, he at last felt the courage to move, and he hoped the terror that he had felt looming over him was gone.

Cautiously, he opened his eyes, listening for any sound of movement. He lifted his head slightly, but only the vast blue sky above came into view. Then, ever so slowly, he turned his head so he could peek over his shoulder. The pungent odor still hung faintly in the air. Certainly, the monster had to be there watching him, waiting to pounce. Fear and panic once again welled up, and he trembled, afraid of what he might see if he stood up in the tall grass.

But each inch that he raised brought only the empty view of the sky, the meadow, and the bony branches of the alder brush whose leaves rustled in the late-afternoon breeze. He summoned all his courage, stood fully upright, and looked around—it was gone. He felt an overwhelming sense of relief. *Has it gone away for good, or was all this just a bad dream?* he wondered.

And then he saw something, next to a flattened patch of grass a few feet away. It was his blood-stained arrow sticking out of the ground. Next to it lay the rabbit he had killed.

Upon realizing it wasn't a dream, Eagle Claw's eyes flashed as he spun around looking in every direction. *Home! I have to get home!* He grabbed his bow, arrow, and the rabbit, and he raced as fast as he could for the village.

Chapter Fourteen

Trouble on the Trail

G*abe was awakened by a curious sound coming* from the side of the mountain above their campsite. The morning sun cast its first rays upon the mountaintops as he searched the area, but Eagle Claw was nowhere to be seen. Grabbing his gun, he climbed to investigate the strange sound.

As he approached a rocky promontory that jutted from the mountain, he noticed through the trees the figure of a man sitting over a small fire with his arms raised, softly chanting in a foreign tongue. He crept closer and, as he'd suspected, recognized Eagle Claw. Gabe drew near and asked, "What are you doing?"

Surprised, Eagle Claw jerked sideways and spun around with his knife drawn. When he saw Gabe, he sighed deeply, then composed himself. "You're getting good at sneaking up on things, eh?"

Gabe felt a twinge of guilt, realizing the brave was apparently praying. "I'm sorry ... sir," Gabe replied, clearing his throat.

Without another word, Eagle Claw sheathed his knife and picked up the tuft of sage smoldering by the fire. He waved it around himself and continued his prayerful chanting. Gabe listened and watched as the smoke from the sage drifted up and disappeared. Looking out at the scenery from the lofty vantage point, he could see why Eagle Claw had chosen this spot to pray. The majestic mountains in all their

109

glory revealed the presence of a higher power, and as Gabe took it all in, he thought of his father and mother and how they had struggled to point him toward the things of God despite his stubborn apathy and frequent indifference.

When Eagle Claw had finished, Gabe asked, "What do you pray for?"

Eagle Claw paused for a moment as he snuffed out the tuft of sage. "I pray to the Great Spirit, the Creator of all things—earth, sky, water, and all living creatures. I pray for my people, for my family. I pray for our safety on the journey home and peace from our enemies."

Eagle Claw's words cut Gabe to the quick. He hadn't heard a prayer since his father had given thanks for their morning meal on the day they'd had gotten into a fight over his father's rifle, followed by Gabe's contentious departure from the farm. The young trapper recalled trying to give an awkward prayer of thanks on the momentous occasion when he'd killed his first elk, but Branch and Choteau had ridiculed him.

Since then, he had given up on praying, his fleeting thoughts of God an irksome reminder of his waywardness and the frailty of the faith he had so easily cast aside. But the sight of the noble Eagle Claw with his hands lifted, his beseeching eyes peering into the heavens as if looking into the very eyes of God, had delivered a piercing stab—a severing of soul and spirit, joints and marrow, convicting Gabe to the bone.

His prayer complete, Eagle Claw rose and headed back to camp with Gabe close behind. But even as Gabe thought soberly about what he'd just witnessed, his growling stomach soon made the spirit grow weak and the flesh strong as they approached their camp.

"What's for breakfast?" he asked.

Eagle Claw snorted, then laughed dryly. "Breakfast? What's breakfast?" he scoffed.

"You know—food, grub, that stuff you eat in the morning after you wake up. I'm so hungry, I could eat a wormy old grizzly bear."

"I know what breakfast is. We don't have time. The trail calls. We can eat later."

"Eat later?" Gabe said, dumbfounded.

"Yes, later. I sometimes go days without food. It's easy. You just think of something besides food."

Gabe, however, wasn't accustomed to such a meager diet, and the tidbit of rabbit the night before had done little to stave off his incessant hunger.

"Sorry, but I need to eat something. I'll go get us another rabbit," Gabe insisted as he grabbed his rifle.

"No. No gunfire yet. The Blackfeet use this trail, and they could make trouble for us. Ever use a bow?" Eagle Claw retrieved and strung his bow, then gestured toward a rotting stump some thirty feet away. "Let me show you. You hold it here, in the middle below this mark. The notch on the back of the arrow fits in the middle of the string, like this. Pull the string to your cheek ... and release." Eagle Claw sent the arrow into the stump. "See? It's easy. Now, you try."

Gabe took the bow and held it awkwardly in his hand. It was well made, with stout limbs cloaked with tanned rattlesnake skins sewn tight for added protection. He fumbled with the arrow as he tried to nock it on the string, but it slipped off his fingers and fell to the ground. Determined to succeed, he tried again, and again. Finally, he managed to get off an awkward shot, surprised at how difficult it was to pull the string to full draw, and missed the target by a wide margin.

"What?" he remarked, perplexed by his errant shot. Then, he saw the slight grin on Eagle Claw's face. No—he would not allow the brave to laugh at him. "I'm not ready to give this up just yet. I'm gonna figure this out."

Eagle Claw folded his arms. "I'm impressed by your determination. It's good that you want to learn how to shoot the bow—a weapon most white men consider inferior. Perhaps the trail can wait. You practice while I catch breakfast."

Puzzled, Gabe said, "Won't you need your bow?"

Eagle Claw shook his head, not bothering to explain, then turned and disappeared into the forest.

Gabe took another shot and was pleased when he hit the base of the stump. He retrieved the arrow and stepped back a bit farther, then continued practicing until his arms grew weary and sore. He had never seen an arrow up close and always wondered how such a primitive-looking weapon could be effective in killing game. He held up the flint-tipped arrow and examined it closely, noticing how the tip of the flint broadhead was deceptively sharp.

Nocking an arrow, he drew back the bow and released the string in one fluid motion, pleased when he hit the stump dead center. He was finally getting a good feel for the weapon. Taking one step toward the target, he heard the click of a rifle behind him and froze when he remembered Eagle Claw had left camp unarmed. Gabe spun around to find himself looking down the barrel of a rifle held by a fierce-looking Indian not more than five paces away. Gabe stood stock-still, stunned when three others emerged like stealthy cougars from their hiding places and surrounded him. Gabe dropped the bow and held up his hands. They were on him in a flash.

Trying to reason with them, he blurted, "Wait! What do you—?" but before he could finish his question, the four wrestled him to the ground, gagged him, and tied him fast to a nearby tree. It all happened so fast that Gabe didn't have time to process what was happening. Sitting against the tree with his feet and hands tied, he suddenly realized the precarious nature of his situation and a wave of panic swept over him.

Immediately, the men began speaking to each other in a native tongue. Their faces were covered in war paint, but they appeared to be in good spirits as they laughed and spoke in congenial tones, which put Gabe somewhat at ease. One of them was staring at Eagle Claw's horses tethered to nearby trees. *Maybe they only want the horses,* Gabe thought. It wasn't until he spotted one of the braves rummaging through his belongings that he tried to holler and wriggle free. He knew it was one thing to be without a horse, and another entirely to be without a weapon or critical survival gear. He bit down hard on the gag and tried pulling his hands free, but they had done a fine job of lashing his wrists. His struggles drew the braves' attention, and they sauntered over and stood in front of him.

"White man like to shoot bow, eh? Crow like to shoot *you!*" one exclaimed in broken English with a laugh, poking his finger in Gabe's chest.

The leader held up the bow. "You mighty warrior, eh?" he said, drawing laughter from the others.

One of them took notice of the bow's intricate workmanship and commented to his companions, "Very nice bow!" Turning to Gabe, he asked, "You make?"

Gabe glared and tried vainly to talk through the gag. As they huddled around gawking at the bow, it began to dawn on him that they might have darker motives than stealing horses. He struggled against the cords that bit into his wrists until they went completely numb, as if they'd been cut off, and all that remained were stumps.

The leader retrieved a large clump of moss and placed it atop Gabe's head, but he shook it free. "Tie his head," the brave said, scowling.

One of the others grabbed a piece of rope and wound it around Gabe's neck, pulling his head tightly against the tree as he struggled to breathe. The clump of moss was placed back on his head, where it rested like a helmet with strings of brown roots drooping over his ears and eyes, partially blocking his vision.

The leader grabbed some arrows, paced off ten steps, and marked a toe line with a stick. "Now, we will see true warrior!" he said gleefully.

They snickered as Gabe tried desperately to wriggle free and laughed when he squinted his eyes shut and mumbled a prayer. Gabe held his breath as the Crow warrior released the arrow, hitting the moss dead center, a mere inch above his head. Their jeering suddenly seemed far off, drowned out by the sound of his heart throbbing like a drum inside his chest and echoing in his ears.

The leader smiled with self-assurance, then approached Gabe amid the mishmash of prattle and laughter. The humor previously written on his face had vanished, and after carefully loosening the arrow imbedded into the bark, he removed it and tossed the clump of moss aside. Reaching down, he plucked a charred stick from the nearby campfire. Gabe tried to struggle against the cord wrapped across his neck, but that only made it tighter, nearly choking him.

The leader came near and squatted low, then looked into Gabe's eyes with a steely hatred. "Now, you die, white man." With the charred stick, he smeared a circular mark on Gabe's forehead.

Suddenly, Gabe realized the man was making a bull's-eye. As the leader stepped back to the toe line, the stark reality of what was happening came into full view—he was about to be killed. He closed his eyes and fought for air against the gag, a million memories screaming through his mind, one after the other, stopping on a singular vivid childhood recollection, as if it were happening all over again.

His father was weeping and kneeling next to Lilly, the milk cow, his head on her shoulder and his hand covering Lilly's side, blood bubbling through his fingers with each breath. His mother sat on the ground next to them with her head and shoulders drooping, her arms hanging limply, oblivious to the flecks of blood that sprayed her white cotton dress that draped on the ground around her like a puffy cloud.

Young Gabe forced himself to turn his head toward Lilly. Through his teared eyes, he could see her long, thick tongue lolling out as it reached vainly for air, the blood pouring from her nose in a thick, crimson stream.

The raucous laughter of the men placing wagers on the shot distracted Gabe from the memory, and he opened his eyes as the leader stood at the toe line. He nocked an arrow and focused on the dark spot he had smeared on Gabe's forehead. He drew back on the string and took aim. Gabe felt himself relax in deathly resignation as a thousand regrets poured from the recesses of his mind into his soul.

Just then, the moment before the arrow was shot, the whir of a hatchet broke the silence, and Gabe looked up just as it struck the leader squarely on the temple with a dull, wet thump. Instantly, his fingers relaxed, and the arrow was released. Gabe flinched as the blade of the broadhead grazed the top of his head and stuck in the tree behind him. The brave dropped to his knees, rigid, then fell face-first to the ground.

For a moment, the other men stood in shock as their leader lay twitching spasmodically. Then, in a heartbeat, they exploded into action and scrambled for their weapons. Gabe sat dumbfounded as the melee unfolded before him. To his relief and surprise, the leader—the one who had been about to kill him—lay dead with a hatchet buried in his head. The three others had grabbed their rifles and were taking aim in the direction from which the hatchet had been thrown, ready to fire at the slightest movement.

From his own vantage point, Gabe was able to glimpse Eagle Claw hiding behind an enormous larch tree. The brave slipped off his buckskin shirt, then ran a broken branch through both arms. Quickly, he swung it from behind the tree, which drew instant gunfire, several bullets punching holes through the shirt. As soon as the shots rang out, Eagle Claw sprinted toward the braves as they worked to reload.

The closest man looked up as Eagle Claw charged toward him. He had no time to finish reloading. He dropped his rifle, pulled out his knife, and threw it at Eagle Claw as he bore down, but the Kootenai man dodged the whirling blade and simultaneously grabbed one of the arrows lying on the ground. He lunged and thrust hard toward the soft spot just under the Crow's sternum, the arrow penetrating deep into his chest. The Crow collapsed, holding onto the arrow, groaning as he struggled to breathe.

The closer of the two remaining men was nearly done reloading when Eagle Claw pulled his beavertail dag knife from the scabbard tucked inside his belt. He dove forward and buried it to the hilt in the Crow man's chest. The man yelled, spun away, and rolled on the ground, the knife still sticking into him.

The fourth warrior had just finished reloading when Gabe heard the unmistakable click as the brave cocked his rifle to fire. Eagle Claw lunged at the first warrior he had killed, pulled the hatchet from his head, and in one swift whirling motion hurled it toward the remaining brave, striking him squarely in the forehead with the pike end of the ax, which buried deep into his skull. The rifle discharged as he fell to the ground, the bullet narrowly missing Eagle Claw. In less than a minute, the fight was over, and four Crow men lay scattered across the campsite.

Eagle Claw seemed remarkably calm when Gabe glanced over at him. "You okay?" the brave said.

Gabe nodded, looking up at the arrow that had parted his hair. Except for the minor cut from the broadhead that had nicked his scalp, he was rattled but uninjured.

The Crow man Eagle Claw had skewered with the arrow was still alive. He was crawling, reaching for his rifle, which was lying with the ramrod still sticking out of the barrel, just out of reach. Eagle Claw casually walked over and pulled the hatchet from the forehead of the man he had just killed, then approached the one he had wounded.

"Not a good day for you, eh?" he said, and with a quick swing of his hatchet, he dispatched the man with a deep, penetrating blow to the head. He worked the handle of the hatchet back and forth to loosen it before pulling it out, followed by a spray of blood from the gruesome wound. The Crow man lay still, except for the diminishing jerk of an arm and leg. Eagle Claw bent and wiped the sticky, pink residue from his hatchet onto the brave's legging before tucking it back in his belt, then retrieved his knife from the other brave, who now lay motionless.

Gabe sat stunned by the efficient manner which Eagle Claw had dispatched the marauders. He looked up, feeling a sense of vulnerability as Eagle Claw approached. The spattering of blood, the fierce look in his eye, and the bloody beavertail dag in his hand caused a lump to form in Gabe's throat and made him shift apprehensively.

But fear turned to relief when Eagle Claw calmly reached behind the tree and cut the cords binding his hands and neck. When the gag tied over his mouth was cut, Gabe breathed deeply and sighed as if the air were a gulp of cool spring water that quenched his thirst, then he quickly untied the cords around his ankles and jumped to his feet.

"Thank you! *Ahhh!* I thought I was a dead man. Thank you, God," said Gabe, looking to the sky as he paced back and forth with nervous energy.

"They are Crow," Eagle Claw remarked.

"Crow? I haven't heard of many Crow around these parts."

Irreverently, Eagle Claw pulled back the head of a dead brave to show his face. "They wear the paint of a Crow raiding party." He then pulled out his knife and peeled off the scalp in one swift movement. Gabe looked on, bewildered, while he did the same with the other three dead men.

"Why do you take their scalps?"

"If I don't, someone else will—either Blackfeet or grizzly bears. Besides, they are good for trade." He stared at Gabe. "Why do you look at me that way? I am not a 'savage,' Gabe Bauman. I am a civilized human being. Trust me, where they are going, they won't be needing their scalps or their belongings."

He tied the scalps neatly together and hung them off his saddle horn. "We need to pack up and leave—now. We can eat later. The gunfire may attract more trouble."

Gabe didn't argue. The growling in his stomach was now but a whimper after nearly getting killed and witnessing the bloody skirmish.

Eagle Claw hastily searched the dead warriors but didn't find much of value. He examined their rifles, but when he found them to be in poor condition, he tossed them aside. He bundled the few useful items he had found before loading them on his horse. "You start packing, and I'll be right back—and this time, pay attention," he warned.

"Yes, sir." Without hesitation, Gabe grabbed his rifle and kept it near while breaking camp.

A couple of minutes later, Eagle Claw returned, wearing his bullet-riddled buckskin shirt and carrying two dead grouse he had killed for breakfast.

"Hey! How'd you get those without your bow?"

Eagle Claw smiled. "An old Kootenai trick. Someday, I might show you."

Soon, they had the horses packed and were heading back to the main trail. Farther down the mountain, they found the Crow horses, tied securely to trees by their lead ropes. Two of the animals had scabbards containing bows and arrows tethered to their saddle horns.

"These two horses show the marks of the Blackfeet," Eagle Claw said, pointing to their intricate bridles and the markings painted on their necks and hindquarters. "The Blackfeet don't take kindly to horse thieves."

The two matching Appaloosa horses were healthy with coats that glistened, the dappled skin of their hindquarters channel-etched, as if slabs of muscle had been stacked one atop another. They were plains horses—the Blackfeet called them buffalo runners—and as Gabe took note of their excellent conformation, he could easily see they were no prairie mongrels. They had been the beneficiaries of extra attention and special training, perhaps owned by a mighty warrior, chief, or Elder.

Eagle Claw dismounted and approached one of them. "Easy," he said softly. He reached to untie it, as if to let it run free, then stopped. He patted the horse on its muscular neck and cheek, then began stroking it while he spoke, using Kootenai words. The animal seemed perfectly content with his affection. A few minutes later, he untied both the horses and wasted no time in stringing them head to tail, with their lead ropes tied through a loop he fashioned with the long hair of their tails. After letting the other horses run free, he led the two buffalo runners in single file to his own horse, secured them in the same manner, and mounted his horse with a single jump. In minutes, they were marching down the mountain toward the main trail.

The morning's events weighed heavily on Gabe's mind as they turned onto the main trail and headed west. Once again, he had the uneasy feeling of blindly slipping downward, like in his nightmare, toward the abyss. First, it had been Crooked Bill Branch, and now, the Crow attack. *What next?* he wondered.

He remembered his father's words about being too trusting, and it dawned on him that he knew little about Eagle Claw—aside from the fact the Kootenai warrior had just snuffed four able-bodied warriors right in front of his eyes. This was the second time Eagle Claw had saved his life, and for that, he was grateful. However, seeing the unflinching way he'd just killed the Crow men was a cause for concern, and the way he'd nonchalantly removed their scalps gave rise to a questionable moral turpitude. The last time Gabe had witnessed a scalping was when Branch had scalped the poor Blackfeet boy, and it sickened him.

They rode silently, as if their tongues were somehow wounded casualties of the battle with the Crow. One benefit, however, was that the adrenaline shock from the tumult continued to silence Gabe's growling stomach.

At midday, Eagle Claw turned his horse off the trail toward a grassy flat near a quiet stretch of the Flathead River and dismounted. "This is a good place to rest," he said.

They tied off the horses, built a fire, cooked the grouse, and finally sat down to eat a meal. When Eagle Claw sat back to relax after eating, Gabe saw an opportunity to satisfy his curiosity.

"How far is it to your village?"

"We should arrive in four or five days as long as we don't have any more trouble on the trail to slow us down. It is a long journey, so it varies, eh."

"Will I be welcome there?" Gabe asked hesitantly.

"Yes. My people are friendly."

"How long will they let me stay?"

"You ask too many questions. It will be fine," Eagle Claw said dismissively.

His curt words were vaguely reassuring but didn't assuage Gabe's uneasiness, his fear of the unknown, and his creeping sense of foreboding regarding what lay ahead.

"I have one more question."

"Only one?"

"Why didn't you kill Branch—after he threatened you at the Rendezvous?"

Eagle Claw paused for a moment, gazed ahead as if selecting just the right words, then said, sage-like, "I give you two reasons—two arrows of wisdom for your quiver. The first arrow comes from my father, James: 'There is a time for everything under the sun ... a time for war and a time for peace.' The time at the Rendezvous was not a time for war—it was a time to run. The second arrow of wisdom comes from our village leader, Chief White Cloud: 'To be in control of oneself is to become a human being.' One must learn to master one's impulses—of the eye, the tongue, the hands, the feet."

"I don't understand."

The warrior breathed a heavy sigh and looked Gabe in the eye. "There is a time for war, a time to pull the trigger, but that trouble at the Rendezvous—that was not the time. We would have been killed."

Gabe pondered his words and didn't ask any more questions. After resting and giving their horses a drink, they traveled on, making good time.

ℰ

Eagle Claw thought about Gabe as they rode silently. He could shoot and throw an ax, but the young trapper seemed oblivious to the darker nature of men and had few apparent fighting skills. But he noticed a difference between him and the other trappers—honesty, for he could see no deception in his heart. Perhaps he could teach him how to survive, for surely, Gabe would otherwise not last long on his own.

Three hours later, Eagle Claw decided to turn his horse off the trail. "I want to show you my father's favorite fall hunting ground," he said, smiling. "We always find much game there."

They traveled another mile before breaking through a densely timbered patch of forest into a meadow dotted with stands of poplar and buckbrush, whose leaves had turned a brilliant yellow. But as they rode a short distance farther, it soon became apparent to Eagle Claw that the area was devoid of life.

They approached an abandoned campsite just inside the timber on the edge of the meadow when the cackle of ravens drew his attention. The area around the camp had been thoroughly stomped by horses and men into a muddy mess. Bones of sundry animals were strewn about the meadow, and a pile of deer and elk carcasses lay rotting near the camp. The firepit was cold; next to it lay the bony remnants of half-eaten beaver carcasses. Eagle Claw's emotions turned inward at the gruesome sight, as if someone had run a spear into his very soul. The hunting ground had been thoroughly ruined; the once-verdant, game-rich meadow had vanished, and one half-dead had taken its place. He dismounted and tied off his horse.

"This is why we find no game," said Eagle Claw as he searched with a woeful heart through the mess to assess the damages. The ravens, maggots, and dermestid beetles had been busy working on the rotting carcasses, and only fleshy bones remained.

Gabe walked up and stepped beside him just as he spotted something partially buried under the heap of human detritus. He grabbed a stick, fished it out, and bent to pick it up. In his hand was a rusty, broken beaver trap, and on the underside, the inscription **HBC** was deeply stamped into the metal.

"That stands for Hudson's Bay Company," said Gabe. "A mob of trappers was here."

"Uh-huh. I know what it stands for. My father, James, mocks this Hudson's Bay Company. He says HBC stands for Here Before Christ because they think they are God." Eagle Claw was silent for a moment, still shaken by the repugnant sight. Disgusted, he tossed the trap back into the heap and remarked, "My people used the camp for our fall hunt. The deer and elk we would harvest here got us through many long, cold winters."

He surveyed the familiar meadow and sighed deeply, feeling despondent. With Gabe following, he strode to a nearby tree—a magnificent ponderosa pine. He stooped low and looked closely on the south-facing side of the tree until he found what he was looking for. Barely visible, near the base of the great tree, was a child's carving of four stick figures, the scars mostly healed over from the passage of time. He frowned as he carefully ran his fingers over the etched figures and audibly groaned at the sudden deep stab in the center of his heart.

"I will never forget one of my earliest memories of this place," he said softly, sitting back against the tree. So absorbed in the moment, he barely noticed Gabe, who sat down near him to listen as Eagle Claw recalled that day—when he was young and the meadow, unspoiled.

The campsite, tucked just inside the timber in the lush meadow, was one of their favorite retreats—the surrounding area had plenty of game to hunt and lots of room for children to play. On this bright spring day, young Eagle Claw and his family were sitting around a small campfire, finishing their meal. There was easy laughter and a feeling of togetherness, and Eagle Claw giggled as he saw how tenderly his father placed a yellow wildflower in his mother's hair, and how she tried to smile even though the old wound on her face made it difficult—and how in that moment, her happy eyes smiled for her.

"You children be careful, and don't stray too far," said Singing Bird as he and his sister Dawn scampered off after they had eaten.

Eagle Claw was set on finishing a simple carving of himself and his family on the side of the great pine tree that he had begun earlier in the day. But Dawn quickly grew bored watching him and wandered off into the meadow.

"Claw! Come see what I found," came her high-pitched voice.

In a flash, he was running across the field to where she stood, gazing at something in the tall grass of the meadow. He stopped and looked down into the grass when Dawn pointed at a speckled newborn fawn that lay silent and still. She started to speak, but Eagle Claw put his finger to his lips and said, "Shhhh," for he knew that its mother would be nearby.

They stood and watched the fawn, so small and weak, as it lay still. The only things that moved were its little wet nose as it breathed and its long, dark eyelashes whenever its blue eyes blinked.

It sensed their presence, and its breathing quickened, so Eagle Claw motioned his sister away. Soon, the two of them were hopping and running once again through the meadow.

Only once had Eagle Claw seen his father cry—a single tear when he could not revive a child who got lost one cold winter night and died in his arms. Eagle Claw wondered to himself if it was the sight of the ravaged camp that caused the trembling in his chest and the watering of his eyes? Or was it the result of many marred layers, one atop the other?

He closed his eyes to stifle the rising torrent and suddenly felt nauseated. It was only when he looked up to see Gabe sitting quietly beside him, with a compassionate look on his face, that he realized he'd been talking the entire time, telling the anguished story of that which he'd lost—a doleful eulogy of what once was.

The horses snorted their annoyance at the lingering smell of death and rotting flesh that hung in the air, and they pawed the ground impatiently as if eager to leave the gloomy campsite and meadow. Eagle Claw glanced at the fidgety horses and concurred—he had seen enough. His pleasant childhood memories of this special place were tainted forever by the fetid waste.

Without another word, he mounted his horse, and the two men headed back to the main trail. As they rode, he wondered how his people would make it through the winter without the meat they needed to survive. Ignoring his own rule about silence on the trail, he complained loudly, so the mountains themselves could hear his grievances.

Some of the Elders could also see what was happening—how the collective soul of the land was slowly shriveling, and the web of life was being torn asunder with no way to reconstruct it. It was as though a rampaging herd of buffalo was trampling their heritage and way of life, yet they were powerless to stop it. They could only take shelter and grumble in the darkness of their lodges while the herd shook the ground as it rumbled by—only this herd didn't rumble by. It just kept coming and wouldn't stop.

$\mathcal{A}$ *Hunt*

Eagle Claw seemed to lose track of time as he thought about what he had witnessed at the meadow. The slogging pace of the horses finally told him that they were growing weary. He found a series of lush meadows that offered a good place to camp for the night and graze the animals, so they dismounted, unloaded gear, and hobbled the horses before turning them out to graze.

Eagle Claw gazed at the sky. "We still have some good light," he remarked, squinting to gauge the position of the sun. "We are close enough to my village that the meat won't spoil. Let's go on a hunt."

Gabe smiled and grabbed his old trade musket and possibles bag.

"No. You can use this." Eagle Claw held out his bow and quiver of arrows.

Gabe hesitated. "Are you sure?"

Eagle Claw nodded and handed them to Gabe. They walked quietly through the forest until Eagle Claw detected movement in the timber ahead. It was a feeding doe, and it hadn't spotted them. He turned to Gabe and nodded toward the deer.

When Gabe finally saw it, Eagle Claw motioned him forward then retreated several paces to watch his protégé make the stalk. Gabe closed the distance quickly, then slowed his pace for the final stage. Eagle Claw was impressed to this point, but the stalk was only part of the game; Gabe still had to make a clean shot without being detected.

Eagle Claw halted and waited quietly while Gabe closed in—fifty paces, forty, thirty, until he finally was within range of the deer. When it lowered its head to feed, he drew back the bow and released. At the twang of the bowstring, the doe instinctively ducked, the arrow just clipping the hairs on its back. It quickly darted away. Retrieving the arrow, Gabe walked, hangdog, back to Eagle Claw.

"It was a good stalk, eh? You were close." Gabe's eyes brightened at his words, and his pace quickened. Eagle Claw saw no need in chastising him—he knew the young trapper had received plenty of that from his former associates.

They ventured deeper into the timber until Eagle Claw noticed the flicker of an ear in the dense forest ahead. The brown color of the animal appeared in a patch of greenery within a thick tangle of buckbrush. A flick of its tail identified it as another whitetail deer filling its belly on succulent forage, but this time, it was a buck with impressive antlers. It moved in and out of sight behind the vegetation as it foraged, then vanished into the foliage.

They crept ahead, watching for any sign of the deer, scanning for disturbances of the forest floor that might indicate its travel route. Finally, Eagle Claw found the buck's tracks pressed into some moss. Knowing it had to be close, he pointed to the tracks and motioned for Gabe to follow them while he stayed a few steps behind.

There was a movement ahead in the timber. Gabe stopped and stared at the deer. Eagle Claw peered around his back, and sure enough, there it was—slowly ambling away from them as it browsed. Eagle Claw tapped Gabe on the back and motioned for him to wait. He tested the air with a small feather tied to a strip of rawhide, which indicated the breeze was quartering toward them, and it would carry their scent away from the wary nose of the buck. He motioned for Gabe to continue, and they quietly followed, keeping their distance, until the buck finally crossed a small meadow and bedded down for the day.

The deer had chosen its resting place well—near the edge of the timber overlooking the meadow, where it could easily spot danger. It was a perfect location, except for a bushy juniper tree in the grassy clearing that conveniently offered concealment for the closing stalk and a clean shot. The two quietly circled to the right, in a wide arc, then belly-crawled from the timber and into the clearing toward the juniper tree. Tall grass hid them from sight, and the wind stayed true, carrying their scent away from the buck.

As they crept forward, Eagle Claw noticed their quarry alertly scanning the area for danger. It was clear they wouldn't be able continue without being detected, so he motioned to Gabe to hold up. At once, Gabe's stomach began growling loudly, which Eagle Claw found both annoying and alarming. He tugged on Gabe's sleeve to get his attention, then plucked the leaves from a leafy plant growing next to them and began chewing. Gabe did the same. Almost immediately, the growling of his stomach stopped, much to Eagle Claw's relief.

The buck finally relaxed and lay still, chewing its cud with its eyes half open some twenty yards away, when they finally made it to the juniper. Eagle Claw could see a clear shooting lane through the branches to an unobscured patch of brown behind the buck's front shoulder. He didn't have to tell Gabe—the young man also saw the opening and nocked an arrow for the shot. Gabe cautiously stepped clear of the juniper and pulled back on the bowstring.

The buck opened its eyes at the faint sound of the arrow sliding against the bow. It jerked its head around and tried to stand, but it was too late—the arrow was already on its way. Just as the majestic buck saw the figure of a man, the arrow struck squarely behind its shoulder.

The buck exploded from its bed and tore through the timber, breaking branches as it fled. Its rapid thumping bounds grew fainter as it went deeper into the timber until the forest once again grew silent. Gabe's sudden rapid breathing caused Eagle Claw to wonder if he'd been holding his breath for the entirety of the stalk.

"I think I hit him!" Gabe said exuberantly, as if he'd just finished a footrace.

Eagle Claw hid the humor he felt from Gabe's reaction, slapped him on the back and shouted, "You did hit him. Good shot!"

They approached the spot where the buck had been lying, and Gabe looked skeptical, as if his eyes had deceived him. "I need to see evidence," he said. "Blood!"

Eagle Claw picked up a small tuft of hair and examined it closely. The hairs had been clipped clean, and he smiled, holding it out to show Gabe. A few paces into the timber, they found a fleck of blood—enough to give Gabe hope. But Eagle Claw had no such concern. He was planning on how they would deal with the meat—the hunt was over, and the real work was about to begin.

Not much farther into the forest they found more drops, then a splash of blood, then a spray, until searching for the trail was no longer necessary. They followed the red swath deeper into the forest to where the great deer lay. Gabe stood over it, reverently, awestruck.

"Very good, Gabe Bauman. You did it!" exclaimed Eagle Claw, smiling. He knelt before the buck, raised his hands, and softly sang a prayer of thanks in his native tongue. He was pleased when Gabe bowed his head and folded his hands respectfully until the prayer song was over.

Eagle Claw took his bow from Gabe, turned it gently in his hands, and studied it for a moment. It was his prized possession and the finest bow he had ever made. Its stout limbs stored death energy, enough to make an arrow disappear into a buffalo. Most of all, it was accurate, and helped provide much food for his family and his people.

"I didn't damage it, did I?"

Gabe sounded nervous, but Eagle Claw wasn't looking for damage. It was his way of showing appreciation. Running his fingers along its limbs, he recalled how he carefully crafted the weapon from a single piece of yew. Once again, the implement had performed well, and he drew back on the string to feel its power, remembering his most memorable hunts. After a couple seconds, he relaxed the string and unstrung the bow.

"No. It's in good shape. Let's get the buck back to camp before we lose the sun."

Just as the words left his mouth, a cyclopean cloud billowed over the peaks to the west, angry and dark. Eagle Claw insisted they quicken their pace, and they field-dressed the buck hastily, saving the kidneys, liver, and heart, which they shoved back into the empty body cavity. The rush of adrenaline they both felt from Gabe's successful

stalk made dragging the buck relatively easy, and it didn't take long
for them to reach the camp, just as the wind started to howl.

Eagle Claw didn't have to tell Gabe what to do, and together,
they scurried to gather downed lodgepoles, cut spruce branches, and
build a makeshift hovel big enough to shelter them and their gear,
along with a drying rack. The deer heart was roasting nicely over a
campfire when a cold rain started, and the two hunters looked forward to eating a feast, warm and dry in the comfort of their shelter.

Without delay, Eagle Claw lashed together a meat rack—stout
sticks tied with strips of sinew he had carefully trimmed from the
bucks backstraps. By the time he was finished, a thin black crust
had formed around the heart, and Eagle Claw cut a piece from the
aromatic chunk of muscle. He blew on it to cool it, then took a bite.
It was a bit rubbery at first but easy enough to chew, and its flavor
was rich and strong, like the buck whose blood it had pumped. He
split the heart with Gabe, and they quickly devoured it before trim-
ming meat and adding the strips to the rack.

After the fire had died down, they placed the rack over the coals
and hung more strips of venison on its cross-pieces until it was completely full. Next, they leaned branches against the rack on all sides
to help hold in the heat and the smoke, tucking moss between the
cracks to further seal it.

While the meat smoked, Eagle Claw built another fire, and they
cooked and ate chunks of liver until their bellies could take no more.
Gabe leaned back against a tree and admired the impressive antlers
of the giant buck.

"Thanks, Eagle Claw," the young mountain man said.

"Thanks? No. Thank *you* for getting us some good food, eh?"
He chuckled.

"Thanks for teaching me how to shoot your bow and for letting
me use it."

Eagle Claw was pleasantly surprised at his expression of appreciation
and felt a sudden sense of pride. "You're welcome, Gabe Bauman."

"Have you ever seen a buck this big?" asked Gabe.

"Ah, yes. This is an old one. There used to be more like this, eh.
Not so much now." Eagle Claw grabbed the antlers, looked them over,

and remarked, "This thick piece that comes out of the skull would make a good knife handle, eh? And I could carve some tools out of these sharp tines, maybe even a fish spear or two. Yes, very nice."

"Could you teach me the prayer song?" asked Gabe.

Eagle Claw was startled by the request but was happy to oblige. For the next hour, as the pouring rain weakened into a brisk drizzle, he explained to Gabe what the words meant, and they practiced the song while the meat smoked.

The storm diminished in power, but lingered, and Eagle Claw noticed Gabe's eyelids grow heavy as he lay by the warm fire. When his head bobbed awake for the second time, Eagle Claw suggested he get under his bedroll, which he did, and he was fast asleep within minutes.

Eagle Claw, however, stayed awake to reposition the meat as the layers closest to the fire cooked faster than the others. The drizzle faded as the storm passed by, and the forest once again grew quiet. He leaned back and looked out into the night, then down at Gabe, beginning to snore in his bedroll. It had been a long time since he had felt a sense of brotherhood. An old feeling tugged at his heart, accompanied by tormenting memories that scraped at the scab of an old wound. As he sat watching the flickering flame, the festering wound broke open and began to ooze his spirit-blood. Eagle Claw's only brother, were he still alive, would have been about Gabe's age.

Chapter Sixteen

Brother Lost

Eagle Claw was just a gangly boy of eight years old when a serious problem emerged for his village—not that the Kootenai were unaccustomed to facing problems. However, this crisis threatened the very survival of his village. Someone or something was stealing their fish—the fish that they counted on to feed them through the winter. Most suspected it to be a bear, but some of the old women spoke of an old legend, raving about the demon they called the Skookum. Their chatter reminded Eagle Claw of the incident several years previous, when he'd encountered the strange creature after killing a rabbit.

As if this wasn't enough, Eagle Claw's normal workload was doubled when the Elders gave him the task of gutting fish for the toothless old women who prepared them for the drying racks after he was falsely accused of bad behavior by the other boys.

It began early one morning, when the sounds of angry women rang through the village after they discovered the drying racks had been stripped bare. Most of the able-bodied men were on a hunt, so the Elders in camp summoned the younger boys and remaining men. Suspecting the culprit to be a bear, they built a scaffold, rickety but strong, and placed it amid the tipis, so it could be monitored. It had four legs made from lodgepole pine trees and stood over twenty feet above the ground to protect the precious meat supply from the thief.

White Cloud and Red Elk, the two Elders who had stayed behind to oversee the village, stood with arms crossed looking high up at the drying racks being filled by young Eagle Claw.

Red Elk ordered the older boys spearing fish by the river to pile up rocks around each of the legs of the tower for additional support. They stopped fishing and brought rocks from the river, stacking them around the legs until they were piled to Red Elk's satisfaction. "I am well pleased. The meat should be safe now," said Red Elk. White Cloud nodded in agreement. Then, they both retired to their tipi lodges to nap in the cool shade until the sweltering heat of the midday had passed.

The wiry Eagle Claw clambered down from the scaffold, ran to the cliffs above the falls, hopped onto a wooden platform, and grabbed another large fish caught by the spearmen. With both hands, he lugged it to the edge of the cliff overlooking the river. Shoving a flint knife into its rectum, he slit its belly cleanly to the gills, then made an incision around the gills and pulled out the entrails. He separated the bright orange clumps of fish eggs, then tossed them in a large basket. The wolf-dogs in camp had long since eaten their fill of fish guts, and he didn't want to attract bears, so he tossed the offal into the roiling waters below. Finally, he chopped off the head of the fish with a hatchet and tossed it into a pile with the others. They would be used by the women to make stew or to charbroil over coals for a tasty treat, for there was nothing better than the delicate meat in and around the head of a fish.

Eagle Claw carried the gutted fish to a large, flat rock, where one of the chattering women quickly split the fish in half, making crosscuts in the flesh to help it smoke faster. He went to get another fish when one of the women called out to him—several were now ready for him to haul to the newly-constructed tower. He promptly returned, and a wrinkled Kootenai woman handed him a basketful of pink slabs and impatiently barked at him to hurry. Without argument, he dutifully grabbed the basket and hauled it to the base of the tower. He placed the basket's buckskin strap over his forehead, so the basket rested squarely on his lower back, and started his climb.

Fish slime, dried blood, and scattered fish eggs coated Eagle Claw's bare chest. His sinewy arms were preoccupied climbing the precarious tower with the heavy load, leaving annoying blowflies free to attack, as if they had been buzzing overhead in anticipation of the moment. In vain, he blew at them as they tickled his face and crawled on his chest and shoulders. It was a dirty job, but Eagle Claw was used to doing the dirty jobs, and he did so without complaint—even while the other boys his age ran about playing games, having fun, and often aiming disparaging remarks at him while he worked.

Already, there was a hardness to him, both physically and mentally. The muscles on his frame were lithe, like a wildcat's, and his small hands bore leathery callouses that came from much hard work. Nimbly, he climbed the ladder tied to one of the tower's legs, swung the basket onto the platform, and jumped onto the deck. As he placed the fish on the rack, he looked around for the Elders, but they had gone. He would have to be watchful now, like a wary eagle on its perch.

A snicker and some shuffling came from below the tower. It was Eagle Claw's nemeses, appearing like stealthy ravens approaching a deer carcass after the well-sated wolf had ambled off for a nap. The cruelty of these boys, the ones he wished were his friends, was the reason he often escaped to the nearby woods, where he hunted small game and found peace from the endless harassment.

They saw his very existence as wrong, and his clashing appearance only exacerbated their loathing. They found great pleasure in beating him down with persistent persecutions—taunts and biting words that hurt like blunt-tipped arrows shot from a bow.

At first, Eagle Claw hated himself, angered that he was different from the other boys. Then James explained they were jealous because God had made him special and that they only exploited this uniqueness as a reason to hate—for all hatred is led by the leash of an excuse. When he understood the source of their hate, especially for a benign reason like the color of one's skin, he effectively ignored them, refusing to be dispirited. But this only made them angrier, and they resorted to physical pain to satisfy their twisted itch, and this new wrinkle to their game of torment made them try even harder to catch him by surprise.

What deviled Eagle Claw more than their persistent taunts were the lies they told, aimed at getting him in trouble with the Elders.

This resulted in more work heaped upon him as punishment for crimes he hadn't committed. Even so, he always hurried to finish his tasks, so he could continue his favorite of all activities—playing with his little brother.

Eagle Claw had just placed a fish on one of the racks when he heard the whirl of a rock. He glimpsed a brownish object streaking toward him and instinctively ducked. The bullies and their toadies gathered below, cackling with laughter as the rock sailed over his head.

"Not the big rock, Crowfoot, it'll hurt him bad," said one of them.

"Why not?" Crowfoot said, taking aim again. "Maybe it'll teach him a lesson."

But again, Eagle Claw dodged the missile. He grabbed the platform's thin railing and held on tight as the laughing boys shook the tower and tried pelting him with small rocks. But Eagle Claw was quick, well acclimated to their mischief, and skilled at evading their cruel machinations.

Some of the boys left to find more rocks, which was Eagle Claw's cue to make good his escape. He began to scurry off the tower to safety, when suddenly, from somewhere near his tipi lodge, he heard his mother call out for his toddler brother, who had apparently wandered off.

The women near the river stopped their work and stared, then took a step toward the call. Suddenly, Eagle Claw heard one of the children shriek in pain, followed by the grunting of an animal in the woods beyond the village. The women grabbed their knives and ran to help, but when they got to the edge of the trees, the child's crying had stopped. They paused for a moment, then continued into the woods to where they had heard the sound.

From his vantage point atop the tower, Eagle Claw scanned the area for his brother, and as he did, he saw something bewildering. Among the trees, a long stone's throw away for a man, something looked amiss. He squinted, trying to identify the large, dark object moving through the forest, taller than some of the juniper trees nestled among the larches and bull pines that ringed the camp. At first, he thought it was a bear standing upright, but its head wasn't the right shape or size. As it moved, he got a better glimpse of the hairy mass and instantly recalled his previous encounter several years prior, when he'd killed the rabbit. Eagle Claw's heart raced as the creature appeared near where his brother had cried out.

The boys had returned, rocks in hand, for more malicious entertainment and bruising. Together, two of them threw a large boulder down hard on one of the tower legs. The blow knocked the leg loose, which jerked the tower, causing Eagle Claw to lose his balance and slip on the fish grease. He grabbed one of the posts just in time to prevent himself from sliding off the platform and hung precariously over the edge, his legs dangling in the air. The boys laughed as he pulled himself back up to search for the mysterious creature he has seen, but when he looked again, it was gone.

Changing positions to gain a better view, he scanned the woods as the women looked for the missing child. But still, he could see nothing. "Mother!" he called out frantically.

He spotted her glancing up at him through a gap in the timber, but only for a second before continuing her worried search. He cried out to her again but was cut short when the tower shook violently, and he tumbled over the edge. In a flash, he was airborne. As he fell, he saw a support rail and grabbed for it, his wiry fingers latching on like fishhooks. Desperately, he hung on and looked down at the boys shaking the stand, laughing with sadistic glee over his predicament.

They had gathered around two legs of the tower like demented demons, and they shook the tower again until his grip finally slipped. But with the dexterity of a bobcat, he spun in midair and latched onto part of the framework, clinging by one hand, still ten feet off the ground. The tower swayed as his tormentors laughed and tried to shake him off.

"Come on, white boy! Come down and play!" screamed Crowfoot amid cackles of laughter. Another threw a rock, pelting him on the side of his exposed ribs.

Eagle Claw gritted his teeth, ignored the pain, and looked down on them with disdain. Then, another grabbed a long alder branch lying nearby, with clear intent to poke him and knock him to the ground, but Eagle Claw's reaction was quicker. He swung himself and let go, grabbing one of the tower legs. He slid partway down and let go again, rolling as he hit the ground. They picked up more rocks to throw, but he was already on the run.

They continued tossing rocks, which he skillfully dodged, as they jeered and called him a coward. But he wasn't running from them; he was running for his bow and quiver of arrows that he had hidden behind a nearby log. He hurdled the log, grabbing the bow and arrow without losing stride, and disappeared into the timber. The older boys dared not follow, for they knew what he was capable of with his weapon.

എ

The women frantically searched through the brush and trees for the missing child, cringing at the strange, pungent odor in the air. The dense stand of young jack pines opened into a small clearing just ahead. They hurried toward it but stopped short when their own instinct for survival froze them in their tracks.

A few yards ahead of them, something moved behind a patch of brush. Singing Bird could see the back of a thickly furred animal shifting to and fro as if looking at something on the ground. Her mothering instincts rose like an angry sow grizzly, and she quietly picked up a stout stick with her good hand to use as a club. Several men in her tribe had been attacked and killed by bears over the years, but her only concern now was the safety of her child, and the animal in front of her posed an immediate threat.

She gritted her teeth and took another step but was so focused on the animal that she didn't see a small branch on the path in front of her, and as she stepped down, it snapped with a deafening pop. She quickly raised the club, preparing to do battle. Startled by the noise, the creature rose, and Singing Bird's eyes followed it up and up until it towered over her at twice her height. Immediately, she knew what it was, and paralyzing panic swept over her.

Her sister, standing beside Singing Bird, immediately fainted when it stood and turned toward them. Singing Bird lowered her club, instinctively avoiding eye contact, then dropped it to the ground. She stood staring from the corner of her eye at the enormous mass with a mixture of horror and awe.

Then, she glimpsed something the creature was holding. It looked tiny compared with the giant hand that held it. She saw the blood dripping onto the ground in large, thick drops and shook her head, not wanting to believe what she was seeing as her worst fears materialized. She dropped to her knees, and her shoulders went limp as if her very soul had been ripped from her body.

The creature held her son by one leg as if holding a dead rabbit; his other leg was missing entirely. It looked down at Singing Bird, then at the child dangling lifelessly from its hand. It placed her son in the palm of its other hand for a moment, studying the child with a furrowed brow. Then, it turned and lowered the child to the ground, gently laying him on the soft moss.

Singing Bird trembled violently from the shock, put her head in her hands, and fell prostrate with her face to the ground, weeping bitterly. She cared little of dying now, and she hoped the creature would kill her, as well, to end her pain.

Moments later, as she cried in anguish, she heard a noise to her right. Looking up, she saw the creature silently disappear into the dark woods. She crawled over and picked up her dead child and held him in her arms, his lifeblood dripping down onto her dress as she sobbed and wailed.

༄

Eagle Claw ran swiftly, his feet barely touching the ground. His breath was rapid, every muscle in his body tense and charged with adrenaline as he dodged through the trees. He deftly nocked an arrow as he ran between two juniper trees and then into an opening in the forest. He stopped, breathless, when the women came into view. A few yards ahead of him, his aunt Kicking Horse lay motionless on the ground. Beyond her knelt his mother, wailing, weeping, singing the death song. Her mournful cries were barely audible over his pounding heart, echoing between his temples like a war drum.

She sat at an angle, her body convulsing with each despairing sob, holding something in her arms. He relaxed the tension on his bowstring, which he had pulled back tight when he broke through the trees. Slowly, trembling, he walked toward her, fearful of what he might see. As he drew near, Eagle Claw saw the syrupy stains dripping down upon his mother's buckskin dress.

Suddenly, she turned in fear to see who was approaching. Eagle Claw stepped back in horror. She held a bloody bundle of flesh that he instantly knew was his brother. "No, no!" he cried out. He shook his head and turned away, not wanting to see anything more.

Then, grasping at hope, he thought, *Maybe he's not dead. Maybe he's only hurt.* With trepidation, he stepped forward and peered over her shoulder. There, in her arms, lay the bloodied body of his dead brother. The child's eyes were closed as if in sweet repose, but the horrific violence of his death was evident by dark red trails that streaked across his tiny face.

Tears welled up in Eagle Claw's eyes and with them, a primal rage. His little brother was gone, and with him, any hope for a lifelong friend. Eagle Claw felt his heart being torn in half, just as his brother's leg had been torn from his body. All his plans and dreams that revolved around his brother were gone—stolen. He had longed for the time when he could teach him how to fish, hunt, and survive in their hostile world. Most of all, his brother had become the embodiment of the very thing Eagle Claw had been denied—brotherhood. A sense of loneliness and emptiness hit him like a war hammer, and fanged reality sank its teeth into Eagle Claw's heart—he was all alone now.

He clutched his bow tightly, as if it had ceased being an inanimate object and had now become a loyal friend. Together, they would exact their revenge. Looking at the ground through his tears, he could see the indistinct sign where the creature had made its exit—a disturbance in the mossy ground. Step by careful step, he followed the tracks. It wasn't a hard trail to follow—a broken twig, a turning over of rocks, and the occasional deep impression in the soft moss. However, its trail became more difficult to follow when it passed through hard ground. Then, abruptly, he came across a more clearly defined footprint in a patch of soft dirt. He squatted to study the unusual track. The print was enormous, and it appeared to have claws—long claws like those of a grizzly bear. *Surely this is the track of the Skookum*, he thought. He paused and considered turning back to get help, doubtful his small bow and arrow would be adequate against such a beast, but his anger gave him false confidence and drove him onward.

He had gone a half mile or so when the animal's tracks passed into a grassy meadow, where tracking became difficult. But when the track re-entered the timber and approached a nearby stream, a hideous odor stopped him short.

Again, he thought of the creature he had encountered several years before when hunting rabbits and the stories of the legend he'd heard around the campfire. He recalled what the Elders had told him when he described what he had seen near the spring. They said it was the Big Man, to leave it be, and stay away from that area. Some of the old women then scolded him for straying too far from camp. They told him it was a cannibal and that if he kept wandering off alone in the woods, it would kill him and eat him alive. He thought about what it had done to his brother. *The old women were right.*

At once, his confidence vanished. He trembled and froze, fearfully searching the forest ahead for any sign of the creature. His shaking body wouldn't allow him to take another step, and he backed away until he was near the edge of the meadow before turning and running as fast as he could—to the safety of the camp.

In the days that followed, the entire camp rang with the mournful lament of the death song, and a dark pall enveloped the people. Eagle Claw wallowed in bitterness and hatred toward the other boys who had gotten him in trouble, for if he hadn't been punished by the Elders, he would have been playing with his brother as usual, and the toddler wouldn't have wandered away that fateful day.

But he felt hatred for more than just the boys who had tormented him. Amid his grief and anger, Eagle Claw could not stop thinking about the track in the soft dirt, and as he did, his hatred for the beast grew stronger.

The men conferred together on the matter. Some of the Elders considered the creature to be Big Medicine, saying disaster would come upon them if they we were to kill or harm it. But Eagle Claw didn't care what the Elders or anyone else thought about the beast. The sight of his dead brother in his mother's arms and the sound of her wails had changed everything. He made a vow to himself—that someday, when he was bigger and stronger, he would hunt it down and kill it.

Chapter Seventeen

Blackfeet

*G*abe had slept well. Eagle Claw knew because he was awake most of the night listening to his irksome snoring. But Eagle Claw's own disturbing thoughts about his brother's death were the main source of his restlessness. It seemed each time he closed his eyes, haunting images jolted him awake. Eventually, Gabe woke and sniffed the air like a hungry badger, craning his nose toward the smell of the smoked meat.

"Good. Finally awake. Your turn to tend to the meat," said Eagle Claw impassively. He had piled the finished strips atop a piece of tanned deer hide near the smoke rack. The other strips were hanging on the rack above the fire with still another heap waiting to be hung.

"When they get dry like these, take them off and put new ones on the rack, and try not to eat them all," he joked dryly.

"Yes, sir!" Gabe said, grabbing a piece to chew on.

Eagle Claw then gave his full attention to the deer hide that he had stretched out on the ground and scraped during the night. He held the deer's skull by its rack and began mashing the brains through a hole in the back of the skull, where the vertebrae had been attached. For this gory task, he used a piece of alder he had cut and shaped into a small spatula. He poked and prodded through the opening into the cavity until the brains had turned into a fleshy, pink pulp. He then scooped out the globs of brain matter onto the deer hide.

"I see you already caught the horses," said Gabe, pointing to where they were tied nearby, already saddled for the trail.

"Yes," Eagle Claw replied. "I just need to finish this task, and we can be on our way."

"What are you doing?" asked Gabe.

Eagle Claw worked the spatula until every bit of brain matter from the skull had been removed. "This hide must be tanned before the brains go bad. It's a good hide, eh? It will make for a good shirt or breeches, so I can't let it go to waste. The brain of a deer is just enough to tan its own hide."

Gabe sat next to him and watched as he spread out the brain pulp and worked it into the hide. "Can I help?"

"Sure. You must work hard to get the brains into the hide. That's what makes the leather soft." He pressed down on the brained hide with a flattened piece of alder. Soon, the two of them were massaging the brain matter into the hide.

Gabe and Eagle Claw continued working the hide when suddenly, the click of a rifle hammer caused them both to stop. Swiftly, they turned to see two men aiming rifles at them at point-blank range. Eagle Claw immediately recognized them as Blackfeet—well-armed and painted for war.

Eagle Claw instinctively took a step toward his rifle resting on a log several paces away but gave up on that idea when a third brave emerged from the brush nearby, ready to fire.

The Blackfeet had the two of them hopelessly surrounded, and Eagle Claw knew there was nothing they could do. He scanned the group, contemplating a counterattack, but there was no way to avoid a deadly volley of gunfire. He relinquished any desire to fight when three more Blackfeet men emerged from their hiding places, making a total of six in the war party.

"You stole our horses!" exclaimed the apparent leader in his native tongue.

Eagle Claw was well versed in the Blackfeet tongue, having been taught the language by his father, and he was relieved that the

Blackfeet man was talking instead of shooting. That was a good sign. "No!" he replied boldly. "A party of Crows ambushed us. We were lucky to get out alive. I have their scalps to prove it. We found their horses tied farther down the trail. Take them if they are yours, and their scalps as well."

The leader cocked his head, surprised he spoke fluently in his native Blackfeet language. But, undeterred, the brave didn't let them off easily. He motioned for his men to retrieve the horses and said tersely, "You trap beaver on Blackfeet land?"

"No, we only travel through Blackfeet land to get to our fish camp."

One of the men laughed, mocking him. "You go to fish with the women?"

"Yes. They fish with the women, while we hunt buffalo," said the leader to the laughter of the other braves.

Eagle Claw didn't react to their derision, knowing that when the winters grew long, he and other young Kootenai men would sneak over the high mountains to hunt buffalo on the Blackfeet hunting grounds.

He glanced at Gabe, who was clearly getting nervous and fidgety. He couldn't blame him. They had just survived the Crow attack, and now, they were helplessly surrounded by a war party of notorious Blackfeet with their rifles aimed and ready to fire at the slightest provocation.

"What's he saying?" Gabe said loudly.

The leader looked at Gabe and parroted in stilted English, "'What's he saying?' I just said we are going to scalp you and feed you to the ravens!" His comrades roared with laughter, understanding enough English to get the joke.

Gabe visibly reacted to the false threat, his eyes grew wide, and he suddenly blurted, "Tobacco! We'll give you tobacco!"

Eagle Claw groaned with frustration. He knew that the Blackfeet had no intention of killing them; otherwise, they would already be dead. The leader exchanged smiles with his men, and a few of them laughed while he motioned for one of the braves to accept the tobacco.

Reluctantly, Eagle Claw retrieved his last rope of tobacco from his parfleche and handed it over in disgust. The brave gave it to his leader, who roughly grabbed it, then smelled it and smiled. He nodded to the other braves and said in Blackfeet, "If the white man wants to give us tobacco, how can we say no?" The Blackfeet men chuckled to themselves.

"What's he saying?" Gabe asked again.

"They all think you are a very friendly white man to give them my tobacco," said Eagle Claw wryly.

The Blackfeet leader looked at Eagle Claw angrily and spoke this time in clear English. "You speak good English, White Warrior. Maybe you are more white than warrior, eh?"

The other braves chuckled at his attempt at word play, but Eagle Claw clenched his jaw and looked away. He hated to be called by that name. The irony, in Eagle Claw's mind, was that the cocky brave had probably learned to speak English from Eagle Claw's father James, who spent years with the Blackfeet trying to teach them the Word of God.

"Look at me!" demanded the leader.

Eagle Claw turned his head and stared him in the eye.

"I am Two Kills of the Blackfeet Nation. Remember me, White Warrior." He stepped closer to Eagle Claw, and the Blackfeet men once again took aim.

Two Kills reached out and touched them both on the shoulder with the braided quirt looped around his wrist. "Today, I count coup. If we ever meet again, you and your friend will die, and your scalps will hang from my saddle."

Eagle Claw was relieved he was only counting coup, a shrewd act that would win him praise from his Elders. But he also took his threat seriously, for he could see Two Kills was no common warrior.

Two Kills went to the dried meat piled on the deerskin, took a bite, then grabbed a handful. "Tell your people anyone trapping beaver on Blackfeet land makes war with us." Then, he took the scalps hanging from the saddle horn on Eagle Claw's horse and put them on his own. He looked over the two appaloosas that his men had untied. After satisfying himself they were in good condition, the group wasted no time mounting their horses to leave. Two Kills thrust his rifle above his head and shouted, *"Kiyiyiyiyi!"* and they rode off down the trail, whooping and hollering.

Gabe breathed a sigh of relief as the Blackfeet disappeared into the timber. "Are we gonna make it to the fish camp alive?"

"Trouble has come to the mountains. Everyone wants beaver. Their fur has become … like gold. But there is only one problem with this—only a few beavers remain. And this only makes everyone want them even more. First, the French came from Canada, then the whites from the east, and now, even the Crow make trouble here. What will come of this place—my home? Already, the game grows scarce. This used to be a peaceful trail. We used to travel here often when I was a small boy to trade with the Blackfeet. But now—now it has become a trail of death, and the Blackfeet stand against us and want to make war."

Eagle Claw pulled the stakes around the deer hide they had been working on and rolled it up to be finished it later. The incident had given him a heightened sense of urgency, and they quickly gathered their gear in silence, packed the horses, and left.

As they headed down the trail, a squall blew into the valley, pelting them with tiny beads of graupel. The icy wind and scolding pellets chilled them to the bone and turned the trail into a bumpy ribbon of white—a rude reminder of the coming winter.

Thankfully, the storm ended as quickly as it had begun. Within an hour after the sun had climbed over the mountain peaks, the great orb re-established its dominion, and it wasn't long thereafter that the gleaming white blanket of pellets melted and vanished into the earth. But Eagle Claw could sense the faint weakening of autumn and the gathering strength of winter. The sobering trepidation of the struggles that lay ahead weighed heavily upon him.

Chapter Eighteen

Fish Camp

Eagle Claw's words echoed in Gabe's mind, causing him to think of home, where life was tranquil and routine without the daily threat of imminent death. He couldn't think of any words to console the Kootenai man. There was no arguing the threats facing his people—threats neither of them could control.

Already, he had survived two near misses on the trail—confrontations that were nothing like what he had expected a "skirmish" to be. In both humiliating cases, he hadn't fired a single shot, and the enemy had gotten the upper hand before he could even shoulder his rifle. A spirit of war was in the air, and despite Eagle Claw's assurances, Gabe now worried how the Kootenai would respond to his presence when they finally arrived at their village.

They had traveled hard for three days since their unnerving encounter with the Blackfeet, with little to eat besides dried deer meat. The blistering pace cut an entire day off their journey, and Gabe was saddle-sore. But there was no slowing Eagle Claw; it was obvious he wanted to get home in a hurry. Fortunately, it was an empty moon, which made night travel problematic; otherwise, the determined brave probably would have marched both night and day. Despite his fears, Gabe was relieved when the winding trail broke through the forest into a clearing, and he could see wispy streams of smoke rising from the fish camp. The dozen or so tipis were situated next to a pristine river graced with a series of scenic waterfalls. Several people worked atop platforms using long, thin spears to skewer fish, while women cleaned and hung them on drying racks. The sight was a warm welcome after the arduous, dangerous journey.

"We really made it—and we still have our scalps," Gabe said, elated.

But Eagle Claw said nothing. He sat up in his saddle, scanning the village intently.

As they entered the encampment, a small boy with a tiny bow and arrow yelped in a high-pitched voice and came running. Eagle Claw dismounted and plucked the boy off the ground, hugged him, and held him tightly in his arms.

The smudge-faced tyke squeaked something in the Kootenai tongue. Eagle Claw laughed and replied in English, "Yes. We will eat well tonight, my Little Buck."

His wife, an attractive Kootenai woman, emerged from their lodge with a welcoming smile, approached Eagle Claw gracefully, and gave him a hug. They greeted one another in their own tongue. Her pleasant demeanor and gentle voice put Gabe at ease.

"This is Gabe Bauman," said Eagle Claw to her, motioning to Gabe.

"I am Spotted Doe," she said in labored English, then smiled and nodded respectfully at Gabe. "Greetings."

"Pleased to meet you, ma'am."

Out of respect to Gabe, Eagle Claw spoke in English, saying, "Gabe was successful on our return trip and shot a deer. We had to leave in haste, so we weren't able to smoke all the meat, and the hide will need to be tanned."

Spotted Doe nodded and said, "That is good news. I will tend to it." She smiled at Gabe to acknowledge his success while a couple of younger braves unpacked the horses.

The scene seemed surreal. Gabe had only known Eagle Claw as a stoic warrior, skilled in the art of hunting and killing. But now, he saw a different side to him, a fatherly tenderness that seemed antithetical to the stalwart image he'd displayed while on the trail.

Other villagers heard the commotion and began filtering toward them. Familiar faces from the Rendezvous appeared: the bearded white man approached from the river holding two large fish, and the disfigured woman with the white streak in her hair emerged from her lodge and limped over with her staff in hand to greet them.

"Welcome. I am Eagle Claw's father, James," he said, reaching out his fish-slimed hand to greet Gabe.

"I am happy to meet you, sir!" Gabe extended his own hand without flinching.

The woman with the white-streaked hair, however, seemed to look through him as if he weren't there, and spoke only to Eagle Claw in their native tongue. Her words were measured, but firm, the concerned look on her face speaking volumes as she reached out and fingered the bullet holes in his buckskin shirt. Eagle Claw spoke to her lovingly, and he gently placed his hand on her shoulder to reassure her. She nodded, but the concerned look remained. Then, without another word, she slowly turned and limped back to her lodge, humming softly.

Eagle Claw took a step toward her, as if he wanted to comfort her and assuage her worries, then took a deep breath, turned to James, and asked, "Did you tell the Elders what we saw at the Rendezvous?"

"Yes. I told them about the trappers."

"And what did they say?"

"You already know the answer—they said they wanted to smoke on it."

Eagle Claw clenched his jaw and spoke boldly: "While they smoke, our enemies make sport of us, sneaking behind us like coyotes in the night, and nothing ever gets done."

"Yes. I understand how you feel."

"They plan to return and trap beaver on our sacred land. We have enough men to destroy them for what they've done and for what they plan to do!"

His father seemed uncomfortable with Eagle Claw's tone and paused as if parsing his words. "We will always fight to protect the ones we love, but we only do so if we have to. It is not up to us to make war or take vengeance—that is the 'sacred ground of God.'"

But Eagle Claw was insistent, and replied, "I want to meet with the Elders myself. I want to tell them what I learned at the Rendezvous and what happened on our journey. Perhaps my words will help them lay down their pipes and pick up their bows."

"Very well," James replied in a calming tone, "They should hear your concerns. I'll tell them you've arrived."

James and Eagle Claw turned their backs to Gabe and lowered their voices to a whisper, speaking in the Kootenai tongue. Gabe took the hint and walked to the cliffs overlooking the river. Several young men stood fishing on a scaffold contraption built above a deep pool below the waterfalls from thin lodgepole pines. The upper platforms were supported by poles three to four inches in diameter and lashed together with rawhide. The long legs of the structure were wedged tightly into the rocks below, firmly anchoring the structures in place. Several long straps fastened to rocks on the banks provided an extra measure of safety. A couple of young men had long dip nets made from carefully woven rawhide, while others used spears to skewer the fish that were gathering their strength to clear the waterfalls and continue upriver to their spawning beds. The fishermen glanced at Gabe every so often, as if curious, but remained on task.

Soon, one of the men pulled a large fish from the river with his dip net, clubbed it on the head, and tossed it aside. Younger children then carried it over to an old woman, who gutted it with a flint-blade knife and prepared it to be smoked. A small tipi had been erected nearby. Inside the open flap were drying racks laden with rows of fish at various stages of cure. In the center was a smoldering fire, which provided curing smoke and heat for the drying process. The entire operation was fascinating.

Eagle Claw approached and placed his hand on Gabe's shoulder. "These are my people. Many years ago, we found this place and have lived off the water's bounty in peace ever since. We find plenty of food here and freedom from our enemies. The river—it is like a big brother that provides for us and protects us." He turned and pointed up at the mountain behind him. "You know that place, eh? Only a few from our village visited the sacred land—even the mighty Blackfeet fear this place."

"The Blackfeet afraid? I thought they feared nothing."

"They only fear 'bad medicine,' and they consider the Skookum—the demon of the forest—to be very bad medicine."

"Well, I've been on that trail that leads back into that sacred country, and I sure didn't see any demons." But even as the words left Gabe's mouth, a dark, looming image flashed across his mind—the large figure that had appeared and disappeared among the stunted spruce when he'd gone to gather the horses on their final moonlit night in the basin.

"Only a few of us have seen the Skookum," said Eagle Claw. "The old ones tell us stories. When our people first found the fish camp, those who wandered too far from camp would sometimes go missing and were never found. Sometimes, fish left out to smoke and dry overnight would be gone in the morning, and they heard strange cries in the night behind our camp coming from the mouth of the canyon.

"Then, one night, it rained, and in the morning, the fish were gone, and it left behind large tracks—the biggest man in our camp could put both feet inside a single footprint. Some of our Elders call him the Big Man and say he means no harm and that his presence is a good omen. Others claim otherwise and say he is a demon and is to be greatly feared."

Remembering the many cock-and-bull stories Branch and Choteau had told him around the campfire, he suspected Eagle Claw was teasing him—poking fun at his youth and inexperience. Gabe felt the thorny pricks of ridicule and laughed dismissively. "Did anyone get a look at this thing? This demon?" He said with a smirk.

But there was no grin on Eagle Claw's face, no sign of jesting, and his words came sharp and biting. "Yes, we have seen it. We saw it just after it killed my brother."

Gabe stopped laughing and felt his face grow flush. He looked toward the falls of the river and struggled to speak; the rebuttal he'd chambered in the breach of his mind fizzled and sputtered. "I—I'm sorry," he said apologetically.

Eagle Claw pursed his lips, as if holding back angry words, then swallowed hard. "Some Elders say he protects us. But he's no protector. He is no Big Man to me, and from that day on, I have called him Skookum—the demon of the forest." He turned abruptly and walked toward his lodge.

Gabe thought soberly about the story as he followed Eagle Claw to his tipi lodge, the rebuke chipping away at his preconceived notions about the legend. As they approached, he noticed several large ram heads resting along the outside wall of the tipi. One of them was missing a horn, with only the white bony core remaining. The one that was intact was enormous, its thick horns making a complete circle and a half.

The tipi appeared small from the outside yet seemed cavernous once inside. It was filled with the welcoming smell of wood smoke, its only light coming from the small doorway, the opening near the peak where the smoke vented, and the flickering fire in the center. Eagle Claw's son sat quietly playing with meticulously carved toy fig-urines: deer, elk, and buffalo fashioned from wood and ram's horn.

Eagle Claw reclined on a dark, thickly furred buffalo robe spread out on the floor. As if on cue, his son pounced on him, and a wres-tling match began in earnest despite his wife's protests in Kootenai, gesturing as if telling them they should go outside to play. Gabe was amused and entertained by the mismatched contest and the child's ultimate victory.

Spotted Doe had prepared a feast to welcome Eagle Claw home. She placed a piece of tanned deer hide on the floor, her movements smooth and graceful like those of a swan. She smiled pleasantly and addressed Gabe. "Sit. Here is fish—eat." Her words were simple and short but were spoken with hypnotic kindness. She handed him an ornately carved wooden bowl full of hearty fish stew.

"Thank you," Gabe said, smiling back. She acknowledged him with a submissive nod. He studied the intricately carved ram's-horn spoon resting in the bowl. *A marvel of artistry*, he thought.

Eagle Claw, watching his reaction, proudly replied, "I carved them myself."

After devouring the delicious stew, Gabe raised his eyes to his surroundings and spied other carved items scattered throughout the tipi. Curious, he got up to examine an odd array of delicately carved animals made from various materials: buffalo and ram horn, and deer, moose, and elk antler. They were all arranged on a wide slab of larch, set off to the side. There were two groups consisting of beaver, warriors, buffalo, and owls. In the first row, near the center of the line of figurines, stood bull and cow elk. Each was positioned on its own little square and faced each other as if prepared for battle.

"What's this?" inquired Gabe.

"That is a game called chess."

"Chest?"

"No. Chess. My father taught us. It is an ancient game, Gabe Bauman, from a land far from here. You don't know this game?"

"Never heard of it."

"We play it mostly during the long winter months when there is little else to do. I have beaten James three times," he stated proudly. "They play this game across the great waters on the other side of the world. Did you know there are other tribes, other lands far across these great waters? My father knows this. He has been there and seen this place—with his own two eyes. Someday, I want to go there to see for myself his homeland. It is called England. It is surrounded by the great waters. They call it an island, and you cannot get there on a horse, only on a ship, a vessel much bigger than a canoe that floats on waters and is pushed by the wind."

Gabe picked up the exquisitely carved bull elk, observing its intricate detail. "I've heard of these waters—an ocean—but have never seen it. But I've heard people sail across it all the time on big ships."

"Yes, yes! You know of this too!" Eagle Claw answered with enthusiasm. He picked up a small roll of buckskin and unrolled it. "I also made these."

Inside were several wooden knives, forks, and spoons, each fashioned with impeccable craftsmanship. "Very well done," remarked Gabe as he sat again, as Spotted Doe refilled his bowl.

The meaty stew included fish, wild onion and tubers, sliced morel mushrooms, and edible greens, with a hint of wild mint added for seasoning. The feast was gratifying after the long journey on the trail, especially after eating strictly meat for the duration of the trek. Gabe was so busy shoveling in the savory stew that he momentarily forgot his manners, oblivious to his loud slurping, chomping, and the trail of stew dripping from his scant beard.

He glanced up and caught Spotted Doe's eye. She pursed her lips slightly, and looked downward, then took a delicate bite of stew. Gabe had witnessed that look before—from his mother. It was a silent critique, but very effective. Conscious stricken, he wiped his sopping beard with his sleeve and took a careful bite, chewing it with his mouth closed. She glanced at him and smiled patiently.

After Gabe had sated his appetite, his curiosity finally got the best of him and he asked Eagle Claw, "The woman you were talking with at the Rendezvous—the tall one. Where is she?"

"That was my sister, Dawn."

"She hunts," added Spotted Doe.

"Your sister?" Gabe blurted. He stared at Eagle Claw, puzzled, trying to digest the idea they were siblings, while Eagle Claw and his wife paused and exchanged glances. Realizing his outburst had been gauche, he quickly pretended to be nonchalant, humming to himself as if suddenly uninterested in the topic. Little more was said, and after the meal Spotted Doe stepped outside and the two weary travelers napped off their feast in the comfort of the tipi.

"Kayayah!"

Gabe opened his eyes and caught a glimpse of a small, brownish flash just before the object landed on his chest with a crash. He instinctively scooted and rolled away, sending the small bundle tumbling. He heard a maniacal laugh, then the brown blur attacked again, pouncing on him, laughing gleefully, then hopping away. Gabe covered his face and sat back, now fully awake. He peeked from behind his forearms. In front of him stood Little Buck, his small bow at full draw. Before Gabe could react, the tiny arrow hit him on the cheek, sticking momentarily in his sparse beard, followed by more delirious laughter. The boy attacked a third time. *"Yip, yip, yip, kayah!"* Gabe fell back, unsure of what to do with the tiny whirl of fury clinging to his chest like a giant tick, pounding him with little fists that felt like bunny hops.

"That's enough, Little Buck!" barked Eagle Claw, who had also been awakened by the commotion. The little warrior laughed and hopped down off Gabe, retrieved his arrow and bow, and began shooting imaginary buffalo.

Spotted Doe stepped into the tipi and announced, "The Elders are meeting now."

Eagle Claw got up at once. "Come on, Gabe. Let's go. You will be my witness." Then, he turned and looked back at Gabe. "He didn't hurt you, did he?"

Gabe grinned at the joke and followed him out of the tipi.

෴

Eagle Claw led Gabe to the distant side of the village. As soon as White Cloud's tipi came into view, his heart began to pound. *Would they listen this time?* He respected White Cloud's wisdom. He was the oldest among the Elders, with an apt name, for his hair was as white as summer nimbus clouds. The old warrior often preferred diplomacy, but Eagle Claw felt strongly that the issue at hand demanded actions, not words.

He sat down next to James, and the braves scooted closer to make room for Gabe. The proceedings began, as they always did, with the lighting of the pipe, which was passed among the Elders: Arrow Heart, Red Elk, and Chief White Cloud. After each had taken a smoke, the meeting began.

"Tell us what you heard, Eagle Claw," stated Arrow Heart, speaking in the Kootenai tongue.

"The trapper known as Crooked Branch is coming here with a band of trappers to catch the beaver in the sacred canyon. I do not lie. This man, Gabe Bauman, is my witness."

Arrow Heart gave James permission to speak and asked him to translate.

"Is this true, Gabe Bauman?" asked James. "Is the man they call Crooked Branch planning on bringing men here to trap beaver?"

"Yes. Eagle Claw speaks the truth," replied Gabe solemnly.

James translated his words into the Kootenai tongue, and the Elders looked at each other with disconcerted glances, mulling this news.

Eagle Claw felt his spine stiffen as they tarried and made no reply. Finally, he raised his voice: "Brave Elders, we must prepare to fight! It has already started, wise fathers; we are already being pushed aside. We passed through the meadows where we have our fall hunt, and our old camp was piled with the carcasses of dead deer and elk. We found no game there! What will we do when the deep winter snows come, and we have no food? How will we feed our wives, our children? Do you not remember what happens when the winters grow long and we run out of meat? When these trappers finish catching all the beaver, we will have no choice but to leave our women and children unprotected and make the dangerous journey over the mountains to the Blackfeet lands to hunt buffalo."

A surge of confidence swelled within him when the tipi abruptly filled with murmuring, and the few young men, eager to prove themselves in battle, called for war against the trappers.

But then, Arrow Heart spoke up. "How can we fight against our enemies when our numbers are so few?" Eagle Claw clenched his jaw and held his tongue. *Surely White Cloud understands the seriousness of the danger,* he thought, and he waited patiently for the Elder to speak.

The pipe was passed again to Chief White Cloud. The room grew silent. After several puffs, he cleared his throat and spoke with a gravelly voice in the Kootenai tongue—slowly, as if caressing every word.

"We have long lived in peace here with both man and beast. We take what the Creator of the earth, sky, and water gives us to live. Others have come, many moons ago. They tried to hunt and take game from this land and from the sacred canyon beyond our village. Those who tried were either never seen again or vowed never to return. The men you speak of—they know nothing of the danger that faces them. They only care about their furs and their coins—things you cannot even eat. They grab for this and grab for that, until all is gone, but what will they do in the end? What they seek will only end in their demise. The Big Man will be watching them. They will not be able to hide from him. He watches over those who show proper respect and brings harm to those who don't.

When I was a young man, I ventured there, into the sacred canyon, when winter meat ran low. I killed a deer, then gave thanks to the Creator for this food, which would save my family from starvation.

But I became lost in a terrible snowstorm. I walked until my legs could go no farther, then lay down in the snow to die.

As I lay there freezing, something startled me, and when my eyes blinked open, there stood the Big Man. I did not know what to do, for my legs were too weak to run. The Big Man just stood above me, watching me, as if wanting something. I reached into my bag and pulled out some dried meat and handed it to him. He took it, then smelled it, and ate until he had eaten all the food in my bag. I thought to myself, 'Surely now I am a dead man,' so I closed my eyes, sang the death song, and fell into a deep sleep. When I awoke, the storm had stopped, and some braves were rubbing snow in my face to rouse me. It was night, I was lying next to my lodge, and the deer I had shot was on the ground beside to me. The braves took me into my lodge and warmed me by the fire, then gave me water and food to help me recover. I fell asleep again, and when I awoke in the morning, I rose and walked outside, happy to be alive. And there, in the snow by my lodge, were the tracks of the Big Man heading back into the canyon.

A few years later, my son asked me, 'Father, shall we go and visit the Big Man and thank him for saving you?' But I told him, 'You cannot visit the Big Man's lodge, as you would visit a brother or sister. He likes to be left alone, and if you leave the Big Man alone, he will leave you alone. He only reveals himself when he so chooses.'"

Then, White Cloud's tone grew dark and sagacious. "The Big Man makes his camp deep in the forest—beyond our reach—in the far country. He is our protector to ward away intruders. This creature walked the earth when the world was young. This is the Big Man of old, the one who walks at night, the one who goes unseen, watching from the shadows. He is not one to be meddled with."

A pall fell over the men inside the tipi. Eagle Claw saw their growing fear and the momentum of his argument fading. Frustration welled up inside him, and he blurted, "The creature that lives in the canyon is a killer! He is no protector. He is no friend of ours! Do you forget what he did to my brother?"

Red Elk spoke for the first time, saying, "That is enough! Those are bold words, Eagle Claw, but perhaps not very wise. I remember when two Blackfeet warriors ventured into the sacred canyon many moons ago. They had heard about the legend of the Skookum, and they came to prove their manhood—to prove their bravery and kill the legend. They were the strongest of warriors, these warriors of the plains. And though we urged them not to venture into that place, they would not hear our words.

"'Why should we listen to you?' they scoffed. 'You who fish like women for your food?' We watched and waited for them to come back until twice the empty moon grew full, but they never returned."

White Cloud looked Eagle Claw in the eye. "I am sympathetic to your loss and your anger," he said, "but you must heed my words. These white men who seek the beaver's pelt will be like the two Blackfeet warriors. Let them sneak in there if they dare. Do not hold them back. The Big Man will decide their fate. If they are honorable, they will return unharmed. If not, then their flesh and bones will feed the raven and the bear."

Eagle Claw's heart sank, and a lump formed in his throat. The other men had wilted under the spell of White Cloud's words, and once again, he felt alone. The Elders conferred together for several minutes, speaking in hushed tones until a verdict was reached.

Arrow Heart addressed the group. "It has been decided. White Cloud's wisdom, once again, will direct our actions in this matter."

And as the braves nodded in agreement, Eagle Claw shook his head bitterly and stormed from the lodge. White Cloud's kindly story of the Skookum chafed his very soul, causing him to suddenly despise the leader he once held in high regard. Old feelings of abandonment and exclusion filtered into his heart, and he felt the seeds of old resentments sprouting anew.

Marching without a word to his lodge, he threw open the flap and sat down with his legs crossed, rocking back and forth, his forearms tight against his knees. Gabe came in behind him and sat down, away from the fire. Little Buck seemed to sense the tension and scampered under the buffalo blanket, silently peering out, eyes wide.

"What is the matter?" asked Spotted Doe kindly in Kootenai.

Eagle Claw's words were chopped and sharp. "Why must we sit around waiting, always waiting, while our enemies steal our lives away?!"

She placed her hand gently on his shoulder and said, "I am happy you are here. Perhaps you could show our guest how to fish? We are still low and could use his help."

Eagle Claw stopped rocking, calmed by her tender words and the stroking of her hand. He called Little Buck from his hiding place, and the boy crawled into his father's lap for a cuddle.

At length, he said, "Yes. There are important things to do here. Why will nobody listen to me, my wife? Why are they so blind?"

"Perhaps, in time, they will see what you see—like the mist that hides the river until the morning sun drives it away."

Eagle Claw's anger subsided at her gentle and wise words—but not his resolve. "If these men come, I will fight them—by myself if I have to."

$\mathcal{R}apist$

André *Choteau sat with his legs outstretched, warm-*ing his feet by the fire and quietly stewing over Branch's newly concocted plan. Outwardly, he took pains to appear as Branch's yes-man, a "pangle-wangle" who always went with the flow.

But on the inside, he was always running the numbers, refraining from excesses, not throwing his money around wildly on strong drink or gambling. He'd saved most of his earnings, cached it in several locations near the trail to the Missouri River, and was planning to head back east after this latest haul, find a good woman, buy some land, and settle down.

Despite Choteau's misgivings, Branch had cajoled him into taking one more excursion into the remote basin where they'd found the mother lode of beaver—a final payday before hanging up his traps for good. The decision was made easier with the addition of two extra guns—Jones and Johnson. But now, with Gabe gone, that meant only one extra gun, and Choteau was starting to have reservations about venturing back to the strange, foreboding basin.

That evening, the mountain men, Indians, and traders had sat around the campfire, whooping it up with one more big benjo on the final night of the Rendezvous. As the night wore on, they gradually transitioned from obnoxious to half-rats drunk to incoherent. One by one, they staggered into the darkness to their tents and tipis, a few sips away from drinking themselves completely unconscious. The few who hadn't left lay scattered, stone still, like corpses around the large campfire.

From time to time, Choteau would glance at Branch, who was lying back against a log next to him, to check whether he'd fallen asleep. Branch had insisted on staying one more night for some good swilling before heading back into the mountains. This time, when Choteau looked up, he noticed several opportunistic Indian women in the shadows, inching toward the large campfire. He guessed their motive: to imbibe any residual spirits remaining in the brown jugs that lay tipped and scattered around the fire. It wasn't difficult for them to find what they were looking for, and after securing several unattended jugs, they sat down on a log, giggling among themselves like church bells as they shared the potent elixir.

Choteau observed that Branch was awake now, leaning deeper against the log and eyeing the women as they chattered to each other. It didn't take long for the amber potion to cast its spell on them, which only made Branch seem even more intrigued. Choteau had witnessed him taking his liberties with women before, so he knew the weathered trapper was no flapdoodle. Branch appeared particularly intrigued by the one with the large breasts.

Soon, the distant voices of the trappers became muted, and the dark silence of night enveloped the encampment—the only noises came from the tittering, whiskey-drinking women. At length, the big-breasted woman rose and went to her husband, who lay passed out near the fire, and began shaking him, trying to get him to wake up. When he wouldn't move, she shook her head and laughed, then wobbled toward her tipi while the other women stayed and continued drinking and laughing.

Choteau grew nervous about his cohort's intentions but kept silent and still. After a few moments, Branch stood and staggered over to the brave, kicking him hard on the leg to see if he would rouse, but the man didn't move. The whiskey had thoroughly tanked him. The drunken women sitting nearby pointed and laughed at the inanimate man— apparently, everything was funny to them when sotted by the rotgut.

Without hesitation, Branch made his way across the meadow, keeping his distance, as the woman entered a darkened tipi. He glanced around as if checking to make sure no one was watching, then lifted the flap over the entrance and followed her in.

The other native women staggered even closer to the campfire, obviously more at ease around Choteau than Branch. They giggled at the sounds of rhythmic grunting and whimpering coming from the tipi nearby, oblivious to the brazen crime taking place a mere stone's throw away.

After a few minutes, Choteau heard little more than faint sobs coming from the tipi between breaks in the slurred chatter of the Indian women as they passed the jug from one to another. A moment later, Branch threw open the flap draped over the tipi doorway. He poked his head out and glanced around furtively, then circled well behind the drunk women, keeping his distance from the campfire like a demon afraid to come into the light.

Choteau shook his head. The bastard had gotten away with it yet again—and no doubt felt very satisfied with himself for doing so. Choteau fully expected to hear about the conquest for days to come. But he had grown apathetic to Branch's frequent indiscretions.

As the fire died down, one by one, the women stumbled off to their tipis, and when one paused to vomit, Choteau got up and headed to his campsite. He thought he had given the man ample time to crawl into his bedroll, but much to his dismay, he found Branch sitting near the fire.

Choteau sat down opposite him and sighed deeply. Branch was looking at the fire with a smug grin, like a man who had just stolen something and knew he would never get caught. Choteau expected him to elaborate on what just happened, but instead, he lifted a fresh jug to his lips and proceeded to get good and sozzled. As Choteau climbed into his bedroll, the last thing he saw before drifting off to sleep was the twisted grin of Crooked Bill Branch, which made for a fitful night's rest.

თ

The next morning, Choteau rose early and made coffee. When Johnson and Jones showed up not long afterward, he sent them out to catch the horses as the gut-foundered camp denizens stirred and protested the morning light with pathetic groans. The luster of the Rendezvous had worn thin and, as usual, most had spent what little money they'd earned from their furs on strong drink and wagering. They had tippled Trader Smith's entire supply of illegal whiskey and were now staggering around like groggy grizzly bears emerging from hibernation. Choteau figured that Smith, being familiar with the typical Rendezvous, had calculated when they would run out of the rotgut and had wisely pulled out of camp the prior evening, in the dark of night, along with his profits and the few trade items that remained in his stores. The shrewd trader was wise enough to avoid being around when the last drop was consumed and then face the angry customers stumbling back to his log shack demanding more.

Most of the Indians had left for their native camps scattered far and wide. The only ones who remained were a few hardened holdouts fumbling around for coffee and nursing hangovers in misery.

Choteau waited patiently as Branch tried to wake up, obviously having overfilled with "mother's milk" while reminiscing to himself next to the fire about the fine squaw he had raped. Now, his body would be paying the price for his sins—his soul would pay as well, but Choteau knew Branch cared little about that.

"Oh, damn," groaned Branch as he rolled over and squinted against the bright sun. He grabbed his stomach. "Where's the whiskey? I'm a peg too low!"

Failing a clumsy attempt to stand, he knelt on all fours like a hog and looked around for the nearest bottle. Across from the firepit lay an unfamiliar toped trapper who had stumbled in sometime during the night after Branch had passed out. The ne'er-do-well lay with his mouth agape, his jug of whiskey tucked under his arm, as if he had passed out making love to it. Branch crawled over to him, like a thirsty grizzly, grabbed the jug, and tipped it back, but it was empty—dry as a bone.

Choteau could scarcely remember being so disgusted with Branch, but he kept his thoughts to himself. He poured a cup of coffee and held it out. "Here, you might need to drink this."

Branch looked up and begrudgingly accepted the offering. He guzzled the black tar brew, but as soon as it hit his stomach, he doubled up and puked it out along with the fetid remnants of the previous night's repast, then collapsed to the ground and moaned pitifully. Choteau smiled and stifled a laugh. "Bad case of wooden mouth, eh?"

"Hell yeah." Branch grunted. "Damn blue devils got me!" He turned over and looked around, breathing heavily. "My goddamn head's poundin' like a Blackfeet war drum," he grumbled, shivering. "Where's Johnson and Jones?"

"They're out catching the horses."

"Good." Branch fumbled for his knife and patted it when he found it still secure in its sheath. "I wanna get on the trail as soon as we can. Got miles to cover."

Choteau couldn't help but snicker. "You fit to ride?"

Branch heard the insult, just as Choteau suspected he might. He jerked his head up and sneered, "What? What the hell are ya talkin' about? Of course I'm fit to ride! This ain't the first drunk I ever tied on, and it won't be the last."

He stumbled to his feet and staggered, nearly falling over. His body convulsed and he doubled over in agony, holding his belly as if it were full of biting rattlesnakes. He planted his feet firmly to stay balanced and gulped more coffee, the syrupy serum spilling down the corners of his mouth and onto his beard.

No longer able to hide his disgust, Choteau turned away and walked to the edge of the hill overlooking the prairie. After a few moments, he called back to Branch: "I see them out there! They appear to be lost, just wandering around. I'll go help them."

"Fine," mumbled Branch. "Hurry. I wanna get the hell outta here."

Choteau was fed up with Branch's bottle-ache and sour disposition. He was happy to get away from him and help catch the horses. He strode down the hillside and out onto the prairie, then stopped and shook his head at Jones and Johnson, shambling around like lost sheep, searching vainly for horse tracks.

"There's a track over here!" shouted Choteau.

The two newcomers came stomping over, and Johnson groused,

"Don't be so damn loud, Frenchy. Don't ya know we are in Blackfeet country?"

Johnson looked down at the track and then in the direction where they led. He turned and glanced toward the camp, then changed his tone, "Choteau, me and Jones have been talkin'," he said. "You know, this deal with Crooked Bill sounds almost too good to be true. We're thinking he might be tryin' to swindle us. Fifty-fifty split—are you kiddin' me? I know him better'n that. You don't think he'd be plannin' to double-cross us, do ya?"

Choteau had to think for a moment before answering, which seemed to make them even more nervous. The truth was that Choteau didn't trust Branch as far as he could throw him, and it was only when he promised the addition of more men that Choteau relented and agreed to one last excursion into their newly discovered beaver paradise. At length, he said, "Hell no! Why would you fellows think that of Bill Branch?"

"Tell us the truth. How many beavers do you think we can pull outta there?" asked Jones forcefully.

"More than *you* can count, monsieur!"

They looked at Choteau suspiciously. But without another word, they began following the horse tracks, which led across a wide, grassy flat before dropping into a deep ravine, where they finally found the horses grazing contentedly.

"I'll circle and get behind 'em," said Choteau. "You two stay on this trail here, and if they see me and run, I'll bet they come right back to you, Monsieur Johnson."

They split up, and Choteau circled the horses, dropped into the ravine, and worked his way closer. As he did, he thought more about Johnson's question and what he would do if there came a mutiny, ambush, or double-cross. Whose side would he take—Branch's or the other two? It was a difficult question. He'd seen Branch at his worst and wouldn't put it past him to try a double-cross. And if he could swindle a former partner like Johnson, who was to say he wouldn't do the same to Choteau? He worked through the multitude of different scenarios as he approached the horses. His biggest worry was that Johnson and Jones might bag the entire deal, leaving him and Branch alone. Choteau knew most of the work would then fall on his shoulders—including night watch! And that scenario would be a deal-breaker.

When they finally saw him sneaking toward them, the horses took off in that stiff-legged way hobbled horses run, straight toward Jones and Johnson. They roped the first horse, Juniper, as he emerged from the ravine. Once he was caught, the others gave up any attempt to flee.

"Hold up!" said Choteau firmly as they turned and headed for camp. The two trappers stopped and gave him their attention. Choteau breathed deeply. "I've been thinking about what you said. If Branch tries a double-cross … you can count on me to back you."

The two looked at each other and nodded with satisfaction. They all shook hands on it and headed back to camp.

Branch was sitting on a log, still sipping coffee. As they emerged from the timber with the horses, he growled, "About damn time you three got back here with them horses. I'm gettin' antsy to get on the trail."

Seemingly emboldened after the promise of support from Choteau, Johnson sauntered confidently toward Branch with his barrel chest puffed out. "Look, Branch. Let's get one thing straight before we saddle these horses. I ain't about to take orders from you and get yelled at like you did to that kid. You start in on that kinda shite, and you can forget us goin' with you."

For a moment, Branch's anger looked as if it would flare, but he collected himself and replied with a smile, "That's fine, George. We'll all get along fine. And when you see the beaver we're gonna catch, you'll be grinnin' from ear to ear and damn happy to take orders from me." Johnson continued glaring at him, apparently not satisfied with his reply.

Sensing the tension, Choteau quickly intervened. "All right, then," he said. "Let's get these horses loaded."

Johnson and Jones finally commenced packing and loading the horses with Choteau while Branch looked on, still drinking his coffee.

"Damn that bastard," Johnson whispered when they were out of earshot. "I'm always suspicious of anything he says, 'specially when he grins like that. When I worked with him before, it was always like playin' poker with the devil—with the devil dealin' the cards."

Choteau said nothing but couldn't agree more with Johnson's assessment. While the newcomers were preoccupied with packing the mules and horses, he noticed Branch snatching two bottles of whiskey from Jones's saddlebags, then hiding them in one of his own panniers. Choteau snorted and shook his head when Branch gave him a wink. The man was completely devoid of scruples.

It wasn't until Choteau tied off the last diamond hitch that the stark reality of the situation hit him—they were heading back to the godforsaken basin again and soon a memory started haunting him. It was one he had tried to purge, but it kept popping into his mind—those shining red eyes blinking in the firelight just above the alder brush.

"Choteau!" Branch shouted. "Don't forget that pair of leggings I bought. I hung 'em in that tree behind ya there."

Snapping out of his worrisome brooding, Choteau begrudgingly retrieved the leggings, then tucked them under the diamond hitch he had just tied. Branch somehow managed to saddle his horse and lean against it, moaning miserably as Choteau finished packing and brought him one of the mules to lead.

When he held out the lead rope, Branch doubled over and held his belly. "Damned rotgut! I swear if someone gives me another jug of that rotten cougar piss, I'll run 'im through, and if I ever see that no-account Smith again, I'll shoot him. I swear he put somthin' in it this time. Bastard's tryin' to kill us with that poison of his."

"Well, at least you got rid of the worms, eh?" Choteau said, laughing and handing him the lead rope.

Jones and Johnson rode up as Branch snatched the lead rope with a scowl. He grabbed Bauman's Hawken leaning against the tree next to him and slid it into his scabbard. "You boys ready?" he said with a strained smile. They all nodded. Branch collected himself and clambered clumsily onto his horse. "Let's ride!" he shouted.

As the four of them strung out along the trail, Choteau cast a look back and saw that some of the trappers were carefully watching them as they left the Rendezvous.

Branch saw them too and stared right back with an evil glare. "Don't you dare follow us, you sons o' bitches!" he bellowed. "I'll kill ya just as soon as look at ya!" He bent over, holding his belly.

Later that evening, the four of them sat comfortably around a campfire eating one rabbit while another was skewered through a spit, still cooking over the fire. The trail ride had given them a chance to sober up and clear their senses, and now, Johnson had questions.

"So how long do you think we'll be in there?" he asked Branch.

The reply was quick and pointed. "One week, tops."

Johnson and Jones stared at Choteau, who purposely kept his face impassive. Then, they looked at each other skeptically, but the wary Branch picked up on the silent exchanges.

"You don't believe me?" he said belligerently. Choteau casually got up and worked his way closer to his rifle, sensing there might be a fight.

"Branch, I ain't no greenhorn," Johnson said. "I know from experience it's gonna take longer'n one week of hard trappin' to get a haul like what you just brought to the Rendezvous."

"One week will be enough," Choteau interjected. "Trust me."

Johnson and Jones did not respond, but it was clear they both had serious doubts despite their hunger for the furs.

"You just make sure your skinnin' knives are sharp and ready to go to work," said Branch.

Choteau was relieved a fracas had not developed but began to have doubts about Johnson and Jones. They seemed unusually guarded, and he kept a wary eye on them.

That night, they camped at the Middle Fork and the next night at Nyack Creek.

During the latter part of the morning on the third day, they were moving at a steady pace when Branch came around a bend in the trail and motioned for them to stop. A few hundred yards ahead, a faint plume of smoke rose above the timber. Branch dismounted and gestured for the others to be quiet, then tied off his horse and silently slid the Hawken out of its scabbard. Branch signed for Choteau to dismount and work his way through the forest to see if there might be trouble ahead on the trail.

As Choteau slipped from his horse and crept surreptitiously through the timber, he could hear the muted sound of native voices growing louder. He never shied away from a skirmish; rather, he relished the opportunity. Like trapping, it was an opportunity to take, and there was no easier taking than when a man was lying on the ground dead—no hassles or haggling, just pure taking. He approached and peered through the trees, quickly counted the men, and scanned their possessions.

There were six Blackfeet warriors. They didn't seem in a hurry to go anywhere, and since he was fluent in Blackfeet, Choteau paused for a moment to listen, curious as to their celebratory mood. They sat around the campfire sharing smoked meat and chin-wagging about the horses they had taken and boasting about how they had put a Kootenai warrior and his young white friend in their place before counting coup.

The apparent leader of the group loaded the fire-brick red bowl of his soapstone pipe with tobacco, and the others waited impatiently for their turn. He touched the aromatic contents with a smoldering stick from the fire and puffed. Soon, he had it lit and took a few more long puffs. "Mmm, good tobacco," he commented before handing the pipe to his comrade.

And after taking a couple of deep puffs, the brave said, "It was very nice of that young white man to give us this tobacco." The two laughed.

"Yes, very nice of him," the leader replied. "Maybe these trappers aren't so bad after all."

"I wish all white men were that friendly!" They continued chuckling as they reminisced about their good fortune and passed the pipe back and forth between puffs.

As he returned to the others, the thought crossed Choteau's mind that they might have been talking about young Bauman and the half-breed he had followed from the Rendezvous. But he couldn't see Bauman taking part in the theft of horses, so it didn't add up.

"How many?" Branch whispered when Choteau emerged and approached from the dense timber.

He held up six fingers. "They wear war paint."

"I didn't come here for this, damn it. We're outnumbered," whispered Johnson. "Let's circle, go around 'em, and be on our way."

Branch scowled. "Through all that deadfall? They'll hear us. Besides, we can take 'em! They won't know what hit 'em! We kill four right away, then we won't be outnumbered, will we? What do you think, Choteau?"

"I think we can take them."

Johnson stomped to his horse to fetch his rifle. "Son of a bitch!" he hissed contemptuously. Jones did the same, tucking his hatchet in his belt for the inevitable hand-to-hand combat.

Choteau knew the drill and was already prepared. To him, hunting Indians was easier than getting camp meat, with no gutting or skinning involved except for taking scalps, which wasn't much work at all. He followed in line behind Branch as they silently made their way toward the small band of Blackfeet camped along the trail.

The braves' own laughter drowned out the sound of their rifle hammers clicking. Choteau took aim as the leader said, "You know, I thought he was going to spill his water and wet his breeches," before taking another long drag. They were laughing at the joke when Choteau's first .53-caliber ball caught one of the braves squarely in the chest, knocking him back against a tree. The forest erupted with the sound of gunfire, and the lounging braves scrambled for weapons.

Choteau quickly reloaded amid the chaos and the leader fell back, staring in shock as blood poured through the fingers of his fallen comrade who clutched his chest in agony. Choteau wanted to kill the leader, knowing he most likely had the best rifle and gear, but he darted behind the closest tree as a lead ball smashed against it, throwing bark with a loud *thwap*. The wary brave peeked from behind the tree at him just as Choteau took aim and fired, but he ducked back behind the trunk, again narrowly avoiding the bullet.

While Choteau reloaded, one of the other braves scrambled for his rifle as a slug smacked him on the side of his head, dropping him immediately. Meanwhile, the other Blackfeet were frantically trying to retrieve weapons while their horses jumped and jostled, startled by the sudden mayhem. Then, Johnson aimed and fired, hitting one of the men squarely in the gut just as he lifted his rifle to shoot. He crumpled to the ground in a fetal position, groaning and holding his belly.

Choteau rammed a lead ball down the barrel of his rifle as another brave, tomahawk in hand, lunged for Jones, who fired and missed. Raising his rifle just in time, Jones blocked the swing of the brave's hatchet, which came down hard against the rifle and shattered the stock just behind the trigger.

The momentum of the charge knocked Jones onto the ground, and the brave jumped on top of him, holding down his arm. Choteau shouldered his rifle as the brave raised his hatchet high for the kill, but before he could fire, Branch sent his Green River knife whirling through the air. The blade hit the man squarely through the neck, just under his chin, and he fell back, choking as blood poured from the wound.

The distraction allowed the leader to bolt for the nearest horse. As he mounted it with a single leap, Choteau took careful aim, but just as he fired, the man grabbed the horse's mane, ducked, and swung himself to the far side of the animal, then, using it as a shield, he and the horse bolted through the timber. The horse jumped sideways as a bullet whizzed near its head, but the Blackfeet were expert horsemen, and the man held on like a spring wood tick, one hand clutching the mane and the crook of his knee gripping the withers while the horse fled. Before anyone else could shoot, the leader was out of sight.

Choteau reloaded again and spotted the final brave, the one that appeared to be the youngest, cowering fearfully behind a pine. The brave had seen his leader escape and looked to be waiting for the right moment to make a run for his horse. Jones held his broken rifle wedged in the joint of a tree for stability and had his sights lined up, ready to shoot. But every time the brave peered out from behind the tree, he would pull his head back out of sight before Jones could fire.

The young brave stuck his head out one more time to draw the gunfire, and when he saw the smoke from the gunshot, he pulled his head back, and the bullet splattered against the side of the tree, narrowly missing him. He bolted from his hiding place and sprinted toward the frightened horses. Choteau took aim and fired, cursing when his shot missed the fast-running Blackfeet man. Just as the brave leaped onto a horse from behind, Johnson fired. The lead ball caught him through the spine with an audible *thwack*. Momentum carried him through the air, and he fell against the animal's neck before dropping limply to the ground.

Branch stood and raised the Hawken over his head. "Yeehaw! Now that's what I call good shooting, boys. We got 'em—just like I said."

"What are we gonna do now that one of them got away?" asked Jones. "They're sure to gather more men and come after us."

Choteau listened and waited for Branch to reply, knowing full well there could be dire consequences if the Blackfeet were to form a posse. He surveyed the carnage, trying to determine what new problems the skirmish might bring upon them.

Branch blanched at Jones's disgruntled question suggesting that he had made a poor choice to attack. "Just shut yer trap and start searchin' the dead for valuables," he ordered, which prompted Choteau to quickly do the same.

"You know, he's right," shouted Johnson, undeterred. "This valley's gonna be filled with the sound of war drums!"

Choteau watched as Branch looked at Johnson with a self-assured smile. "That's exactly what I'm hoping for."

Johnson and Jones exchanged befuddled looks. "What the hell do you mean by that?" Jones asked.

"I'm fairly certain we're bein' followed, and if not now, we will be tomorrow—by them other damn trappers from the Rendezvous. They wanna find the jumbos. But they'll get a big surprise if they think they're gonna get through on this trail."

Choteau grabbed one of the dead men by his hair. He grinned as Johnson cringed and looked the other way while he made the first cut along the hairline and peeled back the scalp.

Johnson spoke up. "All right, Branch. If we're gonna do this, we need to ride like hell today and get as far from here as we can. Otherwise, I'm headed south to the Three Forks."

"Oh, don't worry. We know how to ride like hell, don't we, Choteau?"

Choteau smirked. "Yes, monsieur, we do know how to do that." He raised the scalp and let out a war whoop. "*Kayayayayah!* To the victors go the spoils!"

He helped Jones scour the small battlefield for a replacement rifle and tossed him one of the better ones he came across. Jones caught it and looked it over, nodding in satisfaction. Jones then approached one of the fallen braves with his knife and bent down to take his scalp.

But Branch ran up just then, shouting, "Hey! Don't touch that long-haired son of a bitch! I got him, and that scalp is mine!" He pushed Jones aside and straddled the brave from behind. "Johnson, you should teach your boy some manners. Rule number one is never lay claim to a scalp that don't belong to ya. We ain't a buncha damn savages!" He grabbed the slain Indian by the hair and, in one quick motion with the knife, lifted the scalp off his head. Holding it up, he brushed back the long hair, admiring his trophy. "Now, that's a proper scalp job, boys," he declared.

After they had thoroughly scoured the dead braves and their horses for valuables, Jones stepped over and began to untether the Blackfeet horses to set them free.

"What the hell are you doing?!" blurted Branch.

Jones turned to Branch, startled and confused.

"Don't let them critters loose!"

Choteau was familiar with Branch's routine and understood perfectly what he meant and what to do.

Johnson replied indignantly, "We don't need all them horses, Branch. Just more trouble and mouths to feed. Besides, these Indian ponies ain't broke to pack."

"D'you think I'm still wet behind the ears, man? Of course we don't need 'em! But we don't want them damn Blackfeet to have 'em, neither."

Johnson and Jones glanced at each other, stupefied. "Then what do we do with 'em?" Johnson complained. "Kill 'em?"

"Damned right!" replied Branch.

Both Johnson and Jones looked at each other and then at Choteau, their faces frozen in befuddlement at Branch's words. Choteau shook his head impatiently as the two stood dumbfounded. He cast his eyes on the horses, which had now settled down and returned to their normally submissive demeanor. The two spotted appaloosa stallions stood out from the rest, like breathtaking creatures from another world—perfect in their coloring and confirmation. A crashing wave of regret passed over his conscience, but just as quickly, it dissipated like a fleeting vapor.

"This ain't right, Choteau," protested Jones.

"We ain't got all day!" barked Branch as he rearranged his gear and commenced tying a bundle of valuables he'd scoured from the dead Blackfeet to the back of his saddle. "Get on with it."

Choteau felt his neck stiffen as he clenched his fists tightly. Once again, he felt himself being forced into doing something he'd regret later. Though he often disdained Branch—was appalled by him, in truth—he saw him as an avenue to get what he wanted. It was usually a crooked avenue, but a more direct pathway to his goal and he had long since accepted any guilt as part of the price he paid for partnering with the outlaw. Besides, he had found the passage of time an effective device in diminishing the shame of his indiscretions as Branch's accomplice.

"Hurry up! The Blackfeet will be coming," urged Choteau.

"Ah, hell!" shouted Johnson, and he stepped toward the closest horse and took aim at the back of its head.

"Hold it! Damnation!" cried Branch. "Do I have to show you how to do everything?"

Johnson lowered his rifle and looked back, confused, as Branch charged toward him. Branch slowed as he approached the first horse to keep it from jostling, then slipped his Green River knife from its sheath and turned to Jones and Johnson, who stood staring, slack-jawed.

"Rule number one—never waste good lead on horseflesh!" groused Branch. He made one quick cut at the junction of neck and shoulder, where the huge pipeline jugular came closest to the skin, and a geyser of blood pumped onto the ground.

The newcomers seemed paralyzed with shock. Choteau had become skilled at burying his consternation; he had worked long enough with Branch to know that arguing was pointless. Fearing yet another confrontation and possible mutiny, he resigned himself to the inevitable and began working at the far end of the string of horses. By the time he and Branch had finished, the first one's legs were beginning to wobble. It stumbled hard to the left and then the right, finally crashing to the ground and sending the others jumping and rearing, the horrific smell of blood jolting them into chaos. Several pulled back, broke free in the melee, and wheeled around, spraying blood in wide arcs.

Pacified by their momentary sense of freedom, the horses stood staring in dumb disbelief at the betrayal, not realizing they were dead on their feet. The two appaloosas were the last to fall, resisting till the end. Their eyes grew heavy, and their heads drooped, as if about to fall asleep as horses do while standing up. Streams of blood gushed from the precisely made cuts, pooling frothy at their feet. They teetered back and forth until both collapsed together, inseparable in death as in life.

Jones jerked his head down and turned away, retching. Even the more hardened Johnson remained speechless, his anguished eyes stinging from the appalling slaughter. The entire camp glistened, as if from a sudden red downpour.

Choteau swallowed hard and sheathed his knife, not bothering to clean the blade, and forced himself to think of green pastures and the homestead he would someday own. It was the only thing that seemed to wipe away the bloody residue from his thoughts and give succor to his seared conscience. Tomorrow would be another day.

Chapter Twenty

Upper Trail Lookout

*G*abe woke to the sound of jubilant voices outside Eagle Claw's tipi. He struggled to throw off the sweltering buffalo hide blanket he was buried under, then got dressed, opened the buckskin flap, and stepped into the blinding light.

Squinting his aching eyes against the bright morning sun, he could faintly make out a rider talking to Eagle Claw and Spotted Doe. A quartered elk fastened neatly onto the pack horses came into focus first, then the enormous, ivory-tipped branches of the bull's antlers that made the horse carrying them appear ridiculously small.

The sound of a woman's voice jerked Gabe's gawking eyes toward the rider. His eyes met hers, but only for a blink. She quickly looked away, as if angry, then continued talking to Eagle Claw in their native tongue. Gabe quickly forgot about the elk and focused solely on the young woman, transfixed by her beauty, which seemed even more pronounced than he remembered. His heart instantly began pounding harder in his chest, and he felt his face flush and his palms become wet with sweat.

Her raven-black hair had a healthy shine in the early-morning light and draped lazily over her shoulders. She was lithe and very fit, like a sleek doe, which made her womanly features even more pronounced. Distinctive black lashes batted her light brown almond-shaped eyes when she blinked, and her skin was a creamy olive that begged to be touched. Gabe felt a discourteous stiffness in his groin and forced himself to look away for a moment.

The sharp tone of her words seemed incongruous with the soft, beautiful face and alluring lips that spoke them. Gabe collected himself as best he could and stepped forward, eager to be introduced. But as he neared Eagle Claw, she glanced at him, said something biting in Kootenai, and kicked her horse, leading her small pack string with its blood-stained cargo away.

Gabe's smile quickly faded. "So, is that your sister?"

Eagle Claw and Spotted Doe, stone-faced, ignored his question and watched her ride away toward a lone lodgepole pine on the other side of camp, where she dismounted, tied off her horses, and began unpacking. Eagle Claw's father James emerged from the adjacent lodge and started helping her.

"Yes," replied Eagle Claw at length. "That is Dawn—my sister." His voice was strangely enigmatic, difficult to interpret.

The tension had little effect in quieting his pounding heart. He looked at Spotted Doe, trying to catch her eye, hoping her warm smile would drive away the chilly moment. But she didn't even look up. Instead, she lowered her head, tightened the buffalo shawl around her shoulders, and walked gracefully back to the tipi to begin preparing breakfast.

"What's wrong?" asked Gabe. "Should I go help her unload that meat?"

"*No!*" Eagle Claw said sharply. "She needs no help." He turned and strode toward his tipi without saying another word.

Gabe paused for a moment to watch Dawn and James unpack the elk. Once again, his heart mysteriously pounded harder at the very sight of her until she cast him a rebuking glance that stopped it cold.

"Come on, Gabe," said Eagle Claw as he neared his tipi. "We have a big day."

"Why? Are we going on a hunt?"

"No. Dawn saw them."

"Saw who?"

"The Crooked Branch and his men. She saw them on her way back to the village from her hunt. We will watch for them from up there." Eagle Claw pointed to some cliffs on the side of the mountain at the mouth of the sacred canyon.

After breakfast, they packed their possibles bags with lunch and filled buffalo-bladder canteens with water. Spotted Doe and Little Buck gave Eagle Claw a quick hug before the men snatched up the rifles and stepped outside the tipi.

Gabe glanced toward James's lodge, hoping to see her again, but the smoke-stained tipi appeared still and empty. He felt a tug on his pant leg and looked down. There stood Little Buck, his smiling smudged face staring up at Gabe. The child reached up with both arms, his tiny fingers springing irresistibly from his hands.

"Hold. Hold," he said in his little squeaky voice.

Gabe picked up the grinning bundle of energy and was surprised when the tot gave him a hug before squirming out of his arms and running off, hollering as he ran into the lodge and returning in a flash with his toy bow. He stood next to Spotted Doe with one arm around her leg and looked up at her proudly, earnestly playing the role of the man in camp.

Gabe smiled at Spotted Doe, hoping to hide the sudden wave of emotion that stirred within him and watered his eyes. Little Buck's show of affection toward him had taken him by surprise. He blinked, cleared his throat, and swallowed away the shameful feeling. After all, a man in the cold, hard wilderness couldn't afford to have his stony resolve weakened by tenderness—Branch had done well in pounding that crucial concept into his brain. Perhaps that was why it hit him so hard—the tiny loving embrace in his world so empty of human kindness, and he was taken aback by how easily the child had turned his heart to mush. Spotted Doe's reassuring glance and slightly upturned smile let him know she understood.

He followed behind Eagle Claw, startled by his quick pace and long strides. Passing by the last tipi, Gabe was pleasantly surprised to see Dawn waiting for them on the trail.

"This is my new friend, Gabe Bauman," said Eagle Claw, his tone oddly formal.

She turned her pretty head and looked at him blandly, her face devoid of expression.

"Hello, ma'am," replied Gabe, but she paid him no heed.

She and her brother exchanged whispers in Kootenai, then she stepped aside and took a position on the trail behind them. Higher and higher they climbed until they were well above the camp. Gabe kept feeling a gallant impulse to give her a helping hand or offer to carry the bundle she had draped over her shoulder, but her chilly countenance caused him to refrain.

Eagle Claw paused every so often to allow them to catch their breath, which offered Gabe a chance to catch a few surreptitious glimpses of Dawn. Blowing at wisps of hair that swung errantly in her face, she seemed to purposely avoid eye contact with him except for the occasional steely glare. Yet her every movement seemed to call for his undivided attention.

"Toshkatu!" she said impatiently.

Gabe blinked at her peevish glance and whispered to Eagle Claw. "What's she saying?"

"She said, 'Hurry up.'"

Gabe turned to her, smiled awkwardly, and said, "Oh, I'm sorry."

Impatiently, she flicked her fingers back and forth, palm down, to motion him forward. He nodded with a smile and hurried to catch up with Eagle Claw, energized by the Lilliputian breakthrough—she had spoken to him!

A tree with a healed-over blaze that marked an ancient trail came into view, and just beyond it, Eagle Claw turned onto a narrow trail etched on the side of the mountain. Eagle Claw paused for a moment to explain the plan. If his prediction held true, the trappers would be coming in on an old trail that eventually intersected with the main trail into the sacred canyon. To keep their tracks from being detected, he told Gabe to avoid stepping on the trail, and Eagle Claw took pains to carefully cover any disturbances they made.

Gabe could hear her gentle breathing as Dawn climbed just behind him. He found it nearly impossible to focus on their mission, forgetting about Branch and his men, completely distracted by her bewitching magnetism. Gabe followed Eagle Claw up the steep grade to the flat bench on top of cliffs jutting from the mountainside. There they found a secluded vantage point from which they could monitor the trail, concealed behind a tangle of scrub that grew over the ledge. Dawn took her position on the outside of the threesome, as if to use Eagle Claw to safely shield herself from Gabe. He casually sniffed his armpit, wondering whether she perhaps found him foul-smelling, but he couldn't detect anything out of the ordinary. Quietly, they waited.

The hours slowly rolled by, and Gabe eventually succumbed to the heaviness in his eyelids and the hypnotic Kootenai whisperings of the two siblings. After seeing Dawn and hearing her voice, he couldn't help but dream about her.

"*Psst! Psst!* Wake up!" whispered Eagle Claw as he shook Gabe out of his enchanted slumber. "They're coming!" Gabe rubbed his eyes and looked at the sky—it was well past noon. He heard hooves clattering through loose shale, and he bellied closer to the edge, peering down at the trail from behind the shrubs.

"Get down," Eagle Claw urged as he belly-inched closer to the edge of the rocky outcropping.

Their perch was a safe distance from the trail, but even at that, Gabe recognized the familiar figure leading the pack train. "That's Crooked Bill Branch. I'm sure of it," he whispered. Eagle Claw nodded.

One by one, the other riders came into view. Gabe recognized Choteau as well, but it took him a minute to identify the other two from the Rendezvous.

"There's four of them all right," he whispered.

"*Shhhh!*" Dawn hissed.

It was only then that Gabe realized the trail angled upward, cutting across the mountain just below them, which brought the riders dangerously close to the sound of their voices. Through a gap in the brush that grew over the edge of the cliff, he watched and listened to them carefully.

"Hold up," said Branch softly. The other riders stopped and followed his hawkish eyes up the side of the mountain.

"What's got ya spooked, Branch?" said Johnson.

"I think I heard something." Branch looked up, searching every fold and crevasse of the mountainside until Johnson grew impatient.

"Come on, Branch. Ain't nothin' up there," he grumbled. "I feel naked on the side of this damn mountain."

"Shhh!" whispered Branch. After a few minutes of watching and listening, Branch nudged his horse, and they continued until disappearing around a bend in the trail.

When the unwelcome trappers were well out of sight and earshot, the three wasted no time in clambering down the mountain.

೭ఌ

Eagle Claw wrestled with his thoughts and choice of words. Surely now, the Elders would act in the face of trespassers bent on exploiting their resources. They soon entered the village and were met by James, Singing Bird, and Spotted Doe.

"Well, what did you see?" asked James.

"Just as I thought," Eagle Claw said. "Now, there are four. They will have the entire valley trapped out by the first snow."

People seeing the commotion drifted toward the small gathering as they discussed the problem.

"Listen to my words," Eagle Claw said loud enough for everyone to hear. "Soon, these invaders will be crawling all over our mountains like fleas on a fox." Several younger warriors nodded in agreement, and in a short time, the village was buzzing like agitated bees. Sensing their energy, Eagle Claw argued persuasively for a fight. Arrow Heart motioned for them all to be quiet, but the murmuring continued until he finally stood up and shouted, "Silence!"

Once again, Eagle Claw felt frustration building up inside as the Elders huddled together and mumbled among themselves—more useless discussion and inaction. *Would they continue to do nothing while their territory was stripped bare?*

Finally, Arrow Heart addressed the crowd. "This new report we hear is of great concern to us. The Elders will ask for courageous volunteers from among you to go in and drive out these trespassers. We will wait until the moon is full."

Eagle Claw could not contain his emotions any longer and

impulsively spoke out of turn. "We should go *now!* Why wait until the moon is full? By that time, they will have taken many furs." His outburst again stirred up the young braves.

Once again, they were silenced by Arrow Heart. "The moon will give us light to see our way home if we must travel by night. I know you are eager to confront this threat that has come upon us, but a greater threat faces our village. Our meat supply runs low, and we do not have enough to get us through the coming winter. We must immediately prepare for a hunt. We will need everyone's help for success, and we cannot afford to divide our resources. We hunt first, then we will deal with the trespassers."

"We must attack *now*, and after that, we can all go on our hunt!" Eagle Claw fumed.

"The hunt cannot be delayed. The Elders have chosen to wait for the moon. The ancient trail holds many dangers, and it leads where the Big Man roams. We don't wish to trouble him. Perhaps, as White Cloud said, he will deal with these men in the course of time." Arrow Heart stared directly at Eagle Claw, singling him out from the others. He pointed his finger at him and said boldly, "It has been decided. We will go on our hunt and return when the moon is full."

As the crowd dispersed, some of the younger braves lingered. For the first time, his peers were finally listening to him, which only emboldened Eagle Claw even more. Sensing their indignation and urge to fight, he called them close and unveiled his plan to follow Branch and his men into the basin and bring swift justice. He spoke in the Kootenai tongue to the young warriors, quietly, to keep from being overheard. "We can bring this trouble with the trappers to an end now. We don't have to wait until the moon is full. They might be long gone by then."

But they grew silent, some staring down uncomfortably while others looked over their shoulders, and Eagle Claw could sense their growing reluctance, probably worried the Elders might overhear his mutinous words. Eagle Claw grew frustrated by their sudden lack of courage. Dawn finally spoke up and said, ""Eagle Claw is right. There are only four of them. If we don't deal with this trouble now, we will be outnumbered the next time they come here. I saw a gang of thirty on my hunt three days ago. If we decide to fight, you can count me in. But it will take all of us."

Eagle Claw noticed Crowfoot, his childhood nemesis, standing nearby and listening with his arms folded across this chest. He stepped forward and approached the group. Though he was slightly built and scrawny, he always managed to find a way to get under Eagle Claw's skin. He approached in his usual strident manner and wasted no time in airing his thoughts. His words were hard and sharp, like the tip of a spear.

"What are you doing now, Eagle Claw? You heard the Elders. Now, you try to deceive us with your words? You're barely part of us anyway—always leaving us and wandering off into the mountains alone." Crowfoot turned to the other braves and rebuked them for their rebellious spirit. "If you follow him, it will be your undoing."

Rage at Crowfoot's boldness and castigation swept over Eagle Claw. He wanted to grab him by the neck and slam him to the ground. Somehow, he managed to find the inner strength to control his impulses. To add insult to injury, James had recently taken Crowfoot under his wing, to teach him English and the Christian faith, and now, the brave followed his father around like a devoted disciple. He wasn't sure which was more irritating, Crowfoot's annoying newfound deference to the tribal power structure or his undying loyalty to James.

"You speak boldly when you stand behind your friends, Crowfoot. But I'm no longer a small child you can pelt with sticks and rocks whenever you wish. Are you afraid of these trappers? Or are you fearful because you might have to face the Skookum? Either way, you are a coward. As for me, I don't fear these trappers. And as for the Skookum, that demon killed my brother, and I am not afraid to face it—even if I must face it alone."

"Then face it alone," Crowfoot said. "It didn't kill *my* brother. You braves—did it kill *your* brothers? If not, then you have no fight with it. If you go with Eagle Claw, you go against the Elders, and you will get what you deserve for your rebellion."

Then, Crowfoot turned and spoke directly to Eagle Claw. "The Elders are right. You are needed here, Eagle Claw—we need you for the hunt. And as for childhood pranks, you know I have repented of my sins. I am cleansed of them. Like you, I am also no longer a child, and I now have a duty to my people—we all have a duty. Are these not your people, Eagle Claw? What about your family, Spotted Doe, your son?"

The other men stepped back, anticipating trouble. Eagle Claw stepped forward, uncomfortably close to Crowfoot, and looked down at him. *It would be so easy to drop him like brain-shot rabbit*, Eagle Claw thought, clenching his fists. But he only stood there, tight jawed, leaning forward into Crowfoot's rebuke as if standing against the force of a mighty wind.

Crowfoot met his stare and said, "You know I am right," then turned and walked away, as did the other braves, one by one, until only Gabe and Dawn stood beside him. The words of Crowfoot pierced Eagle Claw's heart like arrows. Although they were spoken harshly and seemed hateful, Eagle Claw saw the truth in them, yet they did little to bring peace and calm to the war that raged within him.

"I'm sorry, my brother," said Dawn as she turned and headed toward her lodge. "We must help with the hunt." Once again, Eagle Claw felt alone among his people. He turned and stormed toward his lodge to prepare for the hunt while Gabe followed silently behind him.

Chapter Twenty-One

Chasm

Choteau brought up the rear of the pack train. The horses and mules strung out ahead of him along the trail were beginning to feel the strain from the rapidly rising elevation. All were huffing deeply when Branch stopped at the familiar steep, cliffy abutment—by far the most treacherous section of the primitive trail into the beaver lakes.

Jones and Johnson stared at the steep tight switchback trail that zigzagged up the imposing cliffs, mumbling apprehensively as the horses struggled to maintain their footing on the trail's shifting shale.

"This is crazy!" barked Johnson. "The horses are done in, and so am I."

"I'm goin' back," said Jones. "This trail's no good—damn beaver pelts ain't worth it."

Choteau had spoken privately with Branch earlier and insisted on riding at the back of the pack train, suspecting the cliffs might be a deal-breaker for the newcomers. Branch agreed, knowing they needed all the firepower they could get, and Choteau had made it clear that if Johnson and Jones bailed, so would he. Still on edge from their last excursion, Choteau was more concerned about what lay beyond the cliffs than the cliffs themselves. When Jones turned his horse to head back down the trail, Choteau removed his rifle from its scabbard and cradled it in his arms with his finger on the trigger.

"You're not going anywhere, Monsieur, except up!"

"The hell I am! I ain't goin' up there!" Jones gave his horse a nudge with his heels but pulled back on the reins when he heard the click from the hammer of Choteau's rifle. "Oh, so that's how it's gonna be, is it?"

"You're damned right!" shouted Choteau.

Branch chimed in and hollered, "You leave now, Jones, and you risk bumpin' into those damned Blackfeet. They won't take kindly to you bein' here—a lone white man. They'll pick you off real easy. And if they don't, the Koots will. This is sacred ground, and they've been known to kill trespassers! Scalp ya first though, of course. Then, they'll tie ya to a stake and start a fire under ya, then dance around, watchin' ya burn—real slow."

Choteau put his finger on the trigger as Jones looked with determination down the trail, his jaw clenched, as if he would either make a dash for it or pull his rifle. "Nobody told me this was sacred Injun ground!" shouted Jones.

"Branch is right, Jones," said Johnson. "Those Indians will kill you for sure. We stand a better chance stayin' together."

"You knew about this, didn't ya, Branch?!" Jones hollered. "Why didn't you tell us about this damn trail before?"

Choteau was always amazed how Branch could wheedle his way into a man's brain and move him like a puppeteer, knowing full well the Kootenai would never burn a man alive. The crafty mountain man quickly changed his gruff tone and became more sincere, more diplomatic. "Guess I didn't figure you'd care. These mountains are full of tough trails, and I've been on worse. Trust me, we make it past this rough spot, and the trail's easy the rest of the way. Besides, the real danger's gonna be behind us—Blackfeet. They're too superstitious to come back in here."

Jones looked back down the trail from where they had come and shook his head, cursing. "Shite! Well, then, let's get going." Choteau relaxed as Jones turned his horse and nudged him toward Johnson. He could sense their trepidation as the two newcomers looked up at the cliffs on the side of the mountain. Finally, Jones blurted, "Sacred ground, my ass! I can see plain as day why them Injuns avoid this place."

They continued up the steep trail until the horses began to struggle even more.

"Give 'em hell, boys," shouted Branch from the front of the pack string. "Let those pack horses go and then hang on—they'll follow. And whatever you do, don't look down!" Branch kicked his horse in the ribs with his heels and hung on tightly to its mane. The horse grunted and strained up the steep switchbacks.

Branch's horse sent shards of broken rock and shale showering over the edge of the steep trail, causing a distant clattering far below on the jagged rocks at the bottom of the cliff. The horse slipped and slid off the trail backward toward the cliff's edge, but it was the strongest of the lot and caught an edge with its back hooves. With muscles straining, it huffed back up to the trail, saving Branch from sliding into the abyss. Finally, with nostrils flared the impressive animal powered to the top of the steep ridge, where Branch hopped off and grabbed the lead rope of the pack horse following behind him.

Choteau wasn't worried about Branch, but he held his breath when Johnson began his climb. He urged his horse ahead, a chestnut mare with a big-boned frame and powerful hindquarters. The animal strained and clawed, slipping precariously close to the edge on the last switchback until her hooves caught hold. Johnson dug his heels into her ribs and yelled, "Come on! Get up there!" And with a surge of adrenaline, the stout mare struggled to the top. Choteau breathed a sigh of relief as Johnson looked down from the bench and hollered down to Jones, "Dismount and climb up on foot. I'll catch your horse!"

But it was too late. Jones was already well into his ascent, and it was much too dangerous now for him to attempt a dismount. Johnson urged him on. "Come on. You can do it!" His horse, which Choteau best described as "wormy," struggled more than the others but was making some headway and had cleared the worst section where Johnson's horse had lost its footing. "That's right. You got it," encouraged Johnson. "Just a few more feet."

Suddenly, the rocks broke loose beneath the horse's back hooves. It stumbled, then struggled to regain its footing. Choteau instinctively nudged his horse ahead to begin the climb. Just then, another rock came loose under a front hoof, and Jones' horse went down, sliding down the steep grade toward the edge of the cliff while Jones tried to break free. He yanked his feet from the stirrups and leaped just as his horse slid over the edge of the cliff and disappeared into the chasm below.

Branch joined Johnson, and both looked over the edge with stunned looks of disbelief. A few seconds later, a loud, bone-crunching thump, then another, and another echoed up from the gorge—then silence.

Jones, meanwhile, was clinging precariously to a small sapling that had somehow taken root just below the edge of the cliff. There, he held on for dear life while dangling over the abyss. Choteau dismounted and climbed up the steep embankment to help, but Johnson was closer and quickly worked his way down to help his partner, shouting, "Hang on! I'm coming!" He approached the edge of the steep cliff, reached down to Jones, and held out his hand. "Grab ahold! I'll pull you up."

Choteau made it to them just as Johnson reached down. He grabbed for him, but just as he caught hold, the roots of the small sapling broke free, and his fingers slipped through Johnson's hand. For a fraction of a moment, it seemed to Choteau that Jones was suspended in the air—wide-eyed and gobsmacked. Johnson grabbed for his hand again, but he was a second too late. Terror and hopelessness were etched on Jones's face as he fell downward, downward, screaming as he disappeared into the shadowy void.

The sound of his body crashing against the rocks echoed back with each bounce until he hit steep shale and clattered down the slope to join his horse in the cavernous belly of the beast.

Then, all was quiet except for the stirring of Choteau's horses where he had left them on the trail. He looked back, and they seemed intuitively apprehensive after seeing one of their kind go over the edge of the cliff.

"Dear God in Heaven!" exclaimed Johnson breathlessly as he looked over the edge of the cliff.

"Son of a bitch!" moaned Choteau as he worked his way back to his horses. "Branch, we're back to only three of us now. I didn't agree to this, *tu connard menteur!*"

Johnson peered into the dark cavernous chasm for any sign of his partner, but the ominous maw seemed to have swallowed him whole. "Jones!" he screamed, but there was no reply.

"Get the hell away from that edge, or you'll be joining him!" screamed Choteau.

Johnson turned and began to clamber up the mountain, but he lost his footing and slid back toward the edge. A protruding rock caught him and stopped his downward momentum, or he, too, would have slid into the void. The near miss renewed his determination, and he struggled up to the trail, where Branch stood passively waiting, without even extending a hand to offer assistance. Choteau wasn't surprised. He shook his head in disgust and contemplated his options.

"You comin', Choteau?" hollered Branch, "or do you just wanna stand there gawkin'?"

Choteau clenched his teeth as waves of fear and anger crashed inside his mind. He grabbed the reins of his horse and paused as he looked at the trail heading back down the drainage. His horse and the pack mule behind it stood erect and nervous, with nostrils flared, as if they were thinking the same seditious thought as Choteau. He teetered on the edge of retreat. It would be easy now to turn his horses and head back down the trail. By the fearful looks in their eyes, they wouldn't need much encouragement to run, and Branch might get off a single hasty shot before he was out of range. Under the circumstances, it was a gamble worth taking. He jerked himself into the saddle, but in the split second before turning his horse, as if Branch could read his mind, the mountain man yelled, "Them Blackfeet will be halfway here by now, Frenchy!"

Choteau paused, growling and cursing under his breath. Killing the Blackfeet horses after the skirmish was a big mistake. Now, they would be more determined than ever to exact revenge.

Ignoring the inner voice screaming at him to run, he dismounted, circled behind the animals, then slapped his horse and pack horse on their rumps to drive them up the trail. He wasn't about to make the same mistake as Jones. He stood back, watching, but they stopped after a few steps, too frightened to continue. He picked up a broken branch, approached them from behind, and brought it down on the first horse's rump. *"Hayah! Aller! Animaux stupides!"* The horse lurched ahead and scrambled up the trail to the top, aided by the lighter load, while the pack horse followed close behind. Choteau himself had no worries about the climb. He was physically fit, and the trail was easy for him to navigate on foot. He scrambled to the top without incident and soon joined the others, unable to hide his contempt.

Johnson appeared exhausted and bent over to catch his breath. "This is more'n I bargained for, Branch. I don't care how many beavers we might catch."

Choteau glared at Branch, awaiting his response, but he appeared ho-hum over Jones's abrupt termination, almost as if his demise were fortuitous.

Calmly, Branch said, "You don't know what you're talking about, Johnson. Just you wait. You'll see when we get there. Besides, we're through the roughest section. Like I said, the rest of this trail is easy."

Johnson peered down into the cavernous ravine, removed his wolfskin hat, and ran his fingers through his hair. He began pacing nervously back and forth. "Yeah. It's always 'easy' with you. But I know better. I wonder what other surprises are in store on this godforsaken trail."

Branch looked at Johnson sideways with an evil glint in his eye and a slight upturned smile, and he winked at Choteau after Johnson turned away. Choteau held his tongue but couldn't contain a disparaging snort and shook his head with loathing.

"What about Jones?" asked Johnson.

"Nobody could survive that fall," Branch replied.

"That man's been my partner for five years, and to think I talked him into coming with me on this trip into hell. Damn it, Branch, he at least deserves a decent burial."

"If you wanna climb down to bury what's left of 'im, have at it," Branch said half-heartedly. "Chances are good you'll die, too."

Choteau was about to offer Johnson his assistance in the matter, just to spite Branch, but he thought better of it. Finding and burying Jones would only slow them down. Only one thing occupied

Choteau's mind—making it to the first camp before sundown so he could gather enough firewood to last the night.

As Branch turned his horse up the trail, Johnson again peered toward the chasm, shaking his head. He massaged his temples as sweat dripped down his forehead, staring glumly, reluctant to remount his horse. "What the hell have I gotten myself into?" he muttered.

Choteau's thoughts were clearly one and the same as Johnson's, but the moment for mutiny had come and gone. When he got a glimpse of Branch's piercing gaze as the tyrant turned to look back at them, Choteau said loudly, "Branch is right about one thing—the trail is much easier from here on out."

Johnson mounted his horse, murmuring profanities under his breath while Choteau shoved his foot in the stirrup and threw his leg over the saddle. Once again, he took his position at the end of the pack string.

"Come on, boys. We got beaver to catch!" barked Branch.

Chapter Twenty-Two

The Beast

Two carcasses lay bloodied and mangled among the jagged rocks. Death odors traveled quickly in the pristine mountain air, and within an hour, a few ravens and jays had picked up the scent and managed to find the distorted piles of flesh. They cawed impatiently from the branches of a few pine trees that had somehow found a foothold, eking out a sparse existence among the nooks above the chasm. More gathered until the trees above the corpses morphed black. The hungriest ones flew down and landed on the rocks, sharpening their beaks for the morbid feast to come. But the warier ravens watched and waited from above to ensure their meal was fully dead before ringing the dinner bell with a loud burst of squawking.

The man's body lay with mouth agape, neck contorted at an odd angle, eyes staring blankly at the birds perched overhead. Drying blood and other fleshly matter had spattered on the jagged rocks where he and the horse had landed. Still, no tidbit was to be wasted, even though the belly of the horse had burst open upon impact and sprayed entrails and stomach contents over the rocks in a radius of twenty feet.

The ravens were innately fearful of the man, so they swooped down and began working on the horse with their sharp beaks.

Wherever there was an open wound, they thrust and stabbed. One wise old bird perched on a shattered leg and pecked out the exposed marrow from the hollow of the protruding bone, while the younger ones chose the juicy entrails for their appetizer.

The ravens tended to follow the pecking order of all scavengers: the dominant birds got first choice, while subordinates had to either feast on less palatable offal or wait their turn in nearby trees, watching for oncoming danger until the dominant birds had satisfied their near-relentless hunger.

But the purple jays had no such rules. They were more agile than the ravens and flitted here and there, picking at any loose flesh they could find while skillfully dodging the ravens' territorial attempts to stab them with their long beaks.

The fearless jays targeted the man's corpse, his staring eyeballs pleading for attention. A jay perched on the forehead and began pecking, pecking, pecking until it had partially removed one of the juicy prizes, which hung on by a stretched ligament. It stabbed furiously, trying to get at the thickly congealed fluid inside.

Suddenly, the ravens began squawking noisily. At the sound of an approaching intruder, the jay abruptly abandoned the left eyeball, which snapped back onto the eye socket upon being released. The other jays stopped their pecking and fluttered to the safety of the pines, watching impatiently for the trespasser.

The sound of rocks being dislodged as something climbed the mountain toward them caused the birds to flutter higher in the trees. It soon appeared, saliva dripping from the corner of its mouth as the big hungry griz gazed for a moment at the feast that lay before it. The animal approached the man's body and sniffed at the partially dislocated eyeball before lapping it up, popping it with powerful jaws, then breathing deeply with satisfaction. It looked over at the mangled horse and then up at the steep cliff. Craning its neck, the beast sniffed the pale, rigored face of the man, then latched onto a leg and began dragging him down the ravine toward its lair, where it could feast undisturbed while the jays and ravens voiced their disapproval.

After the creature had departed with its prize, the ravens returned to the horse and resumed feeding while the jays hopped around where the man had lain dead, pecking at the flakes of dried blood and fragments of flesh left behind.

The bottom of the chasm lay on the side of the mountain—a flat alleyway of jagged rocks guarded on both sides by cliffs. It ran flat for fifty or sixty feet before it dropped into a long avalanche chute that extended to the foot of the mountain. At the bottom of the chute lay a tangled mass of timber and debris deposited by successive avalanches. It was here, under this jumble, that the beast had dug its den—an excavation large enough to feed on prey without competition from pesky wolves, coyotes, or ravens. Dirt and brush piled near the entrance hid the lair from any curious passersby that happened to approach from the downhill side of the mountain. Inside, it was surprisingly spacious, with the tangled mass providing an impenetrable ceiling except for a few small openings where thin rays of sunlight found their way in.

The remnants of previous repasts lay scattered about, including a partially devoured porcupine whose prickly hide had been nudged to the side but still had enough putrid flesh remaining to offer a convenient meal for blowflies that buzzed incessantly. A faint beam of light shone on the well-chewed remains of a mountain goat skull, and the stench of carrion permeated throughout.

Partially obscured by the pile of bones lay a human skull, absent the lower jaw. It had been there long enough for maggots and dermestid larvae to pick it clean. The top of the skull was missing, and sequential puncture marks ringing the jagged edge of the opening indicated that the beast had meticulously opened it with its sharp fangs, then licked out the fatty contents.

Wisps of dust dropped through tiny gaps in the ceiling when its denizen dragged its newest prize toward the entrance. The light from the opening was suddenly blocked by the beast, darkening the lair as it backed in.

The man's body lay face up near the entrance, halfway inside the den, still looking blankly up into the sky with one eye, the other socket hollow and dark, where blowflies buzzed about, seeking a safe place to deposit their eggs.

Once inside, the beast grabbed the corpse by the ankle with powerful jaws. With one swift move, it yanked him inside, and within moments came the sounds of breaking bones and grinding teeth. Meanwhile, outside the den, the purple jays that had followed the beast down the mountain, hoping for leftovers, roosted overhead and squawked in jealous protest.

Chapter Twenty-Three

Choteau's Devil

Choteau kept one eye on the trail and the other on the timber as the three trappers plodded along in silence. He wondered what Branch was thinking, what scheme he was planning in that devious mind of his. Now that Jones was gone, only he and Johnson were left to stand against Branch in the event of a double-cross.

Then there was Johnson, a useful idiot to help skin and stretch beaver, who had doubts about the likelihood of a three-way split of their catch. Would Branch summon Choteau to dispatch the burly trapper? Even though the two had been former partners, it wasn't a big stretch of the imagination for Branch to do the honors. Choteau had seen him do it before to those he deemed no longer useful. Hell, Choteau himself had even helped a time or two.

If so, how would he go about doing it? A surprise bullet to the back of the head? A slit of the throat while he slept? Or any number of unfortunate "accidents?" One thing was certain—if Branch indeed was plotting something, it wouldn't happen until *after* they'd trapped everything out. "Let others do the hard work" was another crafty Bill Branch credo, and he had many.

Among Choteau's morbid musings about Johnson came a slithering epiphany—Branch could just as easily flip the coin, and Choteau could find himself in Branch's gunsights, staring down his rifle barrel and at that devilish grin of his. The thought made him even more uneasy, and he found himself thankful to be riding at the back of the pack train, where he could watch them with a wary eye.

But there were other things to worry about besides Branch's diabolical scheming. The uncertainty of what lay ahead kept him alert, unable to shake the prickly feeling that something was watching them. And though he tried to ignore the premonition, his nightmares from their previous excursion beckoned from the recesses of his mind.

He thought about how he had once scoffed, along with Branch, at the crazy Indian tales they'd heard. But he couldn't deny what his own eyes had seen: the shadowy upright figure darting through an opening in the timber, the blinking eyes that reflected an ominous red in the firelight, and the creature perched high in the trees, watching as they rode. Each sighting and proof of its presence was like the cold blade of a knife, peeling away his jeering bias against the Indian legends as cleanly as a good scalping.

Choteau was no greenhorn. He'd tangled with grizzly bear and mountain lion, and his body bore a few scars to prove it. From experience, he knew there was no tarrying in the charge of a griz; it always came straight and true like a charging buffalo, with no wavering to the right or left, offering a clean head shot to the steady of hand. But this creature had kept itself out of clear rifle shot, staying in the shadows, tossing pebbles and rocks from the security of the darkened forest to bedevil and torment. Then, without warning, it revealed itself, with apparent premeditated purpose, towering above the tangled alder brush to threaten and intimidate with those damned gleaming eyes. But just as quickly, it would fade into the forest and disappear.

What had spooked Choteau the most was its sagacious disposition, as if it were just biding its time, patiently waiting for the perfect moment to ambush. The idea that it might be cunning and deliberate enough to plot against a man kept Choteau awake at night, nervously feeding the fire to stave off the darkness and what might be lurking just beyond the reach of its protective light.

As they ventured deeper and deeper toward the angry beating

heart of the mountain, unsettling sounds and images popped into his head with increasing frequency: the thump of a pebble on his bedroll while he tried to sleep, the rustling of alder brush in the dead of night, the blur of a dark figure, and those glowing red eyes. But it was the incident near the lake that haunted him the most. Choteau remembered it well.

⁓

After several nights of anguish and fear from tossed pebbles, Choteau was determined to keep vigil, with his rifle cradled in his lap as he sat near the fire, convinced his tormentor would show himself long enough for him to get a shot. But the nights yawned without incident, and after several evenings of self-imposed guard duty while Branch and Bauman slept, Choteau succumbed to the heaviness of his eyelids and drifted off to sleep.

Flashes of creeping darklings made for fitful rest, and he woke periodically now and then during the late watches of the night. He wondered if he was going crazy. He had heard about mountain men going loony from the loneliness and solitude of the wilderness, and he thought perhaps the steady diet of beaver meat had unknowingly caused a strange hysteria. Worse yet, Branch had often taunted and ridiculed him about his supposed "devil," saying he'd gotten a piece of bad beaver meat, and a worm was eating his brain.

Branch's sarcasm was especially disturbing when the Frenchman remembered a trapper he had once known who liked his meat rare, and how one day, while relieving himself, he pulled a three-foot worm out of his arse. It just kept coming, and with each tug, the man became more hysterical, slipping further and further into a state of madness. He finally pulled the worm in half, with one half coiled in a heap atop his steaming excrement, like a hellish white snake, and the other half still crawling inside him. In his panic, the trapper was barely able to pull up his pants before running down the trail without his rifle, screaming and mumbling unintelligibly. Choteau never saw him again, and ever since Branch had jeered him about the worm, Choteau could almost feel it crawling inside his head, chewing away slowly, inching forward as it ate at his brain.

When Choteau's disturbing thoughts and dreams permitted him no rest, he would pilfer from Branch's whiskey stash hidden in one of the sacks lying next to the pack saddles, watching and waiting for the reappearance of his devil, stoking the campfire until finally swigging himself to sleep.

But the visitor seemed to stop coming around, and, thankfully, they had continued trapping beaver without incident. After a week, Choteau had all but forgotten about his tormentor, and for the first time since the night he'd seen the glowing red eyes hovering above the alders, he began to feel somewhat at home in the high mountain basin. Each morning, the pristine lake near the camp where they trapped beaver was perfectly still, reflecting the mountains like a giant mirror. The picturesque basin began to fill him with a sense of awe, and each day, he basked in the aura of the mountains, more and more at ease amid the grandeur of the high country.

One morning, while reaching to pull out a submerged trapped beaver, Choteau saw an odd reflection just before he disturbed the lake's mirror-like surface. Quickly, he pulled his hands out of the water and waited while it became still. As the ripples vanished, something strange came into focus in the reflection near the shore. It was the head and shoulders of a massive creature, looking down at him from behind with a furrowed brow and eyes set deep, glaring menacingly.

A surge of adrenaline pumped through Choteau's veins, and he leaped forward into the lake, lunging as far as he could into the deeper water to get away from the creature. He spun around to face it, at the same time flailing backwards, away from the shore.

But to his astonishment and relief, nothing was there. He treaded water for a moment, afraid of returning to land. He scanned up and down the alder-choked shoreline, but it appeared safe. The water was soaking into his leathers, weighing him down and causing him to sink. Reluctantly, he paddled back to the shore, shivering from the cold mountain water, and cautiously, he inched onto dry ground and grabbed his rifle, which he had placed a few feet away on a tussock of grass. Cocking back the hammer, he nervously scoured the brush and trees along the bank for any sign of the creature. He braced himself for a charge—but nothing stirred.

He waited at the edge of a thick alder patch, afraid to continue his search, hoping the thing would move and give him a shot. His knees began to shake, and his teeth chattered from the cold. "I must be going mad!" he said aloud. "What's happening to me? Why am I seeing things?" He looked at his trembling free hand and clenched it tightly, trying to still it. Was it trembling from the life-sapping cold or the fear of what he thought he had seen in that reflection?

Backing toward the shoreline where he had left his gear, Choteau dropped to his knees and bent over, grabbing his head as he imagined the worm eating his brain. He cried out from exhaustion, frustration, and pain from the numbing cold that was rapidly rendering his hands into two useless stumps. He worked at massaging them back to life, but still, he could not stop shivering uncontrollably. He needed to build a fire quickly and grabbed for his possibles bag, which contained his fire-starting materials. Finding his strike-a-light, tinder, and flint, he fumbled and fritzed with paralytic fingers until eventually, he managed to get a fire going, then gathered more wood.

Once he had a fire burning, he stripped down and warmed himself until the shivering stopped. After several hours of wringing and working the wetness from his leathers, they were finally dry enough to wear again. He ate some jerky to regain his strength, then lay near the campfire to rest until his eyelids drooped.

The cry of a loon startled him awake. He jumped up, realizing he'd fallen asleep, then remembered the trapped beaver still in the lake. In the excitement, he'd forgotten to retrieve it. He walked to the water's edge, pulled the animal from the water, and reset the trap. After skinning it, he lifted the skinned, heavy carcass and heaved it behind the brush just off the trail. When he returned to the grassy shoreline, he noticed an indistinct footprint pressed into ground. It was so ridiculously large that he had almost failed to see it.

Something enormous and heavy had stepped there, pushing the waist-high grass into a deep depression. Choteau grabbed his gear, loaded the beaver into his trapper's pack, and crept forward until he found another track, then another. He had followed the tracks several yards when he realized he wasn't imagining things. Someone, or something, had been there.

The tracks went through a depression, where moisture had prevented the grass from growing. There, in the middle of the barren spot, was a clear footprint in the mud. A mixture of bewilderment, elation, and fear swept over Choteau at his discovery. He reached down but hesitated before touching it. *Is this real?* he wondered. *Am I still seeing things?* But as he traced the giant track with his fingers and touched the imprint where the toes had pressed deep into the moist earth, it became apparent that he wasn't delusional, to both his delight and horror. He stepped back, scanned his surroundings, and felt a sense of vindication and reassurance that his cognitive abilities were still intact—the worm would not get him yet.

Choteau's mind was clear now, his paranoia gone, but his fear remained. He strode back to camp with purpose and confidence. First, he would build up the fire, so he could easily see danger. Then, with rifle in hand, he would wait by the fire for Branch and tell him about what he had seen and the large tracks he had found.

He hurried on toward the camp, occasionally scanning the area for any sign of movement. But even when he turned to check behind him, he walked backwards to keep himself always moving toward the safety of the camp. His heart raced as he scanned the scattered willow and alder patches on his backtrail; he couldn't shake the feeling that something was watching him. Occasionally, he'd catch a glimpse of movement just inside the heavy canopy of foliage that ran along the creek. It seemed to be moving silently, parallel to his course, keeping pace with him, and he quickened his steps.

എ

A chill went down Choteau's spine as he recalled the strange encounter, as if his buckskins were still soaked through with the icy water he had lunged into. He thought about the perilous trail ahead, and dread made his heart skip a beat.

Past the deathly cliffs, the trail undulated this way and that like a thin, gray serpent. It hugged close to the narrow stream, sometimes parting with it entirely as it wound up the mountain, until the terrain leveled out, and the rushing creek turned into a bubbling brook. Upward it climbed, through timbered ravines full of giant cedars, along steep rocky abutments, and into a broad valley that eventually met the scabrous spine of the mountains, where the lakes lay calm and flat. The occasional snort from one of the horses was the only thing that distracted Choteau from his icy memories.

As they followed the trail toward the first camp, they entered the giant forest of Indian lore. Enormous trees were evenly spaced in this haunting section of the drainage; here, the creek flattened, and an eerie quiet settled upon them.

The sight of the ominous trees jolted Choteau from his troubling thoughts, and again, he sensed something amiss. His eyes came alive with darting glances as he scanned the forest for the creature his instincts told him was watching them. With nervous fingers, he reached for the stock of his rifle to reassure himself it was still there, ready to be used at a moment's notice.

He looked at Johnson, who also seemed to sense something as they entered the forest. An eerie calm descended on them, unnatural and malevolent. Even the vegetation seemed to abruptly change, and huge bunches of thorny devil's club with leaves the size of horse blankets bristled from the creek in great colonies, reaching out to stab unwelcome passersby. The horses appeared profoundly smaller as they plodded through the trees that rose from the earth like the pillars of the gods and disappeared into the heavens. It was in this spot, as they left the remote valley with their first haul of beaver, that Choteau had seen the creature high in the trees.

He was again brought back to reality from his reminiscing when he noticed Branch's lack of alertness. From the back of the pack train, he could see the man rocking back and forth to the lazy cadence of his horse, completely unaware of the potential danger that lurked just out of eyesight. Choteau had come to dread the darkness as much as the creature itself, for the darkness helped conceal it among the shadows of the forest. It was the blackness of night that gave it the courage to haunt the edge of their camp, where its mysterious movements gave evidence of its presence.

A roiling anger churned as he remembered Branch's cynical derision when Choteau had told him what he'd seen. His scoffing gnawed at Choteau like a coyote chewing on a bloody bone, and as they rode, savage thoughts began creeping into his mind and bounced around in his head. Perhaps he would orchestrate his own double-cross against the nefarious mountain man, take the furs, and get the hell out of the godforsaken canyon once and for all.

Branch suddenly stopped and got off his horse.

"This is one strange trail, Branch," remarked Johnson as Branch tied off his horse in silence.

"Why are we stopping here?" Choteau said. "Let's keep moving!"

Branch looked at the two of them with disdain and replied, "When a man's gotta piss, a man's gotta piss. There ain't no two ways about it. Can't very well do it on a horse, now, can I?"

Choteau stirred impatiently in his saddle while Branch casually stepped off the trail. "Please hurry, monsieur."

"I know I got a long broom handle, Frenchy, but if'n I was to whip it out, like my Hawken from its scabbard, I'd still more'n likely splatter my moccasin with piss on account of the way ol' Fleabag jostles me back and forth when he walks." Branch looked over his shoulder grinning as he relieved himself, proud of his rank attempt at comedy.

Johnson glanced back at Choteau, rolling his eyes, and shaking his head with incredulity at Branch's embellished phallic self-glorification. "Perhaps you should join the circus, monsieur," replied Choteau under his breath.

Johnson laughed out loud at his remark while continuing to survey the forest. "Damn! I've never seen trees like these before. I sure hope all this effort's gonna be worth it."

"What's so damn funny, Johnson? Oh, it's gonna be worth it, all right," Branch remarked with a laugh. "I can guarantee you that. Besides, I kinda like this forest. Kinda peaceful."

Choteau gazed up in the lofty trees and felt goosebumps popping up on his arms. "Branch! We need to move if we're going to make camp by nightfall—or turn around and get the hell out of here."

"All right, damn it! Ya want me to piss myself? The way you two are carryin' on, you're startin' to make *me* nervous."

Just then, Choteau heard a faint noise. "*Shhhh!* Be quiet!" he implored, cocking his head in the direction of the sound.

The men listened carefully, but the forest was quiet and still. Branch tied the laces on his breeches, rolled his eyes derisively, and began to untie the reins of his horse. Then, faintly, off in the distance, a tapping sound echoed in their direction.

"Did you hear that? Did you hear that, Branch?!" exclaimed Choteau as he gestured toward the sound. It was a sound he had heard on their previous excursion—a faint knocking.

Branch shrugged. "Yeah, I heard it. Sounds like that carry a long way in the high country. Probably one of them damned Koots trying to mess with us. Don't worry. They ain't comin' back in here. They're afraid of this place."

The horses cocked their ears toward the noise, shifted restlessly, and flung their heads up and down, as if wanting to get moving. Johnson was fidgeting in his saddle impatiently, but he abruptly turned toward the sound when it echoed again high on the mountain. "There's something damn spooky about this place," he said. "I can feel it in my bones. The horses can sense it, too."

Branch gave a testy sigh. "Let's move out, boys."

They had taken only a few steps when a branch fell from high in the trees and landed next to them with a loud crash. The horses startled and jumped sideways.

"Ain't no wind did that, and I'll be damned if any Injun can climb up there!" Johnson shouted as he hurried to catch up to Branch.

Choteau followed, drawing his gun and peering nervously into the forest canopy. They had gone a few hundred yards farther when Branch noticed a deeply cut blaze mark scratched in the bark of a tree eight feet or so off the ground.

"Hey! Take a look," he said, pointing up at a row of deep cuts, still dripping sap.

"That's one helluva bear that made that!" said Johnson.

Choteau had seen blaze marks before. They were territorial warnings often used by dominant bears to ward off competition and let others know they were trespassing.

Johnson looked up gleefully and shouted, "Why didn't you boys tell me there were griz up here?!"

Branch stopped his horse and wheeled around to face Johnson

with a hawkish glare. "Don't get any big ideas, Johnson. I've seen how ya get when you see bear sign. We didn't come here to hunt no damn bear. It's beavers we're after—and that's it!"

Johnson didn't even flinch. "If I get my sights on a bear like that one, there's not a man alive that'll keep me from takin' 'im down. Not you, nor the Frenchy, nor anyone else!"

Choteau saw the evil gleam in Branch's eyes and watched as his left hand slid down to clutch the butt of his rifle. But the man checked his apparent murderous impulse; he gritted his teeth and turned his horse back up the trail. Choteau had seen that look before and knew Johnson had just come within a hair's breadth of meeting his maker.

But Branch was never one to let an opportunity for an insult pass him by. "You dumb cluck, Johnson," he spat. "We don't have time to waste even thinkin' about chasin' bear. Besides, bear hides don't pay worth a beggar's shite!"

Johnson was quick with his rebuttal. "Ha! I can out-trap the both of ya and still get my bear!"

"Fine. But if you're chasin' bear and not tendin' to traps or skinnin', we'll pull everything we catch in your traps toward *our* share of the haul."

"Fair enough," said Johnson gleefully.

Choteau listened quietly to the banter as the shadows grew long. He thought about the look Branch had given Johnson. It hinted at what Branch might have in mind with respect for Johnson's fate. The thought should have put one of his worries at rest, but instead, it only made him more uneasy.

They had ridden hard all day and the final rays of sun reflected off the mountain peaks on the eastern rim of the basin. Choteau remembered a distinctive gnarly pine rising above the thick patch of alder they were riding through and felt a sense of relief—the campsite was just ahead. Beyond it, the forest opened into a sparsely wooded valley with a nearby meadow for the weary horses to graze. The first series of beaver lakes stretched for a quarter of a mile, followed by another section of heavy timber, then several other bodies of water that held beaver farther up the drainage toward the spine of the mountain.

The picturesque basin ringed with rugged snowcapped peaks was a sharp contrast to the timber-choked drainage through which they had just traveled. Stretching across the north end of the lake nearest the camp lay the biggest beaver dam Choteau had ever laid eyes on. It spanned nearly the entire length of the valley—maybe four hundred yards across, by his reckoning.

"So this it, eh?" Johnson asked with a grin.

When Branch didn't answer, Choteau replied, "Yes. This is our first camp. The other is farther up the valley."

"Damn!" said Johnson, impressed by the surrounding scenery. "Now ain't that a spectacle to behold. I can see why them Kootenai call it sacred ground."

"Quit yer gawkin'," Branch barked, "and let's get these animals unloaded and get some grub cookin'—I'm starved."

Choteau had already dismounted and tied both his horses to nearby trees. "I'll gather wood for a fire," he said.

Johnson looked at him curiously. "Why are you so worried about getting a damned fire goin'? There ain't no shortage of wood here."

His lack of urgency chafed at Choteau. "I'll start the fire! You ... you unload and help Branch."

"Damn, Frenchy, a little testy, ain't ya? Go ahead. Leave me to do the heavy work while you go gather sticks."

Choteau ignored him and soon had gathered an armful. Returning with his load, he arranged the wood in the firepit, then noticed Branch on the other side of the brook near the edge of the alders, peering at the ground as if searching for something. *What dirty trick is he up to now?* Choteau wondered.

His feelings of frustration and resentment toward Johnson grew when he noticed him casually unpacking the horses, talking to them as though they were fast friends. "You got over the cliffs just fine, ol' boy. Here I am, fiddlin' around doin' the work of a greenhorn when I could be tryin' to find a good bear track."

Choteau paused to eavesdrop when the trapper lowered his voice and whispered to the horse, "I feel like I'm bein' used, ol' boy—used like a dirty rag. But that Branch won't be jinxin' us, no sirree."

His words were reassuring in one sense: Choteau was still suspicious the two might collude against him, but Johnson's whispered words made that scenario seem less likely.

"Hey, Choteau," Johnson muttered. "What the hell's he doin' over there?" Johnson's eyes were locked on Branch, who was still bending over as if looking for something.

"Not sure," Choteau said. "Why don't you ask him?" But Johnson just shook his head and mumbled to himself while he continued unpacking.

Choteau returned with another load of firewood and was glad to see Johnson had finally unpacked, hobbled, and turned out the horses. By now, it was getting dark, so he retrieved his possibles bag and commenced building a fire, while Johnson looked on.

Branch returned carrying a pannier containing food items. "If you see a copper powder flask lyin' around here somewhere, it's mine. I dunno how, but I lost it the last time we were in here."

"Sure, I'll keep an eye out for it," replied Johnson, sidling up to him. "What's eatin' Frenchy?" he whispered, but Choteau heard him clear as a bell.

"Ah, hell. He's just a little spooked from the last time we camped here."

"Spooked? What the hell for? I seriously doubt an Injun would go to the trouble of comin' way back in here. Hell, I reckon only a barmy-mouthed trapper, ailin' with beaver fever, would do such a thing." Johnson laughed loudly at his self-deprecating humor. Choteau, however, found his observation to be closer to reality, and did not see it as funny.

"You know, Johnson, we've been here less than an hour, and you're already getting on my nerves," groused Branch. "Why don't you stop gawkin' and help out." Branch grabbed one of the box-panniers, situated it near the fire ring, and sat down, while Johnson appeared miffed.

Weary of the tension, Choteau found solace in gathering more firewood. He grabbed his rifle, slung it over his back, and disappeared into the timber. When he returned with another armful, Johnson seemed in an oddly jovial mood. "Choteau, I gotta hand it to ya! Ya sure know how to gather firewood. And how to build a big fire, too—but does it need to be that big? I guess ya never know when the loup-garou's gonna pop out and grab yuz!"

Choteau ignored the sardonic jab but wondered how he was going to manage to last for a week without murdering the loud-mouthed Johnson. Immediately, he figured Branch must have told Johnson his entire "ghost story"—or, at least, Branch's version of it.

They cooked up a quick batch of grub and, as usual, Branch wasted no time getting to bed. He no sooner had laid his head down when the snoring commenced. Johnson raised his eyebrows at the slugabed and snorted in disgust at the awful racket coming from under his bedroll.

They sat silently until Choteau finally spoke: "I will sleep close to the fire tonight. I suggest you do the same."

Johnson laughed and replied snidely, "Why? You ain't afraid of that griz, are ya? Ol' Ephraim comes around, I guarantee I'll be a wearin' his claws around my neck come mornin'. I'd sure love to get on the track of the one that blazed that tree back yonder."

Choteau felt the hackles on the back of his neck raise at Johnson's arrogance, and he glared at him disdainfully. "I have no fear of bears, monsieur. But there are things in these woods that I do fear."

"Ha! I know a bear blaze when I see one. And the one that marked that tree is around here somewhere. Ya see these?" Johnson flipped and fiddled with the sweeping necklace of grizzly claws draped over his chest. "Yer lookin' at a bear hunter! Branch was right about you, Frenchy—you are a superstitious one."

Choteau held his tongue and felt for the handle of the knife tucked in his belt as dark thoughts about the pompous Johnson raced through his mind.

Branch stirred in his bedroll and hollered, "Would you two get to bed! We got a big day tomorrow. Gotta get all them traps set."

"All right, all right," Johnson said. "I hear ya. I'm gettin' tired anyway."

Choteau made sure he had enough wood within easy reach to keep the fire going until dawn, then stretched out on his bedroll next to the fire and kept watch.

Johnson fell asleep quickly and soon joined Branch, their snoring a cacophony of snorting and wheezing that could wake the dead.

Choteau wondered, as he warmed himself by the fire, how he would maintain his sanity, and chastised himself again for letting Branch talk him into another misadventure. The loud snoring clashed with the soft calls of a forest owl, but as he lay comfortably warm by the fire, the soft hooting was just enough to lull Choteau to sleep.

The snap of a twig jolted him awake. Nervously, he fumbled for his rifle while scanning the heavy alder patch across the creek for the source of the noise. Without taking his eyes off the alders, he pulled the hammer back, then shouldered his rifle, ready to fire at the slightest movement. The minutes ticked by, but the forest was still. He sat back against a log lying next to him and kept vigil, feeding the fire until his eyes grew heavy again, and his body's need for sleep overcame his fear of lurking night creatures.

The tinny sound of clanking dishes startled Choteau from his slumber. He sat up quickly and looked around, clutching his rifle, but it was only Branch rummaging through a sack for a cast-iron skillet to cook some flapjacks for breakfast.

"All you boys do is sleep, sleep, sleep. Ain't you two hungry yet?" Branch's gruff voice was more effective than an alarm bell, and soon, they were up and moving.

After breakfast, they placed all their traps around the lake. They checked them as they returned to camp and were surprised to find a half a dozen beaver already caught in their traps. They dispatched them with rocks and clubs, skinned as many as time would allow, and packed the rest for camp food. Once at camp, they stretched the skins on loops of alder, and later that evening, Johnson had one of the skinned rodents cooking nicely over the fire.

Branch tore a leg off the beaver and took a bite. "Well, boys," he said while chewing a mouthful. "We did it. Got every damned one of them traps out, and we already have beaver!"

For the first time since arriving, Choteau felt hopeful. "If our luck holds out, we're gonna have one hell of a catch tomorrow," he said, smiling. His thoughts drifted once again to the homestead he dreamed about and the cabin he would build.

Johnson was working at peeling the skin off the last beaver. "Gotta hand it to ya, Branch—you were right. I ain't never seen more beaver lodges in all my time in the Rockies, and I been all over this country." He lifted the giant pelt with his bloodied hands and stretched it out to get an idea its full size. "Hell, I ain't never seen a pelt like this, either. It's bigger'n a jumbo!"

"That's one helluva skinnin' job, Johnson," said Branch. "Trust me, you'll have more just like that one before we're done."

An unfamiliar piercing noise shattered the calm. Choteau was savvy to strange sounds in the forest: the thud of a pinecone dropped from the treetop by a squirrel or the crash of a falling tree in a windstorm. But this sound was altogether different. It was a strange animal cry—and much too close for comfort.

"What the hell was that?!" blurted Johnson.

Choteau's excitement over the beaver catch was short-lived, and he snatched up his rifle as fear once again gripped him. He glared at Branch, wanting to shout, "I told you so!" But he remained silent.

Then came a loud *whack!* that echoed across the basin, only this time, the sound came from farther to the left. "Now there are two!" barked Choteau. His heart raced as he recalled their previous expedition—the tormenting had returned. His heart began to race, and he could feel himself grow tense.

"What in tarnation's goin' on here?" shouted Johnson, squinting hard into the darkness, trying to catch a glimpse of whatever it was that deviled them.

"Just like before," said Choteau with a slight quiver in his voice.

Johnson grabbed his rifle and got behind a tree. "Who could have followed us?"

"Nothing followed us," said Choteau. "There's something living in these woods. There's something wild out there that's been watching us. And it's not a bear!"

Johnson turned to him, bewildered. "Well, I've got a little present for whatever it is." He shouldered his rifle and prepared to shoot.

Whack! This time the sound was within rifle range.

"Hey! You dirty son of a bitch! Step out, ya coward, and I'll fill ya full of lead!" Johnson took aim in the general direction of the sound and fired into the darkness. A fiery plume burst from his rifle and lit the surrounding area. Then, all went silent.

"Get another one ready," Branch told him. "There could be more'n one of 'em out there."

Johnson reloaded his rifle to prepare for another shot in the event of an attack.

"Gabe, is that you?!" hollered Branch. "If it's you, Bauman, I'm gonna put a hole through ya with this here Hawken of mine, you jealous bastard!"

Choteau listened carefully, but the only sounds came from his own nervous breathing. He hadn't thought about Bauman. Aside from the Kootenai, Gabe was the only one who knew how to get to the beaver dams, and he had certainly seemed angry enough to do so after Branch took his Hawken. But the youth wasn't a killer and didn't seem cunning enough to seek revenge. They waited for a reply, but nothing stirred, the darkness suddenly seemed darker, and the picturesque basin grew foreboding. Choteau couldn't seem to control the quaking in his voice as he blurted, "It's ... it's the loup-garou, the Wild Man, the Skookum! Just as the Indians said!"

"Quiet, Frenchy," Branch growled as he scanned the surrounding area. "It's gotta either be them trappers from the Rendezvous, the Koots, or that twirp Bauman and his Injun friend."

"I can deal with them trappers an' Koots, but I don't know about no Skookum," said Johnson. "That's the craziest talk I ever heard."

"You will eat those words, my friend, I promise you that. You will see," said Choteau. Johnson's puffed-chested bravado and square stance made it seem he was ready to tackle any beast of the forest—but Choteau could see the fear in his eyes.

"It's gotta be those damned Injuns trying to scare us outta here. Well, let me tell ya, boys—I don't scare so easy!" Johnson's boasted, then laughed nervously.

They waited and waited for a response and a possible charge, but it never came. Finally, after the minutes stretched into an hour, they lowered their rifles and eased from their hiding places. It didn't take Choteau much convincing to get Johnson to help him gather more wood. After they built up the fire, he and Johnson kept watch until morning.

Chapter Twenty-Four

Strange Track

Deep in the sacred Kootenai basin, the animals began to stir with the approaching dawn. A herd of elk that had silently drifted into the meadow to feed during the night were now nibbling their way back to their daytime, bedding areas on the timbered mountainside. A beaver slapped its tail on the water at the far end of the lake to protest the presence of a wolf dining on one of the skinned beaver carcasses that had been left near the shore.

Johnson groaned and stretched before coming to his senses, then threw off his bedroll and looked around for danger. He sighed with relief to see Choteau dutifully posting guard, sitting next to the fire with his rifle resting in his lap. After four days of hard trapping, he was sick of taking turns keeping vigil but nonetheless glad to have the superstitious Frenchman in camp. Fortunately, whatever it was that tormented them on their first night had left them in peace.

"You boys ready to catch more fur?" mumbled Branch from inside his bedroll.

"Ready? Hell!" replied Johnson. "I'm fit as a mountain mule and ready to skin more jumbos. With all the beaver we've caught, I might even go find me a bear."

Branch yawned and threw off his bedroll, got up, and staggered toward the coffee Choteau had made. "We need to check for Injun sign before we leave."

"Already done," Choteau said. "I backtracked on the trail for a mile. No tracks, and the horses are fine."

"Glad to hear that," said Branch. "Grab some jerky and hard tack, and let's check them traps. Johnson, you take the west side of the lake."

"I know the routine, Branch. You don't have to tell me every damned day," he replied, perturbed at Branch's penchant for giving orders, even when unnecessary.

Johnson looked out toward the peaceful lake. Except for the ripple made by a swimming beaver, it lay flat and mirror-like. They marched from camp and split at the lakeshore—Choteau and Branch veering left, Johnson right. As he walked along the lake, Johnson scanned the terrain for any sign of Indians and studied the ground carefully for tracks, but he saw only those of a lone wolf that had trotted through during the night. Soon, he found the well-used game trail winding around the lake and followed it.

He had walked several hundred yards when in the distance echoed the celebratory whoops of Bill Branch. "*Yeehaw! We got more jumbos!*" Johnson turned to see Branch and Choteau standing atop a beaver lodge holding up four huge beavers.

"Jumbos. Humph! I'll show you a jumbo, you crooked son of a bitch," muttered Johnson. "I find the bear that made that blaze back on the trail, and you'll see a *real* jumbo."

Johnson continued along the rim of the lake toward a series of traps he had moved to a new location the day before. The faint game trail undulated down to lake level, where muddy bogs made it easier for an animal to leave a track. He approached one of these narrow bogs, took two quick steps, and leaped across to drier ground.

Midway through his jump, on the edge of the bog, an unusual imprint caught his eye. He took a few steps toward the traps, then abruptly stopped, stood straight up, and turned around. He was used to seeing animal tracks, but this one demanded closer inspection. It didn't take long to locate it—the enormous track was nearly twenty inches long. Exuberance and trepidation clashed as he examined the track, thinking surely it had been made by the king of bears. The back half of the track was pressed into the mud, and the front part had caught a grassy tussock, which was embedded several inches in the soft soil. Johnson figured it had to have been made by the same bear that made the blaze mark along the trail they'd ridden past the day before. But a griz that made a track this size could cause a lot of problems: destroy a camp, tear up pelts, or devour all the camp food; not to mention kill a man outright.

The track was freshly made, and the beast had to be nearby, perhaps drawn by the smell of beaver carcasses. He felt the impulse to follow it but hesitated—the other two would be furious. Perhaps, if he got lucky and was patient, he might be able to eventually shoot the bruin right in camp. But he'd probably need backup firepower at such close range—a bear that size would require a lot of killing.

The more he studied the track, the more curious he became. Experience had told him a bear would sometimes step with its back foot into the track made by the front paw, making it appear as a single enormous print.

But this track didn't seem to fit that the standard scenario. Bears generally walked on all fours, and the tracks were usually closer together and staggered wide. Why weren't there more footprints? It was as if the bear had meticulously jumped across the bog on one leg, and a big boar griz would never bother with that—it would just plow straight through.

Johnson knelt and pulled the grass from the tussock that had been pressed into the soil, then stood up, perplexed. A griz distinguished itself by leaving telltale marks with its six-inch claws well ahead of its toe tracks, but this imprint bore no such impressions. He stroked his beard, and as he thought hard, the pesky notion of Choteau's devil whispered in his ear, dashed across his mind, and vanished. *Not even a devil could make a track that large, and certainly not a man,* he thought. *It had to be a bear.*

He fought his way through the dense cover toward the line of beaver lodges that hugged the west side of the lake. But thoughts of the behemoth track tugged at his subconscious, veering him, step by step, off his intended course. Soon, he was fighting through a tangled patch of alder brush that was blocking his way, heading toward a ridge overlooking the basin. There, he could gain a strategic vantage point and perchance spot the bruin that had made the track. It was slow going, but eventually, he won the battle against the stubborn tangle and emerged atop the ridge, where he had a commanding view of the lake and the surrounding area.

On the water, he could see the first of a series of beaver lodges, where the traps had been set the previous day, and his two comrades standing on one of the lodges on the opposite side of the lake, checking traps. He turned and faced the opposite ridge to the southwest, where lay another long stretch of alders extending from the base of the mountain to the lakeshore below. It was the perfect place for a big bear to fatten up on huckleberries unmolested. Johnson paused, watching hopefully for any sign of the beast, but his eager eyes failed to conjure anything moving among the mosaic of greenery.

Begrudgingly, he turned to make his way to the beaver lodge when he noticed something out of place in his peripheral vision and stopped abruptly. His eyes darted ravenously and somehow caught a glimpse of a distinct dark patch amid the wide swath of foliage cascading toward the lake.

Johnson backed up and stared downhill for a moment. It was perhaps only fifty yards away, and it wasn't moving—maybe a dead stump peeking through the green? A hunk of black rock chipped from one of the granite teeth high above? Craning his head to the right, then the left, it was difficult to identify the object amid the tangle of vegetation. Suddenly, the dark patch disappeared and reappeared in the gaps between the alders. Whatever it was, it was now moving, and if it was moving, it was surely alive. He tightened his grip on his rifle, as if to remind himself that his trusty bear killer was still in his grasp.

His eyes had never lied to him in the light of day, and they now clearly told him an animal was present in the shallow ravine below him, well within his rifle's killing power. It was dark, like a bear, and within the general proximity of the giant track he'd found. That was all the evidence he needed, and his heart began thumping with lustful anticipation. He crouched silently, not taking his eyes off the brown patch, and pulled back the hammer of his rifle until it clicked into place. The animal must have heard the noise because the dark splotch suddenly stopped moving and remained perfectly still.

$\backsim$

The sharp click caused the big Gray to freeze. Looking up through the tangle of brush, devil's club, and alder, he could see a man-beast holding a fire-stick. The Younger turned his head slightly and eyed the Gray, who held up an open hand, signaling for him to remain still.

The Gray saw the man-beast peering intently as he slowly pointed the fire-stick at them. Sensing danger, he flicked his fingers at the Younger, who immediately turned to run, but was struck by something and fell. At the same time, a loud blast made the Gray's ears ring. The Gray stood for a moment, confused when the Younger cried out with a deep, guttural groan. Just as he reached down to help him, the Younger got to his feet, and again tried to run. The Gray followed close behind, but the dense alders grabbed at the Younger's knees and slowed him. The Gray decided to cut in front of him, breaking through the brambles like a giant buffalo, snapping any branches that barred their exit as if they were dried kindling. He moved quickly, but the Younger lagged behind, and after they had gone some distance, he finally stopped altogether. The Gray turned to check on him to find him cupping his hand over his side, with blood oozing through his fingers. The Younger was staring at his hand now covered with blood. His legs were wobbly, like vines that climbed the forest trees, with no strength or stiffness to them. Just before he collapsed, the Gray grabbed him under his shoulder, pulled him upright, and they continued their escape. The Gray knew where to take him: a safe place where he could rest, higher up the mountain. It didn't take long for them to cover the distance.

The opening of the cave wasn't wide enough for the two of them walking abreast, so the Gray wrapped his arms around the Younger's chest and backed into the cave. Once inside, he gently placed the Younger on a thick bedding of pine needles closer to the back of the main cave chamber. The Younger groaned from the pain and curled up in a ball, clutching his side, blood still oozing through his fingers as he clutched the wound. Gently, the Gray patted his son's shoulder, making reassuring coos and clicking sounds. The Younger lay his head back and grimaced, once again cupping his hand over the wound.

The Gray left the cave and, after a short time, returned with two handfuls of plants he had gathered. He dropped them, squatted down, and mashed them into a moist pulp between two rocks.

With gentle fingers, the Gray moved the Younger's hand and placed the poultice he had made onto the wound, stopping the blood flow. When the Gray was younger and suffered an injury, his mother had used the mixture to help the healing process and stop the red juice flowing from his skin.

∽

Suddenly, Johnson heard his name ringing through the stillness of the basin.

"*Johnsaaan!*" Branch was hollering at the top of his lungs. His booming voice echoed across the lake and bounced off the surrounding mountainsides eerily: "*Johnsaaan!* ... *Johnsaaan* ... *Johnsaaan* ..."

Johnson finished reloading his rifle and looked down at his shaking hands. "I hear ya, Branch," he muttered, his voice trembling.

For the first time, his eyes had betrayed him and had told him a lie: "Had to be that bear. Had to be!" Thoughts of what he'd seen flashed again and again—*something* had been running through the opening, something that didn't run like a bear, something that ran upright, like a man. "It was surely that goddamned bear!" he said out loud, as if to rebuke the inner voice that was telling him otherwise. And then, he damned his eyes—he damned them straight to hell and set out for the bear.

Stiffening his spine, he crept down through the brush to where the bear had been standing when he took the shot. He soon found a drop of blood on an alder leaf and laughed a crazed laugh as he rubbed the red smear between his shaking thumb and finger. "Ain't no demon! I knew I hit him! I got you, you big bastard. You're mine, now."

He had taken a few more paces along the escape route when a horrific stench enveloped him. "Damn! What's that ungodly smell?" he said aloud.

Again, from across the lake came the faint hollering of Branch and the resounding echoes. *"Johnsaaan!... Johnsaaan ... Johnsaaan ..."*

Johnson reluctantly clambered back to the top of the ridge and shouted back to Branch, *"Bear!"*

A few seconds later, Branch yelled, *"Bullshite!... Bullshite... Bullshite ..."*

"All right, all right. I'll check the damned traps," Johnson muttered. "I gotta let him stiffen up anyways."

He marked the location of the blood trail and reluctantly made his way to the first beaver lodge, where he pulled on the chain of the trap with all his might. After considerable effort, he managed to drag an enormous dead beaver onto the lodge.

"Damn!" he exclaimed as he looked over the giant rodent. "He's purt-near bear sized." He pulled up the other trap, which also held a huge beaver. "I think this un's half griz!" he shouted.

From across the lake, Branch raised his hand and waved. Johnson felt relieved at his response. The catch seemed to satisfy the roguish trapper that Johnson was sufficiently back on task. Johnson reset the traps, dragged the two beaver onto the shore, and quickly skinned them. He continued along the lake checking the other traps, which also held beaver. Johnson was a master skinner, but in his eagerness to get back on the blood trail of the bear he shot, he performed the gruesome task even quicker, casting the skinned carcasses aside and throwing the skins in his pack.

After checking all the traps and skinning all the beaver, he tied together the pelts he couldn't fit in his pack and lugged them back to where he'd found the blood, dropping them all in a heap. "Well," he said to himself with satisfaction, "now it's time to do me some trackin'."

He fought his way back up the ravine and found where he'd marked the blood trail. Looking closely, he found a drop here, a fleck there—a sketchy blood trail for such a big animal. However, it wasn't hard to follow the escape route from the debris kicked up and the trail of broken branches.

Johnson was puzzled about the lack of blood. He even got down on his hands and knees and scoured the ground beneath the vegetation but found the tracking to be even more difficult. When at last he stood and turned around, he spotted something on the wide leaves of the thorny devil's club that grew just below eye level—a large splash of blood. Even more puzzled, he took a few steps and found some yet higher on the vegetation.

"What the hell?" he murmured.

His trek up the trail revealed more and more blood at eye level. He moved cautiously, the brief glimpse of the creature as it made its escape popping in and out of his mind like an annoying, chattering squirrel. For the first time as a bear hunter, a wave of fear crept into his bones, and a perverse thought came to him—perhaps his eyes had been telling the truth.

But even while he perished the thought, his thumb instinctively pulled back the hammer on his rifle until it clicked into place. It was a comforting sound that stroked his troubled mind, one that always put him at ease when following up on a wounded griz.

The blood trail continued up the mountain through stands of alder snapped like matchsticks. His pace slowed, and his courage drained like a throat-cut deer. He paused and considered retreating, but when he thought of the blaze mark and a new row of giant bear claws to add to his collection, he pressed on, for bragging rights surely lay on the trail just ahead.

As he climbed higher and higher, the brush gradually gave way to pines, then to a scree slope that climbed to the base of the mountain. Johnson stopped and looked up at the mountain's sharp peaks jutting skyward like the teeth of a giant primordial dragon, hoping the wounded bear didn't have the strength to climb. He followed the blood trail across the scree slope to a rocky face, where a wide slit in the mountain led to a cave. Johnson approached with caution. Beads of sweat coalesced on his brow and dripped from his nose as he neared the entrance, his finger still pressing against the trigger of his rifle, his breaths short and trembling.

Then, he noticed a smear of blood at the entrance. Nervously, he stepped into the narrow passageway leading into the cavern. Without warning, from inside the cave came a deep, guttural scream that seemed to shake the granite walls of the entrance: *"Yeeeaaaaaaaaaa!"*

Johnson stumbled and tripped, falling backwards to the ground.

He scooted back on the sharp shale with his rifle pointed into the darkness of the cavern, oblivious to the sharp edges that scraped his legs. Another primal cry sent shivers down his spine, and he wriggled out of the entrance and scrambled to his feet. He backed away, trembling, still pointing his rifle at the cave opening until he had retreated a safe distance.

Thankfully, the beast hadn't charged, but it was certainly holed up in that cave. The sound was like no bear he'd ever heard, but he damned the thought—there was the blaze mark, the dark patch of fur. It was a griz, and that was all there was to it. Anything else was lunacy, and Johnson wasn't about to go down the crazed madcap path of André Choteau.

Johnson understood the death of things more than he understood the life of things, and the blood trail told him death was near—for a beast only has so much blood to bleed. The wound he'd made simply needed a bit more time to do its work. Patience. He would wait and bide his time while the beast bled and the bullet wound festered, leading it to a slow but sure death. The worst-case scenario would be that it would die during the night and could be easily retrieved in the morning—but he wanted the claws, and he wanted them now. Johnson could almost see the necklace of six-inchers draped around his neck.

Then, he thought about Branch and Choteau—backup firepower! In the exhilarating chaos of the hunt, it hadn't occurred to him that they might want to join him. With the day still young, maybe he could persuade them to help him finish off the beast now instead of waiting until the next morning.

As he retraced his steps, he tried to avert his eyes from the mysterious blood splotches marked impossibly high on the brush. He pacified himself with thoughts of the claws and the necklace and was pleased with his new plan.

He finally arrived at the lakeshore where he had left his pack and the bundle of beaver skins. Johnson threw them over his shoulder and climbed to the place where he had taken the shot, then retraced the sequence of events. He paused for a moment and stared at the opening the creature had passed through. It wasn't such a hard thing to do—to blink away what his damned lying eyes had seen. Like magic, in an instant, the leggy mass had become a bear. Yes, it surely was a bear. Johnson turned and lugged his pelts toward the camp, feeling very satisfied with himself.

Chapter Twenty-Five

Blackfeet Posse

T*wo Kills rode hard and pushed his horse to the* point of exhaustion after the surprise ambush on the trail. After days of riding, he finally stopped and dismounted on a high bench near Marias Pass to watch his backtrail, hoping some of his fellow men had survived. But he waited in vain. After half a day's rest, he finally mounted his buffalo runner and continued toward home.

He arrived at the Blackfeet village just as the sun dipped behind the mountains. Soon, the wailing moans of grieving mothers and wives drifted across the dusky hills and valleys like the icy winds that sweep across the northern plains in the dead of winter. By the next day, he had organized a posse of determined men to hunt down the murderers.

Two Kills' only thought was for revenge. He and nearly a dozen other Blackfeet warriors rode quietly and with single-minded purpose, their faces painted for war. The only thing that would quench their rage was the scalps of the trappers who had killed their brothers, and they were determined to annihilate the men or die trying.

The leader of the posse was Bloody Hand, a name earned from the many scalps he had taken. His younger brother was one of the men slaughtered during Crooked Branch's ambush, so he had a score to settle.

Two Kills rode in a daze, reliving over and over the two minutes of chaos until he lost track of time and orientation. A stirring on the forest floor up ahead jolted him to his senses. Squawking ravens had marked the scene of the battle, picking away at the maelstrom of exposed flesh, and when they flew away in a fluttering black mass, what remained was more than the hardened braves could stomach.

Two Kills found a quiet spot, sat, and cut off a section of his hair before singing the doleful death song, remembering his fellow braves—and the men who killed them. Though their faces were unfamiliar, they were firmly etched in his brain. He recognized one that he had seen previously at a spring Rendezvous—the man they called Crooked Branch.

They took the time to pay homage to the fallen men, and the next morning, they took up the trail. Not long after striking out, Bloody Hand motioned for them to stop and summoned Two Kills, who was gifted in the art of reading sign.

The brave swung his leg over the withers of his black-and-white paint mustang and nimbly jumped off. His horse stood stock-still as he walked up the trail to study the tracks. Fortunately, there had been little traffic on the trail to cover their tracks since the ambush. "It is them," he said in the Blackfeet tongue. "The track is still good. We will find them."

Bloody Hand kicked his horse ahead and commanded, "Let's go!" The other warriors tucked in behind and followed him down the trail. The tracks were distinct and easy to read, and Two Kills felt confident they would find the murderers and have their revenge.

Four more days of hard riding brought them all the way to the trail above the Kootenai village. There, they stopped and watched from a rocky point above the camp to ascertain that none of the trappers were mingling among the villagers. They had been watching for nearly an hour and had spotted one white man, and though he could not forget the faces of the men who had attacked and slaughtered his brothers, Two Kills couldn't be certain the man was one of them—he had to get closer. The skilled brave understood the Kootenai tongue, so Bloody Hand sent him in to spy on them and determine his identity. Upon Two Kills' signal, they would make their move on the unsuspecting Kootenai village.

Using the timber for cover, Two Kills circled the encampment and crept close to the men fishing from the platforms near the river where he had last seen the white man. Sure enough, he was still there, along with a half dozen braves scattered about, using spears and nets to catch fish below the waterfalls.

It wasn't hard to recognize the Kootenai man teaching the man how to spear fish—he was the White Warrior. In addition, Two Kills felt immediate disappointment that the white man wasn't among the attackers either, fairly certain that he was the one who had so readily handed over the tobacco when Two Kills and his men had surrounded them on the trail. But he had to be sure.

As he studied the white man, his attention was diverted by a young woman who had joined them. She carried a long trident and commenced spearing fish with amazing skill. Two Kills soon found himself thoroughly distracted by her—his hatred and mission blurred by her alluring features and figure. He studied her and listened carefully, surprised they were speaking English.

"You and your friend did very well on the hunt. I was surprised," the attractive young woman said. "I'm worried though about James and the other braves. They should have returned by now."

The White Warrior answered her: "Perhaps they didn't do as well and need more time to find game. If they don't return soon, you can join Gabe and me to go look for them. So, you finally decided to help us fish, eh?"

"Only to show you how to *properly* do it."

Two Kills was amused by her spunk and struggled to contain a laugh. They seemed to be involved in a contest with the other braves, for one shouted, "It's not fair. You have three to our two!"

The White Warrior answered, "What's the matter, Crowfoot? Afraid to be bested by a woman?"

She immediately speared several good-sized fish, which she pulled in, hand over hand, and tossed behind her while the men watched. The fish flopped and thrashed about precariously near the edge of the platform.

"Okay, fishwoman, so you know how to spear a fish. Do you know how to club one over the head?" said the White Warrior. But she only smiled contemptuously and kept spearing.

Suddenly, one of the men on the other platform cried out and pointed into the water, yelling, "Sturgeon!" Everyone dropped their spears, rushed to the edge of the platform and began chanting, "Eagle Claw! Eagle Claw! Eagle Claw!"

The White Warrior turned to his white friend and said, "Keep clubbing the fish, so they won't flop back into the river."

The woman stopped spearing, then folded her arms and said, "Be careful!" as the White Warrior removed his leather shirt and tossed it aside. He grabbed the end of the rope coiled at the edge of the platform and, without blinking, dove headlong into the swirling waters.

Two Kills watched, bemused, as the seconds turned into minutes. Just when a couple of men seemed poised to jump in after him, a huge, odd-looking fish leaped out of the water, with the White Warrior clinging to its back. It was lined with large, bony scales, and its length was over twice that of the brave, who stabbed it hard as the fish leaped, its blood staining the foaming waters red. The man and the fish submerged, then resurfaced, and the brave quickly tied the rope around its tail. Two other men pulled hard on the rope, and soon, others joined in as the White Warrior swam to the bank with his knife clenched in his teeth.

Once ashore, he sheathed his knife and grabbed the rope to help the others pull the enormous fish up the bank. Two Kills stared, his mouth agape, as half a dozen Kootenai men carried the fish up to the women amid raucous laughter and smiles. The White Warrior walked close behind the procession as youngsters gathered round him, cheering their hero.

The white trapper, meanwhile, seemed content to watch from the platform with the pretty Kootenai woman, who only said, "That's my brother!" and continued fishing.

She skewered another and tossed it on the deck behind her. He tried to pick up the flopping fish, but it slipped from his hands and landed near her feet. Just as she lifted her foot to drive the spear down on another one, the fish on the deck flopped again before he could grab it, and she stepped on its slimy body.

In an instant, her feet flew out from underneath her. She landed hard, hitting her head on the platform with a loud crack, her legs and hips dangling precariously over the edge of the platform. She'd been knocked out cold by the fall. The white man lunged for her hand but was a second too late, and she slid off the edge and into the churning water below.

Without thinking, Two Kills sprang to his feet to help, hitting his head on one of the branches of the tree he'd hunkered under, which stopped him short. He dropped to his knees and rubbed his head vigorously. When he again looked through the branches of the tree, the trapper was diving in after her.

They disappeared under the water, parting a large school of fish that came together again after they vanished. Soon, the White Warrior returned and saw the others yelling and pointing to the water. He sprinted, jumped off the platform, and plunged into the froth below.

It seemed like an hour, but it was less than a minute when the young trapper broke the surface of the water farther downstream. He swam to the bank, dragging the unconscious woman behind him by her long hair. He reached the steep bank where he scooped her up, draped her over his shoulder, and carefully climbed out on the rocks. Her wet leather breeches drawn tight against her skin revealed a perfectly formed rump perched atop his shoulder, and her leather shirt fell in a wrinkled mass as her arms dangled loosely behind the trapper. Two Kills' eyes grew wide as the edge of her well-formed breast peeked around her lithe frame.

The white man, who seemed pleased with his prize, was hauling her up out of the rocks to flat ground when suddenly she came to life, coughing up water. She adjusted her leather shirt to cover herself and within seconds she was thrashing and hitting and screaming, "Put me down!"

There was no hesitation. He unceremoniously plopped her onto the ground. Even from a distance, Two Kills could see the anger on her face when she scooted back, as if a bear or puma had grabbed her.

"Sorry, ma'am," the white man replied awkwardly. She sat for a moment looking up at him but said nothing. Then, still coughing, she abruptly got up and stumbled away, wringing the water from her hair. As she left, the white man reached toward her, fumbling for words. "I—I'm happy to save your life, ma'am." She did not reply.

The other young braves who had been fishing had already rushed to the river's edge where the White Warrior had just resurfaced. With a look of concern, he hollered, "Did you get her?"

"Yes, she's all right!" shouted the white trapper, panting. "Very much ... alive." Two Kills wasn't sure if his hesitation was due to his breathlessness or perhaps her feisty reaction to his rescue.

Then the one they called Crowfoot reached out to help the White Warrior from the river. But he lurched back into the icy water, as if he preferred to remain there rather than touching the hand of Crowfoot. He treaded water, glaring at Crowfoot until his would-be rescuer shook his head and walked away. A different man then helped him out of the water.

"These Kootenai are a strange people," whispered Two Kills.

Entertained by the hubbub, he had forgotten all about signaling his Blackfeet men. Suddenly, his warriors appeared—seemingly from nowhere—catching the Kootenai unawares and sending them scrambling for weapons. Two Kills observed covertly as the White Warrior and the white man snuck into the timber and circled toward his Blackfeet comrades, no doubt trying to get to their weapons and engage in battle. The two stopped and watched from behind the cover of a small patch of pines. Two Kills crept in behind them and waited. As he did, he saw his leader Bloody Hand come into view, nudging his horse forward while the well-armed Blackfeet warriors were poised, ready to fire at a moment's notice.

∽

Eagle Claw motioned to Gabe to lie prone, and they hid and watched as the situation unfolded. The Blackfeet had come upon them quickly and had probably been watching and studying them. As luck would have it, Eagle Claw had left his weapons in his lodge, and he had no clear path to retrieve them without attracting possible gunfire.

"What do they want?" asked Gabe.

"Shhh. Listen."

He nodded toward Arrow Heart, who had heard the commotion and was running toward the Blackfeet warriors with his rifle. Arrow Heart motioned for the braves, armed with hatchets and bows, to lower their weapons and stand back. He placed his rifle on the ground by his feet to show he was no threat, then used sign language to inquire, "Why do you come here painted for war? We have no quarrel with the Blackfeet."

Bloody Hand replied in Blackfeet with an imperious tone, "I am Bloody Hand, leader of the Blackfeet warriors. Are you the chief who leads this tribe of women and children?"

Arrow Heart did not speak Blackfeet, but Singing Bird was nearby, and she understood the warrior clearly. "Chief White Cloud leads us," she said. "I will summon him." She motioned for a boy to run and get White Cloud. In short order, the wise old Elder hobbled out of his lodge to join Arrow Heart.

Bloody Hand nudged his horse forward with a tap of his heels. He looked down at White Cloud and spoke with boldness. "Chief White Cloud, speak the truth."

Singing Bird translated and White Cloud answered, "Yes. Yes. I will speak the truth."

"I am Bloody Hand of the Blackfeet tribe. We come seeking four white men who ambushed and killed our warriors. Their trail leads here. Turn them over to us now, and we will spare your village."

"What did he say?" asked White Cloud. Singing Bird repeated the message in the Kootenai language, and he said, "The men you seek are not here." He pointed up the mountain. "They passed through to the sacred lands to trap beaver."

"And you let them trap the beaver on your sacred grounds?" Bloody Hand looked incredulous.

Eagle Claw had understood the exchange clearly and could wait no longer. He ordered Gabe to stay still and emerged from their hiding spot in the forest. "White Cloud speaks the truth!" he declared in the Blackfeet tongue. "The men you seek are not here."

Suddenly, a scuffling came from the nearby timber. Eagle Claw turned and sighed in frustration as a brave emerged with Gabe, holding a rifle to his back.

"You think I don't have eyes in my head? Look! What about him?" Bloody Hand pointed with his rifle at Gabe and the brave holding him hostage. "Two Kills, is he not one of them?"

The Blackfeet men quickly raised their rifles, aiming directly at the Kootenai villagers.

"Don't shoot!" shouted Two Kills as he stepped clear. "This man isn't one of them!"

"Where are the other trappers?" demanded Bloody Hand. "Turn them over now, or we will attack and burn this village to the ground."

Eagle Claw stepped forward and spoke boldly. "Your brave speaks the truth! This white man rides with me. We did not kill any Blackfeet men!"

"You Kootenai! You trade beaver with the white trappers until your bellies are fat! Why should we believe anything you say?" Bloody Hand let out a loud war whoop and his men took aim.

"Listen to me!" shouted Eagle Claw. "I saw these trappers you seek. They rode into the sacred land without our permission—and they have yet to return."

Bloody Hand's jaws were clenched, and his horse shifted to the left and right in anticipation of battle. Eagle Claw knew his village was outgunned. It was clear to see they were painted for war, angry, and thirsting for revenge.

The Blackfeet leader raised his hand and appeared ready to signal his men to fire. "Wait!" Eagle Claw said. "To show you I speak the truth, I will guide you to the waters where they seek the beaver."

Bloody Hand paused, considering this offer. Slowly, his anger subsided, and he motioned for his men to stand down. "The offer you make is honorable," he said. But he pointed his finger at Gabe and added, "He must come too, and if we don't find the men we seek, we will take his scalp." He turned his horse and as he rode back to his men, he called over his shoulder to Eagle Claw, "Prepare to leave now. And you must leave your weapons here!"

Dawn had run to get her bow and arrow, and now stood with an arrow nocked. Having also heard the words of Bloody Hand, she was ready to fight. Eagle Claw motioned for her to put her bow down lest she provoke an attack and bring upon them the wrath of the Blackfeet.

The Blackfeet sounded a war whoop and as they disappeared into the timber. Dawn pleaded with the Kootenai men, "Why don't we fight them now? You heard what they said."

Arrow Heart replied, "No! Our numbers are small. Most of the men are still gone on the hunt. Even if we drive them back, they will only bring more Blackfeet warriors and kill our people. White Cloud and Eagle Claw are right. We must do what they ask."

The village was soon alive with activity. Spotted Doe ran to prepare food and supplies for Eagle Claw and Gabe, while Eagle Claw explained the situation to Gabe. Soon, she emerged from her lodge with the sacks, handed them to Eagle Claw and Gabe, and said, "Be strong, my husband, and may the Great Spirit protect you."

He reached for her and held her tight, then stooped down to hug Little Buck, wondering if he would ever see his family again. A wave of sadness swept over him, but he contained his emotions and quickly mounted his horse. He trotted over to Arrow Heart and White Cloud and said, "If we fail to find the trappers, the Blackfeet may come and destroy everyone in this camp. Flee to the Tobacco Plains, so you can warn the others to prepare for battle. Don't wait for us. We'll find our way out."

Arrow Heart nodded. "We will send a runner after the hunting party, so when they are finished, they will know not to return here."

White Cloud nodded in agreement just as Gabe rode up and joined him. Together, they headed toward the band of waiting Blackfeet.

Chapter Twenty-Six

Raven's Feast

Gabe's position on the trail was just in front of Eagle Claw, roughly in the middle of the string of twelve Blackfeet warriors. Once again, he was bewildered at how he'd managed to inexplicably find himself in yet another life-threatening situation. While they rode, Eagle Claw had explained that Branch and his men had attacked and killed their unsuspecting Blackfeet men along with their horses, and they were determined to mete out vengeance. To make matters worse, their leader had said that Gabe's scalp—a physical attribute he'd always considered to be one of his finest—was up for grabs, and he would only keep it if they were successful. They were weaponless, and he felt naked and vulnerable. As they pressed deeper into the toothy jaws of the mountain, a sense of doom hung over him like a storm cloud, growing stronger as they pressed on.

The cold reality of the situation caused him to think not only about his uncertain future, but also his reckless past. His combative parting confrontation with his father, his mother's distressing sobs, and the weight of unamended sins pressing on his shoulders—all were becoming increasingly burdensome in the face of his possible demise.

When he was younger, he had once watched a murderer in a blindfold get escorted to the gallows to be hanged in the village near their farm. Afterward, Gabe had always wondered what was going through the murderer's mind as he stumbled blindly up the short stairway toward the hangman's noose. Now, he knew that feeling, at least in some semblance. But in Gabe's case, he wasn't offered the courtesy of a blindfold, and he had to endure the long, slow march toward the deathly gallows of the sacred canyon.

The voice of Bill Branch quoting his verses of poetry kept repeating in his mind. Occasionally, they touched a poignant nerve. His ability to string words into an ornate tapestry was the only quality of the man that he found semi-interesting. As they moved steadily ahead, Gabe came up with a simple poem to help bide the time and get the crusty mountain man's voice out of his head:

> *Kentucky, oh Kentucky! Verdant land of birth,*
>
> *Humble rolling hills of magnolia and mirth.*
>
> *Placid lakes of silver, and rivers of gold—*
>
> *I yearn for thee, Kentucky, my sweet land of old.*
>
> *A wicked foreign path lies beneath me now;*
>
> *I hereby curse my restless legs and lustful brow.*
>
> *To death, dark death, I rightly go;*
>
> *My stubborn wandering eye hath decreed it so.*

ᏅᎣ

Eagle Claw knew why the Blackfeet warriors were pushing the pace— revenge. Eagle Claw had traveled the trail once before. For the first couple miles, it wound its way up the mountain, sometimes skirting dangerous cliffs, but always leading upward. Several hours after leaving the fish camp, they stopped on the side of the mountain, just below a dangerous series of switchbacks. After this obstacle, traveling would be much easier. But before starting the climb, a mountain updraft brought with it the repulsive, rank odor of rotting flesh to Eagle Claw's nostrils.

He turned in his saddle toward Gabe. "Do you smell that?" he asked, wrinkling his nose.

"Yes. I smell it. Something happened here—something bad."

Bloody Hand ordered everyone to dismount. He gazed down into a steep ravine cut on the side of the mountain, then ordered Two Kills to take their hostages into the chasm, along with two other braves, to investigate the odor. Bloody Hand took up the rear as the group worked their way down the steep grade with their rifles slung over their shoulders. The rest of the men stayed behind with the horses.

The smell grew stronger as they descended into the ravine. Glancing back, Eagle Claw noted that Two Kills looked nervous. Before long, they heard ravens cackling and saw dried patches of blood on the jagged rocks below. As they continued to descend, there came the sound of buzzing flies and the flutter of ravens' wings.

"There!" said Two Kills as a dozen ravens flapped away from their feasting, landing in nearby trees jutting from cliffy footholds to await the intruders' departure and resume their foul repast. The men crept toward a small ledge and cautiously peered over.

The steep grade came to an abrupt stop, and the ravine flattened out for fifty feet, with cliffs on both sides, like a dark hidden pocket on the side of the mountain, then drained into an avalanche chute that descended steeply down the crag. There among the jagged rocks lay the remnants of an animal—a bony mass buzzing with flies. Eagle Claw was accustomed to seeing the aftermath of death, but he found the mangled horse and the fetid smell that hung in the air truly revolting. Much of it had been picked clean by scavengers, but enough flesh remained on the ribs and bones for the ravens to peck at. Maggots were busy taking care of rotting remnants that even the ravens refused to eat.

Gabe was cringing at the squirming mass of maggots as they devoured the putrefied innards. The other men, too, recoiled at the ghastly sight and the stomach-turning stench. "It fell from up there." Gabe plugged his nose and pointed to the steep trail carved into the cliffs above them. "I've been up there, and that's one dangerous trail. It must have slipped and fell." Eagle Claw nodded in agreement.

"The mountain is against them, White Warrior," Two Kills said with satisfaction. "This is a good sign for us."

They descended a few more steps to the floor of the chasm for a closer inspection. Eagle Claw picked up a loose chunk of moss that had been dislodged from a rock. "Something was dragged off that way," he said, pointing down the ravine.

The Blackfeet seemed eager to get away from the offensive smell. Nevertheless, they followed the drag marks a few paces until they came to a mangled and bloodied hat lying among the rocks. Two Kills picked up the hat to inspect it, but when he unfolded it, a pile of wriggling maggots that had been feasting on fleshy tidbits inside rolled out onto his hand.

"*Aaaahhh!*" He recoiled in horror, flinging the hat down and shaking his hands again and again. Though the squirming larvae had all fallen to his feet, he continued shaking his hands and wiping them on his pants, as if they still remained.

Eagle Claw stifled a chuckle. "There's one of your trappers," he said, smiling.

Gabe shivered in disgust and grimaced at the spasmodic wrigglers trying to clamber blindly up Two Kills' moccasin. The brave jumped back and grabbed a piece of moss, then furiously wiped slimy bits of pinkish brain matter from his hand.

Eagle Claw turned away to hide his impulsive smile and took a few steps to where the ravine dropped down the mountain. "I sense bad medicine was at work in this place—very bad medicine." Two Kills huffed and stepped beside him, then followed the drag marks with his eyes until they vanished farther down the mountain.

Sensing his bemusement, the brave looked at him with a broad grin on his face and said, "I have heard stories of this mountain, White Warrior. For your sakes, I hope they are not true since you have no weapons to defend yourselves." Then, Bloody Hand motioned for everyone to climb back to the horses.

When they arrived back on the trail, Eagle Claw turned to the leader and said, "It would be better to walk the horses." Bloody Hand looked up at the cliffs ahead and didn't argue. The others followed his lead, and one by one, they picked their way through the dangerous set of switchbacks until reaching the top of the bench.

"I hate this part of the trail," Gabe whispered to Eagle Claw. "Isn't there a better way in here?"

Eagle Claw kept an eye on the horse in front of him as it struggled to maintain its footing. "The horses are strong. They will make it."

Fortunately, the entire group finally made it safely to the top. There, the slope of the mountain tapered, and the trail became more conducive to safe travel on horseback.

Later that day, they approached the giant cedar forest. It was clear that the Blackfeet men had never seen such enormous trees. They soon began to whisper to each other with a hint of awe and trepidation in their voices. Eagle Claw's ears perked when someone used the word *Skookum*.

"I'm amazed every time I see these big trees," said Gabe as he stared at the enormous obelisks that rose from the forest floor as if to hold the sky in place.

Eagle Claw sensed an opportunity and spoke loudly in the Blackfeet tongue: "The Elders told us stories of these giant trees when I was a child. The legend tells how the Skookum planted these trees. It is his forest, and they were planted as a warning to keep out."

"What did you just say?" whispered Gabe curiously.

"Just planting a seed. They fear the Skookum."

The Blackfeet chattering continued more earnestly, and some of the warriors began checking over their shoulders for danger. Seeing the growing panic among his men, Bloody Hand spoke boldly and scoffed. "You won't scare us with your stories of your Skookum. We Blackfeet are fearless warriors, not cowards!"

But this time, the men did not respond with a raised fist and a war whoop. Instead, they sat passively in their saddles and held their tongues. The mention of the Skookum seemed to fill them with dread. Bloody Hand approached Red Hawk, who appeared to be the main instigator, and scolded him in front of the others. Red Hawk scowled and nodded grudgingly, then Bloody Hand waved him angrily to the front of the pack string. The brave kicked his horse in the ribs, his face contorted with rage as he fumed over the leader's rebuke while the other riders tucked in closely behind him.

Bloody Hand turned his horse off the trail and let the other riders pass by, then stopped in front of Gabe and Eagle Claw and spoke to them in English, saying, "My men sense bad spirits on this trail. They grow fearful. Do not frighten them with your stories, or we will leave you and your friend here—dead—and continue on without you."

"I'm not intimidated by threats," Eagle Claw said. He then changed the subject abruptly: "Do you smell that?"

Bloody Hand sniffed the forest air. "A wise and mighty warrior, and yet you don't know the smell of a skunk?"

"That is not a skunk," replied Eagle Claw. "I know that smell. It is the Skookum. Before this is over, the beast will test the courage of you and your men. Perhaps he will let us pass through and not seek revenge for our trespass ... perhaps not."

"Skookum or no Skookum, if we fail, then you fail—and so will your people."

Eagle Claw looked soberly at Gabe, then turned back to Bloody Hand. "Very well. But you have been warned."

Chapter Twenty-Seven

Sidetracked

*J*ohnson approached the camp with his haul of beaver, rehearsing how he could persuade his trapping partners to help retrieve his bear. Branch and Choteau appeared to be in good spirits as he staggered into camp with the heavy load of fur. The jug of whiskey sitting on a nearby log partially explained their jovial mood.

"It's about time you showed up," Branch said as Johnson dropped the pile of beaver fur in a heap.

"Got 'em skinned already. All I gotta do is stretch 'em."

"Not a bad haul," remarked Choteau.

"Not a bad haul? I done made some big beaver catches in my time, but this is one to brag about! Hell, to be honest, I ain't never made a haul like this in my entire life," Johnson boasted. "In fact, I know a lot of trappers, but I ain't bumped into one yet who's trapped this many beavers in a single day."

Branch laughed as he grabbed the corner of the buckskin tarpaulin that covered the pile of skinned beaver pelts and flung it aside. "Damn! You weren't jokin', man! You were right. This is the mother lode!"

"Okay then, I'll get to work stretchin' hides." Johnson grabbed an alder branch, bending it into a loop to stretch a pelt. He smiled congenially, but Branch only cocked his head and squinted skeptically at Johnson's sudden friendliness. Persuading him to help with the bear might be tougher than he realized. Johnson cleared his throat, forced another cheerful smile, and broached the topic. "If'n I get these stretched, I might need some help gettin' that bear outta that cave he went and died in."

Choteau stopped fleshing the beaver he was working on and blurted question after question: "Are you sure you hit him good? Did you get a good look? How big was it? Are you sure it was a bear?"

Johnson was careful not to say anything that might scare away potential reinforcements. "Oh, I hit him hard—real hard. Bled like a stuck pig, too. I left him breathin' his last up in that damned cave. You should see the swath he made bustin' through them alders when he lit out. Lord-a-mercy." Johnson noticed Choteau's curiosity and leveraged it to his advantage. "Hell, Choteau. I'll even give ya one of his claws if you help me retrieve him. Must be six inches long."

The offer of a claw was all it took. "Very well, then, I'll help you get your bear," Choteau said. "But only if I get that claw."

Branch continued to look wary and doubtful, so Johnson was surprised when he said, "You get them all stretched, and then I'll see about helpin' you get that bear." Branch snickered, then gave Choteau a sideways glance and a wink, adding, "But it'll be a cold day in hell when you can get all them beaver stretched before we lose daylight."

Johnson was familiar with Branch's sketchy conditions of negotiation and could see through his counterfeit promise—just more pushing buttons and pulling levers to extract more work from him. But this time, Johnson took his words as a challenge. He took off his ornate jacket and leather shirt, folded and placed them neatly on the fallen log near the campfire, and rolled up the shirtsleeves of his cotton undershirt. After sharpening his knife, he became a blur of muscle and steel, his hands working with the skill of a trained surgeon as he fleshed and stretched hide after hide.

Johnson hated to sweat, but after several hours, his cotton undershirt was soaked. It was a tolerable irritation, for even more than proving Branch wrong, his mind was focused on one thing—getting help to retrieve his bear. Meanwhile, Choteau and Branch took turns sipping the whiskey jug and tried to out-boast each other with tall tales.

Johnson stretched the last beaver in his pile and tossed it with the others. "That's the last one in my pile—fifty-six!"

"*Whooo-wheee!*" shouted Branch. He rose and walked straight over to the beaver lake, completely disrobed, and jumped into the chilly water. "It's a great day for my annual bath!" He dunked for a few seconds and then stood and shook the water from his graying hair like a wet dog. Johnson stared for a moment at his battle-scarred body, then groaned with disgust when the clear water of the lake turned dingy brown as it filtered through his matted hair and ran down his back.

Johnson wondered with a quiver of revulsion whether the fleas and ticks crawling around under Branch's helmet of hair were bothered by the sudden shock of frigid water, or if they were too blotto to care after sucking Branch's whiskey-tainted blood.

Triumphantly looking across the water, Branch raised his arms in victory. "*Whooo-wheee!*" he yelled again. Choteau was obviously feeling his oats from Branch's whiskey and joined in the celebration. He disrobed, tossed aside his buckskin garments, and, in typical toady fashion, jumped into the water and yelled, "*Yaaaahhh!*" Their sinewy naked bodies appeared snow-white when contrasted with their grime-browned faces and hands.

"You crazy-ass bastards!" shouted Johnson. He waited impatiently, pacing as they splashed around like buffoons.

Branch finally got out of the water and dressed hurriedly after his glacial bath. He lay with his back against a log next to the fire to warm himself. Johnson wiped his sweaty brow and donned his leather shirt. "We got time to go get that bear I shot. I bet he's good an' stiff by now an' ready for skinnin'."

Branch glanced at the sun and repositioned his hat to better shade his face. "We don't give two shits about that bear. I done told ya, we're here for beaver. Besides, I'm kinda likin' it here by the fire."

Johnson stepped toward Branch, hands clenched for a fight, and shouted, "You promised you'd help me get that bear!"

Branch glanced at him sideways. "If you're such a great bear hunter, why do you need us? Go fetch him yourself. Besides, we was planning on breakin' camp and movin' on up to the next beaver hole—the *real* mother lode of plew."

"What about you, Choteau? You still want that bear claw?" asked Johnson. Choteau paused for a moment and took another sip of whiskey. Finally, he replied, "Like I said, I will go for the claw."

Branch sat up straight, and Johnson felt a grin spreading across his face, knowing full well Branch couldn't stand the idea of him and Choteau working together as a team, which could lead to things— collusion, mutiny, or double-cross.

Grudgingly clambering to his feet, Branch said, "All right. But we better double-time it. I don't wanna be fumblin' around on that trail to the next camp in the dark."

Johnson stepped back and folded his arms, pleased that he'd been able to outmaneuver the crafty mountain man.

"Well? Don't just stand there. Let's make this quick—we got beaver to catch!", growled Branch.

"Now, you're talkin'!" said Johnson. He cheerfully put on his folded leather shirt and jacket and added a couple of bear fat-soaked torch rags to his possibles bag. "All right, boys. Follow me."

Johnson paused at the creek to thoroughly scrub his hands while Branch grumbled and complained. "Cleanliness is next to godliness, Branch—a philosophy you don't appear to subscribe to. As a matter of fact, I'm told that's in the Bible." Johnson felt smug as he flipped the water off his hands.

"That ain't in the Bible," Branch scoffed as they continued toward the blood trail.

"Oh, I believe it is."

"Are you a bettin' man, Johnson?"

Johnson didn't care much for the Good Book. In fact, he'd much rather face an angry griz than an open Bible—especially when it spoke of judgment and repentance. But he had heard a preacher remark about cleanliness once. It was the only time he ever said *amen* to anything a preacher had to say. Certainly, it had to be written in there somewhere. But Branch's self-assured rebuttal made him hold his tongue. He wasn't interested in losing a bet to the likes of Crooked Bill Branch.

"So, tell me again, Johnson," said Choteau. "Did you get a good look at this ... this ... bear?"

"I got a pretty good look at 'im. He plowed through the brush like a heart-shot buffalo. I hit 'im hard, too. Like I said, he bled like a son of a bitch."

"I can't wait to see him up close," said Choteau.

"If he's as big as I think, you'll earn that bear claw helpin' me pack out his hide." Johnson began humming a song to distract from his pesky doubts. "Of course it was a bear," he muttered to himself. But Choteau's pause before he said the word *bear* kept needling him.

"What did you say?" asked Choteau.

"What? Nothin'. We're almost there." As they approached the bloody spoor, Johnson crowed, "See?!" He pointed to the blotch of blood as if he'd discovered gold.

They continued to find blood—lots of blood. It had dried now and turned dark, but it was still easy to follow.

"You hit him good, eh?" Choteau stooped and studied one of the snapped alders with great interest.

"Why the hell is this blood so high on the brush?" Branch said as he looked at a dark smear at eye level.

"You know, I asked myself the same damn question," Johnson replied hesitantly. "I ain't figured it out yet. It's an oddity … I don't know what to make of it."

They passed through a nearly impenetrable patch of alders where the beast had broken through, leaving more large, snapped branches on either side of its path. Again, Branch and Choteau paused.

"Hold up, Johnson!" barked Branch.

Johnson turned and faced them as Branch reached up and pulled a long strand of black hair—over six inches long—from one of the alder branches. He ran it through his fingers, then smelled it. "What the hell kind of bear did you shoot anyhow? I damn sure ain't never seen hair like this on a bear, and I've killed some big griz in my time. Are you sure you didn't shoot one of our horses?"

"All the horses were grazing together in the meadow this morning," said Choteau, dead-faced, apparently not realizing Branch was being facetious.

Johnson looked at the hair and felt a wave of doubt. Clenching his teeth, he beat back his fears and rolled his eyes.

"I told you he's one big son of a bitch," said Johnson angrily. But the question kept churning inside, causing him more uncertainty. He steeled himself, resisting what his eyes had seen, refusing to recall anything but a bear as it ran through the opening in the trees.

Branch squinted at him, looking skeptical. "Alright. Carry on. We don't have all day!" Johnson turned back up the blood trail, marching past the brush, timber, and scree until they finally approached the cave, where the wounded creature had taken refuge.

Johnson had grabbed a stout alder branch along the trail. He wrapped it with one of the oil-soaked rags, then lit it with his strike-a-light. He gave it to Choteau and said, "Hold this up for me, so's I can see to shoot. It's dark as the bowels of hell in there."

"He's still bleedin' good," Branch whispered as he stared, looking perplexed at the smear of blood at eye level on the rock wall near the entrance. "Be ready to pull that trigger. Them griz can soak up a lot of lead." The wary trapper then took a safe position well behind them as they entered the cave.

Johnson stepped forward with his rifle cocked and ready. Just a few feet ahead, the narrow entrance opened into a large chamber. He could sense Choteau's hesitation as he crept forward. Beads of sweat dripped down his face, and he tensed himself for a close-range shot.

He had killed charging bears before and bore the scars from the few occasions when one had still had enough life to take a swipe or two before giving up the ghost. Now, he stood again at the precipice, one more step toward the moment he lived for, and the singular reason he loved hunting big bears—the deadly final moments of a stalk when it came down to one shot, and that one shot meant life or death. This was the climax of the stalk, when the heart quickened, and the adrenaline surged—the ageless collision of man and beast, hopefully culminating in the death of the latter. The final victory brought with it the fleeting but glorious moment of euphoria, invincibility, and domination.

Impatiently, he motioned for Choteau to move closer, so he could illuminate the dark chamber where he suspected the bear lay waiting. With each step, more of the chamber came into view. His finger tightened on the trigger, anticipating a charge. Just one more step.

But as the entire chamber was revealed, one thing was clear—the cave was empty. "Hold that torch over here, Choteau," Johnson whispered. The Frenchman stepped forward while Johnson feverishly scanned every crevice and corner of the cavern, but there was simply no bear to slay.

"Damn it!" he yelled. Removing his wolfskin hat, he wiped the sweat from his forehead and stepped forward to an enormous bed of pine needles that covered half the chamber floor. "He was here!" he exclaimed, pointing to a large patch of dried blood.

"Yes. He was here all right," said Choteau, his voice quivering with fear as Branch stepped into the chamber behind them to survey the situation.

Suddenly Choteau gasped. "Come over here, both of you," he said. There, on a rocky ledge, the light of his torch revealed several objects.

"What the hell?" Branch said.

"I'll be damned," Johnson chimed in.

On the ledge were several familiar articles, placed almost as if on display: a rusted old knife, a trap, some tattered buckskin clothing, a powder flask, and a few other quirky objects of no value.

Then, Branch yelped, "Hey! That's my missing powder flask!" He jerked it from the rock shelf and inspected the shiny copper container for functionality. He scratched his head. "This don't make any sense."

"Maybe an Indian or trapper used this cave," offered Choteau.

"Yeah," said Branch. "Maybe the dirty bastard that's been tryin' to spook us outta here."

Choteau reached up and removed a beaver trap from the ledge. "This is in good shape. I don't know any trapper worth his salt who would leave behind a perfectly good trap."

"Well, he must be one ornery son of a bitch to put up with the skunk that's been livin' in this cave!" said Branch.

"If this is a man-cave, where's the firepit?" asked Johnson, looking around the cave for other oddities.

"Lemme see that," said Branch, grabbing the trap from Choteau's hand and turning it over. "Gimme some light." Choteau lowered the torch so they could all see the trap in detail. There, etched on the bottom of the trap, were the initials *B.B.*

"Hey! This here is one of my traps," Branch said. "Why in tarnation is it in here?"

"Don't you remember when we first trapped this basin?" said Choteau. "We were missing one of our traps! Remember? You thought Bauman lost it on purpose, so you docked his pay and scolded him good."

Branch paused for a moment. "Hey. You're right. We was missin' one—and here it is! Wouldn't put it past that piece of shite Bauman to try and scare us off! If Bauman was in here, looks like you drew blood on him, and I hope ya gut-shot that bastard."

Johnson rolled his eyes but didn't bother commenting; it wasn't worth another verbal wrangle with the argumentative, pettifogging Bill Branch. He had seen enough and began backing out of the cave, followed by Choteau. Devoid of light, the cavern suddenly became even more sinister, prompting Branch to follow them out. Johnson squinted as his eyes adjusted to the waning daylight.

"Don't matter if it's a man or a bear, Johnson. Looks like you didn't hit him hard as you thought, mighty bear hunter!" Johnson felt embarrassed, but made sure not to show it, glaring back as Branch railed. He wanted to bark right back at him, but it was clear Branch was hot with anger—the veins on his neck bulging as he spat out the words. "I can't believe you drug us all the way up here for this bullshite!"

"Branch is right, Monsieur Johnson—flesh wound. I guess you are not such a great bear hunter after all," scoffed Choteau.

The words hit his pride like a slap in the face, and he felt his face grow hot with anger at Choteau's insult. "Flesh wound, my ass. I hit 'im square. Look at all this blood." He pointed to the large splash of blood near the cave entrance. It was enough to take a rebuke from Branch, but he drew the line with the Frenchman. "Gimme that damn torch!" he demanded, grabbing it from Choteau's hand. He stomped back into the cave, looked around angrily one last time, then tossed the flame onto the large bed of pine needles.

He quickly exited the cave and following him like an eerie black ghost came belching smoke from the bed of pine needles he had set on fire. He stumbled toward the others, muttering to himself as he watched it burn: "That bastard won't be usin' this cave anytime soon! I swore I hit him hard. He's gotta be lyin' dead somewhere." He shielded his eyes and looked up at the mountain, hoping to see movement in the few treeless patches on the wooded slopes.

"Are you sure it was a bear?" asked Choteau.

"Damn it to hell!" shouted Johnson defensively, as much to convince himself as the other two. "If you ask me that again, I'll brain ya! Of course it was a bear! You think I don't know what a bear looks like?!" Gritting his teeth, he marched ahead of the others back to the camp, grumbling under his breath.

After arriving at their camp, Johnson stewed while he packed to leave. Choteau seemed especially eager to depart and made fast work of saddling the horses for their departure for the next camp deeper into the basin.

He listened half-heartedly as Branch went over the details of their plan to trap several lakes, heavy with beaver, tucked next to the spine of the mountain. There, they would the trap the area clean and then return to the first camp to catch any remaining beaver that had previously eluded them.

After packing, Johnson looked up at the mountain, where wisps of smoke still emanated from the cave he had set ablaze.

"No bear claw for me today," Choteau said in a regretful tone as he glanced up at the smoke.

"Maybe we could circle above the cave and try to cut a fresh blood trail," Johnson said. "How far to the next camp?" The words sounded inane even as he spoke them, vainly hoping the promise of a bear claw still carried weight.

"Six or seven hours, I'd guess, maybe more if we have delays," said Choteau. "But do you really think me a fool? I don't want a bear claw bad enough to hike around after a wounded griz, and Branch will be terribly angry if you leave to try and find it."

Johnson knew it was a lost cause, but he had to ask, and Choteau's words helped bring him to his senses and assuage his frustration. "I still can't believe we didn't find that bear dead as a wedge in that cave.

I don't understand it. I know I hit 'im good. .53-caliber Hawken at close range? Hell, that'd stop a buffalo. Just don't make any sense."

"Many things don't make sense here, my friend," replied Choteau, scanning the surrounding forest as if something were watching.

Chapter Twenty-Eight

Healing Place

*I*nside the timber near a ledge high on the mountain, the Gray looked down at his injured son with concern, then bent down, tenderly picked up the Younger in his arms, and carried him even higher up the mountain.

The Gray climbed with long strides toward his peaceful resting place tucked in a secluded hollow near the spring on the upper third of the mountain. He arrived at the nook and gently lay the Younger on a blanket of moss. Then, cupping his hands on each side of his mouth, he let out a soft cry that started low, changed octaves, and finished with a high pitch.

A few seconds later, from not far away came a short reply. The Gray sat next to the Younger, scooped some water from the spring, and held it to his mouth. The Younger opened his eyes and took a small sip before uttering a bird-like warble. The Gray replied with a deep purring sound. The Younger bared his teeth and grimaced as he held his hand over the wound. Branches snapped as something large moved down the slope toward them, but neither bothered looking up, for they both knew who was approaching.

The Alpha parted the alder brush and came upon them quickly, then knelt and moved the Younger's hand away from the wound.

Looking up at the Gray with wide-eyed concern, she uttered a series of worried grunts and warbles.

The Gray moved and sat on a nearby log, staring with a blank expression that hid a roiling distress from the unsettling pandemonium. He turned and forced himself to watch the Alpha tending to the Younger. He was hot with fever and drops of sweat beaded on his forehead. His mother soaked a wad of moss in the spring and placed it on his forehead, then leaned in and sniffed the bloody mat of fur on the Younger's rib cage. Carefully, she moved the blood-clotted hair until she got down to the wound itself. Coagulating blood oozed from the neat, round hole. When she put her finger over it, he winced. She quickly moved her finger, and again, it began oozing.

The Gray turned away and put his elbow on his knee, then cupped his hand under his chin in dark contemplation as the Alpha continued tending to him.

She furrowed her brow and grunted at the Gray. He abruptly left and returned with several items: a sticky chunk of juniper sap, a handful of yarrow, and a substantial wad of spider web.

He watched as she carefully placed her mouth over the wound. Slowly, she began to suck out the infection and clotted blood cooking inside him. The Younger opened his eyes and clenched his teeth against the pain. Grimacing, she spit globs of pus and blood into the spring before rinsing out her mouth. She took the items from the Gray and made a new poultice, which she placed on the wound and gently pushed into the hole. In seconds, the wound stopped bleeding.

The long shadow of the mountain crept upon the opposite ridge as the sun eased its way toward the west. Before long, the fever broke, and the Younger began to shiver from the sudden drop in his body temperature. The Gray sat on the log pensively and looked down at his son as the Alpha curled up next to him to hold him and keep him warm against the chill of the mountain.

The Gray blinked and looked at the ground, then at his massive hands. His prominent brow furrowed. He opened his clenched fists, palms up, and ran his fingers over scars long healed. If his hands could talk, they would tell many stories; they would tell of lonely mountains climbed in the dead of winter when all creatures either slept or had migrated far from winter's deadly grasp; they would tell of ice-filled, flooded rivers crossed in the heart of spring runoff; they would tell of brutal battles won against claw and fang, and they would tell of the man-creature he had carried one wintery night—all the way to his village on the big river far below. What incredible stories his weathered hands would tell if they could only speak, but only the scars bore silent witness to them.

A grim duty called, and he wondered what new tales his hands would tell after the dread of night had passed. Perhaps ones better left untold—a dark secret kept between himself and the night.

As he stared at his hands, they appeared to turn ominous as the final rays of sunlight glanced off the tips of the mountains. The Gray studied his massive fingers as they opened and closed tightly against his palms, forming giant fists as hard as stone. He relaxed his hands and gazed at his wounded son. *"John ... saan,"* he uttered in a low, guttural voice.

The Alpha female looked up at him hesitantly and uttered a calming coo. He glanced again at his hands and huffed deeply and urgently: *Humph! Garooo! Hu! Hu! Hu!*

She needed no prodding. The time for watching was over, for blood had been spilled—the blood of her son. She patted the Younger, then rose from her position beside him. Resolutely, she headed north while the Gray disappeared into the darkening depths of the valley.

The Gray traveled halfway down the mountain, skirted the base of the cliffs on the western edge of the drainage for a mile until he picked up a familiar scent, and made a beeline for its source. His walk was purposeful, without confusion, hesitation, or fear. His long strides covered the ground quickly, and his massive feet spread his weight evenly, which helped him travel silently. And as he thought about his son's injury and pain, there came a slow simmering that made his hulking frame swell and his muscles harden like the stony mountains he called home.

It didn't take him long to reach the valley floor, where he crept through dense alders toward the first camp. As he approached, it became apparent that something had changed. For the past several nights, he'd been spying on the man-creatures and was familiar with their noises. But the clanking of metal and tools, the caustic laughing, and angry shouting were now conspicuously absent. He peered through the brush, eyes burning with fury and fists clenched in anger, but they were nowhere to be seen.

The Gray looked to the right and left after emerging from the brushy barrier of alders next to the first camp, then cautiously approached the firepit. He picked up a smoldering branch and studied it carefully, mesmerized by the wisps of smoke emanating from the tip before tossing it back in the ashes.

He turned to the pile of skinned beaver carcasses, still crawling with flies. The sight made him seethe, and he snorted as if to rid the smell from his nostrils. He stomped to the pile, picked up one of the carcasses by the tail, and hurled it high above the pines on the other side of the alders. The release of tension made him feel better, much better, and he continued tossing, sending them whirling through the air until none remained. He looked around for something else to throw or break and spied a young pine tree perhaps twelve feet tall. He grabbed it at waist level, snapped it with a twist of his wrist, and hurled it aside with a grunt. He found other trees and either snapped them in half or ripped them out by their roots until his rage was quelled, then he sat on a stump to rest his arms on his knees.

But while his body rested, his mind began racing, and violent thoughts stewed and simmered like a smoking cauldron as he thought about the man-beasts. He used to watch the ones that camped far below along the big river when he was younger. Eventually, though, he grew bored with the pastime and thought best to leave them alone. The man-beasts were strange, mostly hairless except for their heads, and they wore odd coverings. They were also loud and aggressive, so he preferred to keep a safe distance.

But after what they had done to his son, he no longer saw them as a curiosity. Like the grizzly bear, mountain lion, or wolf pack, he realized they meant to cause harm. He looked down at the bloodied, matted grass where the pile of beaver carcasses once lay, and as the darkness settled on the mountain valley, he was certain the man-beasts were his enemies.

As he was thinking, a sound alerted him, and his head snapped to attention. He turned and looked down the drainage as something approached from below. Soon, he heard the sounds of hooved animals—many hooved animals—coming up the trail and growing louder: the familiar squeak of a saddle, the soft chatter of man-beasts, and the snorting of horses. There were many more now, and he quietly slipped into the forest to spy on them and perhaps find the one he hunted.

Chapter Twenty-Nine

The Omen and the Mutiny

O*ne by one, the riders coughed and cringed at the* lingering skunky smell that suddenly permeated the trail. The horses' reaction was more pronounced—they instinctively locked their legs and came to an abrupt stop, quivering with fear.

Eagle Claw scanned the area, noticing the trampled grass and campfire just ahead—the unmistakable signs of the trapper's camp. But it appeared abandoned.

"The horses! They sense danger!" shouted one of the braves as his horse tried to turn back down the trail.

Bloody Hand dismounted, pulled his rifle from its scabbard, and cautiously approached the fire pit. Keeping one eye on the surrounding brush, he knelt and hovered his hand over the smoldering ashes. "They were here today," he said.

"And so was a skunk," added one of the braves.

Eagle Claw winked at Gabe, who had pulled up next to him, and translated. "He said the skunk was here today. That skunk sure does get around, eh?"

Two Kills dismounted and studied the trail. "They went up the canyon. The tracks are fresh. Only a few hours old."

"Darkness comes. We will camp here tonight," said Bloody Hand. The other braves dismounted, gathered wood, and rekindled the fire to give light and keep warm as the night settled in around them like a shroud.

"I don't think they're near here," Gabe said to Eagle Claw. "Branch would have fired by now."

"Yes, he would have fired on us. There is a devil in him."

Gabe nodded his agreement.

One of the men gathering firewood from the forest opposite the creek returned with a skinned beaver in hand, explaining that he had tripped over it. The Blackfeet soon had it skewered on a spit over the fire.

"Where did you find the beaver?" asked Two Kills.

"It was lying up on the mountain." The man pointed at the timbered slope well over eighty yards away.

Just then, several other braves emerged with firewood and more skinned beavers. The Blackfeet warriors exchanged incredulous glances, but Bloody Hand brushed off the coincidence, saying, "Maybe a bear or coyote scattered them."

Eagle Claw noticed a glint of blood on the vegetation. He made a small torch from one of the smoldering branches and took a closer look. "Looks like they trapped here for a while," he said as he held the torch over the bloody, matted grass.

A few braves strode over to investigate. "Lots of blood," replied Red Hawk. "But the bodies of the beaver are gone. It makes no sense why they would scatter them about." He looked nervously at the others.

"Yes. Strange," remarked one of the men, then together, they stood staring fearfully into the darkening forest.

Bloody Hand weighed in. "Enough of this talk! Tomorrow, we will catch up with them. We have them boxed in. They can't take their horses over these mountains."

One of the braves walked a few paces from the fire, staring down intently. After relieving himself, he knelt close to the ground and called to the others, "Look at this!"

As Eagle Claw looked down at the discovery, old memories came rushing in and flooded his thoughts. There, pressed into the dirt, was a large depression in the shape of a footprint. He remembered the track made by the creature that killed his brother. Certainly, this must be the same devil that haunted his dreams. But there was only one difference between the two tracks—this one didn't appear to have claws. He stepped a few paces toward the creek and said, "Come look at this, Bloody Hand."

In unison, they all got up and approached Two Kills, then stood in silent bewilderment at the destruction. All around the camp, jutting from the ground, were remnants of trees that had been snapped, broken, or ripped out of the ground, roots and all.

"No hatchet did that," Eagle Claw said as he inspected one of the snapped trees. He noticed something odd hanging from one of the splintered branches and plucked it off for a closer look. Walking to the light of the fire, he examined several long strands of the thick, grayish hair. He smelled it and instantly knew where it came from.

The suspicious braves looked around at the damaged trees. Red Hawk, ignoring Bloody Hand's rebuke and promise of punishment for causing fear in the men, spoke boldly: "All this is an omen. This is the work of the Skookum. We are all in danger."

"No!" Bloody Hand said. "We must remember our mission and not worry about old women's tales." He paused for a moment, pacing back and forth in desperate contemplation. "Their horses may have been tied here, and they could have spooked and pulled these trees out." But Eagle Claw noticed the fear in his eyes and the hesitation in his voice.

"What did he say?" asked Gabe.

Annoyed, Eagle Claw frowned at Gabe and said, "Some Blackfeet gibberish about a Skookum. But then again, you don't believe in that nonsense, eh? Here, smell this." He held out the strands of hair he had found and placed them under Gabe's nose. Gabe winced at the pungent musk, then peered at the odorous strands and picked one to study it more closely.

"Ever see a track like that?" Eagle Claw pointed with his foot toward the enormous imprint in front of them. Gabe kneeled and gawked at the track, stubbornly silent.

The night was closing in, and soon, the men were preparing their beds. A breeze filtered through the trees carrying a baleful whisper that seemed to start at the very uppermost parts of the pine and spruce. It grew stronger with each passing minute until it became a moan, and tiny embers from the fire began to take flight, dancing like fireflies until swallowed by the darkness.

Then came a sorrowful wail. It started slowly, but as the wind picked up the forest gradually came alive with a mournful lament. The wind had set the trees in motion, bark on bark, jangling into a cacophony of spectral voices. One by one, the braves repositioned themselves closer to the fire as the macabre serenade enveloped them like a thick blanket.

"I hear voices," said one of the men fearfully.

The others sat still, listening intently, as if the sounds were indeed the voices of braves long past, summoned by the night to haunt the darkened forest. Eagle Claw saw their fear and could not resist. "It is the spirits of Kootenai men, long dead, who haunt this forest," he said in an ominous tone. "At night, they come down off the mountain to dance with the Skookum. Then, they sneak about on this trail, and together, they hunt for trespassers."

"Nonsense!" said Bloody Hand in frantic rebuke. "It's just the trees rubbing together in the wind."

Eagle Claw stifled a smile as the braves stared wide-eyed, searching the forest. He knelt by the campfire while Gabe loosened the leather cords around his bedroll and unrolled it on the ground. The beaver sizzling over the fire was only half cooked when the ravenous men began carving it up to slake their hunger and distract from their uneasiness. Blood dripped from their chins as they bit and chomped like hungry wolves.

"Do you want some?" one of the men asked Eagle Claw.

"No. I like my beaver well-cooked. I'll wait." Then, he whispered to Gabe, "I don't want to get worms, either." He sat on a horse blanket, leaned against a log, and stretched out his legs. As he watched the firelight dance, he thought of Spotted Doe and her gentle touch and wondered if he'd ever see her beautiful face again. Soon, he dozed off and dreamed he was back in his lodge, once more in her embrace.

He hadn't been sleeping long when he was awakened by a commotion. The braves were all standing next to the fire, armed with their rifles, murmuring and pointing into the forest in the same general direction.

"What's wrong?!" Eagle Claw said in a loud voice. He didn't have to wait for Gabe to reply. Farther up the canyon came an eerie sound.

Garooo! Garooo! It was followed by what seemed like angry, almost maniacal chatter. *Uh-ha-uh-ha-uh!* The sound was not far away, yet even above the gusting wind, it was clear and distinct in the thin mountain air.

The unhinged braves listened intently. The minutes ticked by when, all at once, from across the creek in the timber not a hundred yards away came another disturbing sound. It started as a low, almost imperceptible vibration and grew into a deep growl, as if emanating from the pit of hell itself. Eagle Claw felt it seep into the soles of his moccasin-clad feet, raising goosebumps as it traveled snake-like up his legs.

All rifles swung in unison toward the horrific growl. Then came a loud snap of a branch. It was close—just across the creek.

Bloody Hand spoke rapidly: "Don't fire unless you see movement!"

The men waited and waited, searching and listening, ready to fire, but the forest grew silent.

Eagle Claw couldn't help but read the fear written on the faces of the Blackfeet men, the cracks in their otherwise impenetrable shields of courage. They took turns keeping watch through the night, but underneath their thin veneer of bravery was a panic borne of superstition and fear—the seeds of mutiny.

↔

Like Eagle Claw, Red Hawk also sensed their fear. In fact, he was watching and hoping for it. He had heard threatening animal sounds before from powerful creatures like the grizzly bear, wolf, and mountain lion. But the guttural emanation was unknown to him, like something from the underworld. It made him think of one thing—the Skookum, and the wrathful growl made clear its intentions—to bite, claw, crush, and kill.

Initially, Red Hawk had been eager to help exact revenge upon the trappers, but the once-virtuous mission had taken a malefic tone, and now, he wished he hadn't volunteered. He didn't want any part of the Skookum. As a boy, he had heard plenty of stories about the creature from his father and grandfather—stories that brought on cold sweats and night terrors.

Even more significant was the fact that his wife was about to give birth to their first child, and his obligation was to her and to his fledgling family. Even if they were to return immediately, it would still mean they'd have been gone over two weeks. His horse was tired; he was tired, and the imminent threat fueled the idea he'd been mulling all day.

Midway through his watch, when Bloody Hand was fully asleep, Red Hawk quietly went around to the braves and whispered his plan. He was happy to find that they, too, were ready to abandon the mission, at least for now, and were frustrated with Bloody Hand's bullheaded determination to find the trappers who had ambushed their men, no matter what the cost. Red Hawk let Two Kills sleep undisturbed, thinking he would tell Bloody Hand and disrupt the plan.

Their leader's revenge went beyond reason, inflamed even hotter by the field of dead horses they had found along the trail—two of which were Bloody Hand's prized appaloosa buffalo runners. It appeared to Red Hawk that Bloody Hand was willing to endanger everyone in order to mete out vengeance, and it was becoming clear that the mission had charged over a cliff, jaded by Bloody Hand's recklessness and thirst for revenge. Why risk the deaths of more men at the hand of the Skookum when all they needed to do was wait near the Kootenai village for the trappers to return?

Red Hawk also resented Bloody Hand's insinuation that he was a coward. Red Hawk had always been fearless in battle, but he also understood that victory in battle was achieved with wisdom and forethought. Bloody Hand had cast this aside, and the mission had now become a fool's errand, sure to end in their demise. The voice of reason inside Red Hawk's head told him to retreat down the main trail and to do so with haste.

The wind helped cover any unintentional noises as they quietly rose and grabbed their gear, while Two Kills, Bloody Hand, and the white trapper snored loudly. Then, quietly, they faded into the forest.

Their horses had filled their bellies in the mountain pasture adjacent to the camp and offered no resistance to capture, as if they wanted to leave just as badly as the braves. After catching their mounts, the ten warriors circled wide to avoid waking Bloody Hand and Two Kills, then merged onto the trail a safe distance from their camp. The half-moon had risen and cleared the mountains, illuminating the trail and surrounding timber with a silvery cast. It provided plenty of light to permit slow travel as they made good their escape.

Farther down the trail, Red Hawk caught a glimpse of a shadow on the sidehill parallel to the trail. He jerked his horse to an abrupt stop.

"What's the matter? Why are we stopping?" asked one of the braves.

"I thought I saw something." Red Hawk pointed at the gap in the timber where he had noticed the dark flash move through a small moonlit opening. "Keep your eyes open," he warned. "Something's out there." He heeled his horse, and they continued alertly down the trail.

They were about to push through a tight spot between a large bull pine and a rocky abutment that ran alongside the trail when Red Hawk's horse abruptly stopped and would go no farther, its ears perked, legs trembling. Red Hawk kicked hard until his horse begrudgingly moved toward the bull pine, with the other animals following close behind. But as he neared the tree, his horse again balked and refused to move forward, no matter how hard he kicked.

Frustrated, Red Hawk ordered the next man in line, Little Foot, to take the lead. The brave kicked his horse hard and it lurched forward, as if the bull pine were about to grab them. Suddenly—*swoosh!*—*whack!* Little Foot cartwheeled off his horse and sailed through the air, landing lifeless with a lumpy thud amid the rocks and deadfall.

His horse spun, and the entire group of riders scattered like flushed quail, diving into the deadfall-choked timber. After fighting through the mishmash of fallen logs to a clear piece of ground, they regrouped in the moonlight to discuss the situation. Most of them were rattled and confused.

"Tell us what's happening." asked one of the braves. "Where is Little Foot?"

Red Hawk, who had been riding immediately behind him, replied, "Little Foot was attacked. I didn't see what it was. Something hit him by the big tree along the trail, and he just went sailing. Whatever it was, I think it killed him. We must circle and go around the danger."

Two of the braves wanted to immediately abandon their escape plan and return to the camp. They were turning to leave when a fist-sized rock struck one of them in the head with a dull crunch, sending him flying off his horse onto the ground.

Again, the men scattered, bolting into the forest in fearful panic, each man for himself. Red Hawk guided his horse clumsily through the deadfall, trying to get his bearings in the dim moonlight. He stopped when he heard a muffled scream, followed by the sound of horse hooves crashing in the timber—then silence. Not long after, he heard footfalls from one of the horses and someone whispering his name from somewhere within a dense stand of spruce. He moved carefully toward the sound with his rifle ready.

After several minutes, Moccasin, one of the men who had helped him organize the mutiny, came into view. As he approached with caution, another brave cried out—then sudden silence.

"What did you see? What's happening?" whispered Red Hawk.

"I saw it. The thing. The Skookum. It killed Running Badger." The brave's voice was trembling.

"It's stalking us—one by one," said Red Hawk. "We have to get out of here."

Just then, a panicked horse squealed, and a brave's cry for help was cut short by yet another loud whack and thump as he hit the ground, followed by the sound of hoofbeats fading into the night. The braves froze as again a menacing growl emanated from the timber not far from where they stood. Then came a rustling whirl, followed by a thump and the horrific sound of breaking bones, and more of the same whirls and thumps, again and again, as if something or someone was being flailed hard against the ground, over and over. Suddenly, the noises stopped.

Red Hawk shot a glance at Moccasin as a dark blur swept him off his horse, which wheeled and bolted riderless into the timber, crashing away on a dead run. Red Hawk's horse reared at the same time, sending him and his rifle flying in different directions. He crashed against a fallen log, knocking the wind out of him.

Slowly, he got up, holding his belly. Hearing a muted shuffling, he looked up, and there stood the Skookum a mere ten yards away, towering over the unconscious Moccasin in the pale moonlight. The creature reached down and picked the brave off the ground by his arms. Just as Moccasin started to regain consciousness, the enormous black beast pulled his arms taut. There was a loud pop and a dreadful ripping, and Moccasin fell to the ground, his arms still clutched in the creature's hands.

The man moaned once and fell silent. Red Hawk huddled in the shadow of a juniper, watching in shock. Had he seen what he thought he'd just seen? Had that thing just ripped Moccasin's arms off, as if he were a mouse or squirrel? But when the towering creature huffed and tossed the arms aside casually, Red Hawk knew his eyes had not lied. He began to shake in terror, and his heart raced uncontrollably as a flood of adrenaline poured through his veins.

The great black beast took a step away, looked over its shoulder, and cast its eyes upon Red Hawk crouching at the base of the juniper. Before it could turn around, Red Hawk bolted, hurdling over deadfall, weaving around trees, trying desperately to distance himself from it. He ran like he had never run before, but no matter how hard he ran, it seemed as if he was running through thick, chalky water that turned to mud with each stride. He could sense the beast getting closer and closer, breathing down his neck, its massive hand reaching for him. Would this be his last step, his last heartbeat? Would it rip him apart as it had ripped apart Moccasin?

Then, as he hurdled a fallen log, a memory of his wife winged across his mind. She was sitting with her legs tucked beneath her, the light from the fire inside their lodge flickering softly on her round belly. She took his hand, smiling, and placed it there gently on that warm, soft sanctuary of life. Then he felt it—lightly at first, then a sharp kick, as if her child, his child, wanted out, to breathe, to run, to live.

And as Red Hawk ran himself breathless, he prayed a silent prayer: "*No!* Stay there! Stay where you will be warm and safe. Don't leave your safe abode for this one, where monsters lurk and hunt men in the ashen light of the moon."

He rounded a tree and could see another brave just ahead, atop his horse near the edge of the abutment. Hopefully, the brave had a rifle and could get a shot at the monster before it caught him. He glanced over his shoulder, but to his astonishment, the creature was no longer there.

He turned back toward the brave just in time to see a thick piece of broken log hurtle through the air from somewhere in the forest. It struck the brave with a bone-crunching thud, knocking him off his horse, which turned and bolted. Red Hawk skidded to a stop. There, not thirty yards away, stood the Skookum. It was standing above the brave, who moaned and tried to rise. But the Skookum reached down, grabbed him by the ankle, and flung him in a wide circle before smashing him on the ground with a sickening thud.

Then, it turned and came swiftly for Red Hawk. He had only one way out, and he took it, leaping off the abutment to the rocks below. He was certain he heard a rock whistle past him just as he jumped. He landed hard, heard and felt the bone snap in his lower leg, and rolled to the bottom, stopping against the base of a bushy juniper.

He tried to run, but immediately fell. It was no use—he couldn't run. He crawled under the tangle of juniper like a scared rabbit and stayed motionless as a passing cloud blocked the moon, and death's dark shadow enveloped the basin.

A minute passed, and he heard soft footfalls, like the gentle padding of a rabbit. Suddenly, there it was, towering above him, black against the backdrop of starlight. The cloud whisked by, and the moonlight lit the creature's dour face. Red Hawk tried desperately to keep his breathing in control and remain as still as possible to calm his pounding heart. Imperceptibly slowly, Red Hawk turned his eyes upward to see its face, its eyes. They sparkled in the moonlight and were clear and sagacious; it's breathing relaxed and almost undetectable. It blinked once as it glanced up at the moon, inexplicably placid. Then, its eyes suddenly became animated, searching the area, and it sniffed the air as if trying to catch Red Hawk's scent. Red Hawk understood its movements completely, for he had done the same thing on many occasions when on the hunt, except now, he had become the rabbit, and the dogged determination written on the face of the hunter made him tremble.

From somewhere in the thick timber came the sound of horse hooves struggling over deadfall. Red Hawk blinked, and the Skookum was gone. A minute later came the panicked screech of a horse and the wail of its rider, both cut short with the sound of a crash.

He waited under the juniper, panic-stricken, wondering what he should do. His leg was broken, he had no horse, and his rifle was lost somewhere in the timber. His instincts told him the creature was determined and would be back to search for him. Then, he saw it—the black shadow of a small cave near the base of the abutment. He heard another scream from somewhere in the timber. He quickly scrambled out from under the juniper, ignoring the pain, and hobbled over to the cave. Without hesitation, he crawled inside the opening.

Inside the entrance, the narrow cave disappeared into darkness. He wondered what lay deeper in the crevice. Anything could be there: rattlesnakes, a den of coyotes, bobcat, or maybe even a mountain lion waiting for him to draw near before it struck at him. Perhaps the Skookum wouldn't come back. Perhaps it couldn't reach him if it did return, or maybe it would be too big to fit inside the small cave. He wriggled in a few feet farther and sat back against the cave wall. A heavy, dull pain coursed through his body when his leg shifted, the broken bones grating together as he carefully pulled it away from the entrance and shifted to face the opposite wall. He was uncomfortable, and the pain in his leg was growing stronger as the adrenaline and shock gradually wore off.

An hour must have passed before he heard a rustling outside the cave, and a fleeting shadow momentarily blocked the moonlight seeping into the opening. A few minutes later, the shadow moved past from the opposite direction. Red Hawk stared nervously at the entrance, feeling the trembling once again take over his body.

At the uppermost rim of the cave opening, a line of darkness appeared against the starlight. Then, slowly, like the falling of an evil moon, it descended, growing larger ... and larger. Red Hawk's heart raced as the silhouette of a massive head slowly came into view. Could it reach him? Was he in far enough?

In the next instant, there was a deep grunt that seemed to shake the walls of the cave. Red Hawk instinctively lunged away from the massive black arm that reached in, grabbing blindly. The cave grew tighter as he crawled in deeper. He felt a brush against his foot and heard another grunt behind him as the arm reached greedily for him with wide sweeps, scattering rocks as it groped. He squirmed, worm-like, into the tight orifice, his buckskin shirt catching on the stony floor like an anchor holding him back. He must go deeper— deeper into the safety of the darkness, deeper into the protecting womb of the mountain.

His breathing became chopped, and the walls of the cavern hugged his chest, yet he could still hear the creature, feel the vibrations from its powerful arms clawing ravenously, its guttural breaths just behind him, lusting for the kill. *Farther, farther, I must go farther!*

He crawled an inch, two inches, three, until his head grazed the rocky ceiling with each wriggle forward. Then, with his out-stretched hands, he felt an edge on the floor of the passageway. He squirmed forward, found a handhold, and pulled himself through the ever-tightening hollow. As he squeezed himself through, his body blocked the scant moonlight illuminating the cave. Ahead was an empty blackness; for a moment, he thought about what danger the darkness might hold. Would he fall off the edge into a deep abyss, never to return, never again to see the light of day? A rock tumbled through the opening behind him, hitting his foot; his hesitation vanished in an instant, and he lurched forward, over the edge, and into the void.

He thumped to the bottom and sat back against the rim of a shallow chamber, then wept in relief. He had fallen only a few feet and he was alive, but most important, the creature couldn't reach him now. There was hope now that he would see his wife again. Yes, he would see her again—and his child.

Gradually, his rapid breathing subsided, and his heart stopped pounding. With the narrow passage now clear, he could faintly see the wall of the chamber across from him, the moonlight painting a softer brush of black against its rocky face. Then came a worrisome sound from the opening of the cave—the clatter of a large, dropped rock, then another, and another. And as they dropped, the lighter brush of black faded into pure darkness. But just before the last glint of moonlight was snuffed, there came the familiar growl of a cougar from inside the cave's chamber, just a few yards away from him.

Red Hawk inched back and sat tightly against the ledge below the entrance, thinking any moment it would pounce, imagining its claws sinking into his flesh and its sharp teeth biting down on his exposed neck. He couldn't tell how long he waited with the cougar in the lightless tomb, but it did not attack. It may have been less than an hour, but it seemed like days. The only thing he could figure was that both he and the cougar had one thing in common: they both feared the thing that had driven them there, and they were in a mutually beneficial truce brought on by sheer terror.

But when Red Hawk heard it yawn, lick its teeth, and smack its lips, he decided he'd worn out his welcome. He wriggled back through the tight opening, his leg throbbing, then managed to push away enough of the rocks covering the entrance to emerge. He found a sturdy piece of lodgepole and used it as a makeshift crutch, then headed down the trail, as fast as his good leg and crutch could take him.

The morning sun had yet to rise when Gabe woke up. He shivered from the cold night air and rekindled the fire. He glanced down at Eagle Claw, then scanned the area. For the first time since they had left the Kootenai village, he was hopeful. Two Kills heard him toss a log in the fire and got up, then looked around nervously. Gabe smiled to himself and stared into the fire. Two Kills prodded Bloody Hand's heavy buffalo blanket and woke him up loudly. Foggy-eyed, Bloody Hand threw off the blanket, grabbed his rifle, and pointed it toward the alder brush on the other side of the creek until he realized there was no danger.

The sound of Two Kills' sharp voice also roused Eagle Claw, and he quickly sat up. Two Kills spoke angrily, waving his arms and his rifle, gesturing wildly. Bloody Hand grew enraged and spoke back even louder.

Gabe already knew what they were talking about. "Where did they go?" he whispered to Eagle Claw.

"The must have left during the night, back down the canyon. They fear the Skookum. I could see it in their eyes."

Gabe watched silently as Bloody Hand looked around in astonishment, seeing that his men had abandoned their mission. He appeared embarrassed, and rightly so. For weeks, Gabe heard stories about the ferocity of the Blackfeet, but now, they had been exposed as cowards, skulking away in the dead of night like coyotes with their tails tucked between their legs.

They continued arguing back and forth in the Blackfeet tongue. "What are they saying?" he whispered to Eagle Claw.

"The one they call Two Kills wants to leave with the others. He said they no longer have an advantage over the trappers. They only have two guns to the trappers' three." They continued arguing back and forth until Bloody Hand reached for his rifle.

Finally, Two Kills huffed in frustration, grabbed his rifle, and disappeared into the timber. "Is he leaving, too? What's going on?" asked Gabe.

"He is off to check the horses. He will be back. This is the only trail in and out. The new plan is wait for the trappers to come down this trail and ambush them."

"But that could take days. What about food?"

"Bloody Hand said we have plenty of beaver to eat, and we have time. They will take turns watching the trail."

Bloody Hand sat several paces away, holding his rifle tightly. He seemed lost until suddenly he looked up and to Gabe's surprise, rebuked them in English: "Stop whispering!"

After an hour or so, Two Kills returned with four horses. He tied them close, and, once again, the chattering between the two Blackfeet began. Then, as if their captives had suddenly become compatriots, Two Kills confided to Gabe and Eagle Claw in English and said, "The horses are scattered. I was lucky to find these."

Bloody Hand rebuked him angrily, and they exchanged terse words until Two Kills finally stomped away and sat down opposite them by the fire, his rifle cradled in his lap.

Gabe felt a sudden urge to speak to him, but before he could utter a single word, Two Kills glared at him and said, "I'm hungry, white man. Go find us a beaver for breakfast. If you don't come back soon, the White Warrior dies."

Gabe sat for a moment, bewildered and confused. He glanced at Eagle Claw, then Two Kills, but neither were smiling. Gabe got up and hurried toward the timber, still wondering if the Blackfeet man's deathly threat was real or just spoken in frustration. It seemed draconian—to kill a man for lack of a breakfast—but he didn't want to test him.

He climbed the steep fifty-foot bank on the opposite side of the creek and stopped at the top. Ahead of him, the mountain sloped more gradually, the trees a mixture of mature fir with stands of younger trees, ten or twelve feet tall, bunched in scattered pockets. He felt naked without his rifle and took a hesitant step when he remembered the strange track and the fearful growl that had emanated from the forest the night before. Farther ahead grew a dark patch of timber. It seemed the most likely place where the growl had come from. He crept ahead, scanning the forest floor in the dim pre-dawn light—all he needed was one beaver, just one beaver.

Blocking his way stood a stand of young fir that appeared to run parallel to the drainage. Summoning his courage, Gabe fought his way through it until the forest opened again, and he continued up the mountain until he looked up, and there in front of him stood the dark patch of timber. He had been so focused looking for a beaver, he somehow had lost track of where his footsteps were leading him.

As he stared into the blackness, he felt the hair rise on the back of his neck. The trees seemed to have a life of their own, almost as if the forest itself were breathing. He stepped back and felt something slippery under foot. Looking down into the knee-high foliage, he was ecstatic to find he had stumbled upon one of the beaver carcasses. It was a smaller one, probably born the previous spring, with minimal raven pocks, but it would do just fine. After all, Two Kills hadn't specified that it had to be a big one. He turned back down the mountain as an unsettling sensation came over him—the feeling that something was watching him. He paused to listen, then heard a faint rustling behind him in the shadowy timber. He spun around and scanned the dark pre-dawn forest. The rustling stopped, and an ominous silence blanketed the mountain, swallowing the faint noises from the camp below. Gabe cocked his ears and picked up the subtle sound of something creeping toward him. A tingling sensation sent shivers up and down his spine as the faint sound of low breathing drifted from somewhere behind the dark curtain of trees. Then came the low vibration of a growl. Goosebumps sprang up all over his body, and a voice inside seemed to scream between his temples, telling him that there were places on this earth where the sons of men were not welcome—and this was one of them.

His heart thumped with fear as something large approached, causing the tops of the pines to sway.

Whatever it was, it was close and headed straight toward him. He quickly turned, beaver in hand, and ran. Glancing over his shoulder, he expected to see a grizzly closing in. Instead, he got a glimpse of a looming figure twisting through the dense timber, approaching fast.

He broke into an all-out sprint, as fast as his legs could carry him. Behind him came a low grunt and the sound of running footsteps closing rapidly. He careened ahead, dodging trees as the sounds of deep huffing got louder, as if it were right behind him. Branches slapped him in the face as he busted through a stand of young fir trees. He picked up speed once in the clear and felt the earth shake when something large landed just behind him to his right, as if his pursuer had simply leaped over the stand of fir he had just crashed through.

Ahead was a line of large, tightly spaced trees. As Gabe dove between them, he heard the footsteps veer to skirt the obstacle. He hurtled down the mountain toward a small ledge overlooking the creek and leaped just as he felt a brush of air on the nape of his neck from the violent swing of something heavy.

As he jumped, Gabe flung the beaver aside, surprised it was still in his hands, and grabbed for the branch of a fast-approaching bull pine. Latching on, it bent under his weight, then snapped at the climax of momentum, sending him crashing into the patch of alders below.

The alders broke his fall, but when he landed it knocked the wind out of him. He scrambled to his feet, fighting for air, and stumbled ahead, across the creek and through the remaining tangle of brush and willows. He tripped and fell as he scrambled forward in view of the camp, and when he broke through, everyone was standing watching him—Two Kills and Bloody Hand with rifles shouldered.

"Where is my breakfast?" asked Two Kills incredulously.

Breathless, Gabe pointed behind him and gasped. "I—I found one. I dropped it there. Don't kill Eagle Claw. Just—just let me catch my breath."

"You are fast, white man," remarked Two Kills, grinning. "See, White Warrior, how bad your friend wants to save you? Or maybe he is just very hungry?"

"What happened? Why were you running?" asked Eagle Claw.

Gabe, bent over, hands on his knees, breathing hard.

"Gabe?"

"I don't know. I—I thought I saw something. I don't know, Eagle Claw. It happened so fast. Something came after me—quickly, so I ran. I couldn't tell what it was. Everything was a blur. But it tried to get me."

"Are you okay?"

"Yes, I'm okay. No broken bones that I can tell."

"The white man appears whiter than usual," joked Two Kills.

"He is called Gabe," replied Eagle Claw firmly.

"Well, then—Gabe! Go back and get the beaver."

Gabe walked cautiously. At least this time, he was within sight of the camp. He picked up a club-sized length of a broken larch bough and glanced back at Eagle Claw. Eagle Claw appeared worried; his lips pursed with anticipation. Gabe continued, working his way through the tangle of alder and up the steep bank. Peering up, he spied the shiny carcass of the dead beaver. He expected his pursuer to pop over the ledge at any moment as he drew closer. It was within grabbing distance now. Gabe lunged, picked it up and bolted back down the steep grade.

They were both relieved when he approached Two Kills with the beaver. He grabbed it, ran it through with a skewer, then positioned it over the coals.

"So, they call you Gabe, eh?" Two Kills said. "What is the meaning of this name?"

"It's short for Gabriel—the death angel of God," Gabe replied, glaring at the man.

"Angel? What is *angel*?" he asked.

Eagle Claw chimed in before Gabe had a chance to answer. "It means a powerful spirit, a messenger to bring death to the wicked or help to the good."

"Ah. Well, it is good name. But you do not appear like death spirit to me," Two Kills said with a chuckle.

Gabe studied the Blackfeet warrior, picking up on his sudden change in demeanor—how he suddenly seemed more cordial, almost friendly. He had even begun speaking in English, almost as if the fearful events of the night and the mutiny of their braves had, by necessity, caused him to want to form an alliance. The thought crossed his mind that perhaps the two Blackfeet men needed them more than they were letting on.

Gabe plopped down by the fire to regain his composure. Everyone grew silent for a moment. Eagle Claw sat back against a tree with his arms on his knees directly across the fire from Two Kills. Watching the two of them staring at each other, Gabe was hard-pressed to think they weren't related: the same wiry frame, sharp eyes, and alert demeanor. The only things distinctly different were Eagle Claw's lighter hair and unique eye color.

Bloody Hand broke the tension and the silence. "What about you, White Warrior? What is your real name?"

"Eagle Claw," he stated proudly.

"A very good name," said Two Kills. "My grandfather's name was Flying Eagle."

As the men shared a meal of rancid, over-aged beaver, the chit-chat, intended to ward away the sense of foreboding, chipped away at their adversarial walls. Soon, they realized they had more in common than they thought—including their fear of what might be waiting in the darkness of the woods and their shared enemy in Crooked Bill Branch and his men.

$\mathscr{A}$ *Hasty* $\mathscr{R}$*etreat*

The villagers had risen early at the Kootenai fish camp and were scurrying about packing and loading their belongings. The Elders had conferred and agreed with one thing Eagle Claw had said: their fish camp had become vulnerable, and the Blackfeet could easily have wiped them out—and possibly still could when they returned.

They had a big day ahead of them as they prepared to make a hasty retreat to the Tobacco Plains, where they would join another band and marshal their resources to form a defensive bulwark against possible attack.

The older women prepared a morning meal and packed enough food for their long trek, while the younger women arranged their sparse belongings into bundles to be hauled with pack horses and travois. The older men were also busy, wrapping and bundling smoked fish in buckskin tarpaulins, and the younger braves were catching the remaining horses feeding in a nearby meadow. The trail to the Tobacco Plains meandered north along the same river that flowed near the fish camp. They worked quickly, for it was a difficult three-day march to their winter camp.

Dawn had most of her items prepared and packed, but she wasn't clothed in the draping buckskin dresses the other women wore.

Instead, she wore a pair of form-fitting elk-leather breeches she had made herself, along with a pair of knee-high moccasins adorned with beads ornately stitched in a pattern of wild roses.

She hadn't slept well, tossing and turning with dreams of the Blackfeet holding down Eagle Claw and Gabe while they scalped them alive. She respected the Elders but was incensed by their apparent lack of concern over their well-being. She often thought about Running Bear, the brother she had lost, and wondered what her life would have been like if he were alive—if he hadn't wandered off on that fateful day. Now, Eagle Claw had volunteered to guide the Blackfeet into the sacred lands, putting himself at risk for the benefit of the tribe. Even more troubling was that they were traveling to where the Skookum lived, the same creature that had killed Running Bear. The very idea of it seemed wrong-headed and unfair. She hatched a plan to covertly drift back from the others on the trail and peel off from the main group once they were well underway, then journey into the sacred canyon alone to help free her brother.

Eagle claw's friend Gabe Bauman was also in danger, and though she would never openly admit it, she felt she owed him a life debt after he had saved her from drowning. Though she battled her feelings, it was becoming more difficult to maintain her chilly demeanor toward the young mountain man. He was polite, patient, and unusually tolerant of her generally scornful attitude toward him, and she was beginning to feel guilty for shunning him and treating him so harshly. It bothered her much more than she had expected, especially after Singing Bird said he had "a good heart."

Dawn noticed Singing Bird's suspicious glances as she readied her horse for the trail, how her face blanched at the sight of her embroidered leggings, which Dawn only wore as a good-luck talisman during their community hunts or whenever they had to face their enemies on the field of battle.

"Why do you dress like this, my daughter?" Singing Bird said. "What is happening in that pretty head of yours? We need you here to help us get safely to the Tobacco Plains."

Dawn heard her voice but ignored her words as she removed her bow from its scabbard to inspect the sinew bowstring, hoping her mother would refocus her all-seeing eyes on something else. Dawn examined her arrows, which were tipped with skillfully crafted flint broadheads, sharp enough to be used for shaving. Everything appeared to be in good condition and ready for use. But when she began inspecting her rifle, Singing Bird asked pointedly, "You don't wish to answer me?"

"I think you already know the answer to your questions." Dawn turned away and looked toward the sacred canyon.

"What about us? What about the word of the Elders?" Singing Bird continued.

Dawn felt a welling of indignation, making her heart race. *Had she forgotten about Running Bear, viciously killed at the hands of the Skookum?* She tried controlling her words, but they spilled over. "What about Eagle Claw, my only brother—and your only son? Does it not worry you that he is in grave danger? It appears I am the only one who cares about his welfare!"

Singing Bird gasped. Her expression became downcast, and her eyes saddened at the cutting words. Immediately, Dawn felt regretful, for she spoke them with malice—sharp arrows that pierced her mother's heart, aimed to bring shame for Singing Bird's apparent disregard for Eagle Claw's well-being.

"He is my only son," Singing Bird said, regaining her composure, "and you, my only daughter. You are safe here with us, but if you leave, you will both be in danger. You need not worry about Eagle Claw. He can take care of himself."

Dawn took a measured breath, strengthening her own resolve. "I must do what I must do. I'm not going to just ride off and let the Blackfeet kill and scalp my brother. And I know he would do the thing same for me."

Singing Bird shook her head in frustration. "Yes, you are strong, and you are brave. But this—this takes a different kind of strong and a different kind of brave. Are you strong enough and brave enough to trust the wisdom of the Elders and let the Great Father answer your prayers?"

"Perhaps *I* am the answer to my prayers," Dawn said firmly but respectfully.

Singing Bird stepped back and looked at her daughter lovingly, as only a mother can do. "I know how you feel, my dear child. Many times, your father went out to hunt or to fight, and many times, I thought I'd never see him again. I had to be strong—but being strong wasn't enough. I had to learn to conquer my fears, to trust in the Great Spirit."

Suddenly, a cold gust of wind blew in from the canyon, a raven cawed as it flew overhead, and Singing Bird's pupils grew black. She took a frail step toward the sacred canyon and gazed as if in a trance. Dawn joined her, trying to see what she was looking at.

"What is it, Mother? What do you see?"

"Darkness comes upon us—I see death in the speckled clouds."

Dawn looked at the sky. "But Mother, there are no clouds in the sky."

The sound of horses approaching from the west sent everyone scrambling for weapons and broke Singing Bird from her trance. But when the riders emerged, everyone was relieved to see it was James and Crowfoot.

"Father, you're back!" shouted Dawn.

The runner had found the hunting party and told them how the Blackfeet had taken Eagle Claw and his friend as hostages, then ventured into the sacred land seeking revenge against the trappers. When James heard the report, he immediately abandoned the hunt and returned to the fish camp.

Dawn and Singing Bird hurried forward to greet James, who dismounted and gave Singing Bird a hug. "I'm so glad you are here!" she said.

"Where are the others?" Dawn asked, hoping more men might join her in searching for Eagle Claw.

"When we got the message, I sent the other hunters on to the Tobacco Plains," James replied. Her father glanced down at her attire and the bow and arrow that lay upon her bundle of belongings. "It looks like you are well prepared, daughter. But we are not going to war yet," he said as he gave her a hug.

"You made it back just in time," Singing Bird said. "We will soon be ready to leave."

She gave Dawn a subtle pleading look, clearly hoping her words would persuade her to reconsider her plans. Dawn felt the tug of her mother's words but stiffened her spine against them. She finished rolling up her supplies, tied them tightly, and fastened them behind the saddle of her horse.

Within minutes, the village had finished packing, and everyone was lined up on the trail. White Cloud gave the signal, and they began the long trek north. Dawn didn't want to create a scene in front of the Elders or engender an argument with her father in front of the tribe, so she gradually drifted back until she was near the end of the procession. After a half hour of riding, they approached the sharp turn on the trail, where she had planned to make her move. She spoke casually with the braves bringing up the rear, then abruptly excused herself, telling them she needed to "answer nature's call." As soon as the procession disappeared around the corner on the trail, she turned and headed the opposite direction.

Once she became confident that nobody was following her, she thought about the ordeal in front of her, fighting back fear and doubt. She had just passed through the fish camp and was heading to the trail leading into the sacred land when she heard the unmistakable sound of hoofbeats approaching from behind. Looking back, she saw James and Crowfoot clearing the timber and heading toward her.

"I'm not going to the Tobacco Plains without my brother," said Dawn firmly as they galloped up to her, their horses foamy with sweat, chests heaving, and nostrils flared.

"We are not coming to bring you back, daughter. We are coming to help you."

Dawn relaxed in her saddle, gave a small smile, and choked back her emotions. She turned her horse up the trail and they fell in behind her.

The many tracks of the Blackfeet horses were easy to follow. They paused near the creek that flowed from the sacred canyon to water the horses and let them rest before the arduous climb up the cliffs.

"This will be a tough climb," said James. "I hope the animals are up to the task." He dismounted and studied the cliffy switchbacks farther up the mountain.

"If they can't make it, I will continue on foot," Dawn said with determination as she dismounted. Neither James nor Crowfoot replied, but as the horses watered, the men looked at the cliffs again and then at each other. She could see the doubt written on their faces and the misgivings in the squint of their eyes.

"If the horses can't make it up there, I think we are both willing to make the climb and help—even if these legs of mine aren't as young as they used to be," James finally said.

Dawn smiled gratefully. "Thank you, Father."

The sound of falling rocks brought everyone to attention, and they quickly retrieved their weapons for a possible fight. A Blackfeet warrior hobbled into view, using a broken piece of lodgepole pine for a crutch. They could see he was unarmed, so they lowered their weapons as he limped toward them down the mountain. As he approached, he looked up and, to Dawn's surprise, seemed relieved to see them. Immediately, he lowered himself to the ground and lay panting.

"Be careful, Father," urged Dawn as James approached the man.

"What is your name?" asked James in the Blackfeet tongue.

"I am Red Hawk."

"Here. Have some water," said James.

The brave seemed relieved to hear his own language. Dawn understood enough Blackfeet to get the gist of what they were saying. He was thirsty and drank nearly all of James's water supply. Somewhat surprised, James said, "There is much water in this ravine. Why did you not drink?"

Red Hawk handed the canteen back to James, struggling to get the words out from sheer exhaustion. "Could not stop. The demon … I saw it … I saw what it did. The demon got them!" he cried out hysterically.

Dawn thought she understood what he said, but hoped she was wrong, that she had misinterpreted his dark words. "What's he saying? Where's Eagle Claw?"

"What do you mean, 'the demon got them?'" asked James.

"The … the demon of the forest … the Skookum. Don't go back there. It will kill you. This trail only leads to death!"

Dawn felt the blood drain from her face at the word *Skookum*. She sat with her arms propped together on her knees, feeling as if her spirit had been torn in two.

"He said the Skookum will kill us," James told her.

She nodded. "I know what he said," she replied. Dawn hid her head in her hands and wished it was all just a bad dream.

"What about our two men?" James pressed the Blackfeet man. "The white man and Eagle Claw, the White Warrior?"

"I don't know. They stayed at the camp. We tried to flee from the Skookum, but it hunted us down. I don't know where they are."

"He said he doesn't know what happened to Eagle Claw," James translated.

Dawn looked up and stared at the brave, then rose with a surge of new hope. "Eagle Claw and Gabe could still be back in there?" she said, hopefully. Dawn marched to her horse, rifle in hand, with renewed determination. "What are you waiting for, Father? Let's go!"

"Hold on a minute," replied James. To Dawn's chagrin, her father knelt and spoke compassionately to the wounded man. "You stay here and wait for us. We are going to try and find them."

"No! No!" cried Red Hawk. "I won't wait here. I will go. Away from this demon mountain!"

"But your leg—it's broken and needs a splint."

Before James could say anything else, the man scrambled upright and continued hobbling down the trail. Suddenly, he tripped and fell, groaning from the pain. Dawn sighed impatiently as James ran to help the brave and calm him down, reassuring him that he would be okay and that they would help him get back to his village.

Dawn waited grudgingly while James fashioned a splint, perturbed how her father could so easily wander into the dingy realm of helping an enemy in need. In her mind, there was no such thing as shades of gray, only stark black and white. An enemy was an enemy and should be treated as such. In theory, she understood the concept espoused by her father, to "love thy enemy," but the principle he regularly taught made no sense in her pragmatic mind. She could never understand the logic behind showing mercy to the unmerciful; after all, it was the Blackfeet who had threatened to destroy their village. She huffed and clenched her jaw when James gave the brave some food and told him to wait at the fish camp, assuring him he would be safest there. She shook her head in disgust when the man agreed, then slowly limped down the trail.

"What are we going to do?" asked Crowfoot fearfully, as if hoping James would come to his senses and follow the wiser path of the Blackfeet man. "The Big Man they call Skookum surely waits ahead near the trail to destroy anyone who ventures into his territory."

James and Dawn looked on as the brave struggled painfully down the trail, wincing with each step.

"Whatever happened to that man," James said, "it has put the fear of God in him. I've never seen a Blackfeet man act that way before."

Dawn mounted her horse and kicked him in the ribs. "*Hiya!*" she barked—a subtle rebuke of Crowfoot's trepidation and her father's mercy. As her horse powered up the mountain, she glanced over her shoulder to make sure James and Crowfoot were following.

It wasn't long before the horses began struggling to keep their footing as they ascended the steeper section of the trail, and they dismounted before it became too treacherous.

Suddenly, Dawn's keen nose detected a foul odor. "What's causing that smell?"

"Not sure. Something's dead down there," replied Crowfoot, staring into the deep gorge.

"We don't have time to investigate," Dawn said as she looked at the cliffs ahead of them. "We must keep moving."

"I know these horses—they're mates," said James. "Tie off his reins and give him a swat, and the others will follow him right up."

Dawn didn't hesitate. After tying off the reins, she gave her horse a good smack on the rump, and it shot up the trail. The three horses dug in with their powerful hindquarters and climbed up the rocky switchback trail until they finally reached the top.

"Now, the question is, can I make it?" said James.

"I'm not worried one bit about that," replied Dawn. They scrambled up the trail to the horses waiting patiently for them at the top.

Dawn was pleased when she noticed the trail flatten—it would make traveling much faster. The only thing that kept her from wanting to kick her horse into a gallop was what the Blackfeet man had told them about the Skookum. Even as they moved steadily toward their goal, an eerie chill crept into her bones. She wondered whether James and Crowfoot felt it—the quiet, impending presence of death. They had ridden several miles when Crowfoot stopped on the trail.

"Hold up," he said as he dismounted. "I see something."

Dawn and James got off their horses and tied them off, then followed him through a maze of deadfall until the flutter of ravens stopped them short. Ahead, wedged tightly against a fallen pine, lay a mangled body.

Crowfoot tried to roll him over, but there was no stiffness to the red mass—just the crackling of broken bones. He and James each grabbed and rolled the sprawling, bloody heap. It was difficult to decide who or what it was—aside from his hands and feet, there wasn't much to indicate a person had once lived inside the gruesome pile of torn skin and broken bones. Dawn surmised it must have been one of the Blackfeet men because the hair was much too dark to be Eagle Claw or Bauman. She was mortified at the sight.

"God have mercy on his soul," said James.

"What could have done this?" asked Crowfoot, scanning the surrounding forest with a grimace etched on his face. "It must be true. The legend. What man would do such a thing?"

The discovery splashed cold water upon the fading embers of Dawn's hope. She continued up the trail slower now, her zeal squelched by the horrific sight. James offered a prayer for courage after they all felt the sensation that something was watching from the shadows. They rode alert now, and more tightly together, drawing strength from each other.

Farther up the trail, they saw more ravens and found another dead brave—his severed arms lying next to him, as if his wrists had been tied with ropes and pulled off his body with a pair of horses. Aside from his hideously dismembered body, this one hadn't been pulverized quite as badly, and it was easy to identify that it wasn't Eagle Claw or Gabe.

Dawn felt the blood drain from her face and let James take the lead. Slowly, they inched up the trail. Before long, they found a third body, skewered like a scarecrow on a fir tree that had been snapped in half. The jagged end of the pike was sticking up through the pocket between his neck and shoulder. The three gathered round the corpse, its eyes rigored wide in fear, mouth agape as if frozen at the apex of terror.

Dawn felt a surge of fear-induced trembling and turned to see Crowfoot pale with anxiety, as if he were about to fracture and lose his grip on reality. James, on the other hand, appeared pragmatic and unmoved by the mutilated bodies that lay scattered throughout the timber—more puzzled than fearful.

"This is like a battlefield," said James. "Only there are no gunshot or stab wounds."

"What do we do, Father?" asked Dawn as she fidgeted nervously with the horse's reins.

"We continue in faith. A man did not—could not—do this. If there is a demon in this forest, as Red Hawk said, then only God can help us."

For the first time since she had made her personal vow to help Eagle Claw and his friend, Dawn's confidence faltered, and she felt a widening chink in her otherwise impenetrable armor of courage. Concern for her brother's safety had been supplanted by an innate fear born of survival and self-preservation.

"There is plenty of water and grass for the horses," James continued. "I think we should let them rest and search the area to get a better idea of a body count. And pray that Eagle Claw and his friend are not among them."

"I agree," said Crowfoot. "If Eagle Claw and Gabe are wounded and holed up somewhere in this timber, we'd be just riding past them if we keep going."

"Very well, but we must stick together," Dawn said firmly.

"Agreed," James said. "Let's spread apart, but not too far, and keep within sight of each other, so we can cover more ground."

They searched for several hours, combing the area on each side of the trail, finding more random bloody carnage. One man's neck had been snapped, and his head twisted completely around so that he faced the opposite direction of his torso; another was skewered with a broken tree limb with his eyes scratched out; still others had been pounded beyond description. Fortunately, none of the ill-fated victims were Eagle Claw or Gabe. After they'd found nine corpses, Dawn noticed that even her stalwart father appeared to have a case of bilious ague. They returned to their horses well before dark, built a fire, and let their stomachs settle before eating dinner.

As they were preparing their camp for sleeping, an enraged animal cry came twisting and writhing toward them like a fiendish devil.

They stopped and turned toward it. But nobody asked what it was, for they all instinctively knew the answer.

"Do we have enough wood for the fire?" asked James.

Without another word, they began gathering wood, rifles in hand.

Chapter Thirty-One

Messy Camp

*B*ranch and his men arrived at the next campsite well after dark, built a quick fire, and settled in. The following morning, Choteau woke from a fitful night's rest, stirred by his nightmares about the mysterious troublemaker who seemed determined to spook them out of the basin. The placid virgin lakes ringed with beaver lodges at the far end of the basin quickly became a strong distraction from his disturbing thoughts. They could now look up from their camp and see the impressive beaver dam. Half a dozen enormous, furred rodents swam back and forth on the still waters with mouthfuls of branches, blissfully ignorant of their coming demise.

After a quick breakfast washed down with a slosh of gritty coffee, they prepared to set their traps. Choteau skewered a skinned beaver and placed it above the pile of glowing coals in the firepit. It would be ready to eat for lunch by the time they returned.

It was a cool, crisp morning, and a thin layer of ice had formed along the grassy lakeshore. After several hours of setting the traps, the men marched back to their new campsite in single file, following the game trail that ran along the shoreline until it merged with the small stream gurgling near their camp. The beaver had been working diligently, evidenced by the many willows and alders they had felled, and the freshly gnawed branches piled in underwater food caches near their lodges to help get them through the winter.

Choteau's fears were momentarily quelled, supplanted by his ongoing fantasy of his new log cabin situated near a placid stream somewhere far from the mountains. His daydream was always the same: watching a few cows grazing contentedly in a pasture carpeted in verdure, and the gentle wind rustling through a fresh crop of corn reaching skyward from rich black soil, while he rocked back and forth on the porch of his cabin. His mind whirled through another long series of calculations, approximations, and speculations over how much money he would make on the beaver furs and how quickly he could make his bucolic dreams come true.

"If luck is on our side, we'll soon be skinnin' jumbos," said Branch as they hiked toward their camp.

Just then, a swimming beaver expressed his feelings toward the trespassers with a dissenting slap of its big flat tail. It was so loud it even startled Branch. "Oh, we'll be busy for sure," Johnson said, puffing out his chest. "No doubt about it. Bet you a Green River knife I'll be skinnin' that one, too."

Choteau felt the sudden urge to challenge the pompous trapper, but he held his tongue.

As the men approached the camp, it became abundantly clear that something was amiss. The first thing that met them was the annoying odor that had seemed to come and go ever since they had entered the drainage. It was a smell Choteau knew all too well, once again resurrecting his worst nightmares. The horses off in the distance had stopped grazing and were standing at attention, alertly staring at the men as they approached the camp.

"Do you smell that?" Choteau said nervously.

But Branch and Johnson didn't respond. They were walking several paces ahead of him, their eyes transfixed on the camp as it came into full view—a shocking tangle of pots, bedrolls, and horse tack scattered in disarray. Their pace quickened as they drew closer.

The evidence was unmistakable, and Choteau quickly realized once again that they were not alone in the remote basin. Whatever had deviled them at the first camp had followed them to the second and had now boldly paid them a visit while they were away setting traps. Choteau carefully studied the destruction, for things hadn't simply been rummaged through in the typical fashion of a hungry bear. Whatever tore through their camp did so in anger and was trying to send them a clear message.

"Damnation!" exclaimed Johnson. "The bear that did this must be close by, and by the looks of this mess, he's madder'n hell and bent on mischief."

Branch stood stupefied, scratching his head and mumbling to himself. Finally, he said, "Well, if it's that bear you shot, all ya did was piss him off. Damn it! That's all we need—a bear problem. I blame you for this, Johnson! You just couldn't leave the griz well enough alone, could ya?"

Choteau stood in stunned silence, hands on his hips, until Branch barked, "Choteau! Check the furs!" He ran to their bundles of beaver fur and examined them. Surprisingly, not only were they all accounted for, but they were unmolested and intact. He gazed in resignation at the mess, knowing most of the cleanup would fall on his shoulders. Approaching the firepit, he remarked, "What bear wouldn't bother to devour a nicely-cooked beaver?"

Branch examined the beaver Choteau had placed over the coals for roasting before they had left to set their traps. "Well, maybe he wasn't hungry," he said sarcastically.

Choteau shook his head as Branch stubbornly conjured yet another "rational" explanation, grasping idiotically for anything to support the flimsy theory that the vandal could be anything but a bear.

Choteau pointed up at the branches of a nearby tree and hollered, "Hey, Monsieur Johnson! Do you know how to climb a tree?"

"What kinda fool question is that?" Johnson barked.

"Well, that appears to be your bedroll up there. Looks like your bear not only doesn't like you, but he knows how to throw your things as well."

Johnson snorted with derision and stared at his bedroll hanging from a limb well beyond reach. He was cutting a long alder branch to try and retrieve it when Choteau suddenly felt the familiar, unwelcome sensation that they were being watched. An icy chill crept under his garments as he scanned the timbered areas around the camp.

"You gonna stand there all day watchin' the timber, or you gonna help get this mess picked up?" Branch said gruffly.

"Something is not right about this, Branch," replied Choteau, "and you know it."

Branch ignored him and commenced gathering firewood without debate, but his silence told Choteau that Branch also knew something was amiss. Choteau leaned his gun against a fallen log near the firepit, where he could grab it on a moment's notice, and began picking up items that had been strewn about.

After a few minutes, Johnson was finally able to dislodge his bedroll. He peered at something on the ground and scratched his chin before kneeling and studying the thing more closely. "What do you make of this?" he asked.

Choteau went over to see what he was looking at.

"Don't seem like any griz track I've ever seen. No claw prints," said Johnson. But Choteau had seen the enormous track before, and its presence in the camp only reinforced his suspicions and fears.

Branch dropped his armful of firewood in a heap near the campfire and joined them to examine the track, stroking his dingy beard. Choteau chuckled incredulously when Branch seemed stubbornly unwilling to admit what his eyes were telling him. "Damn clawless griz?" he asked dismissively, then changed the subject: "You boys hungry?"

Johnson squinted up at Choteau, then back at the track, bewilderment written on his face. Choteau took a few paces and scanned the area until he noticed something odd about a tree he had previously leaned his rifle against. It was a young spruce about ten feet tall with a trunk of four inches in diameter, but it had been snapped in half, its white inner core exposed in jagged shards.

He decided to test the obstinate Branch: "Since you're the expert on all animal sign, Monsieur Branch, can you please explain how this tree got snapped? There has been no strong wind this day, and this tree wasn't broken when we left camp this morning to set traps."

"You mean like those over there?" said Johnson, pointing to half a dozen others around the camp that had also been snapped in half.

Reluctantly, Branch walked over to examine them, his arms folded across his chest contemptuously. But after a minute of silent staring, he looked out across the creek toward the brushy alder that grew eight feet tall along its banks. For the first time, Branch seemed to teeter, as if lost in confounded cogitation.

Choteau continued picking up the messy camp, holding scant hope for a rational explanation outside of what he already knew. Finally, he couldn't take any more of Branch's adjournment of reality. He looked squarely at him and said, "I think we both know it hasn't been a bear, Injuns, or even Bauman that's been haunting our camp."

To Choteau's surprise, Branch didn't argue. Instead, he continued standing stalk still and silent, as if the tide had suddenly turned, and any word to the contrary would make him look like a complete idiot. At length, he nodded to Choteau and said, "Go help him gather up some firewood, Johnson, while I watch the camp."

Choteau grabbed his ax and rifle before cautiously heading into the scattered spruce to gather more firewood, alert for danger, mentally preparing himself for another long night. Johnson followed him into the woods, grumbling under his breath, obviously chafed from Branch's order giving.

Choteau peeked through the timber and spied Branch retrieving a flask of whiskey from his stash before sitting down next to the fire. No surprise there—Branch always preferred to drink alone, so he wouldn't be pressed to share with either Choteau or Johnson. But there was something else written in the subtle looseness in how he moved and plopped down against the log. Choteau could see it clearly. Branch was shrewdly adding everything up—the jumbled mess, the horrendous odor, the broken spruce, and the enormous footprint. It wasn't a celebratory reach for the rotgut. On the contrary, it seemed Branch preferred to wash away his worries in whiskey rather than capitulate and surrender to the naked truth— that something more terrifying than a bear or a man was watching and waiting.

Choteau continued his search and soon found an enormous fallen spruce in the nearby woods. It had been lying where it had fallen a few years earlier, so the wood was well seasoned for burning. He lifted his ax and began chopping off branches. The sound of each whack echoed down the canyon.

Johnson stood by, watching. Still awkwardly holding to the absurd bear theory, he laughed and remarked, "What's got ya spooked this time, Frenchy? If that bear comes back, don't worry—I'll be ready for 'im."

Choteau stopped chopping and turned to address Johnson head on. "You think I'm afraid of a bear?" He pointed his ax at Johnson as he spoke. "What did this to our camp was no bear. And whatever it was sent us a clear message—it wants us gone!"

Johnson tightened his lips, unable to refute him, vaguely penitent. Choteau noticed that, for the first time, Johnson didn't offer another inane excuse, either. He continued, chopping more aggressively now.

The conspicuous tension seemed to needle Johnson. Finally, he blustered, "Gimme that ax, and I'll show ya how it's done."

"Fine by me. Have at it." Choteau handed him the ax and stood back a few paces to watch.

From the lack of callouses on his hands, it was clear to Choteau that Johnson was a stranger to ax work—probably any strenuous work, for that matter. For whatever reason, perhaps the chance to impress someone with his natural physical prowess, he lit into the tree with zeal, large chunks flying off with each blow as he released his pent-up anxiety. Choteau looked on, hands on his hips, more impressed with Johnson's gusto than his skill with an ax.

The two of them cut and hauled wood until they had a substantial pile of logs and kindling stacked for the night. They hurried back into the timber for one more load, and Johnson began chopping some of the larger pieces when Choteau noticed something odd. The whack of the ax seemed to echo back to them with each chop. "Hold it. Stop!" he shouted to Johnson. He cocked his ear toward the echoing sound.

Sweating profusely and breathing heavily from the exertion, Johnson blurted, "What's the matter now, Frenchy? Afraid of me showing ya how to properly swing an ax?" But when Choteau didn't reply, he finally paused to listen.

Off in the distance, somewhere up on the mountain, came the sharp sound of something hitting a tree. This time both men heard it. Every few seconds it repeated: *whack! ... whack! ... whack!*

"What do ya make of it?" asked Johnson. "Kootenai? Blackfeet?"

"You should know better! The Kootenai won't come back here," Choteau scolded. "And if they were Blackfeet, we'd be dead by now. Come on. Let's get back to camp."

The two mountain men picked up the firewood they had cut and hurried back toward the relative safety of the camp, each checking over his shoulder for any sign of danger lurking behind them.

Chapter Thirty-Two

*A*ttack

*T*wilight descended just as Choteau and Johnson approached camp with their final load of firewood. Choteau couldn't help but notice how the conniving, skilamalinking Branch scrambled to hide his flask of whiskey as they cleared the trees, then nonchalantly sat next to the fire with his book of poetry to await their arrival.

But Choteau could see from Branch's body language that he was out of sorts and not in a jovial mood—mainly by the way he stared morosely at his verses. As Choteau drew near, he overheard the crusty trapper's somber recital and listened with as much respect as he could muster.

> *From restless slumber I arose,*
>
> *The glow of love in me immersed.*
>
> *A golden ring for her I'd give,*
>
> *I'd humbly bow, my words rehearsed.*
>
> *On bended knee I made my pledge,*
>
> *Undying love ne'er to betray.*
>
> *But she surprised my flooding eyes,*
>
> *Then turned and slipped way.*

Choteau had seen it before, when, on occasion, Branch would slip into a blue remorse and wallow aimlessly in deep regret. Whenever it happened, he always tried to give him his space until the bleary spell passed. Usually, by the next morning, he would have regained his typical snarling disposition.

Johnson, on the other hand, had no such etiquette and blundered loudly into camp, threw down his load of wood, and marched straight for Branch.

"Did you hear that sound?!" blurted Johnson urgently.

"Yeah, I heard it," replied Branch dryly with a whiskey-slur, somewhat perturbed as he thumbed through his verses.

Choteau stepped toward the campfire and before he could unload his armful of wood, a primal cry came from the darkening forest. He dropped the firewood, lunged for his rifle, and quickly took aim into the shadows from where the sound had come.

"What the hell was that?" said Johnson. He followed Choteau's lead, grabbing and shouldering his rifle.

"Skookum!" said Branch, laughing sarcastically. "What else could it be? Damn drainage is full of 'em."

Choteau ducked behind a tree and glanced over at Branch, unsure if it was the whiskey talking, or if Branch had suddenly had an epiphany. He appeared somewhat loopy, but when Branch reached for his rifle and rested it in the crook of his arm, Choteau felt somewhat vindicated.

"Come on, you bast—"

Branch's words were interrupted by a shrill cry from within the nearby alder thicket. *"Aaaaaaah!"*

The sound made the hair on the nape of Choteau's neck stand on end, and by the looks on the faces of his two partners, it appeared they were finally taking the threat seriously. They turned in unison, aiming their weapons toward the noise, looking for any sign of movement.

It had moved closer now, much closer. Branch was dangerously exposed but perhaps too doped to realize it or care. Finally, he staggered toward a spruce, ducked behind it, and cocked back the hammer of his rifle. Johnson followed his lead and hid behind a thick pine.

"It is happening again, Branch!" Choteau yelled. "I knew it! I knew we should not have come back here!" He peeked from behind the tree as fearful memories of their previous excursion flashed through his mind.

"Branch! I'm serious," blurted Johnson. "What the hell are we dealin' with? Cougar?"

"How in hell do I know what it is?" Branch snarled. "Whatever it is, if I see so much as a twitch, it'll get a .53-caliber surprise." He seemed suddenly sober, the half-rats slur from the whiskey completely gone.

Far off in the distance, the sound of tree-knocking again echoed high on the mountainside. The three of them turned toward the perplexing noise.

"Now it's coming from up yonder," said Johnson.

"Must be more than one of them." Choteau's voice wavered, and his heart raced uncontrollably. Suddenly, a twig snapped from within the thicket. "He's in there," he said, his voice an octave higher. He stared into the shadowy alders, trying to locate any movement, rifle poised and ready to fire. He heard a slight rustling in the dense cover of vegetation, barely perceptible, like a mouse on an erratic course through the underbrush. Suddenly, a tall, shadowy figure darted through one of the openings. But before Choteau could pull the trigger, it disappeared behind the foliage.

Feverishly scanning the undergrowth, he picked out a dark patch that seemed out of place, hovering above the alder. He squinted to try and determine what it was, when without warning, it opened its eyes and then its gaping maw, showing its teeth, then it quickly disappeared.

"It's the loup-garou! I saw it!" cried Choteau. *"I saw it!"*

"Shut up, Frenchy," Branch hissed, his voice filled with rage. "Nobody's gonna get our furs, not Bauman and his Injun friend, not them Koots or Blackfeet, and certainly not no damn Skookum or loup-garou, either!"

The forest grew silent, and the men listened, the only sound coming from the sporadic crackling of the fire. They waited and watched, but nothing stirred.

After several hours, Branch got to itching for another shot of whiskey while Johnson became distracted by his growling stomach. Satisfied the danger had passed, they cautiously moved from their hiding places and occupied themselves—Branch to his whiskey and Johnson to the evening meal.

"I will stand watch," said Choteau, unwilling to move, for he wasn't convinced it was gone.

Choteau sat quietly watching, listening to the chatter of the men, their voices distant and irrelevant. For the first time, he thought about how meaningless it all seemed, wondering how he had gotten to this place so far from where he wanted to be. His thoughts were dismal and forlorn, scolding himself for not listening more closely to the inner voice that he so often brushed aside, letting others direct his steps rather than himself.

Suddenly, from the dark timber quartering away from them, a large rock whistled through the air, striking the fire and scattering the logs and food with an explosion of hot embers that flew like buckshot all over the nearby supplies, kindling them ablaze.

Johnson swung his rifle and quickly fired as he wheeled, then ducked to reload. "*Yeehaw!* That Bauman can really chuck a rock," he crowed, his words dripping with sarcasm. "Sounded like a damn cannonball comin' in!" But Johnson's shaking hands belied his bravado as he fumbled to reload his rifle.

Choteau ducked as another rock hit the tree next to him with enough force to shatter the eight-inch-diameter trunk. The thirty-foot tree shivered at the impact, creaked loudly, then cracked at the point of impact. Choteau dove out of the way as the tree fell with a crash next to him. "We must leave this place!" he shouted.

"Maybe it's that 'breed. He's got one helluva throwin' arm, I'll grant him that!" Half-drunk, Branch broke into loopy laughter as he peered from behind his tree. "Where the hell are them rocks comin' from?" Another one whistled by his head as more supplies smoldered and caught fire.

"Bloody gawd!" Johnson yelped.

"The supplies!" shouted Choteau. Their supplies were their lifeline. Without them, their mission would be over. He ducked and sprinted to put out the burning pile of supplies, grabbed a tarpaulin, and beat out the flames. Another rock zipped through the air, glancing off Choteau's left ear. He fell back, his head racked with pain, the voices of Branch and Johnson drowned by the hollow hum in his ear. He blinked, trying to focus as tiny points of light floated across his spinning blurred surroundings. Instinctively, he backed behind a log and regained his senses, then sat up holding his injured ear, blood oozing through his fingers.

"Damn it all to hell—that's about enough!" hollered Branch. Wheeling in the general direction of the barrage, he fired. The bullet glanced off a tree, and the smoke from his muzzle-loader obscured the scene as a figure ran from behind a large pine and disappeared into the timber.

But Choteau clearly saw it—an enormous upright creature running through a small opening. It stopped for a few seconds, opened its jaws, and growled viciously.

"I saw it!" Johnson yelled as he finished reloading. "I saw it, I tell you!"

"Would you two muttonheads cover me?!" shouted Branch as he jumped from his hiding place and finished beating out scattered embers.

Choteau looked down at his bloodied hand and again felt his injured ear. It was still intact. But the stinging pain on the side of his head and the sight of his own blood had brought him to of the brink of utter panic—and the sight of the creature staring menacingly at him had nudged him over the edge.

Distressing reality came crashing down on him now, like an overwhelming avalanche. Ever since Jones had fallen from the cliff to his death, he had been thinking about a backup plan. Now was the time to act. He knew the trail to the Two Medicine River. He had enough powder and shot to kill game and survive until he reached the plains. From there, he would make a mad dash through Blackfeet country and beeline to the Missouri River. He would gather his hard-earned profits from the caches he had buried along the way, carve out a canoe, head downriver to Fort Union, then hitch a ride from there to St. Louis.

"To hell with you, Branch!" he shouted. "I'm not staying here to die for a few beaver pelts!"

Clutching his rifle, he jumped from his hiding place grabbed his possibles bag and a bundle of food he had already put together, then bolted down the trail.

"Choteau! Get back here!" hollered Branch.

But Choteau quickly found the trail and distanced himself from the mayhem.

෴

Johnson watched as Choteau disappeared, the instinct to run overwhelming. He took a step toward the trail when he felt another rock whiz by his head. He ducked back down, his heart thumping in his chest. At the same time, just as Branch brought down the tarpaulin on the flames, yet another one whistled through the air, nearly striking him.

"Shoot, damn it!" he shouted at Johnson.

Mustering his courage, Johnson rose and fired in the general direction of the incoming missiles. The whistling rocks abruptly stopped coming, and the forest became eerily silent. They watched and waited. "I—I think it's gone this time," he said. "Maybe I hit 'im. I'm a damn good shot, ya know." Johnson's tried to hide his fear, but his voice broke and trembled slightly. He swallowed and coughed deeply to summon his fleeing bravado.

Branch mumbled under his breath as they scanned the dark edges of the forest for any sign of movement. "That would be a miracle," he said snidely as he snuffed a smoldering ember with his moccasin clad foot. "That yellow-bellied French bastard! Fine. Just fine. He won't get a damned penny from all these furs, I guarantee you that!"

The two men inched away from their protective cover and stood for a moment. All was quiet. Cautiously, they set up barricades and tucked their charred, tattered bedrolls tightly behind them. They sat quietly, watching and listening until the fire dwindled, and its light began to ebb.

"Throw another log on that fire, Johnson."

The man is crazy as a loon, Johnson thought. Reluctantly, he reached around the barricade, picked up a branch, and tossed it haphazardly into the fire, causing an eruption of fiery embers.

Branch's angry glare indicated that he was less than impressed, but Johnson could not have cared less. He wasn't about to expose himself and was smart enough to keep a barrier between himself and the incoming deadly missiles. Getting killed by an inglorious rock wasn't how he'd pictured himself dying. He imagined his death in the pursuit of a monstrous griz—a death that would usher him into legendary status, one that would be spoken of with reverence at the Rendezvous for generations to come.

"Ah, hell, cover me!" barked Branch. He threw off his bedroll, stepped around the barricade and grabbed several logs. He dropped one on the fire and quickly sat back down.

"Tell me the truth, Branch. What did you shoot at? Did ya get a good look?"

Branch answered slowly. "Damn trees. Not sure. I only got a glimpse. It was big, that's all I know. Damn whiskey. I swear I'm either addled, or my eyes are playin' tricks on me."

Johnson could no longer deny what his own eyes had seen. He blurted, "I know you think I'm crazy, but I saw it clear as day. Can't say what it was, but it weren't no bear, and it weren't no man, yet it ran upright on two legs. If there's such a thing as a Skookum, that'd be him!"

Branch was staring blankly into the dark timber, but he didn't seem to be looking for danger. He appeared thoughtful, down-hearted, almost ill, as if he were finding it increasingly difficult to swallow the wormy glob of cold, hard facts. Johnson felt it, too—the unnerving reality that something deadly was out there, watching and waiting.

Branch spoke without looking at him: "Okay, I gotta admit one thing, Johnson. I never let on, but last time we trapped in this here valley, there was times I was certain something was a-watchin' me. I thought it was them Kootenai, but now, I'm havin' second thoughts." He rubbed his chin and shook his head. "I ain't never put stock in no damned Injun superstitions. There's gotta be a logical explanation—" He stopped mid-sentence and rubbed his eyes. "Gotta be them damned Kootenai! They're tricksters. Sneaky, connivin' tricksters. Dressed up in bear skins, I'll wager. Can never tell what they're up to, and I'll be damned if I'm gonna be jinked by 'em!"

"That don't make a lick of sense to me, Branch. You're losin' your mind if ya think the Kootenai wouldn't be a gunnin' with rifle and bow at this range—instead, they chuck rocks?" When Branch didn't respond, he continued: "Truth be told, I've had a funny feeling ever since we ventured in here. My eyes weren't playin' tricks on me, I tell ya. I saw it! Them teeth, them eyes! The hair on the back o' my neck is standin' up on end, and I don't scare easy."

"Now, they're gettin' to ya," replied Branch. "They can't be too dangerous if all they can do is chuck rocks!"

But Johnson couldn't deny what his senses were telling him. He knew at gut level that the trapping game was over, and he wished he had bolted down the drainage with Choteau.

They watched and waited, but nothing stirred in the dark forest and brush around camp. A forest owl hooted from its perch, and bats fluttered here and there, picking off the flying bugs attracted by the light of the campfire. The men waited and waited, but the troublemaker did not return.

Finally, after an hour in brooding silence, Branch announced, "Injun or Skookum—I don't give a damn anymore. I'm going to bed." He yawned deeply and added, "They would've attacked by now, seein's how it's just the two of us." He peeked out at the forest from his bedroll and scooted closer to the fire with his rifle loaded and ready. "Maybe one of us hit him after all. But I ain't going in them trees to check till mornin'."

Johnson tried to ignore the cold night air that slowly crept through his garments. He wasn't satisfied it was safe enough to retire for the night, so he sat anxiously, watching behind the protection of the barricade, and shivered under the horse blanket he had draped over his shoulders. He looked over at Branch, who lay comfortably in his bedroll and shook his head in disgust when the crusty trapper promptly commenced with his usual stentorian snoring. Johnson watched until the biting cold began gnawing on his bones. Against his better judgment, he crept near the campfire, sat with his rifle resting in his lap, and warmed his hands.

Branch must have heard him shuffling toward the fire and momentarily paused the cacophony. "Now, you don't go fallin' asleep on me," he mumbled. "I'll take second watch."

Johnson doubted his words. Branch hadn't taken his turn on night watch since they had left the Rendezvous. Sure enough, within minutes, he was snoring again under his patchwork bedroll of animal fur. Johnson looked out into the lonely night and up at the stars. They always seemed brighter in the high country. For a fleeting moment, he felt the peace and majesty of the mountains and forgot about the danger lurking just inside the forest.

His eyes grew weary as the soothing warmth of the fire soaked through his clothes. But something startled him out of his drowsy state. Had he been dreaming? The sound had been faint, almost a whisper, but now, he was fully awake. Grabbing his rifle, he jumped to his feet and ducked behind a tree, swinging the weapon around into shooting position. His eyes darted here and there, looked for the source of the sound, but the only movement came from the flickering shadows cast by the firelight, the only sound from the distant forest owl.

After a while, he stepped closer to the fire and tossed in another log. He sat and watched it catch fire, comforted by the flickering firelight. The hypnotic red tongues lapping at the fresh log always gave him a sense of safety and security whenever he felt the presence of night creatures lurking in the shadows.

Then, he heard it again, only this time, he was fully alert and heard it clearly. It wasn't a loud sound—more like an eerie whisper. It came from high on the mountain, but there could be no mistaking it.

"*John ... saaan,*" came like an otherworldly moan, tickling the tops of the pine trees.

"Branch! Branch!" Johnson shouted, kicking at the leader's leg when he wouldn't respond.

"Wha—what? What the hell?!" Dazed and only half awake, Branch threw off his blanket, clumsily sat up, and shouldered his rifle.

"*Shhhh!* Listen," said Johnson.

Neither man moved a muscle until, off in the distance, it came again: *"John ... saaan!"*

"I'll be damned!" exclaimed Branch. "Gotta be either that yellow-bellied son of a bitch Frenchy or Bauman." He paused, then yelled at the voice, "Come on down, you coward! But ya won't lay a hand on these furs. You're done here now! *Done!* When them Blackfeet get done with ya, you'll be grinnin' at the daisies without your scalp!"

"What's he doin' way up yonder?" said Johnson. "And why in tarnation is he callin' my name like that?"

Branch grinned and hollered at the voice, "Hey, Frenchy! It ain't much fun tryin' to get through on your own in these parts, my friend. Why don't ya head back here, and we'll let bygones be bygones!" But the grin instantly vanished from his face. He looked directly at Johnson with his hawkish eyes and said, "Even if he comes in here waving a white flag, he'll be a comin' for fur. Shoot 'im dead, ya hear? Shoot him *dead.*"

The moon broke over the peaks, and an ominous stillness crept into the valley—even the owl stopped its hooting. Once again, Johnson felt a chill, but it wasn't from the cold night air. It was as if a dark, primal presence encircled the basin like a specter, reaching through his clothing with icy fingers to stab with its sharp claws. Johnson shivered, as if to drive the cold demons from his garments, then draped his wool horse blanket over his shoulders and huddled closer to the fire.

Chapter Thirty-Three

Choteau's Run

Choteau had been steadily making his way down the canyon, running hard for the first quarter mile. Even though the moon brightened the landscape, the shadows from the forest often obscured its light, and he frequently stumbled, until finally, he slowed to a jog and then to a hurried walk.

Just when he was getting into a good rhythm, something shuffled in the timber along the trail, where the mountain sloped sharply toward the creek. He stopped dead in his tracks and listened. The shuffling sound continued for a second before stopping. Immediately, his heart raced even harder, as he sensed a phantom presence.

He took four or five more steps and stopped. Again, the shuffling steps continued for a second, then ceased. Something was following him, moving parallel as he moved down the trail. The sound came from behind the alders that grew along the creek—perhaps fifty yards away. Choteau broke into a panicked run, fueled by a surge of adrenaline.

He had sprinted a hundred yards when clouds drifted over the peaks, blocking the moonlight. Suddenly, Choteau could no longer see the trail, and he crashed blindly through the forest as he desperately tried to distance himself from whatever was stalking him. He had never been a religious man, but he found himself breaking into a prayer as he stumbled and tripped over deadfall. It was a pleading, beseeching supplication to ward away demons and protect him from the creature—the loup-garou he'd seen with his own two eyes.

As he lurched ahead, his quivering breath sent plumes of steam into the cool night air, and his legs burned from fatigue. Suddenly, he came to a steep slope, rising above the creek. Without warning, he stepped into the dark shadow of a tree and tripped on a large root, causing him to roll off the steep embankment, through a patch of devil's club, and all the way down to the creek below.

"Damn it!" he blurted as hundreds of spiny thorns pierced through his leathers and stabbed the exposed skin on his face, hands, and neck.

But even worse, somewhere during the tumble, he had lost his rifle, food, and possibles bag. He groped blindly for them among the devil's club, but the thorns bit at his fingers and hands like hornets, sending their burning tinctures of poison into his skin. He thought about going back to the trappers' camp, but then he'd have to face Branch. The monster was behind him now. *Or is it?* he suddenly wondered. His new goal was simple—to get out of the drainage at any cost.

He felt naked and vulnerable without his rifle, but when he heard faint footsteps approaching, he abandoned any hope of finding it in the mishmash of undergrowth and deadfall. His immediate problem was that he had lost the trail. He got to his feet and followed the creek down the canyon, picking his way over deadfall and the rough, broken ground at the bottom of the ravine, knowing the creek would eventually empty into the Kootenai River. All he had to do was get to the waterfalls—and away from the damned Skookum.

He stopped to rest next to a giant fir tree growing just shy of the creek's edge. He bent over, hands on his knees, panting for air while trying to listen for footfalls. Hearing none, he closed his eyes and remembered the sweetheart he had met at a tavern in Montreal. Although she was just a dingy trollop, she had somehow transformed into a princess inside his fear-addled mind. And although she'd cost him his last three dollars on that memorable night, he suddenly longed for her, certain she was smitten with him. Now, he felt pangs of regret that he'd left her for the thrill of adventure and the frivolous lure of fortune.

"Adventure and treasures be damned," he whispered under his breath. "I'm going back to Montreal!" His mind was perfectly clear now. No need for calculations and recalculations. There had never been a time when he was so certain about his direction and the course he would take to get there after picking up his hidden caches of money along the way.

Choteau wasn't sure how long he'd rested next to the tree, but when he opened his eyes and looked up, the thin veil of clouds that had been hovering over the mountains was gone, and everything around him seemed illuminated. He looked at the moon shining brightly through the trees in the old-growth forest and smiled; traveling would be much easier now.

To his left, he spotted the faint shadow of the trail. His heart leaped with euphoric joy. The forest was still, with no sign of anything following him. For the first time since he had left the camp in a panic, he felt at ease, and a sense of relief filled him with renewed energy for the shuffling steps had gone away. Perhaps it had been just a scurrying rabbit or a curious coyote.

He stood and stretched his back, which was tender and sore from his tumble through the devil's club. He stepped around the tree toward the trail. Just as he was considering backtracking to find his rifle and possibles bag, he heard the sharp sound of a snapping twig. It wasn't particularly loud, but a gunshot would have been less startling in the eerie moonlit forest. He froze in his tracks, listening intently for footsteps while horrifying thoughts raced through his mind. He prayed to God it was a deer or even a bear. He could deal with that—but not the loup-garou, not the Skookum, the forest demon, the legend of old who stole small children and ate them alive.

Too afraid to turn around, Choteau closed his eyes and listened, but the only sound came from his pounding heart and the gently bubbling creek. After several minutes, he calmed down, and his fear subsided. He had just taken another step toward the trail when a pungent odor wafted into his nostrils. He stopped and sniffed the air, hoping it was only his imagination, but grimaced as the scent grew stronger. He waited for several more minutes, trembling and listening intently, but the forest was still and quiet. His mouth went dry, and his blood grew cold as he again sensed an ominous presence nearby.

Now frantic, he searched the ground for something, anything he could use to defend himself—a rock or a broken branch—but he could find nothing. As he looked down, a slowly creeping shadow cast by the moonlight emerged at his feet, growing larger and larger until it enveloped and consumed his own shadow. He bolted toward the faint, silvery trail on his right, fueled with pure terror, the instinct for survival governing his every stride as his legs churned down the path.

The lifesaving silvery trail seemed clearer now, or perhaps his eyes had adjusted to the monochromatic surroundings. He ran faster than he could ever remember, hoping, praying that the scattered clouds would sail clear of the precious moon, so it would continue to illuminate his escape route. After a minute or two, his breathing grew heavy, his chest heaved, and his leg muscles began to cramp again.

Chancing a look back, he fully expected to see the creature, but to his relief, there was nothing but the silhouette of the pines and the brilliant orb overhead. He stopped, put his hands on his knees, and breathed deeply. When he recovered enough to stand upright, he again studied his back trail for any signs of danger, but it was clear, and the night was still and calm. But though all was quiet, and there appeared no danger in sight, the skunky smell still hung persistently in the air. Choteau cursed himself for dropping his rifle.

After one last look, he turned to head down the trail. The remnants of a large, tree trunk partially obstructed his path, and he took a step to move around it. Stepping into its long shadow, he stopped dead in his tracks when the shadow on the ground suddenly moved beneath him. Choteau wheeled, looking up. The moon shone directly above and behind the looming monolith, making it difficult to distinguish, so he shielded his eyes and squinted to better see it.

Suddenly, the inanimate object came to life, its enormous arms reaching, its huge hands springing to clutch. With blinding quickness, they sprang and grabbed him by his buckskin coat before he could react. Choteau's head snapped back as he was jerked off the ground. He blinked in petrified fear, losing all senses, except the sight of the thing before him, its deep-set eyes glaring under its furious brow.

Coming to his senses, he grabbed at the giant hand and tried to free himself from its grip, but the fingers felt as thick and hard as stones. He felt his buckskin coat tighten around his chest when the beast clenched its fists. Thrashing feebly, he tried to strike out at it, but his efforts were in vain as he was lifted higher off the ground, his feet dangling in the air. With its other hand, the creature snapped a large branch off a tree next to them, leaving a broken snag several feet long protruding from its trunk. It lifted him higher, until Choteau could feel the jagged snag pressing against his back. He winced with pain when its sharp edges jabbed against him. The mountain man whimpered as he realized his struggle was futile.

The beast looked Choteau directly in the eye and snarled. Then, with one swift move, it slammed him into the spikey snag. He felt the ribs on his back pop, then pop again, as it penetrated clean through his chest. The creature let go, and Choteau hung from the snag, gasping as blood spewed from his mouth and from the wound.

Snarling with a satisfied grin, the beast then mouthed something with a deep, guttural voice that caused Choteau to lift his head, even as he felt his life ebbing away.

"John ... saaan ..."

Choteau's eyes grew heavy, and his breathing became more labored as his lifeblood spilled beneath him. The steady wet warmth oozed down his chest and onto his leather trousers before dripping off his foot. As he looked down, it gleamed in the silvery moonlight, slowing to thick, heavy drops as it coagulated in a tar-like puddle at the base of the tree. Choteau's eyes began to droop as his blood drained from his body.

He looked out at a lavender-painted sunset as he rocked in his chair on the porch, smoking his pipe. His lovely wife was sitting next to him, humming, and knitting a sock while the children played in the waning light.

Just before he breathed his last breaths, he opened his eyes, but the beast was gone. The sound of a distant owl finally broke the deathly stillness of the night as he closed his eyes, and the empty darkness swallowed him whole.

Chapter Thirty-Four

Stealth Attack

J*ohnson had sat up most of the night keeping the* fire going, catching a wink of sleep now and then and thinking how he would break the news to Branch—that he was done, finished, and that he would be leaving with or without him. He dreaded the man's likely reaction, but he weighed his options and decided it would be a safer bet dealing with Branch's wrath than face another night in the accursed beaver camp.

Morning was but a dim hope when he could wait no longer, and he roused Branch, who arose from his bedroll and felt the top of his head. "Well, still got my scalp! See anything?"

"No, thank God!" Johnson said as he tended the fire.

"Got any coffee?"

It was more of an order than a request, which Johnson immediately resented. "Help yourself," replied Johnson.

Branch rolled over, dumped the ashes that had floated into his tin cup during the night, and poured himself some coffee. What he said next caught Johnson unawares.

"You know, Johnson, after sleepin' on it, there ain't no sense in fightin' this situation anymore. We're down to just two guns. Let's take what we got and get the hell outta here. We can always get more men and come back in here. Then, we can really give them beavers hell!"

Johnson sat back, absorbing Branch's unanticipated turnaround. *What in tarnation is in that whiskey?* he thought. Whatever it was, Branch needed more of it. Johnson's dreaded departure speech had been averted, and he answered with enthusiasm: "Yes, sir! I like that idea." He smiled to himself with satisfaction, knowing full well he had no intention of ever returning to the haunted basin with Crooked Bill Branch.

"All right, then, we better get movin', so we can get these furs packed and outta here."

Johnson thought for a second, then shrewdly replied to ensure Branch wouldn't suddenly change his mind. "Yeah ... I agree. Who knows what that damn deserter Frenchy is up to? He might try to sneak in here and steal our fur, or ambush us, or tip off the Injuns—and we could lose the whole lot!"

"You know, Johnson, I ain't hungry. We can eat hardtack this morning for breakfast. Go catch the horses and saddle 'em up. After that, just stay here and guard the fur. And don't go chasin' off after a damn bear! I'm gonna pull the traps we set yesterday an' get my ass back here. If that Frenchman pokes his head out, you plug him, ya hear? Watch for Injuns, too."

Johnson looked down the canyon with a self-assured grin. For the first time, he and Branch agreed on something, and the man's newfound sense of urgency came as a welcome relief. "Yeah, I like that plan."

Without further delay, Branch grabbed the Hawken and an empty trapper's pack for his final foray on the trapline. He stared at the alder brush and heavy timber, searching for danger. "You keep your eyes open now, Johnson, and have everything ready when I get back."

"Don't worry. Those horses'll be ready to go. An' I'll be ready for any son of a bitch that thinks he can steal these pelts. An' if'n that bear shows up, I'll have his hide draped over my saddle before you get here."

It was easy for Johnson to catch the horses. They had inched closer to camp during the night, no doubt directed by their uncanny sixth sense. Johnson wasted no time in saddling them for the pack trip out, loading them with their belongings and the beaver pelts, and performing his assigned duties with stalwart motivation. Anxious to get down the trail, he was ready and waiting, so they could leave as soon as Branch returned.

It was a pleasant, bluebird day, and the morning sun soon thawed the thin layer of frost blanketing the ground, bringing a comforting warmth to the basin. Johnson had a sudden urge for a nip and glanced toward the beaver lakes where Branch was pulling traps before rummaging through Branch's gear for his hidden stash of whiskey. To his dismay, the bottle was already empty.

Then Johnson spied it. Branch's notebook of verses. He always wanted to take a peek to see why Branch seemed always so absorbed with it, but Branch never let anyone touch it. He grabbed it and sat against the fallen log opposite the campfire with a sigh of fatigue from the morning's work. He removed his hat, sat back against a log, and nervously wiped the sweat from his brow before thumbing through the tattered pages, browned and crinkled from years of use. He settled on a passage somewhere in the random middle of the tome and read it out loud in broken sentences. Reading was never his forte:

I saw it,

In midnights darkest doleful gloom.

I felt it,

In icy fangs of winter's wind.

I heard it,

In lonesome howls of distant wolves.

The song of what might have been,

And the child I never knew.

Johnson paused for a moment, puzzled by the words, wondering what they meant. He dismissively laid the book aside on the log behind him. He wasn't much for emotional ideas, romance, or thoughts much deeper than the faint footprint of a griz on hard ground.

"Come on, Branch!" he grumbled, then scooted a log further into the campfire with his foot.

Johnson vainly scanned the forest for any sign of movement, his rifle resting in his lap. He hadn't seen or heard anything since the fracas the night before, which eased his mind somewhat, and soon, the balmy sunshine gave succor from his anxious thoughts. A gentle breeze made its way up the canyon, and the babbling of the nearby brook relaxed him like a baby's lullaby. His eyelids grew heavy until Johnson dozed off to sleep.

A noise jolted him awake. Swinging his rifle toward the sound, Johnson startled a whisky jack that had flown in to scavenge a crumb or two from the campsite. He wheeled and scanned the surrounding area for danger. Relieved to find nothing amiss, he calmed down and watched the bird hop here and there, looking for a scrap of food.

"Hey, little feller. Came back for a little handout, eh?" Johnson picked up a morsel of beaver fat and held it toward the precocious gray bird, which peered at him curiously with eyes black as pitch. The whisky jack didn't hesitate, fluttering toward him and landing on his knee. Then, it hopped up and perched itself on his thumb. It turned its head to the left and right, studying the tidbit of food with its beady eyes.

"Go ahead. You'll like it," whispered Johnson.

The bird skillfully snatched it with its beak and swallowed it, to Johnson's delight. Then the bird cocked its head, looked toward the sky, and fluttered away, as if a hawk were circling overhead.

"Hey! Where ya going?" Johnson sighed and lowered his head. Perhaps he could catch another quick nap before Branch returned. It was dead calm, and his eyelids began to droop again as the sun beat down on his back, warming him into a blissful respite.

As he dozed off, he felt a slight brush on the back of his head, near the nape of his neck, like a slow-creeping tick. He stirred and felt through his hair for a tiny trespasser. "Dirty bastard bugs from hell" was what he called them. They crawled from the earth, from the very depths of hell, he figured, then onto the closest shrub or tall blade of grass, their tiny, hooked legs reaching for any passerby. Once aboard, they would begin their determined journey upward until they found a moist, dark place to sink their teeth: head, armpit, behind the ear, inside an unoccupied navel, or their favorite place of all, the groin area.

On occasion, a tick would go unnoticed, until it became impossible not to after bloating itself with the blood of its victim to the point of bursting. If left long enough, the millions of eggs inside would swell until the thing burst open, whereupon they would hatch a million more of the pesky devils.

Whenever he found one of the nasty swollen varmints, Johnson was careful not to rupture the blood-swollen tick, which looked like a hideously dimpled grape. But one time, he had happened to do just that, releasing thousands of eggs from the little blood-sucking vampires—deep into the nether region of his pubic hair. Three days later, the itching began, and then his horror upon discovering why. A quick scrubbing with some ball-burning lye had done the trick, and from that moment on, he had lived his life on high alert for any sign of the dirty bastard bugs from hell.

After fingering fruitlessly through his hair, Johnson resumed his previously relaxed state. But a moment later, he felt it again, like a warm push of air. He opened his eyes and sat still, wondering why a warm gust would suddenly come from the south when the wind was blowing steadily up the basin from the north. He looked over his shoulder, shading his eyes from the blinding noonday sun. There sat the whisky jack, peering down at him as it perched atop what appeared to be the broken limb of wind-snapped bull pine. The bird cocked its head and peered down at him with one eye.

"Come back, little feller. I got more food for ya." Johnson was reaching for another piece of beaver fat lying nearby when the hackles on the back of his neck stood on end. His sixth sense screamed like a banshee and at the same moment the wind shifted—the smell had returned!

Without hesitating, he reached for his gun, but before he could latch onto it, he was grabbed from behind and whirled around.

Dazed, he felt a rush of air, and his vision blurred. He blinked and found himself staring into two enormous, angry eyes, bloodshot with rage. It all became clear in a fraction of a second, yet the sight of the creature had put him in a momentary state of shock—gone tharn as a rabbit before a bouncing weasel.

The creature had chosen its moment of ambush well upwind with the sun too high to cast its shadow. Johnson was too terrorized to speak or move. Like a surreal nightmare, the flittering whisky jack caused him to avert his eyes for a second. It perched on the beast's shoulder at Johnson's eye level, peering down at him as if he were a morsel of food. But the rank smell of the creature jolted him to his senses. "Put me down, you bastard!" And with all his strength, he struggled to free himself.

The kerfuffle awakened the dozing horses, and when the wind swirled, they snorted and began jostling against their lead ropes, trying to escape. They bucked and kicked but couldn't break free. As Johnson struggled vainly against the beast's powerful grip, he cursed Branch and cursed himself for making the ill-fated choice to enter this basin of horrors, wishing he had run off with Choteau during the night when he'd had a chance.

His kicking and swinging had little effect except to anger the beast even more. From deep within the creature's chest came a growl. It started as a low rumbling and then rose to a crescendo until it opened its mouth and roared, blowing its hot, rancid breath in Johnson's face.

"What the hell are you?!" he bellowed.

The creature relaxed its grip slightly, just for a moment. Looking him squarely in the eye, it gave a maniacal smile, then uttered in a guttural voice, *"John ... saan."*

In a flash, he realized the truth: the mysterious hurled rocks, the huge track, the peculiar noises, the creature that had growled at him from the cave, the creature he had shot at, the creature he had wounded that he'd hoped beyond reason was a bear, the voice that called his name—it now stood before him, glaring with bloodshot eyes. Choteau's loup-garou! The Skookum!

But before Johnson could voice a response, it gripped the top of his head, as if it were an apple, and squeezed. The creature's grip grew tighter and tighter, and Johnson squeezed his eyes shut against the paralyzing pain. Just before he could scream, the massive fingers closed. The sound of his own skull being crushed was the last thing Johnson heard.

∽

The man-beast went limp, and the Gray dropped the body to the ground in a heap. But when it twitched reflexively, he grabbed it by the ankle and flung it against the fallen log, bones breaking sequentially like the clatter of a shale rockslide.

The body lay with its mouth agape and neck perversely dislocated. The Gray kicked it with his massive foot, but there was no response. His rage unsated, he stomped on the carcass, again and again, the bones popping like twigs under his feet.

Abruptly, he stopped, beat his breast, and danced around the corpse, making guttural grunts and squeals until, inadvertently, he stepped on a hard object. He picked the curious implement off the ground and studied it carefully. The Gray recognized it as one of the smoke-sticks the man-beasts had used to throw their deadly rocks—like the one used to harm his son—and he sneered at it and huffed deeply. Giving the wooden end a light twist caused it to snap like a twig. He let out a deep, disapproving *humph* and cast the splintered butt of the implement in the brush.

Intrigued by the mechanism, the Gray moved his fingers down the long metal shaft. One of the parts moved when he touched it, and he heard a click-click. Then, he noticed a curved twig-like object protruding from the opposite side of the smoke-stick. Not knowing its purpose, he touched it gingerly, puzzled how the smoke-stick was able to throw the deadly stones. A faint noise far down canyon brought the Gray to attention, and just as he lifted his head to scan in that direction, he accidentally moved the protruding twig. *KA-BOOM!*

The smoke-stick exploded like thunder, sending belching smoke and flame into his face. The blast singed the hair on the side of his head and a searing pain above his ear rocked him backwards.

The Gray roared loudly and immediately dropped the implement. He held his palm against the side of his pounding head and felt a warm sensation, then pulled his hand away to see that it was covered with blood. He wiped it on some brush before cupping his hand over his ear, for the blast had made his ears ring painfully. Rage swept over him as he looked down at the smoke-stick. He picked it up and swung it hard against the fallen log, bending it into a U-shape. Then, he hurled it over the treetops into the forest.

The Gray felt the side of his head and ran his finger above his ear, then along the painful channel cut by the smoke-stick. He glanced angrily one last time at the man-beast's body and let out a disgusted grunt before heading down the canyon.

$\mathcal{A}$ttack on $\mathcal{B}$loody $Hand$

Gabe sat with *Eagle Claw and Two Kills around* the campfire in the early-morning light in relatively good spirits. Bloody Hand stood not far away. They had begun where they'd left off the night before—telling stories into the wee hours. Gabe observed that even Bloody Hand had relaxed somewhat as the hodgepodge group of men filled their bellies on beaver and hovered near the campfire, laughing and telling yarns.

Two Kills had what Gabe's mother would call "the gift of the gab," and he kept them entertained with embellished storytelling. One story was quite memorable.

"We are hunting buffalo near the Two Medicine River," Two Kills began, speaking in English for Gabe's benefit, "and we have to camp out overnight. I wake up because my cousin Blue Hawk is jumping up and down and yelling. I say, 'What is the matter with you, cousin?' He keeps jumping and shaking his leg, and soon, a rattlesnake slides out his pant leg." He paused, laughing.

"What happened? Was he okay?" asked Eagle Claw.

"No. It bit him on the end of his puschka!"

"*Aiyaaa!*" Eagle Claw sucked in air at the word.

Gabe shook his head, confused. "What is a puschka?"

"You might call it a 'tool' or 'dick,'" explained Eagle Claw, pointing his finger out from his crotch.

Gabe shifted and groaned in empathy. Bloody Hand stood listening with one foot on a fallen log, chuckling to himself.

"Blue Hawk told me the venom must be sucked out," Two Kills continued, "then he showed me the bite. I say, 'I know you are my cousin and I care very much for you, but you really must see the Medicine Man for that. We need to hurry and get you to Yellow Horse.' So we mount our horses and rode like the wind. Soon, we arrived at Yellow Horse's lodge and called out for him. He walked out of his tipi and asked what we need. Blue Hawk is doubled over in pain, so I told him, 'Snake bite.' Yellow Horse said to me, 'You stupid idiot, why did you not just suck out the poison? Do I have to show you how to do everything?' I helped Blue Hawk off his horse, and he pulled down his pants for Yellow Horse so he can suck out the venom. Yellow Horse took one look and walked away toward his lodge. Blue Hawk yelled, 'Where are you going?' Without turning around Yellow Horse said, 'Sorry, Blue Hawk ... but you are going to die.'"

The three of them burst out laughing while Bloody Hand chuckled once and shook his head, a faint upturn on one corner of his mouth fracturing in his normally stony demeanor.

The faint echo of a rifle shot from far back in the basin rippled down the canyon.

"*Ssshh!* Quiet!" barked Bloody Hand.

Everyone stopped laughing to listen, and Two Kills rose, holding his rifle. Gabe's ears perked up in the direction of the drainage.

"It sounded far off," said Two Kills.

"Yes," Bloody Hand said. "Let's mount up and move closer."

Two Kills stood guard while Gabe and Eagle Claw caught the horses and prepared them for the trail. Within minutes, they were mounted and ready.

"Be alert now!" demanded Bloody Hand. "We don't know what to expect." He took the lead just ahead of Gabe and Eagle Claw, while Two Kills brought up the rear.

Cautiously, Gabe nudged his horse ahead, and the small group slowly moved up the trail. They had traveled a half mile when the narrow path cut along a sidehill just above the creek, then passed through some dense timber before emerging into a small clearing. Bloody Hand's horse came to a stop, its ears perked, apparently alerted to an unseen danger. The brave nudged it forward, but instead, it stepped backwards, away from the opening in the trees. He craned forward to see what could be spooking the animal. Apparently satisfied nothing was there, he dug his heels into its ribs and whipped it on the rump with his braided quirt. Once more, it stalled and tried to turn back. Finally, he was able to coax the horse just inside the clearing, but it would go no farther. Gabe's horse also balked and didn't want to leave the security of the stand of spruce trees. It snorted and planted its hooves, legs quivering.

Again, Bloody Hand scanned the area. Seeing nothing, he grumbled something angrily in Blackfeet, ignored his horse's warnings, and instead of turning around, he dismounted and pulled his rifle from its scabbard. From the furious look on his face, Gabe thought for a moment Bloody Hand might cock his rifle and shoot the horse between the eyes. He glanced back at Eagle Claw, who sat in his saddle with his arms crossed and shaking his head, his body language expressing concern and disapproval of Bloody Hand's stubbornness.

But Bloody Hand paid no attention to the others. He tugged on the reins, trying again to get his horse to move forward. This time, his horse reared up, thrashing its front legs, then spun and broke free as it tried to escape back down the trail. With quick hands, Gabe caught its reins and held fast. Bloody Hand angrily grabbed them from Gabe and pulled the horse back into the clearing.

Two Kills nudged his horse past Gabe to help. His horse seemed more willing to enter the clearing, and Bloody Hand was finally able to nudge his own horse closer.

As the two spoke in the Blackfeet tongue, Gabe noticed something big moving in the alders across the creek, some twenty yards away. "Look!" he cried out, pointing. "Something's in there!"

Suddenly, a primal roar came from the alders, sending all the horses into a frenzy. Bloody Hand's terrified horse reared up again, thrashing its forelegs before landing on all fours, spinning toward the safety of the timber as the creature stepped from behind the trees in full view. Bloody Hand struggled to hang onto its reins as the horse pulled him back toward the trees.

Two Kills shouted, "It's the Skookum!" In a frenzy, his horse spun and bucked, sending him flying into an outcropping of jagged rocks just off the trail.

Gabe heard a loud pop when he landed, followed by a pained moan. Two Kill's horse crashed past him, bucking and bolting down the trail, with Bloody Hand's horse close behind. Gabe calmed his horse and peered out from just inside the timber. Bloody Hand's eyes were locked onto something near the creek, his expression stunned and etched with confusion. Gabe followed his gaze as Eagle Claw nudged his horse alongside his. Simultaneously, they saw the creature's unmistakable outline—a dark, grayish hairy head and two hulking shoulders just inside the foliage and two angry eyes glaring at them from the jumble of brush and alders.

The moment of bewilderment passed in a heartbeat when Bloody Hand instinctively raised his rifle, took aim, and fired. But the beast disappeared in a flash. Nevertheless, Bloody Hand let out a victory cry. "*Kai yai!* I shot it! I killed the Skookum!"

Two Kills sat up grimacing, reaching for his contorted leg as Bloody Hand turned to his fellow brave with a smile of victory on his face. "Are you injured?"

Gabe saw it first, and then Eagle Claw—a brown whirl sailing out of the brush—but before either could call out a warning, a four-foot-long snag whistled straight for Bloody Hand. It smacked into his midsection with a hollow thump, sending him flying and impaling him against the base of a fir tree. Their horses reared and spun, fighting to join the two others that had fled back down the trail. Gabe and Eagle Claw somehow managed to turn them back around. Bloody Hand lay against the tree, coughing up blood as he struggled to breathe after being skewered clean through, convulsing in the throes of death.

Eagle Claw dismounted, tied off his horse, and raced toward them. He scooped up Two Kills' rifle, which had been dropped when the horse bucked him off, then wheeled to face the creature. Gabe followed his lead, then noticed Two Kills trying to wriggle across the boulders toward Bloody Hand's rifle. Gabe dashed over and beat him to it. He then swiftly retrieved Bloody Hand's leather ammo purse and reloaded.

They watched and waited, but the creature did not emerge. Breathless from the chaos, Gabe took in the situation: behind him lay Bloody Hand dead against a tree, impaled by the large snag, and Two Kills lay nearby with a badly injured leg. The strange turn of events had happened so fast, Gabe could scarcely believe it—he and Eagle Claw were now well-armed and free to retreat down the trail.

They studied the alder brush, worried the creature might still be watching them, but the only sound and movement came from the bubbling creek and Two Kills' groaning. Eagle Claw kept watch as Gabe cautiously stepped toward Bloody Hand and removed his knife and hatchet.

Then, he approached Two Kills, and was surprised when he pulled his knife, scooted back on the rocks, and pointed it at Gabe. "Easy. I'm not going to hurt you." Gabe's words didn't seem to change Two Kills defensive posture brought on by the sudden reversal of power. Eagle Claw stepped closer and smiled. In a flash, he snatched the weapon from his hands and handed it to Gabe.

Gabe examined the Green River knife; it was in good condition with an improvised but well-made elk-horn handle. He tucked it under his belt as Eagle Claw stared down at Two Kills. The jovial disposition they'd grown accustomed to over the past twenty-four hours had vanished in the mayhem, and Two Kills sat back against the boulders like a wounded prairie rattler poised to strike.

"That leg needs attention," said Gabe. "Let me take a look." The brave grabbed his leg just above the knee, his face contorted. When he did, the lower leg twisted unnaturally, and he hollered out in anguish. Gabe carefully felt the leg, squeezing gently up and down his calf.

"It's not broken, but his knee is loose, like he badly tore something," said Gabe.

"Can you make a splint?" asked Eagle Claw as he hunkered down next to him. "Do you think you can walk on it?"

The injured man relaxed somewhat once he realized they weren't going to harm him. He lay back, wincing as he clutched his leg. "I don't think so. I felt it pop when I landed."

Gabe found several stout branches and began making a splint. "I think that thing is still here in the brush. I can still smell it," he said.

Eagle Claw scanned the timber for several moments before answering. "Maybe ... maybe not," he said. "Look at the horses. They've calmed down. I think it's gone. We would have seen or heard it by now. I'm going to find its track and see what direction it went. You stay here with Two Kills and watch the horses. If something happens to me, do not wait. Get him on my horse and ride out of here as fast as you can."

"Very well," replied Gabe.

Two Kills looked perplexed—his defensive posture had been replaced by contemplation.

"You ... you are going to help me stay alive?"

"The Kootenai are peace-loving. We kill only when necessary," Eagle Claw said in a somber voice before cautiously walking to the spot where the creature had stood on the other side of the creek. He took another step and disappeared into the thick alders as he searched for the track.

After splinting Two Kills' leg, Gabe double-checked the horses, making sure they were well secured, then stepped out of the trees and stared at the dead Blackfeet warrior. Drops of blood congealed in a pool next to him, his face ashen. Bloody Hand, once strong and proud, now lay undeniably dead, killed by the Kootenai legend, in a way Gabe never thought possible—with a stick, just like Eagle Claw had killed the grouse.

Gabe glanced at Two Kills, in severe pain but clearly happy to be alive. The brave forced a glance at his fallen leader, then looked down and shook his head in bewilderment. He seemed indeed fortunate to have only been thrown from his horse.

After a few minutes, Eagle Claw returned.

"What did you find?" asked Gabe.

"The tracks head up the canyon."

"Let's get out of here. We're no match for that thing."

"Are you forgetting about Branch and his men? For the sake of my people, they must be driven out."

Gabe looked down at the ground sheepishly and breathed a fearful sigh. He was convinced now, after seeing the Skookum, that it was the creature that had chased him through the woods that morning. He remembered how fast it closed in on him and felt its power with each of its heavy footfalls. Its murderous intentions were now perfectly clear. More than anything, he wanted to retreat to safety. Looking down at Bloody Hand, sallow in death, it seemed there was only one choice.

But, as Eagle Claw stood awaiting his reply, Gabe recalled his near brushes with death at the Crow raid and the Rendezvous, and how Eagle Claw had saved him. With apprehension, he finally nodded and replied, "Okay. Let's do it."

They removed the branch impaling Bloody Hand, lugged the body to a hollow among the deadfall, and then covered it with branches. It was the best they could do under the circumstances. Then, they built a fire, gathering enough wood to keep it burning for the remainder of the day and through the night if necessary, and they helped Two Kills move to the safety of the fire.

Eagle Claw addressed Two Kills. "You will be safe here."

"No! Don't leave me alone. Take me with you. My leg is better now."

"You will only slow us down. The Skookum has gone up the canyon. Don't worry, Two Kills. We will come back for you. I give you my word."

The Blackfeet man tried to get up but stumbled on the uneven ground and fell back, grimacing with pain.

"See? Now, stay here and rest. Here," said Eagle Claw as he tossed him a knife.

The weapon seemed to pacify the brave, and he sat back against the rock, moaning quietly as Gabe turned and followed Eagle Claw up the canyon.

ↄ◠ↄ

An hour later, Dawn and the others rounded a tight curve in the trail and suddenly came upon a small campfire. The gentle mountain breeze had blown its blue-gray smoke up the canyon, away from their keen noses. She pulled her rifle from its scabbard and dismounted.

She didn't have to tell her father or Crowfoot what to do. They were off their horses immediately, weapons in hand. After they tethered their horses, they quietly crept ahead, but the campsite appeared vacant.

"This fire has been tended to recently. Whoever made it must have left not long ago," she said softly.

"Perhaps, the rifle shot we heard came from here," said Crowfoot gesturing toward the clearing.

"Be ready," James added. "The fire is fresh, and they may have heard us coming. Be ready for an ambush."

"There is enough wood gathered here for two days!" Crowfoot exclaimed loudly.

Dawn looked at the large pile of wood. "Very strange. Maybe they had the same experience we had."

Her father circled the area and suddenly grew alarmed. "Look. Blood—and lots of it. There was a skirmish here."

Dawn stepped over and frowned at the blood spattered on the rocks just off the trail. "Yes. That explains the two horses that ran by us."

"Those were Blackfeet horses," added Crowfoot.

Dawn followed behind her father as he cautiously tracked faint drag marks until they came to a pile of brush.

"Look, Father." There, protruding from under the debris, was a moccasin-clad foot. He carefully uncovered it and she recognized the body immediately. "It's their leader. The man who spoke to us at the fish camp. Look at that big hole in him. He was killed without a gun or knife—just like the others."

"Let's make a quick search around the camp. There may be more bodies."

Dawn was about to step onto one of the large boulders near the campfire when a Blackfeet warrior emerged from his hiding place behind it, scooting backwards on the rocks. She shouldered her rifle and took aim.

"Don't shoot!" he shouted.

It quickly became apparent that he had no rifle, and his leg was badly injured, so she lowered her weapon. "Tell us what happened here," said Dawn firmly as the others joined her.

They listened in disbelief as Two Kills explained their encounter with the Skookum, how it had ambushed them, and how Gabe and Eagle Claw had gone up the trail. Dawn was elated to hear they were still alive, and after they discussed the situation, Crowfoot agreed to stay with Two Kills to keep watch and make sure the fire was well tended as Dawn and her father continued up the trail to find Gabe and Eagle Claw.

∾

The sharp bark of gunfire was always a rude sound in the wilderness, one that made Bill Branch stop dead in his tracks, as if an alarm bell had gone off. A gunshot meant possible danger, and it was always a toss of the coin whether it was friend or foe who had pulled the trigger.

What worried Branch, as he stood listening at the far end of the beaver lake, was that he hadn't heard just one shot, but two. The closest rifle report came from the vicinity of their camp, and for the first time, he hoped Johnson had finally gotten his bear or whatever it was that had been vexing them.

The second shot was but a distant moan far down the valley. His first thought was that it came from Choteau, perhaps fending off a bear. His second thought was more worrisome—what if it had come from a band of angry Kootenai, or even worse, Blackfeet?

Branch hefted the heavy load of pelts and traps over his shoulder. Staggering toward camp, he cursed Choteau for deserting them and leaving him to do the hard work. Without Choteau's help, it had taken much longer than usual, and it was noon by the time he had finished pulling all the traps and skinning his catch. Along with his growing desire to make a hasty retreat, he couldn't stop fretting about the precious beaver pelts, worried the pack string might be heading down the canyon behind the tow of the Blackfeet or Kootenai. His determination motivated him to cover the ground without resting, and he was both exhausted and relieved when he saw the string of horses tethered and loaded as he approached the campsite. Strangely, Johnson wasn't up and moving, but Branch figured the layabout was probably snoozing somewhere nearby in the sunshine.

The horses Johnson had saddled and packed were skittish and jumped sideways when Branch dropped his load of clanking traps and beaver plew. Their uneasy demeanor prompted him to grab his rifle with both hands, and, with his finger on the hammer, he crept toward the campfire where Johnson liked to nap. There was no sign of him there, either. Branch squinted hard, scanning the surrounding area for any sign of him.

"I'm not waitin' for ya," he muttered. "No, sir. I wager you're chasin' some worthless stinkin' bear, and I ain't a-waitin'."

Suddenly, something out of place caught his eye. From a distance it appeared to be Johnson's moccasin, just on the other side of the large fallen log near the campfire, perhaps a nice place to nap out of the wind. "Sleepin' again? Damned slugabed!" shouted Branch, but there was no reply.

He moved closer, then stopped short when the carnage came into full view. The body, if it could even be called that, had been pulverized into a bloody mass, the blood churned in with dirt to form a reddish muck, irresistible to blowflies that took flight in a swarm as he approached. If it hadn't been for Johnson's bear-claw necklace protruding morbidly from the corpse, he'd hardly recognize it as a man, its face a gory mash of brains, flesh, and hair, its blood-soaked arms and legs fractured and contorted. Branch gulped when closer inspection revealed a couple of fingers poking out from the pulpy mound like someone rising from the grave. The head had been pounded flat, with one of the eyeballs popped completely out of its socket, as if peeking at the world like a bizarre creature emerging from the pit of Hades.

"What in the name o' God did this?" Branch said out loud, clenching his rifle tighter. One time, he'd seen a man after a herd of buffalo had trampled him, and he'd looked a sight better than what was left of Johnson.

"Son of a bitch!" Branch blurted as shock gave way to reality. In a flash, he spun around with his rifle, defensive, looking in every direction for the killer. He figured whatever it was, it had to be close, probably watching him at that very moment. He'd heard of Indians sometimes mutilating an enemy, but what lay on the other side of the log was certainly the work of a devil.

He studied the churned-up soil around Johnson, inching along until he finally found an unmistakable footprint. Befuddled, he squinted hard and stared. It was the same enormous print Johnson had shown him the previous day. What Branch had refused to believe for so long at last became obvious, and the smell that hung in the air around the camp like a palpable fog left no doubt as to the identity of the culprit. The rank odor made Branch wince. He backed away toward the horses as he scanned the forest for any sign of the creature.

He suddenly became starkly aware of his solitude, which made him feel impotent and vulnerable. There was now no mistaking what he was up against, and a menacing terror grew, crawling up and down his spine like a hissing rattlesnake.

There was no more time for tarrying or debate. The Skookum had been stalking them, and it had come back for Johnson. It was neither the Blackfeet nor the Kootenai, for no human could have done what had been done to Johnson. It was the damned demon of the forest, Choteau's loup-garou. Branch suspected it was now stalking him; he could sense its presence. He cocked his rifle and cautiously backed up until he reached the horses, keeping his eyes glued to the dense willows and alder patch he suspected was the creature's most likely hiding place.

Carefully and methodically, he loaded his pack full of traps into the empty panniers on one of the pack horses, fastened the bundle of beaver pelts he'd just retrieved to the top of the pack, then untied the reins. He strung the animals out in single file in preparation for the trek down the trail, meticulously tying them together head to tail using their braided rawhide lead ropes.

By the time he finished, the long shadows of the mountains began encroaching into the basin. It would be a push to get clear of the long drainage by nightfall. But it could be done if all went as planned and there were no delays. Quickly, he mounted his horse, and scanned the camp one last time before setting out.

He was just about to kick his horse down the trail when something caught his eye. It was his book of poems resting on the log near Johnson's bloodied remains. He cursed Johnson under his breath, then cursed himself for not seeing it sooner. Branch instinctively began to dismount, then glanced at the jostling pack string loaded heavy with beaver plew, all set and ready to go with the horses anxiously snorting for the trail. Branch gritted his teeth and kicked his horse hard.

"Let's get the hell outta here!" he barked. He glanced back one last time, envious of the mountain breeze gently turning the pages of his book of verses as if the spirit of the mountain had absconded it to snicker at his heart-rendered words.

Branch turned away from it, back toward the trail, sternly glaring ahead. *It was nothing!* he thought to himself. "Just a worthless book of scribbles. That's all it was anyhow. Bloody scribbles!" he growled.

He angrily heeled his horse, as if distancing himself from the camp brought a balm to the piercing stab in his heart. Branch placed his rifle in the crook of his left arm, pointing it toward the alders lining the creek, his finger on the trigger.

He made a hasty retreat, keeping a watchful eye for any sign of danger, and as he distanced himself from the bloody horror, he began to relax and contemplate his good fortune. He had a pack train full of beaver pelts all to himself and just enough daylight remaining to make good his escape. And he was alive.

Chapter Thirty-Six

Broken Branch

Gabe's mind was a blur, and his body was fatigued from the chaos of the Skookum attack. But adrenaline still coursed through his veins as his aching eyes searched the forest for movement and any sign of the creature. Eagle Claw certainly wasn't asleep in the saddle, either, and he kept placing his hand on the butt of his rifle or clutching his tomahawk as they rode cautiously and, above all, quietly up the trail.

Gabe was so focused on searching the timber that he nearly forgot about Branch and his men, and when he recognized an enormous fir tree along the trail, he knew they were not more than a mile from the second camp. He strained his ears, hoping to hear the noisy mountain men before they could see them. Gabe noticed a vague catch in the gait of his horse—a hesitating step that signaled something approaching. He stared straight ahead, pulled back on the reins, and stopped when the animal's ears cocked forward toward an imperceptible sound.

"Hold up," he whispered to Eagle Claw. "Something's coming down the trail."

Eagle Claw stopped his horse, and they listened carefully, but all was quiet. "I don't hear anything," he whispered back.

"Neither do I. But my horse does. Something's got him spooked."

Eagle Claw dismounted and motioned for Gabe to do the same. They led their horses off the trail, hitching them to trees before getting into position. *This is it*, Gabe thought as his breath quickened, and his heart raced. *My first skirmish with a gun in my hand—and it's with Crooked Bill Branch!* He ducked behind a large pine and clutched Bloody Hand's rust-pitted rifle so hard, his knuckles turned white. He looked down at the weapon skeptically. If not for the many notches carved up and down its stock, he would have had serious doubts regarding its potency, let alone its functionality.

The forest was quiet and still, and they crept forward steadily, using the trees for cover. They had gone fifty yards when Gabe saw movement ahead, a short distance off the trail in the timber. He motioned to Eagle Claw, pointing at a large bull pine just ahead. Together, they climbed over a swath of downed trees to where Gabe had spotted the movement. As they approached, several ravens fluttered away with startled cackles and caws. A few steps closer, and the sound of buzzing blowflies gave a grim hint of what lay ahead. The wind suddenly shifted and removed all doubt: the stench of death knocked Gabe back a step.

Nearing the tree, he saw a dark, tar-like streak running along its trunk. He tracked it with his eyes, stepped around the tree, and stumbled back at the horrific sight. To his shock, there hung André Choteau, suspended from a broken snag, skewered clean through, hanging several feet off the ground. The ravens had done a thorough job on his face—both eye sockets were pecked clean, the lips were trimmed back to the bone, showing yellowed teeth, and even the ears had been neatly picked away. It was only Choteau's thick black beard and familiar attire that left no doubt in Gabe's mind that it was the Frenchman.

He was so stunned by the sight he didn't notice that Eagle Claw had continued ahead. He hurried to catch up to him, dumbfounded that he seemed unaffected by the gruesome sight that had left Gabe feeling slack-jawed and speechless. Suddenly, the relic he clutched in his hands seemed like a useless toy, and he hoped and prayed Eagle Claw would abandon this foolhardy endeavor. But just when he was about to tell him his thoughts on the matter, the squeaking of horse tack and the sound of distant footfalls farther up the drainage redirected his attention. Once again, he and Eagle Claw steeled themselves for a bloody confrontation.

ભ્

Branch led the pack train down the trail steadily now; the horses and mules had found an efficient rhythm and pace. As he distanced himself from the ghastly sight of what was left of Johnson, his stubbornly practical mind began to kick in, reasoning away his fears, diffusing his once certainty of what had killed Johnson, and surrendering the misdeed to other possibilities.

As the horses moved down the drainage, he began to worry himself with thoughts of the Kootenai, the Blackfeet, or perhaps even other trappers who might be waiting to ambush him and take his furs, figuring they would attack only after he'd done the hard work of packing everything safely all the way to the Kootenai River. He felt less and less confident as he hurried down the trail, gripping his rifle even tighter.

After he had ridden twenty minutes, he looked back at the pack string as the animals navigated a bend in the trail to make sure the loads were traveling well. He got a head count on the horses. "Five. Excellent." he whispered, as if to reassure himself with the sound of his own voice.

As his horse passed under a tree, he was jerked out of his saddle and lifted upward in a blur. He felt a rush of air across his face, and tree branches whizzed by—as if he were flying. Far below, his horses snorted and scattered like quail as he was lifted ever higher. Something had a hold on him by his hair and head. He reached up awkwardly and felt an enormous hand clenching down, but he couldn't break free.

Branch's head jerked as he was violently spun around. He blinked in disbelief when he found himself staring into the glaring eyes of the Skookum, its massive hand now wrapped around his throat. It growled as Branch struggled to breathe, his feet dangling in the air. He felt a disturbing pull in his neck and a shifting of vertebrae, as if the weight of his body threatened to separate itself from his head.

He grabbed onto the creature's hairy wrist and pulled himself up to relieve the pressure. He glanced down to see its large feet balanced precariously on tree limbs fifty feet above the forest floor. The creature pulled Branch close, opened its mouth wide—its teeth stained dark, the canines sharp and menacing—and its hot breath blew back Branch's hair as it roared in his face.

Consumed with panic, Branch tried hitting the creature's hands, but it was like hitting gnarled stumps. He drew out his Green River knife, but before he could attempt a stab, the beast grabbed him by the wrist and wrenched his arm, sending the knife clanging off branches until it hit the earth below.

Branch looked down to judge the distance to the ground, figuring he would rather risk the fall than be smashed to a pulp like Johnson had been. He drew his leg up and pulled out the extra knife he kept tucked in the scabbard on his calf, then sank it deep into the forearm of the creature and pulled it out in one fluid motion.

"*Aaaaargh!*" the creature shrieked, releasing its grip on Branch and clutching its forearm as blood oozed through its fingers.

Branch landed hard on the closest limb and desperately hung on. Struggling to keep his grip, he fumbled and dropped his bloodied knife, which followed the path of his Green River and landed among the rocks.

He looked at the ground far below and then up at the creature, distracted momentarily as it examined its freshly wounded forearm. Branch felt his fingers weakening and his grip beginning to falter. *Maybe I can catch the next branch down*, he thought. Feeling the brush of the Skookum's hand as it reached down to grab him, he let go of the branch. He grappled for the next branch, but his hands slipped free and he hurtled to the earth, bouncing off the bigger branches and breaking the smaller ones until he finally hit the rocky ground with a thud.

⁓

Within seconds, the Gray was standing over the unconscious man-beast, whose leg was fractured badly, a jagged bone sticking out the side of his leather garment and his skull bleeding profusely from a head wound. The Gray looked at his aching, bloodied forearm and huffed angrily. He kicked at the man-beast's body, but it didn't move. The Gray's anger welled up from the painful wound, and he stood for a moment, holding his arm to further stop the bleeding. He was lifting his foot to stomp on the man-beast's head when he heard a strange noise not far down the valley. He spun around to face the threat, ready for an attack, but whatever had made the noise had yet to come into view. He stared intently down the trail for a moment until he noticed movement, then he silently vanished into the timber.

కా

Gabe and Eagle Claw heard the fierce roar coming from somewhere up ahead. It put them on guard and slowed their progress to a crawl as they expected trouble at any moment. Then came the sound of breaking branches and the thump of something heavy hitting the ground. Eagle Claw gestured to Gabe to be ready to shoot, and they moved silently up the trail with their rifles cocked and ready. Eagle Claw's face had taken on a stony countenance, one Gabe hadn't seen since the skirmish with the Crow Indians. Then came the sound of footfalls and the grinding of gravelly rocks under hoof, and a riderless horse trotted toward them, followed by another.

"Hey, that's Juniper," whispered Gabe. He lunged for the reins as the horse tried to scoot past, and he was dragged several feet before he could stop Juniper. He spoke calmly, with soothing words: "Hey, boy. It's me, your old buddy." As Gabe looked him over, his eyes were suddenly drawn to the Hawken rifle hanging from the scabbard on Branch's saddle. He tied off the horse and grabbed the rifle, overwhelmed with emotion.

"You are reunited," Eagle Claw said quietly.

Soon, another horse came into view, which Eagle Claw caught and secured while Gabe carefully examined the rifle, confirming it was indeed the prized Hawken that Branch had taken from him. He smiled and stifled his urge to shout for joy.

Eagle Claw whispered, "*Shhh!* They are close."

They inched ahead until Gabe spotted something. They skirted to the left, and soon, a man's leg came into view, protruding from behind the base of a tree. He nodded at Eagle Claw, and they moved in with rifles raised.

As the body came into full view, Gabe recognized it was none other than Crooked Bill Branch, lying motionless, alive but obviously injured with blood oozing from a nasty head wound somewhere under his pile of graying hair. But even more grim was his broken left leg, contorted perversely, with a thigh bone protruding a couple of inches through his leather pants. The trapper was just starting to come to and groaned as he became increasingly conscious of his pain.

Gabe whispered a warning as they approached: "Watch out, Eagle Claw. He'll jink you."

Eagle Claw kicked away the knife lying next to the man, but it was unnecessary. Branch groaned again and blinked, struggling to regain full consciousness, squinting as he looked up at them.

"Well, if it isn't Crooked Bill Branch," said Gabe. "Sad to see you this way—such a mighty mountain man and all. I'll be taking back my Hawken that you stole."

"Bauman? Is that you?" Branch grimaced. "Mother of God! *Arghh* ... my leg!"

"I have been told you are touched by powerful spirits—that you can't be killed," said Eagle Claw. "It appears that those stories I heard were wrong. You don't look very well, Crooked Bill Branch."

Branch blinked up at the two men. "Gabe," he muttered. "Thank God ... thank God you're here. Oh! My leg!" He struggled to speak, mumbling incoherently, "Wuh ... whi ... wild ..."

Eagle Claw turned to Gabe. "What's he saying?"

But Branch's eyes grew big and he pointed up, muttering more loudly and frantically until he finally blurted, "Wuh ... wild man!"

"Nice try, Branch," Gabe said. "We're not falling for your tricks again. I ain't no greenhorn anymore."

As Branch continued pointing manically at the tree above them, a flake of bark fell and landed in his lap. Eagle Claw looked at Gabe, and they reacted simultaneously. Shouldering their rifles, they took aim into the upper canopy and were momentarily stunned, for standing on a branch fifty feet above them was the Skookum, holding his wrist and casually looking down on them.

Gabe stared in disbelief as the creature exploded into action with the nimbleness of a cat. It leaped up and grabbed a higher branch, then swung to safety behind the trunk from where it peered down at them. While Gabe gawked, petrified, Eagle Claw hesitated for only a fraction of a second before firing. But the creature was much too quick. It ducked behind the tree and disappeared before the bullet whizzed by its head.

While Eagle Claw quickly reloaded he barked "Why didn't you shoot?!" he shouted.

"I don't know. It—it looked like a man."

"*Man?* That demon killed my brother!"

In the chaos of the moment, they had forgotten all about Branch. "Help ... help me. Please don't leave me here with that thing," moaned the trapper pitifully.

But Gabe ignored his pleading cries and circled the tree behind Eagle Claw as he reloaded, searching intently for the beast, but it had vanished.

Eagle Claw carefully examined the ground below the tree and soon found a drop of blood, then another. "I must have hit him," he announced. "See? Here's blood."

The sight of the Skookum's blood seemed to transform Eagle Claw into something dark and animal-like. As if the hope of revenge had set him aflame. "Come on," he urged. "Let's kill this thing."

But Gabe hesitated and stopped in his tracks. "Please don't go after it," he finally replied. "It will only kill us both."

Eagle Claw scowled but said nothing as Gabe relaxed the hammer of his rifle and cradled it in the crook of his arm.

"I can't do it," Gabe went on, more firmly now. In his heart and mind he knew—without even knowing how he knew—that revenge was not the solution. "The Elders were right. We should just leave the thing alone."

"Very well. I will kill it myself! Catch the horses and lead them back down the trail. I'll catch up."

"Don't do this, Eagle Claw. Let it be. You can't win."

"You sound like the cowardly Blackfeet!" Eagle Claw scoffed. Gabe breathed a frustrating sigh. There was no convincing him. He was determined to kill the creature, and the stubborn brave continued scouring the forest floor for more blood.

Eagle Claw's harsh words stung Gabe, and he almost relented. But a still voice echoed from somewhere in his conscious, and this time, he listened to it. Eagle Claw grimaced disdainfully and stomped away from Gabe without a word, disappearing into the forest as he searched for the creature.

"Help ... please help me ..."

Gabe stopped and glanced at his former boss. He remembered the words the murderous villain used to preach and stepped closer until Branch noticed him and looked up.

"Gabe. Help me."

"Why? You don't need my help, Crooked Bill. You just need to 'toughen up,' 'rub a little dirt on it, and you'll eventually heal.' I'll be leaving now—just 'doin' as I'm told.' Gotta go catch them horses, ya know."

"No! Don't leave me here. Please!"

"Oh, and don't worry about your horses. Just crawl on down to the Tobacco Plains. Maybe they'll be waiting for you there. Who knows? Maybe when Eagle Claw gets finished tracking that Skookum, he'll come back to put you out of your misery. I've seen his scalping work firsthand. I'm sure he'll do a fine job." Gabe clenched his jaws and massaged the hammer of the Hawken, thinking how easy it would be to put a ball right between the degenerate trapper's eyes now that fate had taken a dramatic turn against him. "Don't you see what trouble you've caused? Was it all worth it? All this for a few extra coins in your pocket?" He turned to walk away as Branch moaned pitifully. The sound was unnerving. He paused and tried to ignore the guilt that trickled into his conscious. He glanced back at the badly contorted leg. He looked down and briefly remembered his mother and father—the goodness they tried to instill in him. Gabe sighed deeply, then returned to face the man.

"You don't deserve any help. If the shoe was on the other foot, you would've slit my throat and laughed at me while I bled out." He picked up a stick, broke it in half, and shoved it in Branch's mouth. "Bite down on this."

Gabe wasn't gentle when he jerked the leg straight to reset the broken bone, and Branch hollered loudly through the branch in his mouth. Gabe made a splint and tied it tightly together. He even left Branch some jerky, but that was all the mercy his heart could muster. With the Hawken in hand, Gabe marched down the trail to gather the horses and wait for Eagle Claw as Crooked Branch's moans faded in the distance.

Chapter Thirty-Seven

Tracking Time

*L*ike a hungry fox hunting for a field mouse, Eagle Claw scoured the forest floor, searching vainly for any clues to determine the Skookum's escape path. But it seemed the blood trail had simply vanished. He looked up into the trees but saw nothing except the heavy branches of tall pines.

Suddenly, the sound of tumbling rocks on the trail broke the silence and he spun around, his finger on the trigger. To his relief, clomping down the trail was the remainder of Branch's pack string, which had separated from the group during the mayhem and seemed eager to leave the basin. They ambled down the trail, but Eagle Claw made no effort to stop them, knowing Gabe would catch them when they caught up with the other animals.

As the horses and mules loaded high with beaver plew trotted past, he heard Branch moaning at a higher octave of self-pity. He remembered James telling him, "All men are redeemable." Eagle Claw had his doubts. The words offered hope, redemption, a second chance for evil men like Branch, who didn't deserve such. Branch seemed more like an animal than a man—more vicious than a griz, more cunning than a wolf, and more venomous than an agitated rattlesnake. Yet strangely, the words of redemption echoed with an annoying stubbornness in the back of Eagle Claw's mind.

He would deal with Branch later and continued diligently, searching for a fresh sign, his brother's blood crying out to him from the grave. The creature had to be here somewhere—it couldn't have just disappeared. But even after using years of finely-honed tracking skills, Eagle Claw could not find the blood trail, and he found himself growing increasingly frustrated. He combed the area in ever-widening circles, but to no avail. *How could a beast so large leave no sign?*

Determined to have his revenge, he continued until, finally, he found what he was looking for—a tiny drop of blood on the leaf of a forest fern, then, a few steps farther, another. Now, he knew the general direction the beast had traveled, and his spirits were renewed.

The sparse drops of blood were difficult to find, but eventually, it was clear they were leading up the mountain toward a heavily forested bench. Eagle Claw's gut told him that if the Skookum was injured badly, it would most likely be holed up in the dark timber, where it could watch its backtrail and position itself for a final attack.

Eagle Claw's senses went on high alert, and his adrenaline surged as he closed in. He crept forward, his rifle shouldered and ready to fire. He followed the scattered drops of blood up the sidehill until it leveled off onto the bench. The blood trail led toward an ancient cedar tree directly ahead of him. A smear of blood where the beast had braced himself against the trunk of the tree caused him to stop and take pause. He watched for any movement, but even searching the forest canopy revealed nothing. As he listened in silence, goosebumps rose on his arms, and the hair on the nape of his neck bristled. It had to be there, just in front of him on the opposite side of the giant cedar, listening and waiting for him to move within striking range.

Closer and closer he crept until the pungent smell of the creature told him it was near, within killing range. Every fiber of Eagle Claw's muscles coiled, like a spring trap ready to snap, and as he slowly circled to the right, beads of sweat dripped from his forehead, and years of pent-up bitterness, hate, and revenge quickened his heart. The moment of his dreams was at hand. The long hunger of vengeance would finally be sated, for today, the demon of the forest would surely die.

One more step would bring him clear for the shot. With his finger tight against the trigger, he sprang forward to shoot.

To his astonishment, nothing was there. He looked left, then right, then wheeled in a circle, but the forest was quiet and still. Peering again at the canopy above revealed only an impenetrable network of branches. Eagle Claw stepped away from the base of the tree and knelt.

His heart jumped. The creature had finally left a clear footprint in the softer dirt near the base of the tree. Several drops of fresh blood gave evidence that it had to be nearby. Alongside it was a pulpy, green chunk of organic material, still wet with fresh blood. He studied the wad and upon smelling it immediately recognized the medicinal smell of wolf's bane and goldenrod, healing plants his people had used for generations.

Eagle Claw knelt and studied the footprint more closely. He remembered tracking the creature after it had killed his brother, and the clear footprint it had left behind with its long claws cut into the mud like knives. Like the track they had found at the first camp, this one also had no claw marks. Each toe was pleasantly rounded, without the fearful armament he expected to see. As he pondered the mystery, a single pine needle lightly landed on the ground next to the impression. Eagle Claw's heart raced, and his eyes grew wide. Spinning around, he looked up just as a huge, dark mass came hurtling toward him from above.

Instinctively, he dove as the beast landed next to him with a thud that shook the ground. He tried to roll to his left in order to swing his rifle to shoot but found himself pinned against the tree. He managed to roll just enough to get his rifle free, only to realize he wasn't leaning against a tree—but against the monstrous leg of the Skookum. Panic swept over him as the beast glared down at him.

He pulled his gun up to shoot, but it was jerked from his hands in an instant. The beast appeared wise to the fighting tricks and weapons of men. For a second, Eagle Claw looked up at it, and it looked down at him. In a flash, he pulled his knife from his ankle sheath and sunk it into the beast's foot.

"*Yaaaargh!*" it cried as it jumped aside, clutching its foot.

Eagle Claw sprang to his feet and fled for his life. Every muscle strained to put distance between himself and the Skookum. He looked over his shoulder after fifty yards, sensing it wasn't chasing him, and looked back. Maybe the stab to its foot had stopped it. But the creature stepped into view, holding Eagle Claw's rifle, which looked small in its hand. Without hesitation, it swung his rifle against a tree, shattering it to pieces. Eagle Claw ducked as the broken butt of the stock went whizzing mere inches from his head and bounced off the pine tree next to him.

It took him by surprise, and he stumbled and fell, then got up and raced down the mountain toward the trail, jumping over fallen logs and gaining speed with each stride. Suddenly, he was jerked sideways when his possibles bag caught on a branch, knocking him off balance. He flung the impediment aside as he weaved his way through alder patches, dodging trees and hurdling deadfall. He was running steadily and smoothly now, not like a panicked deer but a speeding antelope. As he distanced himself from the Skookum, his hope of survival grew, which helped him gain even more momentum. He recognized the main trail coming into view just ahead of him and reached it in a few more strides. Now, he picked up even more speed with no obstacles in his path. His heart pounded wildly in his chest. If he could only make it to Gabe and the horses, he would be safe.

He glanced back, relieved to see nothing following him. Turning his head back to face the trail as he ran, he smacked into something hard. The collision knocked him from his feet, and he had a brief weightless sensation as if he was flying, followed immediately by the jarring impact when he bounced off a fallen log and landed with a thud, knocking the wind from his lungs. He lay on the ground gasping for air, certain he had run into the thick branch of a bull pine.

His head throbbed, his vision was blurred, and little spots of light floated everywhere. He rolled onto his stomach and put his hand over his face, only to discover that it was numb. Removing his hand, he dimly saw that it was wet with blood. He tried to look up, but everything was spinning, and he had lost all sense of direction and equilibrium. Blinking to regain his vision seemed to make the vertigo only worse, but he managed to make out the blurred figure of a man looking down at him.

"Gabe! Is that you?" he blurted breathlessly.

To keep from puking, he struggled to get up on his knees, still gasping for air. His vision cleared for a moment, and he lifted his head. There on the ground in front of him, two enormous hairy feet came in and out of focus. Each appeared as big as a beaver, with toes as large as stone war hammers. Eagle Claw felt woozy, and the world began to spin around and around just before he collapsed in a heap.

Chapter Thirty-Eight

The Man-Child

The Gray stared down at the man-beast lying curled up at his feet and immediately recognized his distinct features—the lighter color of his hair and eyes, the unique tint of his skin. His memory took him back to a day long ago, when the warm rays of an autumn sun had melted the hoar frost that coated the trees on the upper reaches of the mountains. Soon, deep snows would come to the high country, and the Gray would seek shelter to sleep through the long winter.

On that day, the heat from the morning sun had lifted the aroma of smoked fish from the village near the waterfalls, the rich odor wafting on the rising currents of air until finally reaching the mountaintops and the nose of the Gray. His stomach grumbled from a sudden craving for the fish's rich pink meat that would help build a layer of fat to sustain him during winter's icy reign.

He dropped down to the river and followed it upstream to the place where the man-beasts lived. On many occasions, the Gray had watched them from just inside the edge of the forest, amused by their curious ways. Then, late at night, when they all were asleep, he would sneak into their camp to grab a fish or two from their drying racks. Sometimes, he would observe them as they scurried about in the light of day, but only for brief periods. They were often loud in their ways, and the many strange things they did were confusing and generally made no sense.

On that warm autumn day, as he approached the village and watched them from the safety of the timber, he detected a familiar smell—one that made his hackles stand on end. Sniffing the air, he stopped chewing and dropped the handful of wild onions he had picked along the way, then circled upwind toward the odor.

The shrill cry of a man-child stopped him in his tracks. The Gray changed course and headed directly for the sound, which originated from somewhere within the forest of stunted juniper trees that grew near the village. He normally maintained a safe distance during daylight, but on this occasion, the cry of the man-child triggered a primal instinct that drew him toward the sound. But the crying suddenly ceased. Just ahead, through the brush and trees, he could see the bristling silvery hair of his mortal enemy: a grizzly bear.

This bear made its home on the edge of the Gray's territory. They had battled before, when the bear was younger, which resulted in the bear burrowing into its lair to heal from the injuries inflicted by the Gray. But the bear had grown stronger and bolder with age—bold enough to encroach where it didn't belong, and it was time for the Gray to teach it another lesson.

The Gray had the advantage of surprise, but as he moved to attack, a twig snapped under his foot, and the bear wheeled to engage its attacker. The beast immediately recognized the familiar frame of the Gray and paused its charge. An eruption of noise from the village startled the bruin, and it bolted into the timber.

The Gray lumbered ahead into the small clearing, and there on the ground, he beheld a bloodied man-child. He nudged it gently with his foot, but it didn't move. The eyes were wide open, but lifeless. Kneeling, he touched it, but again, it did not respond. He lifted the man-child carefully by a leg to inspect the wound more closely and saw immediately that the bear had bitten off its other leg.

A scream behind him startled the Gray, and he stood, still holding the child by its remaining leg. But seeing the terror and sadness on the woman's face, he placed it down gently and slipped back into the timber.

The Gray watched from his hiding place as the woman wept over the dead child. Suddenly, another man-child leaped through the trees behind her. It was the one with the light brown hair, the one he had often observed, the same man-child who had killed the rabbit with sharp flying sticks, then lain still like a fawn hiding from danger.

He remembered when he had stood above the peculiar man-child lying in the tall grass, its hairless chest moving in and out as it breathed. He had found the dead rabbit and the sharp, pointed stick the man-child had used to kill it.

Hesitantly, he had bent down and used the stick to part some of the grass draping over the man-child and get a better view. He studied it closer, then smelled it. So small and weak it was! The man-child seemed to sense the movement close to its head and winced slightly when a blade of tussock grass brushed across its face, but it remained still.

He quietly laid the rabbit near him, poked the pointed stick into the ground, then climbed a nearby tree, waiting and watching until the man-child finally rose and ran as fast as it could to its village. He remembered being amazed at how such a small creature could be so crafty: pretending to be dead to avoid harm. After that, the Gray had learned to keep his distance from the villagers, watching them from afar until he lost interest in their busy, noisy ways.

As he looked down at the man-beast now, it was clear that it had grown bigger and stronger. The Gray recalled other occasions when it was young. He had observed from the cover of the trees how the man-child had been mistreated and pushed aside by the others. He felt an odd connection to it; he understood the struggle—the feeling of being pushed away.

As he thought about these things, the last vestiges of his anger dissipated. He knelt to study the man-beast carefully, sniffed to confirm his suspicions, then uttered a loud *"Humph!"* But it remained motionless. The Gray rose and sniffed the air before looking down the canyon. Far in the distance, farther down the trail, came a faint call. He quickly disappeared into the timber and headed toward it.

❧

Gabe caught Branch's horses and mules when they trotted toward him, then tied their lead ropes to nearby trees to keep them from running off. They seemed relieved to see the other members of the herd and offered no resistance. Then, he built a fire and gathered enough wood to keep it kindled, hoping Eagle Claw would soon return. As he waited, he couldn't stop thinking about his encounter with the Skookum, replaying the sequence of events over and over in his mind.

He picked up the Hawken and examined it closely, remembering how the ruthless Bill Branch had coveted and stolen it. But it was his now, all his. He ran his fingers along the barrel, and as he did, a memory was triggered of how he used to do the same thing with his father's Kentucky rifle when he was a boy.

On the day he left for St. Louis, he had gathered all the items he'd prepared for the journey and bundled them together, tucked neatly into a pack he'd specially made for the trip. His father was gone from the house, and he remembered telling his mother he was going to hunt rabbits, which was, of course, a barefaced lie. She also failed to realize he had switched rifles when she wasn't looking, exchanging his squirrel gun with his father's Kentucky rifle hanging above the fireplace.

He had nearly reached the gate where his friend sat waiting when he saw his father walking toward him from the grain field, as if he had appeared from nowhere. But his father's smile turned to a frown when he glanced down and spotted his rifle clutched tightly in Gabe's hands.

When he figured out what his son was up to, his father approached and tried to wrest the rifle from his hands, but Gabe was nineteen years old and had grown strong. He had to have it where he was going—never mind that it wasn't his. After all, he could hardly kill a buffalo with a squirrel gun, for Heaven's sake! He twisted hard and somehow wrenched the rifle from his father's hands, the momentum cracking the barrel down hard against his father's face and nose.

The haunting image of his anguished mother flashed across his mind. She had come running from the cabin toward him, and as she drew near, Gabe backed away. But she wasn't running to Gabe. She stopped short and knelt over his father, the tears streaming from her face mixed with panic as she tried to help him. His father lay there, his rifle on the ground at his feet, struggling to rise.

Weeping, she helped his father so he could sit, then turned to Gabe. Her eyes pierced into his soul. He stepped back, horrified at what he had done, his friend pulling him away, hollering for him to run. That was when she'd said, through her sobs, the two words that had haunted him ever after and kept him awake so many nights: "Just go!"

And so he had gone. Farther and farther, running past the gate, through the field, and then into the forest and beyond, far away to the freedom of the mountains, far away from his home and his transgression. Each day, he ran farther and faster, until his mother and father were completely gone from his mind's eye, mere pinpricks in time. But it seemed no matter how far he ran, he couldn't outrun that memory. It kept catching him from behind, grabbing him and not letting go.

As Gabe thought about the incident, a disturbing revelation crept into his conscience with the deliberation of a spider. Perhaps he had more in common with Crooked Bill Branch than he had ever wanted to admit. Perhaps, the hatred he felt toward Branch was somehow linked with the hatred he had for himself and for what he had done— his blatant lies and his attempt to steal something that wasn't his.

The thought crossed his mind that perhaps he was just a younger version of Crooked Bill Branch: villains on the same path, separated only by time and space; a dark kinship that needled incessantly, tapping him on the shoulder, whispering in his ear, reminding him that he wasn't really that much different from Branch.

As Gabe's mind drifted deeper into the darker chasms of his soul, he felt as though he were back in his familiar nightmare, trapped once again in the river of sand sliding toward oblivion, taking him hopelessly downward, down into the black hole and the shuffling hungries waiting there for him.

His encounter with the Skookum had made him feel small, insignificant, and humbled. For the first time, he saw himself as he really was—and he didn't like what he saw. As he waited for Eagle Claw, he contemplated the path he'd been walking. He searched his soul for answers and examined his heart without the protective shield of excuses or blame, taking full responsibility for his actions.

As he sat in deep thought, the warmth of the fire settled in, and he dozed off. He dreamed he was standing at a fork in the trail. On the one side stood Bill Branch and his ilk smiling and cheering him to join them, with demons leering over their shoulders. The other path led to his mother and father, who stood stoically, patiently waiting for him to make his choice. Although the right path to take seemed obvious, he had a palpable reluctance to take either, as if choosing one was just as difficult as the other, that facing his transgression was somehow equivalent to choosing death.

The wood crackled and popped and woke him from his slumber. He reflected on the meaning behind the dream and determined it was meant to teach him about a different kind of courage, that choosing to do the right thing sometimes meant facing the truth of one's own ugliness. He silently prayed for this courage—the courage to face the cold, hard reality of himself.

The sun inched its way toward the western horizon, which made Gabe feel ill at ease, wondering what terrors the coming darkness would bring. Pacing and feeding the fire, he continually glanced at the trail, hoping for Eagle Claw's return, wondering whether he had made the right decision to leave him. They were both alone and vulnerable now, and the giant creature could be anywhere, perhaps watching him now in the shadows of the forest.

As the evening breezes began moving up the canyon, the pungent smell of death found its way to Gabe's nostrils. His first thought was that it was the dead beaver from the first camp, but the stench was much stronger now, as if the entire valley had become enveloped in a morbid fog of extermination. Gabe gathered more wood and placed it near the fire, then inspected the stacks of beaver plew and retightened them—anything to keep his mind off the creature and the coming darkness.

As he replayed the events of the day, he remembered Eagle Claw's stories and regretted that he had paid little heed to them, dismissing them as legend. There was no doubt in his mind now. He had seen the thing for himself—with his own eyes. He had smelled it and seen its blood on the ground. He had witnessed how it moved through the trees and what it had done to Bloody Hand, Choteau, and Branch. Wild Man, Big Man, Skookum—it really didn't matter to him what they called it. All Gabe knew was that he didn't care to ever see another one. But the thought of Eagle Claw going up against the creature without his help brought feelings of regret and guilt. At the same time, he saw no malice in the giant creature's eyes. But most of all, it looked human, and he somehow could not bring himself to shoot it. Conflicting emotions crashed together in Gabe's mind like two great buffalo locked in battle. He kept returning to that split second when the creature had peered down at him from the tree with that look in its eyes—like it understood. Not like an animal understands, but like a man.

But the words of Eagle Claw kept ringing in his ears: "That thing killed my brother!" Gabe's mind flashed back to the gruesome scavenged face of Choteau. What if his inner voice was lying to him? What if the creature really is a devil? A rat's nest of contorted thoughts churned in his mind, and he clutched his rifle closer. Before he consciously realized it, his eyes began searching the darkening forest beyond the light—fearfully, just as Choteau had done.

Not far down the canyon, rapid footfalls gave warning to Gabe that something was approaching. The sound of clattering rocks on the trail signaled that it was no small animal. His only thought was of the creature, and he immediately cocked back the hammer of his Hawken and swung it toward the noise. It was coming through the timber now; trees moved as a bulky mass pushed through.

It's big! Gabe thought fearfully. *It's the Skookum! Maybe it's killed Eagle Claw and is now hunting me!* He clenched his jaw and shouldered his rifle, aiming at the spot where the Skookum would emerge from the trees and into the open. He began squeezing the trigger just as the creature was about to break through the brush.

Suddenly, a horse and rider came into view. *Dawn!* Hastily, he lowered his rifle, feeling the blood drain from his face as he realized he had nearly shot her. He was both sickened by his carelessness and overjoyed to see Dawn instead of the creature.

"Gabe!" she shouted as she dismounted. "Where's Eagle Claw?"

He set his rifle down as if it had burned his fingers and put his shaking hands to his head.

"Where's Eagle Claw?" she repeated as James emerged from the trees.

Gabe finally found his voice and looked up. "Hallelujah," he said, lifting his eyes Heavenward for a brief moment, "am I glad to see you two!"

"Glad you're safe!" said James. "Where's Eagle Claw?"

"He told me to wait here for him."

"What do you mean, wait for him? What's he doing? When will he be back?" demanded Dawn.

"I don't know …" He hesitated, unsure of how to explain the bizarre events of the day and Eagle Claw's vengeful mission. "I—I don't know when he'll return. He didn't say. Soon, I hope."

James dismounted, tied off his horse, and strode to the fire. "What happened, Gabe?" he said with pragmatic concern. "We found dead warriors all up and down the trail."

"What?" asked Gabe incredulously.

"We think it was the Skookum. It killed them all," Dawn said. "They looked like they were all Blackfeet."

"What about Two Kills? Is he all right?"

"He's in a lot of pain but alive. We left Crowfoot with him," James said.

Gabe moved closer to the comforting fire as he struggled to understand, sensing now more than ever, that perhaps he had made the wrong choice. Perhaps he had left Eagle Claw to meet his doom. Gabe's voice cracked, "He's gone after it."

James said, "What do you mean, he's gone after it?"

"The Skookum, the Wild Man, or whatever it is you call it. It's real. I saw it … we saw it … both of us. Eagle Claw shot at it and then we found blood. I tried to talk him out of going after it, but he wouldn't listen. I couldn't go along with it. I … I couldn't do it. I couldn't shoot."

Gabe felt a wave of guilt. He glanced at Dawn, who scowled at him furiously. Her piercing glare made him look away, driving him yet deeper into shame and disgrace. James stared blankly into the fire, no doubt contemplating their next move. But there was no such hesitation with Dawn. In a flash, she mounted her horse and was cantering up the canyon trail. James and Gabe quickly mounted and followed her with Eagle Claw's horse in tow.

Chapter Thirty-Nine

Judgment Seat

Eagle Claw slowly regained consciousness. He strug-
gled to his feet, stumbled, and nearly fell before staggering to a nearby
fallen log to sit down. After the fog in his brain lifted, he limped
over to the Skookum tracks and saw them heading down the canyon.
Why had it let him live? Perhaps it had left him for dead? But now,
the creature was heading down the canyon, directly toward Gabe.

Eagle Claw felt naked without a weapon. He remembered his knife
and possibles bag. There was no way to fight against the Skookum
without arming himself with something. Since the Skookum had
gone down the canyon, he was compelled to backtrack and try to
at least find his knife.

After a few hundred yards, he found his possibles bag. His head
pounded as he struggled to climb back up to the bench where he'd
been ambushed by the Skookum. Not far from the edge of the bench
lay his knife, still wet with blood. Lying next to it were several broken
shards of rifle stock, and fifty yards farther, he could see the glint of
his rifle barrel, bent useless. He walked over and picked it up. A chill
ran down his spine, and goosebumps popped up on his forearms as
he ran his fingers along the tight arc of the barrel, awestruck by the
creature's strength.

He dropped off the bench and headed back down the slope, then noticed the butt of his rifle lying on the ground. He mumbled to himself, dumbfounded, as he remembered when it went whizzing by his head as he made his escape.

As he thought about the strength and power of the Skookum, he heard faint moaning. In the melee and confusion, he had forgotten all about Bill Branch, whom they had left lying injured by the trail. A wave of indignation swept over him and, along with it, the bothersome itch of vengeance. He immediately changed course and headed straight toward the outlaw who had started all this trouble in the first place.

Eagle Claw had dispatched wounded men before. It wasn't something he relished—taking a helpless man's life. But in the case of Crooked Bill Branch, he looked forward to it with pleasure. Terminating the outlaw seemed like a perfectly just and rational thing to do. The trespasser was now vulnerable and exposed. It would be an easy kill.

Branch's moans and cries for help grew louder as Eagle Claw drew closer. The miscreant soon came into view, still leaning against the base of the giant bull pine.

"Gabe! Please help me. Please. I'm sorry. I'm sorry for what I did to ya and how I treated ya. Don't leave me here to die. Please!"

Silently, Eagle Claw withdrew his beavertail dag knife before moving in for the kill, looking for a clear path to his throat. He was just about to spring toward the trapper when he looked down and saw the faint glint of Branch's knife lying among the rocks. He sheathed his dag and slipped over to pick it up—the sweet irony of killing Branch with the very knife he'd probably used to kill so many others was irresistible.

"I knew you'd come back, Gabe. I knew it," Branch carried on. "Yer a good man."

As Eagle Claw smiled and stepped closer, the mountain man sensed his presence, turned his head, and glanced up at him. Eagle Claw looked down on the trapper disdainfully and watched as the mountain man's hope drained from his face.

"Oh. It's you. Come back to finish me, eh?" Branch said pitifully as he leaned his head against the tree and closed his eyes.

He noticed that Branch's leg had been carefully set and splinted—somewhat puzzling considering the severity of the break. But his head wound still oozed blood, forming a thick clot in the man's matted hair, like a downturned horn, with blood still slowly dripping off the tip.

"That's a very nice job of setting and splinting your leg. But you needn't have bothered, Crooked Branch." Eagle Claw paused to rehearse in his mind how he would accomplish the task without getting hit, scratched, or bit. First, he would slip around the tree, then grab Branch by the hair, pull his head back, and slit his throat. Branch would gurgle and cough for a few moments, pass out, and in less than a minute, he would completely bleed out. After the gurgling and kicking stopped, he would take his scalp.

"I didn't set my leg. Gabe did before he left. Yer right, but it don't matter. Hurry and finish me, damn it."

Eagle Claw paused and looked at the splint, then at Branch, the embodiment of evil. There would be no escaping for him this time. His life of murder and greed would now come to a quick and bloody end. Eagle Claw gripped the knife tightly and took another step toward the trapper. But his eyes were once again distracted by the splint—a glaring act of kindness toward an evil man who deserved only death.

Fighting the words of his father that spoke of forgiveness and mercy, he took a half step toward him when the crusty trapper gazed straight ahead and began to speak in a strangely elegant voice, his words laced with sadness and regret.

> *A friend waltzed by the other day*
>
> *To tell of riches far away.*
>
> *Alas, I'd sailed 'cross oceans wide.*
>
> *"I'll find my treasure chest," I'd cried.*
>
> *But in my eager search for gold,*
>
> *Aghast, I found that I'd grown old.*

"Where did I go wrong?" mumbled Branch to himself.

The trapper's penitent words, and the way he spoke them, stopped Eagle Claw in his tracks.

"So close. So close to the end. Those bastards back in ol' England woulda raised a brow at me."

England—it was a word that conjured childhood memories for Eagle Claw. When winter's cold kept them nestled in their lodge, burrowed under buffalo blankets, James had told him many stories of his homeland. It had become Eagle Claw's Nirvana—the fairy-tale land of his dreams, a construct within his mind built piece by piece from James's tales, a land flowing with milk and honey with no wars, disease, biting beasts, or disasters common to the life he and his people led.

He stepped carefully around to face Branch, then sat down and crossed his legs. For the first time, he looked Branch in the eye. The mountain man relaxed when Eagle Claw tucked the Green River knife into his belt and said, "Tell me what you know about England."

Branch appeared befuddled. "England? You wanna know about England? Why would you wanna hear about that steamin' cesspool of excrement?"

Eagle Claw had neither heard of cesspools nor excrement. Were they lavish pools of water, decorated ornately with hanging flowered plants? "Yes, tell me about England," he repeated earnestly. "It is where my father was born. I plan to go there someday. Tell me about it."

Branch laughed and looked up at Eagle Claw, somewhat humored. "Hell, I was born 'n' raised in that snake pit. What's his name? Your father?"

"James Harrison."

"Never heard of him, though I do know of Harrisons in England. It ain't a rare name." Branch paused for a moment and stared blankly, then said, "Been long ago now—I got to think on it. I never dreamed my departin' words would be waxin' 'bout England, of all places, to a half-breed Injun." He paused for a moment, looked Eagle Claw in the eye, and said, "But you are half white, so that's in your favor. All right, I'll tell ya about England."

Branch closed his eyes, took a deep breath, then spoke deliberately, reverting now and then to the English accent he had dropped long ago: "Okay, I'll tell you the good stuff. I remember ... the sweeping, rolling hills of Yorkshire—herds of wooly white sheep grazing placidly in hedge-rimmed pastures of brilliant emerald green ... under a daffodil sun." The steely eyes of the trapper suddenly turned softer, almost sad.

After his initial shock at Branch's new voice, so similar to his father's, Eagle Claw sat back and imagined the idyllic paradise of his childhood daydreams—the place of his father's homeland.

Branch continued: "I remember ... the ornate arched bridges of the Thames and the cobblestone streets of London, the coaches pulled by silvery horses driven by coachmen wearing scarlet frock coats and bright white trousers. The ladies, oh, the ladies, all in long, pastel dresses wrapped in colorful shawls with wide-rimmed bonnets to shade their flawless complexions. The elegant balls! There were many of them. I remember street urchins selling their papers to businessmen and the donkeys pulling carts of produce that lined the marketplace each day. I remember walking the checkered cathedral halls of Westminster Palace.

"And Julia—my Julia, how she could play the piano. I could listen for hours, days, for eternity, to her music that filled my heart to overflowing. I remember the lavender dress and the flowered bonnet she wore the last time we met together. I wrote her a poem and read it to her on that day." He closed his eyes and sighed, then began to recite it.

> *For all the world's wonders grand*
>
> *Fail to match the beauty of your hand.*
>
> *Nor would the bitterness of hemlock sips*
>
> *Sour the perfect sweetness of your lips.*
>
> *Nor would the radiant sunlit skies*
>
> *Quench the starlight twinkling in your eyes.*

Branch drifted away for a moment, lost in the pleasant remembrance of a love long lost. His lips quivered, and his eyes became misty.

"Tell me more," said Eagle Claw earnestly.

A single tear broke free and ran down Branch's cheek. He quickly wiped it away and steeled his emotions. "I know you're going to use that knife on me," he said at length. "But before you do, I want to tell you something, and I don't want you to forget it."

Eagle Claw listened intently but did not reply.

"In my lifetime, I've traveled far and wide, and my eyes have beheld many wonders. And without a blink, I can tell you forthrightly that all the glories of England, if you were to add them all up, would be swallowed whole in one gulp by the Rocky Mountains. This land— this exquisite land—has surely been stamped by the signet ring of the Almighty God."

Eagle Claw pondered his poetic words, uncertain if they had actually emanated from the mouth of the notorious Crooked Bill Branch or from a different Bill Branch, one from a different place, a different time, or even one who perhaps had reached a point of repentance. As he stared at the man, Eagle Claw remembered the Skookum towering over him, wondering why it had allowed him to live, and the words of his father when he had said, "Vengeance is God's sacred ground."

"I deserve to die," Branch said. "Go ahead ... make it quick. I'd rather die by your hand than at the hands of that damned Skookum."

Eagle Claw sat in the judgment seat, looking closely at Crooked Bill Branch and wondering, *What death would be most appropriate? What death would he deserve for all the misery and death he had caused?*

Memories flashed across his mind: his brother's tiny fingers clutching his mother's shriveled hand; his father's reassuring words; White Cloud as he told the story of the Big Man; the ominous, dark figure hovering over him as he lay on the ground. Suddenly, he remembered what White Cloud had said when he told him to let the Big Man decide his fate, that if Branch was "honorable, he will return. If not, then his flesh and bones will feed the raven and the bear."

Eagle Claw stood, put his hand on the handle of the Green River knife, and said, "Perhaps, Bill Branch, we all deserve to die."

Branch furrowed his brow, as if trying to comprehend what he'd just heard. Eagle Claw drew the knife and Branch closed his eyes tight, gulped hard, and lifted his chin. Seconds passed. The forest grew silent. Finally, Eagle Claw stuck the Green River knife in the ground between Branch's legs and turned to leave.

He had gone no more than ten paces when Branch hollered, "Hey! Don't leave me here, damn it!"

Eagle Claw shook his head and smiled, remembering one of his father's wise sayings: *The skunk always stinks, and the rattlesnake always strikes.* He hobbled down the canyon, hoping Gabe was safe and waiting with a fire burning to welcome him as dusk approached.

Eagle Claw had gone only a quarter of a mile when he heard the clatter of hooves. He instinctively ducked behind a tree as a voice called out, "Brother!" He peeked around to find his sister topping a swell in the trail. She jumped off her horse, ran, and embraced him. "We thought you were—"

"Not dead yet, sister," he interrupted before she could finish.

James and Gabe came into view and dismounted. "Are you hurt?" James said.

"Bruised but not broken. I will survive. I see you brought my horse, Gabe Bauman."

"Yes. It's good to see you, my friend."

"And how is Two Kills?"

"Crowfoot is with him," replied Dawn.

Eagle Claw was silent. He mounted his horse, and they all headed down the trail together.

"What happened to your rifle?" asked James.

"It's a long story."

"I can't wait to hear it," said Gabe.

As they hurried down the trail, Eagle Claw thought about his conversation with Bill Branch and felt better that he hadn't killed him, as if a heavy weight had been lifted off his shoulders.

His mind was whirling with the revelation that there was often more to the story than meets the eye. For the first time, he thought about the Skookum without malice and contemplated what White Cloud had said about it—the legend he called the Big Man.

Chapter Forty

Beast Battle

Two Kills sat uncomfortably next to the fire. It didn't matter how he positioned his wounded leg—it throbbed with a deep, biting pain. He thought he'd heard something farther up the canyon a moment ago, but the noise was too far away to be distinguishable. He glanced at the setting sun anxiously as it sank below the western peaks, wondering what the night would bring.

"I'll fill up the water flask," said Crowfoot.

"Hurry," he said as the Kootenai man went to the creek for water. He sat back and gazed at the fire, thinking of his wife and child at their camp on the Two Medicine River. By now, she would have kindled a small fire inside their lodge and would probably be telling a story before bedtime. How he wished he were there to tell his new stories—ones that would be told again and again, if only he could make it out alive.

Crowfoot had just finished filling the flask when a branch snapped inside the alder thicket on the other side of the creek. He swung his rifle in the direction of the sound and slowly backed away. He had moved halfway toward the security of the fire when a large, dark blur burst through the alders and charged straight toward him.

Two Kills sat paralyzed with fear as the grizzly charged at Crowfoot, its six-inch claws churning up clumps of dirt and grass as it bore down. Its lips were curled back, showing its long, yellow fangs as it chomped its jaws. Crowfoot raised his gun and fired at the bear, but the bullet just grazed it and served only to make it angrier and more determined. The grizzly collided with Crowfoot, sending him flying and knocking his rifle into the underbrush. Crowfoot had barely hit the ground when it dove, sinking its teeth into his thigh. He cried out in agony as the bear picked him up and shook him, then dropped him and swatted him hard, raking his back with its claws.

Two Kills quickly forgot about the pain in his leg when the beast spun and stared straight at him. He unsheathed his knife and scooted closer to the fire. But the bruin noticed when Crowfoot reached for a fist-sized rock and quickly turned on *him* once again. He swung hard as the beast lunged for his throat, and the rock landed with an audible crack on its lower jaw. The blow stunned it, and it sat back for a moment, then circled, its eyes glowing demon-red from the firelight. Crowfoot pulled his knife and rose to face the griz. He tripped backwards as it made another lunge for him. He thrust his knife and shielded his face with his other forearm, bracing himself for a deadly bite from powerful jaws.

From seemingly nowhere came a dark, swift movement. The thing charged and collided head on with the bear, which let out a deep *humph* as though the wind had been knocked out of it. Rocks and debris flew from the whirling tangle of fur. Two Kills recognized the shape and form immediately. It was the Skookum, the same creature that attacked and tried to kill him. The ground seemed to tremble as the two powerful creatures fought. Dumbfounded, he asked himself, *What is happening?* He was relieved Crowfoot was still alive, but now, he didn't know who to cheer for, the bear or the Skookum?

"Get over here!" Two Kills yelled to Crowfoot, who was fumbling around, trying to find his rifle buried somewhere in the deadfall. The Kootenai abandoned his search and hurried to the safety of the fire.

With a heavy blow, the Skookum managed to knock the bear backwards. It then picked up a large rock as the bear charged and threw it with both hands, knocking the bear off balance, barely avoiding its raking claws. It scrambled up the nearest tree, with the bear chomping mere inches behind until it had climbed well out of reach.

The great bear circled the tree, growling and huffing. Halfway up the tree, the Skookum looked down and gave a loud cry: *Garooooooh!* From somewhere up the drainage came an answer. The bear looked up the canyon in the direction of the noise and took a hesitating step in the other direction. For a moment, Two Kills thought it was about to leave, but it turned and glared at them, its beady devilish eyes glowing red in the firelight. It took two swaggering steps toward them, growling. They huddled closer, on the opposite side of the fire, gripping their knives tightly for the charge.

Suddenly, a dark gray figure came into view, sprinting through the drainage toward them, leaping deadfall, dodging obstacles, and gaining speed. It was another Skookum. Two Kills sat slack-jawed, amazed at its enormous size. It burst into the small clearing and skidded to a stop next to the creek, its massive chest heaving.

Two Kills could sense Crowfoot was about to run. "Don't go out there, away from the fire," he whispered. "You will not make it out alive if you do."

The griz stood up on its rear legs to intimidate its rival, but the Skookum had the clear size advantage. The grizzly growled menacingly, but the big gray beast let out an ominous roar that seemed to shake the trees, causing Two Kills and Crowfoot to jump. The two creatures began to circle each other, sizing each other up for the battle.

☙

Gabe was riding down the trail in silence as the others talked and chattered. Occasionally, he picked up a slight tremble in Eagle Claw's voice as he spoke about the Skookum. His story seemed incredible, almost too amazing to be believed. But after seeing Choteau impaled on the broken limb and witnessing how the creature was able to climb trees like a squirrel, he no longer questioned any stories about it.

The excited chattering came to an abrupt stop when the sound of a gunshot echoed not far ahead of them. James didn't wait to discuss the matter and took off down the trail toward it, with everyone close behind. Just ahead came the sound of breaking branches and clattering rocks. The sounds grew louder as the soft twilight glow of the campfire came into view.

They covered the remaining distance at a full gallop. Just before rounding the final bend in the trail, they dismounted with weapons drawn. Quickly, they tied off the horses and moved forward along the trail. As they rounded the corner, Gabe stared in disbelief as the melee of two great battling beasts came into view. James raised his rifle to shoot, but Eagle Claw surprisingly stopped him.

"No! Wait!" he said firmly, and they watched, like Roman spectators viewing two great gladiators.

The two hairy hulks merged into a single roiling mass of growling rage. They crashed and rolled through the creek and into the tangle of alders until somehow, the bear went sailing from the alders into the creek. When the Skookum emerged from the alders, the griz charged it with full force and slammed hard into the hulking creature. It shuddered from the impact and was knocked over. The bear was on it in an instant, but the Skookum rolled, grabbed the griz around its midsection, then stood and spun in a complete circle and let the bear go, sending it crashing into a tree.

The grizzly stumbled to its feet and charged with bared teeth, sending debris flying with each footfall as its claws dug into the ground. The Skookum absorbed the full impact of the charge, pushing back on the bear's neck and head to keep it from biting. Once again, they wrestled violently.

Gabe and Dawn raced to keep the agitated horses from pulling free as they bucked and strained against their tethers. "I've got this," she said impatiently. "Go help the others!" Gabe quickly returned and stepped alongside James with his Hawken.

As they wrestled, the Skookum rolled up against a log, jamming its right arm and rendering it useless. The griz seized the moment and quickly pinned the Skookum down. It seemed to let out a gloating *humph* as it opened its mouth wide to bite down on the Skookum's exposed neck for the kill.

As the bear lunged forward, it was tackled from behind and swept away by another Skookum, this one obviously a female that had climbed down from a vantage point in a tree to dive into the fray. They rolled together, a violent mass of fur, muscle, and claw. Just as the bear latched onto her arm, the big male freed itself from beneath the log and sprang toward them. In one swift move, the Skookum snapped a limb from a fallen tree and swung it hard. The blow smacked the side of the grizzly's head, sending it rolling again into the creek.

The bear stumbled to its feet and sat back on its haunches, dazed. But before it could charge again, the male Skookum leaped forward and grabbed it by the neck and hindquarters. The griz roared and swung its head back to bite, but it was no use—it could not reach the Skookum. The big male spun the bear around and around until it was fully off the ground, then hurled it through the trees on the other side of the creek, breaking branches as it crashed through the forest canopy until it landed with a thud.

The female Skookum joined the male, and the two strode across the creek toward the bear, which could be heard running in the opposite direction. Just then, the male turned back and looked angrily at the men.

Fearing an attack, James pulled up his rifle, took aim, and started his squeeze on the trigger. In the fleeting second before the gun went off, a shrouded memory flashed across Gabe's mind.

ↄ⌖

He was kneeling in his family's cabin, his dad's rifle in hand, its barrel propped on the windowsill. Tied to the hitching post outside stood Lilly, lethargically chewing the hay his father had fed her before the daily milking.

Just a boy, he remembered struggling to pull back the hammer, and when it clicked loudly, he glanced through the window on the other side of the cabin to see if his mother, who was outside working in the garden, had heard it. He noticed her pause to listen, for she was a fair shot herself and had heard that familiar click many times. But she must have convinced herself it wasn't what she thought and, to Gabe's relief, continued working the soil, pulling weeds. He poked the rifle out the window and pretended Lilly was a deer and that he was hunting. The last thing he remembered was the look in Lilly's eyes when she stopped chewing her cud and stared right at him. He dismissed the look in her eyes, her knowing look of disapproval.

And after all, Lilly was just a dumb cow, and the rifle certainly wasn't loaded.

He tried not to remember what happened next: the deafening explosion that knocked him to the ground, the smell of gunpowder, and the mad, frantic fog of chaos. Then came an enormous vacuum devoid of all sound except for the loud ringing in his ears, and his trembling, as if someone had grabbed him by the shoulders and had shaken him violently, only nobody was near.

The thing he remembered most, and the thing that haunted him, was that look in Lilly's eye—just before he pulled the trigger.

ε∽∂

The beast glared at James when he took aim, as if it knew the man's deadly intent, then shifted its eyes ever so briefly to Gabe. In the waning dusk and firelight, Gabe remembered that look, the same knowing look that Lilly had given him just before he pulled the trigger on that fateful day. Gabe lunged for James's rifle. But before he could stop him, Eagle Claw reached over and bumped it away from its intended target.

"No!" said Eagle Claw firmly.

The gun went off, and the two creatures stood there, unflinching, after the bullet glanced off the tree above their heads. The male squinted slightly and furrowed its brow, its mouth turned slightly downward. Then, the two of them turned and disappeared into the forest, following the trail of the retreating bear.

James looked at Eagle Claw, thunderstruck, but didn't say a word. Then, the brave looked Gabe in the eye. It was a look Gabe would never forget—a look of mutual understanding and agreement. Something had changed Eagle Claw's mind about the Skookum. Gabe felt his guilt at having left Eagle Claw to fight the creature alone disappear when the brave smiled and nodded knowingly.

Chapter Forty-One

Just Reward

The sounds of the bellowing bear as it made its retreat grew fainter and fainter. The night closed in, and the forest grew still as they huddled around the fire.

"That bear would have killed me if the Skookum hadn't been here," Crowfoot said. "The Skookum saved me!"

James, still apparently miffed from when Eagle Claw disrupted his shot, scowled and barked, "We need to be on guard in case they come back! You saw what the big one did to that griz. I've never seen anything like it."

Again, there was an uncomfortable silence until James's sharp words echoed like a gunshot. "Why did you bump my rifle?" he snapped at Eagle Claw. "We found nine dead braves that looked like they'd been run over by a herd of buffalo!"

Eagle Claw didn't flinch, as if he had expected James' blunt inquiry.

"It could have killed me," Eagle Claw said at length. "—When I tried to hunt it down. But it let me live."

Eagle Claw placed his hand on James's shoulder, met his eye, and said, "Remember the words of White Cloud, my father."

James took a deep breath and softened his tone. "I hope for all of our sakes that you are correct."

Crowfoot was oddly quiet, and his face was ashen as he sat slumped toward the fire. "Are you injured, Crowfoot?" Eagle Claw said.

"The bear raked him good on the back," replied Two Kills. "Bit his leg, too."

Eagle Claw knelt next to Crowfoot to better inspect the injury. "That's a nasty wound." Then, he helped him remove his shirt and began doctoring his wounds.

Gabe watched as Eagle Claw gently tended to Crowfoot, astonished at his sudden transformation.

Gabe looked out at the endless mountain peaks to the west, growing a darker shade of purple as the night closed in. The scattered clouds on the horizon reflected a million shades of red, orange, and blue, with golden rays piercing through openings in the clouds in a glorious display of light.

The sight made him wonder about God, if perhaps God had been with him all along, peering from a distance. Perhaps God was like the Skookum in a way—tossing tiny pebbles from behind the veil to get his attention.

Gabe sat in deep contemplation, wondering to himself about the meaning of it all: *Had God abandoned us, or had we driven Him away, into quiet places of solitude, with our wild, bloodthirsty contraventions?* From the conflict and chaos of the past two months, it seemed more likely to Gabe that He had simply given up and walked away—perhaps to find respite from the rapacious clamoring and endless scheming of mankind.

"We better gather some wood to keep this fire going in case they return to pay us a visit," said James.

Gabe helped gather wood, thinking about his parents and why his father had stopped whipping him after what he had done to Lilly. Perhaps he had finally worn his parents down to the point where they had simply given up and, at least figuratively speaking, walked away. The thought ushered a lonely chill deep within his soul.

His thoughts were a revelation of sorts, and he decided he could no longer blame God for distancing himself. The story of Adam and Eve came to mind and how those first illicit bites from the apple had brought an end to innocence—how everything went downhill from there. Perhaps humankind simply couldn't handle the kind of knowledge they gained after biting into that damned apple. It branded something into hearts and minds like a curse, its pattern weaving its deathly thread through the fabric of humanity, with each successive generation taking more savory bites from the apple, looking vainly for false benefits, foolishly swallowing the poison of their own self-destruction. Then, Gabe came to a sobering epiphany—he'd been biting the apple all along.

Standing under the glaring light of his own self-appraisal, Gabe suddenly saw Crooked Bill Branch in a different light—perhaps the outlaw was just a purer representation of what they all had become, a darker shade of black, and his bites from the apple were just bigger and more ravenous.

Suddenly, Gabe's misdeeds seemed more glaring than before, piercing his soul like a knife in his back that he was unable to reach and remove. He thought of his mother and father, the only two people he knew who truly loved him, and his crimes became clearer and lay heavier upon his shoulders.

Gabe had been so preoccupied with his musings that he'd forgotten his spatial proximity to Dawn and they inadvertently grabbed the same log as they gathered more firewood.

"Oh, sorry," he said, laughing slightly as he let go of the wood.

She smiled and replied, "I am sure it will all get burned tonight no matter who collects it."

Gabe felt his spirits lift. Not only had she spoken in clear English, but they were the first pleasant words she had said to him.

That night, they kept watch, sitting within the protective glow of the firelight. James looked into the heavens and sang the song of thanksgiving and healing. Soon, the others joined in while Gabe listened respectfully. Then, the six of them joined hands, and James led them in a prayer for protection. As the evening wore on, they related their encounters with the Big Man—stories that would be told again and again, to their children and to their children's children.

And as they shared their stories and their food and nursed each other's wounds, Gabe noticed something profound taking place before his very eyes. The things that had kept them apart—fear, anger, bitterness, jealousy, and even the color of their skin—all seemed to disappear into the night, like the fading shadow of the Big Man. They had become children of one Father—a family of human beings.

☙

Higher on the mountain, far above the chaos and death, the injured Younger was recovering quickly under his mother's care. The mixture of ground flora with healing powers that his mother and father had gathered was working well. His fever had completely left him now, and the healing wound had stopped oozing. The Alpha handed him some pine nuts, his favorite food, and he devoured them. The Younger felt stronger now, and his stomach growled with an insatiable hunger.

He leaned against a large rock and closed his eyes. His dream took him back to the ravine along the tranquil lake, where they usually picked berries and dug for edible roots. It had always been a peaceful place—but now it had become his worst nightmare. The loud noise, the burning sensation in his side, the puff of smoke, and other memories of the traumatic moment flashed through his dream. As his father helped him through the dense cover, the Younger caught glimpses of the fierce-faced man-beast, with the smoke-stick pointing at him. The blood, the pain, and the terror of being pursued jolted him awake.

The Alpha female gently removed the poultice on the wound and nodded to show her approval, then cast it aside and replaced it with a fresh one. The Younger made a guttural clucking noise and motioned up the mountain. She replied with reassuring chirps and handed him a handful of huckleberries folded inside a leaf of skunk cabbage. He sat up, thanked her with his eyes, and stood. Slowly, they hiked up the mountain to join the Gray.

Atop the mountain, they could see the outline of the Gray and walked over to stand beside him. They stood there and looked down at a tiny spot of firelight, listening to the faint, drawn-out noises of the man-beasts far below. Then, they turned and looked out over the valley, illuminated by the moon and a billion stars. It was the Younger's favorite spot on the mountain, where he could take in the grandeur all around him. Below lay the peaceful lakes, where he watched beaver as they diligently went about performing their curious duties.

The Gray put his hands on the Younger's shoulder and gave a reassuring purr of consolation. The Younger knew why his father had called them here, and his heart was heavy. As if on cue, they all looked down one last time at the valley they had called home. The moon shone brightly, glinting off the monochromatic snowcapped peaks, illuminating the silvery lakes. His mother sighed and hung her head, and they huddled close and silent before bidding farewell to the world they had grown to know and love.

Then, without further ado, they turned and walked with hesitant steps toward the west and the unknown.

Chapter Forty-Two

Good Riddance

Crooked Bill Branch lay next to the stream, exhausted. His anger sprouted not long after the 'breed had left him to his own fate, and his remorse and contrition had been short-lived. After a week of recuperation, he grew impatient and began a slow hobble down the canyon, aided by a makeshift walking staff. With each painful step, he contemplated various avenues of revenge.

He finally made it to the first camp and feverishly hunted for any scraps of food that might have been left behind. "That damn 'breed!" he muttered. "He'll be the first one I kill when I get outta here! Then, I'll find that bootlicker Bauman an' run him through for takin' my beaver an' leavin' me here to die, then I'll get my horses and pelts!"

After searching in vain for scraps, he cursed his misfortune and sat back against the base of a tree. After a while, he noticed something odd poking out from under a large flat rock a few paces away next to the cold fire pit. He crawled over and lay down next to it, then took his staff and pried the stone away. Hidden under the rock was a leather pouch full of food.

"Aha! Lucky for me, the idiots forgot their food."

He felt better after eating his fill. He fell asleep lazily against the tree, dreaming of how he might find Gabe and get back his rifle, pelts, and horses.

The sudden sound of overturning rocks woke Branch with a jolt. He rubbed his eyes, still in the haze of sleep. The sound of clicking claws on the rocky trail below made him sit up straight. Then, as if from the fog of a nightmare, a grizzly emerged. Strings of saliva stretched from its mouth as it sprinted closer and closer, its massive jaws opening wide and its sharp fangs bright and yellow in the midday sun. Branch stared, stone-faced, as it bore down, then closed his eyes.

Overhead, in the trees above where Branch had been resting, there came a quiet gathering of ravens.

ॐ

Gabe had been right about one thing—the Skookum did not return that night.

Early the next morning, the survivors made their way down the mountain to the fish camp. There, they found Red Hawk, who was relieved to see that Two Kills had made it out alive. Neither of them was fit for their long journey home to the Two Medicine River, so everyone decided they would all stay at the fish camp until the Blackfeet men's injuries had a chance to heal. Eagle Claw, Gabe, Dawn, and James hunted and caught fish, smoking the meat to bide their time while tending to Red Hawk and Two Kills as they healed.

Over the course of time, several of the Blackfeet horses managed to escape the canyon. They would show up randomly among the growing herd that grazed in the meadow near the fish camp.

Gabe's budding feelings for Dawn hadn't changed; they had only grown stronger each day as they fished and hunted near the camp. Each evening, the group would gather around the fire, listening to James read from his tattered Bible. Two Kills' funny stories and Eagle Claw's tales of adventure kept everyone entertained, and they took turns retelling their encounters with the Big Man.

It was a pleasant two weeks, and Gabe found himself thinking less and less about the terror they'd experienced in the canyon, as if it had occurred long ago. The skies were clear, the autumn days warm and healing, and the bonds of brotherhood grew strong as old resentments, bitterness, and bias were set aside—even Eagle Claw and Crowfoot were becoming friends.

But as the days rolled past, Gabe found himself thinking only of Dawn. As Two Kills, Red Hawk, and Crowfoot healed from their wounds and grew stronger each day, Gabe felt a painful heaviness in his heart, for he knew he would not be going with them north to the Tobacco Plains. Like Eagle Claw, the events in the canyon had brought about changes in his heart, and it was time for him to make amends.

Finally, everyone had healed enough to travel. Eagle Claw, Dawn, and James grew silent and sullen when Gabe broke the news to them—that he would escort Two Kills and Red Hawk to their village on the plains, then leave for Kentucky.

The parting was difficult for Eagle Claw, and the heartache was written on his face and in his eyes when he bid Gabe farewell. They had been through much together, and though Gabe was an only child, for the first time, he felt as though he finally had a brother in Eagle Claw. Dawn refused to say goodbye. She walked away and disappeared into the trees next to the fish camp.

Heartbroken, Gabe swallowed hard against his sadness when he finally turned Juniper to leave. He and the Blackfeet had traveled only a few miles on the long trail to the plains when they were startled by the sound of a rider coming up fast behind them. Gabe wheeled his horse, dismounted, and drew his Hawken from its scabbard, only to see Dawn heading toward them at a gallop.

She hopped off her winded horse, frothy with sweat, and removed the bow strapped around her saddle horn. Gabe wasn't sure what to expect as she approached, her hair blown back and her cheeks rosy from the gallop. He braced himself.

She thrust the bow toward him, smiled, and said, "Here. Eagle Claw wanted you to have this."

Gabe didn't know what to say. He knew how much the bow meant to Eagle Claw and felt almost ashamed, too unworthy to accept the gift after all Eagle Claw had done for him. He put his rifle back in its scabbard and tentatively, reluctantly took the bow from her hands. He admired the ornate pattern of beads sewn onto the leather sheath that held the bow. Then, he removed the weapon and ran his fingers along its strong limbs. His eyes grew misty as he thought again about Eagle Claw, remembering how he had taught him how to use the bow, and how the brave had patiently helped guide him to his first bow-killed buck.

He looked up to see Dawn returning quickly to her horse, her usual graceful stride hesitant, as if each determined step whispered with vulnerability.

Gabe wanted to tell her not to go and, instead, to join him on his journey home, but the lump in his throat seemed to paralyze his tongue. She grabbed the reins and paused, then brushed the hair from her face as if to steel herself before mounting her horse. Gabe took an impulsive step toward her, and, as if she had heard that step, she turned and hurried back to him, tears in her eyes.

She reached for him and embraced him. He held her tightly, feeling the tremors from her sobs against his chest. In the next moment, she was on her horse, riding away, disappearing into the forest, the trotting footfalls of her horse growing fainter until the only sound that remained was the breeze through the pine trees.

∾

A week later, Marias Pass was blanketed with snow when they topped out and beheld the plains in the distance. Gabe spent a few days at the Blackfeet village on the Two Medicine River, where he rested Juniper and the pack horses before the long ride to Fort Union. The Blackfeet camp was distraught over the loss of their men but treated him kindly for assisting Two Kills and Red Hawk.

Although it took many weeks, Gabe had plenty to occupy his mind, which made the trek seem surprisingly quick. He found a respectable man at the fort and sold Juniper and his pack horses, then caught a ride down the Missouri on a keelboat, just before winter's chill iced over the river. To his relief, traveling was much faster with the downstream flow of the current than against it.

He trekked from St. Louis to Kentucky on foot, along the way noticing a few new homesteads that had popped up. Gabe's time in the mountains had strengthened both his body and his soul. His pace was steady, and his long strides were unaltered by the likelihood of a chilly reception from his parents. Those fears and anxieties had been thoroughly swept clean somewhere back in the sacred canyon.

His ordeal had ushered a change of heart, as if he had gone into that place one person and had come out another. His foolhardy dreams had been swept away, as though only the power of the Big Man was strong enough to pry the selfish ambitions from his heart.

Gabe had never understood what his father meant when he spoke of being "born again." The very idea had seemed ridiculous until his moment of self-awareness on the mountain when they left the sacred canyon. It was then that he saw himself as he really was—a flawed soul in need of redemption and his parents' forgiveness.

Gabe swallowed hard when he finally stepped toward the gate of their homestead. Throughout his journey, he had stiffened his spine in readiness for his father's harsh rebuke and his mother's chagrin. But he wasn't prepared for their reaction when he finally stepped through the front gate of their homestead—how his mother dropped the milk bucket she was carrying, spilling the precious contents on the ground as she ran toward him with tears of joy. Or his father's eyes, opening wide with elation as he dropped the reins of the plow horses, and the way he stumbled as he ran through the furrowed field to greet him with open arms, as if they had been waiting in earnest expectation of his return. It seemed his father had grown smaller in the short time he'd been gone, his mother weaker and frail, as if they'd somehow suffered ill.

Gabe stayed on for nearly a year, helping on the homestead. He remembered Eagle Claw, and how he handled himself with dignity and wisdom. His example gave Gabe the impetus to spend less time talking and more time observing and listening.

His stint working for Branch gave him insight into the darker qualities of men and stood in vivid contrast to his respectable parents. His eyes were open now, and he began to see qualities in his father and mother that he hadn't seen before. Along with that came a new respect and appreciation for them. Likewise, he came to see qualities in his Kentucky chums—those he had previously admired—that were less than savory and wondered why he hadn't seen these foibles before.

Through it all, he came to firmly believe that there is a spirit of goodness and a spirit of evil. They tap eagerly on the door of everyone's heart, and one must learn to only open the door for good, not evil. He was baptized by his father in the river adjacent to their cabin later that next summer and made good his amends to both his parents and to God.

He cut timber and built log cabins for homesteaders moving into the area from back East, eventually saving enough money to purchase an intricately crafted Kentucky muzzle-loader. It was as fine a rifle as anyone in those parts had ever seen, and even his father was envious. He told Gabe, "He must be quite a friend."

The rifled barrel of .60-caliber muzzle-loader was made from the finest steel, and it rested tightly in a full-length curly maple stock. The side plates, patch box, and trigger guard were made from polished brass, and the nose cap, ramrod pipes, and drawdown escutcheons were all made of silver. The crowning touch was an intricate inlay on top of the comb of an eagle clutching a large fish.

But as time went on, his parents watched him grow increasingly restless and aloof. His mother would step outside the cabin after his meal had grown cold, wondering what he was doing sitting alone by a small fire on the edge of the timber long after the sun went down. On occasion, his father was perplexed to find Gabe shooting his Indian bow into a sack of beans he had purchased for a target. They both knew intuitively that he would be leaving again.

It wasn't an easy decision—to again leave the security of his family for the uncertainty and tenuous nature of the frontier. Though it hurt him to see their sadness, he could no longer ignore the call of the mountains. It became so bad that, on rare occasions, he would bring home a beaver and cook it outside over a fire. His parents were polite at first, but eventually, they declined his culinary offering of roasted rodent meat.

It was August when he finally departed. If he hurried, he would make it to the fish camp before the first snows. His departure was much more amicable than before, and this time, his parents bid him farewell with full blessings, tears of sadness, and prayers.

⁓

Gabe had grown bigger, stronger, and wiser. But as he journeyed, he found that some things never changed. The same degenerates manned the keelboat, with the same heinous mob of passengers on board—different faces but nonetheless the same. And when he caught one of the raucous keelboatmen carelessly handling the Kentucky rifle without permission, he grabbed the man's wrist so hard that it snapped like a matchstick. The incident brought an abrupt end to the hubbub and the interest in the ornately decorated rifle.

From the upper reaches of the Missouri, he traveled on foot to the Blackfeet village near the Marias, but when he arrived, they were gone. It took him two days to discover where they had relocated, after which he spent a few days visiting and sharing smoke with Two Kills and Red Hawk.

They kindly gave him a horse. It was an appaloosa buffalo runner with big black spots scattered across its well-muscled hindquarters. He argued for a lesser animal, but Two Kills insisted. Looming dark clouds cresting the mountains threatened to bring snow, so he bid them farewell and headed west toward the Kootenai River.

After a week of hard riding, he rounded the final bend in the trail, but this time, there were no wisps of smoke above the trees to greet him and no tipis spread out on the flat bench above the waterfalls. Gabe looked vainly for tracks, but the thick blanket of snow had removed any sign of human life. Perhaps they had already gone north to their winter camp on the Tobacco Plains.

Gabe tied off his horse and ambled through the barren campsite. Memories of laughing children and bossy old women echoed in his mind, the sight of Eagle Claw hugging his demure wife Spotted Doe, and Little Buck running around shooting imaginary buffalo with his miniature bow and arrow. He walked to the edge of the cliffs where the fishing platforms were tied.

Two of them had come loose from their tethers and had fallen into the roiling waters. The only evidence of their existence was a few broken pieces of lodgepole that lay near the cliffy edge of the river below. Eventually, even those would be washed away when next spring's floods charged down the river. The sight of the disrepair was puzzling.

One platform remained, but the rawhide tethers had rotted, and it was too unstable to step down on. Gabe stood on the rocky edge and reminisced over Eagle Claw and Dawn—their finely-honed movements as they thrust their spears into the churning waters, Eagle Claw's mischievous grin and the impish gleam in Dawn's eye as they tried to outdo each other in catching fish. In his mind's eye he could see Eagle Claw erupting out of the turbulent water with the incredible fish he'd caught single-handedly, the echoes of the braves shouting cheers of triumph as they gathered and carried the great fish away. He smiled at the memories and walked back to his horse.

It didn't take him long to find the well-used trail north to the Tobacco Plains. It followed along the river and was easy to follow. But as he covered mile after mile, he was surprised he hadn't cut a single track.

After Gabe had ridden for two more days, the forest opened into a series of hilly pastures. Several miles later, he smelled smoke from a campfire and followed it north for another mile until a small group of tipis came into view. Except for the wisps of smoke, the village seemed deserted.

A bilious warrior emerged from his tent, holding his rifle defensively as Gabe approached. Gabe held up his hand as a sign of peace and explained that he was looking for the Kootenai village. The warrior said something in garbled Kootenai, then pointed to a shield propped against his tipi. It was painted as white as a cloud and covered with little red speckles, allowing all passersby to interpret the sign with a single glance—*pox*.

Gabe hollered, "Is there anyone here who speaks English?" He repeated his question several times until finally, a warrior stumbled from his tipi.

To Gabe's shock, it was Crowfoot, ashen faced, sallow, and covered with pox. "Go away! Go away!" he cried.

"Crowfoot? Is that you?"

The man squinted hard and shielded his eyes. "Gabe Bauman?"

"Yes! Hello! What has happened? Where is everyone?"

"We are all sick here. The others went north. You must leave. You cannot stay here." He threw up his hands helplessly and ducked back into his tipi.

A heavy feeling came over Gabe like a shroud. He stepped up his pace, traveling north, and soon began to encounter the scaffolds of the dead. They started as groups of three or four, and before long, the stick structures grew into colonies of dozens. Sometimes, they were ornately decorated with spears, arrows, and eagle feathers. Others were more austere, with bones poking out from where ravens had burrowed their sharp beaks through the buckskin and buffalo hide. But the most heartrending evidence of the plague was the smaller platforms that simply held a small buffalo-hide bundle. With each passing funeral scaffold, his heart sank another notch deeper, and the gray cloud hanging over him grew black and foreboding.

He rode for two days up a long valley, then once more crossed the Kootenai River. A heavy snow enveloped the mountains during the second night, adding another foot to the already deep snow. He wondered how difficult finding the trail would be and if he would ever locate their camp. But his horse was strong and plowed ahead through the snow until finally, wisps of smoke above the timber indicated that he was approaching an encampment.

Children stopped their playing as he came into view and scampered into their tipis. Several warriors with bows and spears hurried to block the trail.

"I seek Dawn, Eagle Claw, James!" he yelled. "I am Gabe Bauman."

One of the warriors broke away and disappeared among the tipis. Gabe was elated when James came into view, but his elation faded when he didn't see Dawn and Eagle Claw following him.

"Gabe? Is that you?"

"Yes—James!"

Gabe got off his horse, and to his surprise, James approached him quickly and gave him a hug, as if he were a long-lost son. And as James welcomed him, she came around one of the tipis.

"Dawn!" cried Gabe.

As she tentatively came forward, he opened his arms, and she began running. When she reached him, he saw that she had tears in her eyes, and he embraced her and held her tightly for a long minute.

Finally, he released her. "Where's Eagle Claw?" he asked, grinning with anticipation.

Chapter Forty-Three

Farewell

B*ecause of the deep snows high on the mountain, it* wasn't until the next spring that our mother, Dawn, led our father, Gabe, up to the grave site. Before he passed, Eagle Claw had requested a Christian burial. My mother told my father that her brother could never get past the thought of the ravens pecking at him. He had wanted to be buried higher on the mountain, near some cliffs where he often prayed.

Together, they made the long climb, each step closer to the grave site becoming more painful. Father brought the Kentucky rifle with him and fell to his knees at the foot of the mound of dirt that marked his grave, overcome with grief.

Then, my mother told me, he did something that surprised her: he raised his arms and sang a prayer song, in the Kootenai tongue, with tears streaming down his face. He was inconsolable until Mother tugged on his sleeve and pointed skyward. A majestic golden eagle soared over the peak above them and circled once, letting out a piercing cry before gliding out of sight behind the mountain.

Then, Father lay the fine Kentucky rifle he had brought as a gift next to Eagle Claw's old Hawken that lay atop his grave—the one the Big Man had broken and bent. Each year thereafter, he and Mother visited the grave site, always leaving something behind, always singing the prayer song before leaving.

When we children grew strong enough to make the annual climb to the grave site, we joined our parents to pay homage to our uncle, Eagle Claw. We would sit looking over the Tobacco Plains, and my father would tell us stories of Eagle Claw's brave exploits, and how he fearlessly stalked the Skookum.

Our grandmother, Singing Bird, also contracted the terrible disease, several months after Eagle Claw had passed. One morning after a snowstorm, James woke, and she was gone from his side. He followed her tracks in the snow until they had filled in, then wandered the mountains, searching for weeks, but never found her. Ever since that time, James would go off by himself to some lonely overlook or an isolated pocket of timber to pray, or as some would claim, to talk to her lonesome spirit.

The graceful, soft-spoken Spotted Doe was also infected with the pox during the terrible plague and passed away, so Father and Mother raised Little Buck right alongside me and the other kids.

Years later, when I was big enough to make the journey, we pestered Father until he finally relented and led us on a trek back into the sacred canyon. We had to go afoot because the trail had become too treacherous for horses, and we had to fight through several miles of deadfall, as if the trees had been pushed over onto the trail intentionally. Not far off the trail, along the abutment, we found the cave where Red Hawk had escaped the Skookum, right where he had said it would be.

It was difficult, but somehow, my father also managed to find the first camp, half covered with fallen timber. But the beaver dams that held back the waters of the crystal-clear lake had completely vanished, and all that remained was a wide mud flat ringed with a few collapsed beaver lodges. With no beaver to tend to the dams, the spring floods eventually broke through, and the water drained from the lakes. The high mountain grasses had already begun taking over, and I suspect by now, you wouldn't even know that a beaver had ever lived there.

The second camp wasn't much different. The lake had evaporated into a big mudhole, which was very disappointing to us, because the stories we had heard described it so differently. In fact, the condition of the basin was so contradictory to what we'd been told, it made us wonder if the stories were true.

When we were hiking out, my father showed us the tree from where the Skookum had watched them and the gnarly branch he had stood on. Farther down the trail, Father noticed something lying half buried beneath the pine duff under one of the trees. We didn't know why we hadn't seen it on our way up the trail. Perhaps the angle of sunlight? Who knows? He scuffed away the dirt and leaves and, to our surprise, there lay a human skull staring up at us. For some reason, he didn't want to touch it, nor would he let us touch it, so he grabbed a stick and pried it loose. Oddly enough, the top of the skull had been gnawed through and was missing—you could tell from the ring of puncture marks that ran along the ragged edge of bone that an animal had performed the grisly surgery. I pointed out how the man's teeth looked wolfish. Little Buck and I suspected whose skull it had belonged to from the stories we'd been told. We wanted to keep it as a trophy, but my father would have nothing to do with it. He insisted we leave it there, facing down the trail like a warning sign, and demanded we leave immediately.

An odd thing happened as we were passing through the forest of giant cedars. Father suddenly stopped in his tracks and looked up into the canopy of the trees. A few seconds later, we smelled it—an odor like nothing I've ever smelled before.

He hurried us along, nervously looking up into the forest and over his shoulder. We had no sooner passed through those great trees when the wind picked up. Not long afterward, the trees started "talking," with squeaks and moans that made the hair on the back of our necks stand on end. I could have sworn I heard voices.

By then, it was getting late, and just before we started down the steep section, there came a strange noise from high on the mountain: *Garooooo!* I would have thought it was just another tree squeaking in the wind, but shortly after there came a response in kind from the opposite side of the canyon. We left the sacred canyon and never set foot on that trail again.

The game slowly dwindled away and even the fish had ceased their annual journey upriver. My parents were forced to move our family west and they established a homestead in the Cascade Mountains. They remained on the homestead long after we children had grown up and found our way into the big village of Portland.

Several times a year, we loaded our own kids in the wagon and made the journey to their remote cabin deep in the mountains, and each night, the children gathered round in front of the fireplace to hear the stories, sometimes late into the night.

I confess, there were times when I questioned the legitimacy of some of the old tales, like the ones about my grandmother's strange visions that not even the Elders could interpret, but they never failed to entertain the children.

My parents ... they were something else, those two. They certainly lived a life full of love and adventure; they even hunted with a man who would become president of the United States. But that's another story.

Walter "Running Fox" Bauman

February 6, 1902

GLOSSARY OF
OLD ENGLISH WORDS

arse—variant of ass and asshole

bell-head—head of a penis; fool

benjo—sailor slang for a riotous holiday; a noisy day outdoors

blighter—person or thing to be regarded with contempt or envy

blue devil—the feeling of being hungover after drinking too much (noted in 1823)

bootlicker—same as ass-licker; an obsequious or overly deferential person

bow-wow mutton—a naval term referring to meat so bad it could be dog flesh

church bell—a talkative woman

cussed—cursed or mean

gut-founder—to sink or utterly destroy as to render incapacitated; in horses, a malady caused from over-indulgence—usually of grain—often rendering the horse lame

flapdoodle—a sexually incompetent man who is either too young to have had sex or too old to attempt it

half-rats—partially intoxicated

possibles bag—a satchel of varying materials intended for carrying whatever small gear is necessary for a day's hunt puschka—Blackfeet for "penis"

sauce box—a mouth; could also be called a "tatur trap"

shite—early variant of shit

skilamalink—*skilamalink* dealings are likely held in secret and with questionable moral purpose and they should be avoided

tarnation—used for damnation

go tharn—a person or animal being frozen in terror

toped—drunk; to drink alcohol to excess, especially on a regular basis